FROM ONE HELL TO ANOTHER

FROM ONE HELL
TO ANOTHER

From Fascist Spain,
to war again

* * *

Liz Cowley

&

Donough O'Brien

Matador
9 Priory Business Park,
Wistow Road, Kibworth Beauchamp,
Leicestershire, LE8 0RX
Tel: 0116 279 2299
Email: books@troubador.co.uk
Web: www.troubador.co.uk/matador
Twitter: @matadorbooks

ISBN 978 1789018 813

British Library Cataloguing in Publication Data.
A catalogue record for this book is available from the British Library.

Printed and bound in the UK by TJ International, Padstow, Cornwall
Typeset in 11pt Sabon by Troubador Publishing Ltd, Leicester, UK
Cover design: www.mousematdesign.com

Matador is an imprint of Troubador Publishing Ltd

For the people of Saint-Hippolyte-du-Fort
and all résistants everywhere

THANK YOU

*** * ***

While some of the personalities in this book are fictional, it is based on many real people, places and events.

We would like to thank the following for their memories, input, advice and help:

Otilia Garré (Casales)
Carmen Ouari
Joaquin Garcia, Président d'Association des Anciens Guérilléros FFI du Gard
Anne Marie Garcia
Eloi Martinez Monegal, Président d'ASEREF (Association pour le souvenir de l'exil Républicain Espagnol en France)
Francis Chirat
André Teissier du Cros
Jean-Jacques Bertrand
Alan Ogden
Derek Richardson
Roger Stanton and The WW2 Escape Lines Memorial Society
Les Amis de Clio/Roland Castanet
Bruno Olivieri, Mayor, Saint-Hippolyte-du-Fort
Librairie Coularou, Saint-Hippolyte-du-Fort
John Akeroyd
Major-General Sir Robert Corbett
Sarah Shaw
Luis Duran Rodriguez-Ibañez
Murrough O'Brien

* * *

August, 1944

SHE LAY FLAT IN THE GRASS BEHIND THE BUSHES ON THE RAILWAY embankment, shuffling her position a little. It was already too warm and not very comfortable. And she was terrified.

Behind her the sun was rising above Nîmes, and would be right in the eyes of anyone coming down the road from the west towards her.

But it would be much later, with the sun high in the sky, before Sebastian, her Number Two, tapped her shoulder. She nodded to him, indicating that she had already heard the noise. A motorcycle and sidecar, coming very slowly. The machine-gunner in the sidecar wore dark glasses as he stared around him. She carefully pulled back the Bren gun's cocking handle. Of course, they couldn't hear it above the noise of their engine, but she was still very nervous.

They puttered past under the railway bridge and the silent watchers on the embankment let them go, knowing that 'Carlo' would deal with them two hundred metres behind them.

It was the convoy they wanted. They had heard the distant firing at noon in Durfort and she knew the Germans would have probably broken through the several Maquis ambushes in the streets of Saint-Hippolyte and were now on their way.

Garrison troops from Toulouse or the coast around Bordeaux, the Germans had been content enough sitting in comfortable France – anything but the bloodbath of Russia. Now they were fleeing east, scrambling to escape the Allies, and not just those that were breaking out from Normandy, but now the Americans who had landed *behind them* in the south. They might not be crack troops, but the British had told the Maquis often enough *never* to under-estimate any German troops in a tight spot.

More engine noise. A Kübelwagen jeep drove slowly into view, leading a huge, long column of trucks and other vehicles. She knew her little group must be completely outnumbered. She shivered.

The Kübelwagen will have the officers, and you should always shoot the officers first.

We've all come a very long way.

Carmen gently eased off the safety catch, and waited for the signal.

ONE

* * *

January, 1939

CARMEN CASALES HAD NOT BEEN BORN IN IGUALADA, BUT IN TERUEL MUCH further to the south of Spain, in Aragón. But she had lived in the town nearly all her life, and used to love it, with its narrow little streets, the remains of an old fortress and its pleasant waterside scenery. The family house looked out over the River Anoia, whose water had once been so useful to the leather tanning and textile industries, and walking its banks had once been one of her greatest pleasures along with family trips by train every few months to the exciting and bustling city of Barcelona.

But now, Igualada – like everywhere else in Spain – had been plunged into the horrors of a Civil War, and the once bustling and prosperous town was a completely changed place. The streets were swarming with frightened and desperate refugees, food was running dangerously short, and even a teenage girl could not ignore the rising feeling of dread as the news grew rapidly worse.

She was one of three girls in the family. Carmen was now sixteen, while Otilia was twelve and Juanita only seven. All of them were going to be pretty, but Carmen was already tall and beautiful, and her mother Maria had become a little worried about the way men and boys were beginning to look at her. But these days that was the least of her concerns. Now, in early 1939, with her husband Pedro rarely at home, it was far harder to cope with everyday life or even to know what was going on in the war, being totally illiterate and unable to read the news. All she could do was struggle on and try to keep things as normal as possible.

Pedro had once been a farmer, but in late 1936 the Republican forces had forcibly recruited him into the army – and for some unexplained reason, as an officer. Most regular Spanish army officers had joined the other side – the Nationalist forces of Franco, so the Republic had to make do with any reasonably intelligent man who had not been purged – shot perhaps for being rich, or aristocratic or Catholic. But Pedro had wryly pointed out to his family that the same rather haphazard way of choosing officers had occurred in that other terrible civil war, in America. 'I heard they even grabbed teachers and made them Colonels.'

He had been wounded twice, first at Jarama and then again in the bitter fighting on the Ebro, but had gone back and doggedly fought on, for what was rapidly beginning to look like a lost cause.

Alone with her three daughters, Maria longed for Pedro to be with them.

* * *

MOSCA! MOSCA!

Early one morning, they were woken by little Juanita excitedly shouting at the top of her piping voice.

She was jumping up and down on her bed looking at a plane suddenly banking past the window. Her mother pushed her out of the way and stared outside. At once she knew that it was *not* one of their few surviving little Russian Polikarpov fighters, the ones they all affectionately called 'moscas', or 'flies'. No, this one sounded and looked very different. It didn't have a stubby front, it was much slimmer and there were no familiar red markings – instead, black and white ones.

'GET DOWN!' she suddenly screamed at her daughters.

And, sure enough, the plane came round again and roared over their house, and two deafening explosions came from the nearby town hall. The plane then banked away, climbed and droned off into the hard blue sky.

People started to run past the house towards the smoke and sounds of screaming, desperate to help.

Maria got up cautiously. 'Carmen, *you* come with me! *You two stay where you are. Don't move!* And if another plane comes, get under the bed. *Está claro?*'

Maria and Carmen now hurried nervously up the narrow street towards where the bombs had struck.

There in the plaza in front of the Town Hall was a nightmare scene of utter chaos. Bloodied bodies were lying everywhere – some moving but mostly still, the women's rumpled clothes making them look like bundles of discarded laundry.

And there was one unimaginable horror. Sitting on the steps of the Town Hall was a woman. Her baby was still alive and crying in her arms.

But the mother had no head.

Carmen moaned and was suddenly violently sick before her mother turned her around and coaxed her gently away, knowing it was a sight they would never forget.

But what about the child?

'Stay there!' said Maria to her daughter, who was still shivering with horror. She returned to pick up the crying, blood-covered infant, but suddenly another woman intervened. 'I know her, and the family. I'll take the baby.' As she did so, someone else placed a sheet over the mother's corpse.

Maria returned to her stricken and still shivering daughter, noticing that nurses and doctors were now arriving to administer to the wounded and dying, and knowing that the kindest thing she could do now was to take her back home.

* * *

Two nights later, it was dark when Pedro turned up – quite unexpectedly. His Captain's uniform was faded, dusty and worn, and his face lined with fatigue. He parked a little motorbike in the hall, knowing that even an army machine would be stolen by someone desperate if left outside in the street. He told Maria that the front line of the war was now close enough for him to slip away, and with permission, to see his family for just a few hours. But he had also heard about the bombing.

Maria noticed that he was unshaven, with his moustache and hair unkempt and greying, very different from the once smart officer who had always tried to set an example to his men. He was also limping from his Ebro leg wound. The war had clearly taken its toll.

When he had helped to calm the children and get them to bed, knowing that this was perhaps the last time he would see ever them, he took down the bottle of Spanish brandy that Maria had kept unopened for so long, and poured them both a drink. She then told him about the horrific events at the plaza. Pedro looked very grave.

Maria could not help asking him why the war was so savage, and even why there was a war at all, still shocked and baffled by events, and increasingly frustrated by her limited grasp of what was happening. Pedro sighed and poured them another drink.

'Well, try to remember how it was, Maria. Back when we had the King, Spain was divided right down the middle. The rich, the aristocrats, the church and the army were on one side, and us lot on the other – the poor, the illiterate, the peasants, the industrial workers and the small farmers, like me.'

'But why did everyone hate the Church so much?' interrupted Maria, 'I always rather liked Father Ignacio before he disappeared.'

'Maybe *you* did. But most of us saw the Church as an *enemy*, not a friend. People began to really hate it. And why? Because they saw it as being firmly on the side of the rich. And of course, it ran the *only* schools – which *we* had to pay for. No wonder that half of us are illiterate – like you, sadly. I wish I'd had the time to teach you to read and write.

Then, as you know, we voted in a Republic, and the King went off into exile. And, as I think we all agreed, the new Government did some surprisingly good things. It reduced the power of the Church, built thousands of non-religious schools, and better still – free ones – which is why our three could go to school when we never could. And they even offered autonomy to Catalonia and Viscaya.'

'And wasn't it them that gave women the vote?'

'Yes, that too, and, of course, absolutely none of it pleased the old order, in fact quite the opposite.

Then if you remember, we had another leftist government, but the trouble was that everyone started to quarrel – the Socialists, Communists and Anarchists. It was a total mess. Nothing got done, so no wonder people took things into their own hands. People started getting murdered, riots broke out. The peasants grabbed a million acres, the factories went on strike and – bound to cause trouble – all kinds of hotheads started attacking the Church again.'

Maria was still struggling to understand, impressed as always by her husband's superior knowledge, but suddenly remembering how much he had tried to read about it all, constantly with his head in the papers when at home, and presumably talking to other officers.

'Next minute, saying they were restoring order, the Army revolted, but they couldn't take *all* the cities, especially Madrid. I'll bet Franco probably thought it would be a quick coup, not a war that would drag on for three years – killing so many of us on both sides.

And then, of course, the Germans and Italians pitched in and poured support behind Franco, while we were helped by the International Brigades and backed by Stalin and the Soviet Union – with both the Fascists and the Communists trying out their weapons on us.'

Maria listened patiently, but was becoming desperate. She still didn't really understand despite her best efforts, and didn't consider herself as being a 'Republican' at all, any more than her husband did. Tragically, they just happened to be living in an area that *was* Republican, in fact in Catalonia, which would probably like to break away from Spain altogether if it could.

What she *could* take on board was that the mess was reaching crisis point. By now everyone knew that the Nationalists had fought their way to the Mediterranean above Valencia cutting the Republic in two, and that the counter-offensive on the Ebro had failed. It looked clearly like the beginning of the end, with a huge last offensive now threatening Barcelona. For weeks, refugees had been pouring up from the south and west, bedraggled and starving. Worse, food was very short, and cost twenty times what it used to and what the Nationalists had to pay.

It was quite clearly a catastrophe, and all the blustering propaganda couldn't disguise that, or just how savage the war had become.

Nor were Pedro's next words any comfort. 'Living here in Igualada, up to now in comparative peace, it's hard to understand what's been going on and the real hatreds that have gripped Spain on both sides. As I said, God knows people had some grievances. Half of Spain was illiterate, with peasants without land living on a few pesetas a month, and the rich owning most of the country – all those Dukes and Duchesses treating ordinary people like cattle. And with the Church owning the rest of the land and lots of industry and stealing from the poor.

But it *really* didn't help that, at the beginning, our side went off and killed thousands of priests, monks and nuns. That was unforgivable. I even witnessed some of that for myself to my utter shame, though I never told you before. I wish I didn't have to now.

And on top of all that, they burned down all the churches in Spain that they could – including all fifty-eight in Barcelona. Remember the ruins, the last time we went there?'

Maria nodded despairingly, remembering them all too well. They both suddenly looked up. There was distant thudding. Artillery?

'Now, if *you* were a staunch Catholic, *you'd* hate us. And with Russia's involvement, the other side has been able to label us 'murdering anti-church Reds'. That made the British and French think we'd spark a Communist revolution in *their* countries. So *they* didn't help us. And the Mayor of Alicante even said, 'Should anyone vote for the Right, chop off their right hand and force them to eat it.' *That* wasn't going to reassure the British Ambassador much.

And making matters worse, everything's clouded by propaganda. For instance, I know for a fact that the Germans only killed two or three hundred when they bombed Guernica, bad enough, but not the thousands our side claimed.

I can also tell you that we *weren't* exaggerating when we talked of Franco's people's atrocities. When they took Seville, they shot seven thousand, even more in Cordoba, Badajoz and Malaga. And not just soldiers and militiamen, but loads of others, mostly innocent.

And here the Fascists will hate us even more for wanting a separate Catalan state. So things could be far, far worse. They *know* they'll win, so the gloves will come off completely – they'll be driven by hatred, with no restraint at all.

That's why all those people are going past our windows, tens of thousands streaming north to try to get to France? They wouldn't be doing that if they weren't really afraid.'

Pedro shook his head. 'I can't tell you how worried I am.'

And Maria, sadly, couldn't tell him that she had barely understood half of what he had told her, and that the other half was simply too appalling to take in. But she could tell when he was afraid, and she was now terrified herself.

* * *

'You'll have to leave,' Pedro said wearily, shaking his head. 'You can't stay here any longer, not with horrors like that on our doorstep.'

Leave with three children? Maria made as if to protest, but he raised his hand to stop her.

'The Nationalists are about to break through. There's very little to stop them. Barcelona will fall in a few days, that's for sure. And when they come, those bastards may kill *anyone* they think is Red. And with *even worse* atrocities. As I explained just now, it's been happening all over Spain for months, it's nothing new. And being a woman won't help, especially in your case. You're the wife of a Republican army officer. You absolutely *can't* stay here.'

'But..'

Pedro put up his hand. 'No, please don't argue. You and the girls will have to try and get to France. There are plenty of people there who are sympathetic. I'm sure they'll try and help. And I think I've got somewhere for you to go.'

Maria looked desolate, and suddenly felt horribly alone. 'Can't you come with us?'

'No. I'll have to fight on. Or at least give the *appearance* of fighting on. The Russians, the bastards, are shooting *anyone* who tries to desert, even if it's just to help their families. I only just managed to get a last pass myself. No, I'll hang on a few weeks, then try and get away and follow you.'

He paused, and looked towards the window. They could both now hear more thudding – louder and nearer. Pedro was a man who normally feared nothing. But he was plainly afraid now.

In the darkness of the kitchen, he briefed his fearful wife for several hours about what they should take with them. First, there was the address in southern France of his older cousin Alfonso who had luckily had the forethought to escape Spain a year before. Most important would be the silver coins and gold jewellery that she should tape to her body under the bulky clothing that she'd need to struggle across the snow-swept Pyrenees. With Republican paper money worth nothing, at least there would be something to pay for things – bribe people, get food, maybe even pay rent – that's if they could get across the border.

Pedro left next morning, after a tearful farewell to his family. As his motorcycle disappeared up the street, Maria wondered if she would ever see him again.

TWO

* * *

C ARMEN SOON REALIZED HOW MUCH HER MOTHER WAS GOING TO NEED her. Her two sisters were too young to understand the danger. But even *they* could feel the fear and see the pandemonium, with thousands of wretched people streaming through the town, all heading north towards the mountains.

Two days later, they walked to the railway station early in the morning with two suitcases and some other bundles, the two youngest complaining loudly. Maria fought her way through the throng, and after half an hour returned with tickets. Carmen guessed that such a miracle was due to simple bribery.

A little train wheezed into the station in a cloud of steam, and somehow they found themselves packed in a carriage, all standing up, with Juanita clinging to her mother's leg. Shouts and whistles followed, and suddenly the train lurched out into the countryside. Those near a window could see the roads packed with people, trudging north.

They could hardly move at all, and scarcely breathe. It was stiflingly uncomfortable, but at least, Maria thought, they were moving in the right direction.

However, their extreme discomfort didn't last long, perhaps two hours, because the train stopped at the little town of Figueras, never to move again. Someone shouted up to the windows that bombing had smashed up the track the other side of town, cutting the line to the north. Everyone slowly got out and on to the platform, blinking in the bright sunshine.

Juanita had just started whining that she was hungry and wanted to go home when everyone looked up, hearing the dreaded sound of aircraft. There was an air raid shelter just by the station and men with armbands suddenly started shouting and herding the crowd towards it.

Maria was dutifully following when little Juanita suddenly turned and ran away, off down the road, shouting about 'going home'. Dropping their cases, her family all ran after the little girl, cursing and pleading with her.

They had not gone very far when Juanita stopped in her tracks, staring upwards.

Two planes, big ones with two engines, roared over their heads.

There was a sudden whistling and then huge explosions that knocked them right off their feet. Shaken, they picked themselves out of the dust and looked back. The railway station was demolished and in flames, with their splintered train on its side. Much, much worse, one bomb had gone straight into the shelter.

Clinging together in a state of shock, they went back towards the station. In the road their cases stood forlornly where they had dropped them. Rescuers were desperately trying to get survivors out of the slaughterhouse of the burning shelter, but not many of their fellow passengers of a few minutes ago seemed to be still alive. The few who still *were* simply sat in the road, dazed and covered in blood.

Juanita started to cry. She was not to know that her childish naughtiness had saved her family.

* * *

Maria now understood that everything Pedro had told her was only too true. The quicker they got moving the better, so they picked up their belongings and started to walk. Even the two young ones had stopped complaining. Perhaps the terrible events in Figueras had taught them that there were infinitely worse things than tired feet. They stuck to small country roads to avoid any more air raids, and if any aircraft *did* come near, they all quickly hid in the ditches by the side of the road, or behind the stone walls.

Even on these little roads there seemed to be hundreds of bedraggled people, mostly women and children, and as the snow-covered mountains came into view, mothers quickly began to comprehend the huge challenges ahead, and understand the vast scale of the tragic exodus of which they were just a tiny part.

Reaching the foothills as it was getting dark, Maria realized they should now find shelter and then try to tackle the arduous climb in the morning. A broken-down farmhouse in among cork trees already seemed pretty full, but they managed to squeeze in. In fact, the number of people crowded in meant one blessing – it was quite warm, in contrast with the cold of a January night. Exhausted, they slept reasonably well despite the hard ground, except for Carmen who woke twice from the same nightmare of the headless woman and her crying baby.

The next day, after a meagre breakfast, they set off again, but again frustratingly slowly because Juanita and even Otilia could neither walk very far or fast. But at last their narrow, dusty road joined the main one at La Junquera. Only now could they see how many were trying to get out of Spain. The road was thick with people, as far as the eye could see, mostly civilians, but now joined by a number of bedraggled soldiers, some with their rifles, but mostly not. They now began the long and painfully slow climb. Nobody could go fast. There were far too many children and old people. One old lady, in widow's black, was sitting weeping silently in the mud by the side of the road. There were others, curled up like bundles of clothing in the snow, probably dying – or already dead, and some were pathetically small – obviously infants.

It was hugely distressing, and guilt added to Maria's anguish, knowing that she had to keep moving for the sake of the children, and torn between her duty to them and her natural instinct to stop and offer comfort to weaker refugees, some crying pitifully for help.

She noted that no traffic seemed to be coming the other way, down from the mountains. Perhaps that was a good sign. It might mean that the French were at least keeping the border open at Le Perthus. Somebody had said they had closed it for a while, but had re-opened it, apparently under international pressure. She prayed fervently that this was true.

And while the fleeing throngs must have presented tempting targets, no more Nationalist planes came to machine-gun or bomb them as they had done further south. There was only the occasional one droning high in the sky, plainly watching the scene below. Perhaps, thought Maria, the Nationalists had concluded it was easier to just let the tens of thousands go – to become a feeding and housing problem for the French.

As they climbed, it became colder and colder. Maria tried to carry Juanita for a bit, but she was simply too heavy. So all they could do was go very slowly up the road as it twisted and turned up to the pass at Le Perthus, pausing to rest from time to time. But at last they were there, and approaching the Spanish control point with a limp and faded Republican flag. The barrier was up, and the buildings completely deserted. The fearful police and customs officials had probably joined the exodus into France. There was dazzling white snow on the mountains around them, snow that on the road had been churned to muddy-brown slush by the thousands of feet that had tramped over it.

Two hundred metres further on was France – profound relief at last, and a pleasant surprise as the gendarmes, in their unfamiliar kepis hats and cloaks, waved them through. They walked on and then there were tents with big red crosses on them. A smiling nurse beckoned Maria and her family over, and showed them benches to sit on. She poured out milk for all of them, and then handed the children biscuits, muttering something about 'vitamins' in French. There was hot food too, handed out by friendly French women.

Maria nearly wept with relief.

* * *

Going downhill into France was of course easier, although still frustratingly slow with such young children, and it them took them the rest of another exhausting day to reach a town called Le Boulou. There, things were no longer welcoming. No more helpful women, no reassuring smiles. Just lots of shouting French troops, many of whom seemed to be slovenly-dressed men from some French African colony.

The first thing that happened to the crowds of refugees was that the men were separated from the women, with distressing scenes of crying mothers and children, before they were herded away. Then Maria joined one of the long lines to be processed at desks manned by surly, overworked police officials. She guessed that most of the arrivals would be herded off to some kind of camp, and frantically searched her clothing for that precious French address that Pedro had given her. At the head of the line, she handed it over to a small bald man who scrutinised it. 'Il y a beaucoup des villes appelées Saint-Hippolyte,' he frowned. Then he repeated himself in badly-pronounced Spanish, 'Hay muchas ciudades llamadas Santa-Hippolyte.' But at least it *was* Spanish, to Maria's profound relief

He suddenly looked at the note again. 'Ah, *du Fort!*' He scribbled something on a piece of paper, looked up and handed it to her. 'El tren para Nîmes,' he said gruffly and waved her away, staring rather too hard at Carmen as he did so.

The soldiers ushered them into a very large building, which looked like an old garage. In the poor light of a few dim bulbs they could see that there were old iron beds lined up and a booth at the end where some soup and bread was being served by an almost toothless old French woman. It was very hot, with several pot stoves blazing away, and they had to take off most of the bulky warm clothing they had worn to cross the mountains. Carmen was suddenly worried by that. Though not vain, she knew that she had an exceptional figure and she certainly did *not* welcome the glances that some of the soldiers had been giving her as she waited in the line. It was bad enough to have escaped Franco's notorious Moors without facing more danger here, though of a different sort.

Worse, there seemed to be only one latrine for about a hundred women and children, and a filthy one at that. Sick of the sight of it, early in the morning, Carmen went looking for another one, ending up at the other end of the hall, and wandering about in the half-light behind piles of boxes of car spares.

Suddenly she felt a hand on her shoulder, and spun round to face a large black soldier muttering something she could not understand. But she understood only too well from his breath that he was drunk, and when he pressed up against her it was obvious what he had in mind.

To try to stop him, she shook her head vigorously and was about to scream when he clapped one hand over her mouth and fumbled at his trousers with the other.

Crushed against his sweating body, she saw something glinting at his side. A bayonet! She abandoned her attempts to wrench his hand from her mouth, and lunged for the handle, pulling the blade upwards out of its scabbard. Then, her heart pounding, she swung it back and then forward into somewhere near his stomach.

He gasped with shock and pain, staggered drunkenly, and fell over backwards. Carmen grasped the bayonet with both hands and drove it downwards with all her strength. She missed his groin, but the blade stabbed right through his trousers and his inside leg and pinned him to the wooden floor. Blood started spreading in a dark pool.

'Hijo de puta!' she hissed. He didn't respond. He seemed to have fainted from shock.

Carmen rushed back to where her family was asleep, shaking her mother.

'We have to go to the train *right now!*' When her mother wearily protested, Carmen leaned forward and hurriedly told her about the last few minutes. Maria suddenly realized that all their plans were at risk and shook the young ones awake, ordering them to dress as fast as they could. Thankfully, they at last now seemed sufficiently aware of danger not to argue.

There was a long train waiting. Some of the refugees were already on the platform with railway staff directing them. Carmen showed them the piece of paper and they were sent to the leading carriage, just behind a steam locomotive that was panting gently. The carriage had NIMES written on a sign.

They scrambled inside, with Carmen keeping in the shadows well away from the windows. She and Maria were dreading what might happen if that soldier came looking for her. But gradually more and more refugees turned up, making it harder to find her – mostly women and children, with a handful of men – presumably those who could prove they had somewhere to go.

Time passed. Still no vengeful soldier – or his friends. Maybe he'd gone to a dressing station or hospital to have his wounded leg patched up, or perhaps he was worried about explaining the incident to his officers. Strangely, Carmen had very mixed feelings about the encounter. She was still thoroughly shaken, but at the same time suddenly felt a curious sense of empowerment. For once she had *not* been forced to be the continuous passive victim of appalling events – air raids, defeats, hunger, deprivation – and omnipresent fear. At *last,* she had been able to strike back.

After what seemed like an eternity, but in reality was only about an hour, a whistle came from the engine, and the train slowly moved off to a collective sigh of relief. It steamed through the countryside as the sun rose, with the children looking out and gradually pointing at things, as if slowly recovering from their ordeal. Then the train slowed, and Maria and Carmen became anxious again as it drew to a stop in a station. PERPIGNAN said a sign. Suddenly there was a clanking from the back of the train, but then the engine whistled and they were off once more. An hour later, the same thing happened at another station where the signs said NARBONNE. There was more clanking from the rear of the train, and another whistle before the train pulled out. And at Béziers, it was the same.

By the time they slowed for a station called Montpellier, everyone worked out what was happening. The train was dropping off carriages at each station.

So when it drew into Nîmes, it consisted of just two.

* * *

Maria and her family stood on the platform at Nîmes and looked around them in confusion as loudspeakers announced things they did not understand. It was at that precise moment of frustration that Carmen decided she had to learn French fast, even though many of their fellow passengers were being greeted by Spanish-speaking friends or relatives.

Looking around, they noticed a little crowd gathering round a railway man in uniform, with a Gendarme beside him. And walking over, they were eventually able to produce the paper the official in Le Boulou had given Maria. The railwayman made out some kind of ticket, gave it to her with a smile and pointed at the next platform.

'Attendez. Quatre heures. Saint-Hippolyte. Le train.' He held up four fingers, encouragingly. 'Gracias,' murmured Maria. Was that four hours to wait or four hours' journey time, wondered Carmen? Again she felt thoroughly frustrated, fervently hoping it wouldn't be a four-hour delay.

The family crossed the platform and sat down, and thankfully did not have long to wait. Just twenty minutes later, at four o'clock, a small steam engine with three carriages pulled in.

As the train puffed through the countryside, they were surrounded by chattering, friendly locals, and Carmen and her mother were suddenly acutely embarrassed by their own filthy and probably smelly clothes. For ten long days crossing the mountains, they had barely been able to wash themselves, let alone what they were wearing. But there was no indication of disapproval from the other passengers, who had probably guessed they were part of the huge exodus from Spain. Either that, thought Carmen, or they were extremely polite people.

Now, as the journey continued, her pleasant anticipation of this new country was heightened by the sight of pretty fields and vineyards, little stone houses and horses and carts on the road alongside the branch line. Soon they came to a place called Quissac, and further on, in the fading light, an ancient village called Sauve, and finally the train pulled in to Saint-Hippolyte-du-Fort. The family stood on the platform and watched it steam off, until its red lights disappeared round a curve.

Maria turned to one of the animated women who had shared their carriage, and showed her the piece of paper with Pedro's cousin's address.

'Rue Pasteur? Je le connais bien. Venez avec moi, Madame!' She beckoned for them to follow her.

They set off in the dark with their few belongings, walking down a hill and over a bridge across a river. Just a few metres later, the friendly woman stopped and pointed to the left down a narrow street.

'Rue Pasteur. Votre maison, à cent metres!' She smiled at the family and set off into the centre of the town. 'Gracias!' called Maria to the departing figure. 'No hay de que,' came the reply. So at least *one* person in this place speaks Spanish, thought Carmen. But again she vowed to learn French fast.

THREE

✳ ✳ ✳

IN THE RUE PASTEUR, MARIA KNOCKED ON AN OLD WOODEN DOOR
marked with a faded 36. There was no response. Panicking, she
suddenly remembered that people might be cautious about answering
doors at night if they lived alone. She tried again, for good measure pulling
a cord connected to a bell. To her relief she heard movement inside and
then the door was opened, very cautiously. She immediately recognized
the burly dark-haired man from the old days in Igualada, and clearly far
more quickly than he did her.

'Alfonso, it's *me*, Maria!'

Alfonso hid his shock as best he could, having noticed her torn and
dirty clothes and her matted hair – so different from the neat and well-
groomed woman he remembered from the past, but immediately realizing
the horrors of the trek over the Pyrenees in winter, and with three children,
two of them so young.

'Of course it is!' he said suddenly embarrassed and immediately
embracing her.

'Thank God you made it. I got a letter from Pedro a few weeks ago,
saying you might be coming if things got worse. They obviously did.'

Maria nodded.

'Come in, come in, everyone!' he said, noticing that the two younger
girls were hanging back shyly, clinging to Maria's clothes. 'I'm your uncle
Alfonso. You can call me Uncle Fon.'

Picking up their two suitcases and beckoning for them to follow him,
he was hugely relieved that the family was safe. He had heard horrifying

reports of families escaping from Spain across the mountains, sleeping rough, foraging for food and drinking from ditches. Someone in the café had even told him that there were pathetic bundles of small children lining the route who had died of cold or hunger, and whose parents had been unable to bury them in the frozen ground.

'I live alone now, so there's lots of room. Sadly my wife died soon after we got here. Of flu. Even sadder after getting through the war. It'll be nice to have some company. It can be a bit lonely now.'

He glanced upstairs. 'Anyway, if you'd like to follow me, I'll take up these cases and show you to your bedrooms. You probably haven't slept for ages, at least not in proper beds.

And then you can sit round the fire and get warm while I make you something to eat. You must be starving. There's not much food here at the moment, because I didn't know if and when you'd be coming, but enough to keep the wolf from the door until I get to the market.'

Half an hour later they were all seated around a long pine table in the cosy clutter of the kitchen as Alfonso lifted the lid off a big casserole dish. 'Cassoulet,' he announced. 'A classic French dish. Wait for it to cool down and then tuck in.' He smiled around the table. 'You look as if you need to!'

Maria felt a flood of relief, only wishing that Pedro could be with them.

After supper, all the children, even Carmen, went to bed early, exhausted from the strain of the journey. Maria elected to stay up and talk to Alfonso, both cradling a glass of the local red wine. She noticed his resemblance to Pedro, although looking younger, with none of the stress that she'd last seen on her husband's face. He seemed very friendly and kind.

'I guess you don't know when Pedro will make it?' As soon as the words were out of his mouth, he regretted them. Of course she wouldn't know.

'No.' said Maria sadly 'Or if he even *will*.'

'Let's pray he does.'

Having made one gaffe, he immediately resolved not to make another by telling her what had been all over that day's papers – the disastrous fall of Barcelona and the vast exodus of yet more people trying to get out over the mountains, probably Pedro included. That's if he were lucky enough to be still alive.

But she had to know soon, and know from *him*, not from some Spanish-speaking neighbour she might casually meet in the town.

'I'm sure he'll make it,' he said placing his hand on hers, while not feeling sure at all. 'He's made of very tough stuff. As *you* clearly are. It must have been terrible making that crossing and in this weather.'

'It was. Half the time we had to sleep huddled up together with piles of other people just to keep warm. I was constantly terrified my two youngest were going to get crushed. And getting food and water was a nightmare, picking weeds to eat and even having to cup our hands to drink water from puddles. That's why the children are so thin. It's a miracle they're not ill as well. I can't tell you how relieved I am to be here. And to have a proper bed to go to.

In fact, Alfonso, if you don't mind, I think I'll go up to mine pretty soon.'

'I quite understand.'

Though desperately tired, Maria only slept fitfully that night, thinking about Pedro and then disturbed by Carmen who had slipped into her bed in the small hours, woken by another nightmare about the woman with the baby on the Igualada Town Hall steps.

* * *

At nine the next morning, Alfonso and Maria were alone again in the kitchen – both glad the children were still in bed, and hopefully sleeping off the strain of the journey.

'Let's leave them to lie in,' said Alfonso. 'Then when everyone's up and dressed, we can fetch water for a bath. You'd probably all like one after that horrific journey.'

'I certainly would,' smiled Maria.

There's a fountain down the road where I get the water, one of lots in the town. Nobody's got running water here yet. It's a bit of a struggle getting it back here with enough to fill the tub – several journeys to and fro, but with all of us pitching in, it'll be much easier. 'All hands to the pump' as they say.'

Anyway,' he added, 'did you sleep alright?'

'Fine,' Maria nodded, knowing it was a lie. 'And thanks again for having us. I really hope you won't find us too much of a crowd.'

'Far from it. As I said last night, I've been on my own too long.'

Alfonso suddenly remembered their filthy clothes when arriving at the house and noticed the dirty dress Maria was still in from last night. 'And then when you've all had a bath you can help yourself to my wife's clothes in the cupboard in my room. I've never got around to clearing them out, and they'll probably fit you and Carmen, and then we can buy some new clothes for the youngest later.'

Maria suddenly worried about how she would pay, but as if reading her thoughts he patted her on the shoulder. 'Don't worry about money. I'll pay as a welcome present, and then we can sort out that sort of thing later.' Immediately he regretted saying that. What if she hadn't got any money? And what if Pedro didn't return? Could he afford to finance them all? Somehow, he'd have to.

An hour later, the bath was now full of hot water, heated on the stove, and one by one, everyone was at last able to wash properly before having breakfast and deciding what to do that day.

Despite the horrors of the last six days, Carmen was eager to go exploring, a little annoyed that her mother had insisted on her taking her sisters which would slow her up considerably. The three of them were now strolling around the town – basically one long and wide high street lined with all kinds of shops and attractive three-storey houses with faded shutters painted in different colours, and leading to a big square at the end.

Taking a side street, a surprise discovery was what looked like an old military barracks enclosing a large and elegant courtyard, with a poignant memorial – a statue of a boy soldier cradled in the arms of an angel. Carmen was shocked to see the hundreds of names on the plaques – many of them from the same families, noting too, that many of them were Spanish. She was to find out later from Pedro that it had once been a military school.

By half an hour later, they had been around the local church in the town centre where the three of them decided to say a prayer for their father. They had also discovered an attractive hotel with a small garden called Le Cheval Blanc, and wandering slightly further out of town, a really big Protestant temple, presumably reflecting the large number of people with that faith in the town. Never having met a Protestant in her life, Carmen wondered what differences they had with Catholics, and whether Alfonso would know.

They had then wandered down to the river where a long line of women was busy washing clothes – a job Carmen suddenly dreaded if her mother asked her to help, as she most certainly would with five of them in the house, and six if her father made it.

But in every other respect, Carmen decided that St-Hippolyte-du-Fort seemed a pleasant and friendly enough place to live, and above all it was not plunged into the horrors of war. That, Carmen told herself, was its biggest blessing.

'Learned any French words?' asked Alfonso at supper that evening.

'Loads!' smiled Otilia. 'Rue, église, café, rivière.' Only a slight Spanish accent.

'And pharmacie!' chimed in Juanita. 'And 'boucherie chevaline.''

'Goodness me!' said Maria. 'Whatever's that? It sounds a bit of a mouthful.'

'It is,' laughed Alfonso, 'it's a horse butcher, though I don't touch horse meat myself.'

He turned to the children. 'Goodness, you're doing well! At this rate, you'll soon speak French even better than me! And what's my place of work?' 'Un garage!' they all chimed in.

'And how do you pronounce this town?'

'Saint-Hippolyte-du-Fort!'

'Excellent! But lots of people call it Hippo for short. I certainly do, it's much easier.'

'What's a Protestant?' Carmen asked him.

'Ah, that's a difficult subject.'

As he started explaining, Maria was suddenly frightened that she'd be quickly left behind if she didn't learn the local customs and language fast in this strange new country, and yearned for Pedro more than ever.

FOUR

* * *

THE NEXT DAY WAS BRIGHT AND SUNNY AND NOT TOO COLD FOR THE END OF January. Alfonso had taken them all down the street to the market in the square in front of the Town Hall. It was full of people and with colourful stalls piled high with olives and spices, and many fruits and vegetables they'd never even seen before – or not seen for years. After months of food shortages in Spain they were all amazed by the variety and quantity of the food on offer. Even Juanita and Otilia had been wide-eyed.

Alfonso had sent them back to his house with the provisions, wondering exactly how to convert into francs the silver coins that Maria had insisted on pressing into his hands. Perhaps he could ask one of his Spanish friends in the Café de la Bourse? Someone would probably have exchanged currency before, and might be there on market day. He had pointed out the directions to the café to Maria and now waited for her with a beer in front of him, in the company of a Spanish friend, Luis. The imminent collapse of the Republic made him launch into his usual theme, completely forgetting about converting coinage.

'God, I'm glad I got out a year ago. I *really* didn't like the way things looked at all. A lot of Socialist and Communist hot air. Brave enough, but amateurish. The Republic shouldn't have had to rely on those foreigners – you know, the International Brigades – to bail them out and then try and hold back those German and Italian bastards. They've got all sorts of nationalities on *both* sides – German, English, and Italian. Even the Irish. What a mess! It's an absolute rag-bag.' He paused to reach for his beer.

'And as for our so-called 'friends', only the Mexicans and Poles have been any use. And of course the bloody Russians have got their own aims, not ours. Frankly, I think Stalin just wanted to keep the war going to cause trouble for capitalist countries or something. *And* he got all our damned gold. Those planes and other things he gave us weren't exactly Christmas presents.' He sipped moodily at his drink.

'And Britain was never going to help with that ridiculous Chamberlain idiot with his silly umbrella. Nor the French. Look how they both caved in at Munich.'

Luis nodded. As a simple farmer, most of the time he had little idea what the hell Alfonso was going on about. But he was very fond of his friend and well used to his regular outbursts.

'At least Daladier's French Government is Socialist and has a bit more sympathy.' Alfonso sighed, pouring himself more beer. 'Anyway, it looks as if it's all over. By the way, something important. My cousin's wife and daughters have just pitched up. They escaped across the mountains. Hell of a journey. She told me some pretty awful things. Anyway, I'll be putting them up for a while. Or as long as it takes. She's called Maria. And do me a favour. When she turns up here, please, whatever you do, *don't* mention the mess in Barcelona. I've not got around to telling her yet, and she's frantic about her husband. He's still there.'

He had warned his friend just in time, as only seconds later Maria arrived. After the introductions, Alfonso was wondering when to tell her about the events in Spain. However, things were suddenly taken out of his hands. A grey-haired man came in and looked around the café. Spotting Alfonso and Luis, he quickly came over. Tears were streaming down his face as he sat down, dumping a newspaper on to the table with something in French about BARCELONE in the headline.

'It's all over,' he cried out in Spanish. '*Maldito catastrofé!* Barcelona's gone, and people are streaming into France!'

Maria stared at the paper, not understanding it, but understanding his Spanish words only too well. She burst into sudden tears, with the men playing Belote around her looking up at her with curiosity. Alfonso put his arms around her and guided her to a table outside.

'I'm really sorry about that. I wanted to tell you last night, but I just didn't think you could handle the news right then.'

Maria looked stricken, obviously panicking about Pedro, perhaps fighting and dying in some quixotic last stand. She stared at him bleakly. 'I think I need to go back to the house.'

Alfonso nodded. 'Of course. I'll go with you.'

'No, I'll be all right. Stay with your friends. But next time if there's any news, please tell me. It's better than *not* knowing. I never knew half of what was going on back home.'

* * *

That evening there was plenty on the table, though Maria barely ate a thing – roast chicken and vegetables and a surprisingly long, big loaf. 'Gros pain!' cried out Otilia, picking it up and waving it around – proud of two more French words. She and Juanita chatted animatedly about the town, comparing their different observations and saying how friendly it seemed to be, though Maria stayed all but silent, as did Carmen – both lost in their own thoughts. It was left to Alfonso to chat to the children and add a bit more to their vocabulary.

'That's 'sel,' he said, pointing to the salt, and this is 'poivre'. And this,' he said pointing to his glass of wine, is 'un verre du vin', although you're too young to drink it. And if you want to thank me for dinner, you say 'Merci'.'

'Merci!' chimed in the girls.

At last all the children had gone up to bed, and Alfonso and Maria were left sitting by the fireside.

'Again Maria, I'm *really* sorry about that Spaniard bursting in this morning in the café.'

'It's not your fault.'

There was a long pause before Alfonso changed the subject, desperate to avoid talking about the fall of Barcelona. 'We'll have to get the children into schools, and get them taught French. Luckily, I know some of the teachers in the public one. The Catholic one will be too difficult to get into. Like most Catholic schools, they're pretty against the Republican Spanish right now. I'll ask around in the morning.'

Maria was shocked, never having realized there was such antagonism in France towards the Spanish, or knowing that many of the locals were Protestants. Only much later would she hear of the religious wars and about something called the 'Camisards' Revolt'– and indeed the reason why there was a fort at Saint-Hippolyte-du-Fort at all.

'That would be kind of you.'

'That Carmen of yours, how old is she?'

'Sixteen, nearly seventeen.'

'Nearly seventeen? Almost old enough to be out of school. A lovely-looking girl. But very quiet, isn't she?'

'Tonight she was, but she's not normally like that. She's usually very chirpy, but she's been through a lot just recently. Seen too many things, like I have.'

She recounted in more detail the stories of the headless woman and then of Carmen bayoneting her would-be rapist.

'Por Dios! Well, at least it sounds as if she can look after herself.' He smiled. 'Perhaps we should warn the local boys!'

* * *

Alfonso was as good as his word and had gone to see the school early in the morning. Thankfully, there would be no problem and the three girls could enrol on the following Monday. Maria had already sorted out their meagre clothes and worked out what else she needed to buy in the market or from the little shops.

The news from Spain continued to be appalling. Girona, the last big town in Catalonia, had fallen, so the end was only days away, and rumours abounded that France was about to recognize the Franco regime. By now Maria was asking Alfonso to translate the newspapers for her, and they told a tragic tale. Tens of thousands of people were still pouring over the mountains and into France every day. She was deeply worried about her friends and relations, but her real terror was for Pedro. What had happened to him? Was he even still alive? And now her daughters were all asking the same questions and she hardly knew how to answer.

Adding to her worries, she also realized that she must get some kind of job. The money from those gold and silver coins would soon run out and she hated the idea of herself and her family becoming a burden on Alfonso. But how could she get a job without a word of French?

* * *

Maria had been too exhausted and pre-occupied by other thoughts during her first week at the house to take in much of the surroundings, but now she did for the first time, coming down early to the kitchen in a dressing gown and suddenly shocked by the state of it. The place clearly hadn't had a proper clean-up in years – probably she thought, since Alfonso's wife had died. Piles of old newspapers lay everywhere, the stone sink was almost black and numerous cobwebs trailed from the wooden beams above her. That wasn't even counting the tarnished copper pans hanging on the wall and the heavily-stained wood oven, nor the dusty tiled floor. And opening the shutters to let in the fresh air, she couldn't help noticing that the windows hadn't been cleaned in years.

And she also noticed that the latrine was in dire need of attention and similarly the bath. Clearly, she thought, Alfonso needed a woman in his life, but wondered if it would hurt his pride if she offered to help clean the place up.

But she needn't have worried. Coming into the kitchen, Alfonso immediately solved the problem for her as he glanced around, flicking away a cobweb.

'Sorry this house is all in a bit of a mess. It's not easy to look after with a garage to run and no-one here to help me.'

Maria smiled. 'And more important things to think about. But I'd be really happy to sort things out if you like. Frankly, it would help me take my mind off Pedro and give me something to do. And not speaking French, I'm a bit scared of going out in the town at the moment – and nobody's going to give me a job. Even if I could leave the children – which I can't.'

Alfonso smiled, pulling out a chair from under the table and sitting down. 'Then I'd be most grateful. That's if you don't mind. In fact, it'll be really nice to have a woman's touch here again.'

FIVE

* * *

CARMEN HAD REALLY THROWN HERSELF INTO LEARNING FRENCH, realizing that nobody really spoke anything else in town, except for the handful of other Spanish who had arrived in the last few months. Now she was really working hard, not just at her formal studies at school, but also by reading the papers and listening to the radio whenever she could. Thus she was the first in her immediate family to absorb the news of the worrying signs from the rest of Europe.

In the middle of March, she heard that the Germans had taken over the whole of Czechoslovakia, something that their leader, Hitler, someone she remembered who had armed the Nationalists, had promised the French and the British that he'd never do. All news reports said he could no longer be trusted, and that France had better prepare for war.

Carmen could scarcely bear the thought of that. After three years of a brutal civil war back in Spain, with hundreds of thousands killed or murdered, she recoiled from even the mention of war. Surely nothing was worth such misery? She had never understood the depths of the hatreds back in Spain. Why couldn't people resolve their differences?

By the end of March, the fighting had stopped in Spain, but the refugees kept coming and coming, though not her father whom she thought of constantly, as did her mother – evident from her often sad face. Carmen heard that most of the refugees were being put in camps, and that the conditions were terrible. Was her father in one of them, if he were alive at all? He had been so right to make them leave early and come to this nice little town. But where was *he*?

One Friday, Carmen was buying vegetables in the market, chatting in her limited but fast-improving French to a young man in charge of a vegetable stall. After she had paid, he asked her if she was foreign. She blushed, knowing her accent had given her away. The face that smiled back was very good-looking and friendly.

'I'm from Spain.'

'I thought so,' he said, 'it's a lovely accent. And I hope I hear it again. Maybe next market day?'

'Maybe,' Carmen smiled back.

* * *

There was no doubt that a strange atmosphere was pervading the town. Very few Spanish refugees were now arriving. It was said that most of them were being housed in internment camps, just inside France. Only people who could prove that they had an address to go to were allowed further into the country. Maria knew just how lucky they had been. But why had her husband not turned up, knowing their address? She dreaded the worst.

While the war to the south had stopped, the signs from the north were becoming only too ominous. The Germans seemed to have swallowed Czechoslovakia mostly by bluff – and the talk in the cafés was that once again France might have to fight. There were enough women in the town still dressed in widow's black, and too many sad names on the war memorial, several from the same families, to make that prospect an unbearable one.

Keeping busy helped keep Carmen's mind off things a little, and by now her French was good enough to work part-time in a dress shop, where talking to both the other girls and the customers improved her vocabulary still further. At last she was beginning to communicate without searching for words, and not embarrassed if customers asked her questions.

It greatly worried her that her mother was not making the same effort, doomed to be lonely in this friendly and talkative town. Perhaps it was early days, she comforted herself.

After the third time seeing her in the market, the young man – Pierre – tentatively asked her if she would like to come to a dance the following Saturday, telling her that it was to be held in the Salle des Fêtes in the centre of town, part of the old Military Preparatory School barracks.

'I'll have to ask my mother', she said, feeling instantly foolish that she wouldn't be allowed to make the decision herself, even at seventeen. Perhaps Pierre would think that Spanish parents were over-protective. But he didn't seem to mind.

'What if *I* come and ask her? If you live nearby, I could come round after I've finished here, before I drive back to the farm.'

'Okay,' replied Carmen.

And at about two o'clock there was a knock on the door of number 36, and Pierre came in to meet Maria and Alfonso, bringing them a small basket of fruit. Carmen was nervous at first, especially as she and her uncle had to translate everything to Maria. But it all went well. Pierre was charming and polite, and promised to bring Carmen back to the house by 11 o'clock, told firmly by Alfonso that it would be their last date if they didn't.

* * *

'Are you okay?'

Madame Elaine Puget, the owner of the dress shop, had noticed that Carmen, one of her best assistants, hadn't been herself that day, or the day before – much quieter and surprisingly withdrawn. Obviously something was really worrying her, or maybe she wasn't feeling well. She decided to ask her if anything was wrong, concerned that it might be something to do with her missing father.

'I'm fine,' said Carmen, 'just a bit scared about something. And I'm sorry if that's been showing.'

'Do you want to tell me about it? Maybe I can help.'

Madame Puget had grown fond of Carmen over the past few months, admiring her for the way she had made a real effort with her French, and was so good with the customers. And she knew how difficult it must be not knowing where her father was, if he were alive at all, and with a mother who Carmen had told her was finding it very hard to adapt to life in the town.

Carmen smiled. 'Well, it's not really a big problem. It's just that I've been asked to a dance next Saturday at the Military Barracks, and well, I've got nothing nice to wear, and I don't even know how to dance. I want to go, but I don't want to look a fool or let down my boyfriend. Well, not really a boyfriend, but someone I really like. And now I wish I hadn't said I'd go. And I don't know how to get out of it.'

'Well,' smiled Elaine, 'it's lucky you told me because I think I can help you on both counts. What if we run you up a dress in the next few days? You're a good worker, and I'd be happy to help you. And if it's jazz music, as it almost certainly will be, I know just the sort of dress to make. Something that fits at the top with a nice floaty skirt, because there's lots of spinning around with jazz. You don't want anything too restricting, and...'

Carmen shook her head, and put her hand up to stop her. 'That's really, really kind, Madame, but – well, I don't think I can afford it. A new dress, I mean.'

'*I* can though. And I'd love to make you one, and I will – as a 'thank you' for all your hard work here. I've always missed not having a daughter to make dresses for. Five kids, but all of them sons. It would be a pleasure.

And I can help you with the other problem, too. I and my husband Jacques know how to dance to jazz. In fact, my old man's a bit of a whizz at it. He really fancies himself on the dance floor. If you come over to our house for an hour or two after we close up here – say for the next three or four days – I can play you some jazz on our gramophone and show you the basic steps.'

'Would you?' Carmen was as amazed as she was thrilled, but at the same time slightly embarrassed at the prospect of dancing with her employer, although she quickly realized that that would be far better than being totally embarrassed at the dance. Or not going at all and having to explain why to Pierre.

'I'd be delighted,' smiled Elaine, patting Carmen's shoulder, 'and, we can start today if you like, after we close this afternoon. Go home and tell your mother where you'll be, and

I'll give you your first lesson.'

'I'm really grateful,' said Carmen, 'and if I do some overtime next week, I can start paying for the dress.'

'Don't even think about it,' smiled Elaine. 'A first dance is a big milestone. I remember mine, when I was your age. And it would be a dreadful shame not to go. And a great shame for your beau.'

'I don't know how to thank you.'

Elaine patted her on the shoulder. 'Don't. I can't have one of my best girls worried all week when I can solve the problem. And it will be my pleasure.'

* * *

The Salle des Fêtes was surprisingly big – the dining room, Pierre explained, for the six hundred boys of the old Military Preparatory School. Now it was packed with young people, and Carmen was sure that many of them must have come from all around – not just the country villages nearby like Sauve, Quissac, Ganges and Anduze, but maybe much further. Even on market days in the village she had never seen a crowd like this – nearly all young people with the girls in short dresses like hers. Elaine Puget had really done her proud making such a lovely one, and teaching her how to dance the basic jazz steps. What a shame, she thought, if she'd missed this amazing atmosphere and the band on the stage – apparently a famous swing band down from Paris, where it had been wowing audiences with the latest numbers from America. In the two intervals a local band played – 'La Parisiana Jazz' – headed by a small man, a trumpeter called Maurice Bertrand. Carmen was not to know how important he would be in her life one day.

Pierre soon realized proudly that he had brought the prettiest girl in the room, literally the 'belle of the ball' with her long black hair, flashing dark Spanish eyes, and wonderful red dress. And just as quickly, Carmen was pleased that those dancing lessons had really come into their own. In fact, she had to teach Pierre – not the other way around, while he had to keep fending off his friends from dancing with her too often.

With music like that, everyone wanted to dance, and occasionally Carmen heard the band leader announcing names like Tommy Dorsey, Benny Goodman and Glenn Miller. Whoever they were, they certainly had the knack of creating a fantastic atmosphere, and one she could so easily have missed without Elaine's help.

It was all over too soon. The dance had started early and ended early, presumably to fit with the train times, so there was no problem for Pierre getting her back by eleven o'clock.

Outside number 36, Pierre reached for Carmen and kissed her tenderly on the lips, wishing the evening had gone on far longer and that he didn't have to pull on the doorbell. But five minutes before the deadline he reluctantly did so, waiting until she was seen safely inside by her smiling uncle, who looked at his watch and thanked him for bringing her back on time before shuffling back off down the hall.

Before the door closed, Pierre managed to whisper a few words to Carmen. 'Come to the market on Tuesday. I've got a nice idea.'

Carmen nodded, waiting for him to disappear round the corner before she closed the door.

Her first dance, her first real kiss, her first boyfriend. She was too elated to go straight to bed.

SIX

* * *

'WHY DO YOU HAVE A DIFFERENT NAME TO US?' MARIA ASKED Alfonso, as she brought some letters up from the doorway.

'Well, when I first arrived, I thought it would be better to have a French-sounding one. So I changed it legally to Dubois. A bit silly really, because everyone knows I'm Spanish.'

'So would letters addressed to Casales get to us?'

'Well, yes, I suppose so, if the address was right.'

'It's just I'm shocked we've never had any letters from Spain. Frankly I dread the worst. Day after day, and month after month and nothing comes. You know how frantically worried I've been about Pedro? I'm sorry, I just can't hide it.'

'Yes, I know.' He thought for a moment. 'Let's go to La Poste, and check it out.'

In minutes they were on their way to the Post Office. Alfonso did the talking because Maria was still far from confident about speaking her most basic French, let alone when dealing with anyone she thought was 'in authority'.

'Have you had any letters addressed to Casales, 36, Rue Pasteur?' asked Alfonso.

'Let me see', said the woman behind the counter, and went off to a shelf with some letters on it.

'No, but I *do* have these two, for a Señora Casales – but they were addressed to 63 Rue Pasteur, which turned out to be a derelict house – there's nobody there.'

Maria's heart skipped a beat, hearing her name.

'This *is* Señora Casales,' said Alfonso. 'She's my cousin, and her family are living with me at 36.'

'Well, okay. You can have these letters, and I'll note you're living there, Madame. But please *do* tell everyone it's 36, not 63.'

When they reached the street, Maria quickly ripped open the letters, and cried out with joy. 'Por Dios, they're from Pedro! I can't really read them, but I can see a big 'P' at the bottom. And they're French stamps! He must be *alive* and somewhere in France!'

They hurried to the café so Alfonso could read the letters carefully. In the first one, dated two months earlier, Pedro revealed that he had managed to get away from the last of the fighting and join the exodus across the Pyrenees. But then the French had put him in an internment camp at Argelès-sur-Mer – in winter a bitterly cold and unhealthy place. Only those who could prove they had a French address to go to could get out of the camp. So he had begged Maria to get Alfonso write to him.

In the second, more recent letter, he seemed devastated that Alfonso hadn't written and said that in April he had nearly died of pneumonia, as several of his comrades had. Why hadn't they contacted him? What had gone wrong?

Alfonso thought quickly. 'Pedro obviously got the numbers wrong and didn't know I'd changed my name. I'll tell you what. *I* could write for you, but it'll be much better if we can make it sound official. Let's go to La Mairie right now. I know just the fellow for this.' Maria was hugely relieved, not wishing to admit just she how illiterate she was, though realizing that Alfonso would discover all too soon – that's if he hadn't already.

They walked hurriedly down the hill to the Town Hall and Alfonso asked to see his friend, leaving Maria in the outer office where she waited with anxious impatience.

Alfonso and the official came out half an hour later, an eternity for Maria. Alfonso thanked his friend, who then shook hands with her. 'I hope this helps, Madame.' She looked at the letter, on official Mayor's notepaper and, she was told, addressed to the Commandant at the internment camp. Alfonso quickly translated it for her.

'*This is to certify that Madame Maria Casales now resides at 36, Rue Pasteur, Saint-Hippolyte-du-Fort, GARD, with her three daughters, and would be grateful if her husband, Monsieur Pedro Casales, could be released to come and live with her.*

La Mairie of Saint-Hippolyte hereby approves this.

Albert Monpeyssen, Mayor, Saint-Hippolyte-du-Fort.'

They hurried back up the hill to the Post Office, bought stamps and mailed the letter.

'I'm going to the church to thank God for all this,' Maria said to Alfonso. 'I'll see you at the house. Please don't tell the girls. I want to do that, although I'm really afraid of raising their hopes – and mine.'

* * *

It was a scorching hot August and everyone was seeking the shade in town. The Café de la Bourse was half empty and sleepily quiet. Suddenly someone burst in.

'The Nazis and the Russians have done some kind of deal!'

There were many in the room who had witnessed a decade of the Germans and the Soviets battling each other by proxy, not least in Spain's bloody civil war. For them, any kind of pact was incomprehensible, unless it was to free Hitler to attack Poland. They quickly realized that something terrible was about to happen.

naked wines

www.nakedwines.com Limited,
Norwich, United Kingdom
Email: help@nakedwines.com
www.nakedwines.com/trynaked19

To claim go to **www.nakedwines.com/trynaked19**

| Code | **TEWK75** | Password | **ASP32XYN** |

£75

For **Wine lovers**

Get **£75 to spend on a case of delicious wine**

EAMON FITZGERALD
WINE GUY, NAKEDWINES.COM

CLAIM WITHIN **30 DAYS**   £75 WINE VOUCHER

NAKED WINES IS A CUSTOMER-FUNDED WINE BUSINESS

Our customers fund talented, independent winemakers and get rewarded with delicious wines at wholesale prices in return.

1. Claim...

Your £75 voucher at the address below

2. Choose...

12 bottles of wine from our tasty range

3. Next Day...

Delivery to your door or safe place

www.nakedwines.com/trynaked19

or email help@nakedwines.com

naked wines

Claim your £75 today

- ✓ Get £75 off a case of wine priced £114.99 or more
- ✓ NEXT DAY delivery as standard only £4.99
- ✓ Your money back if you are not totally tantalised
- ✓ NO requirement to join any wine "clubs"

| Code | TEWK75 |
| Password | ASP32XYN |

▦ Claim within **30 days**

SEVEN

* * *

THE 'NICE IDEA' THAT PIERRE HAD MENTIONED TO CARMEN TURNED out to be a surprise picnic up in the mountains. On a gloriously warm Sunday morning, Pierre knocked on the door to collect Carmen, delighted to see that her mother and uncle seemed just as pleased to see him.

'So where are you off to?' asked Alfonso, noticing the dusty pick-up truck outside, the one Pierre obviously used to deliver vegetables to the market.

'I thought Carmen might like to see a bit of the countryside. That's if she doesn't mind coming in my old truck. And if you don't mind me taking her for a picnic,' he added.

'Not if you drive carefully.' He instantly worried if he'd been too lenient, knowing that Spanish daughters were rarely allowed to go out with boys unchaperoned.

'I will,' said Pierre. 'And I know these mountain roads. I never go fast'. He glanced at the truck, laughing. 'Anyway, I can't in that old thing!'

'At least it works,' he grinned as he helped Carmen into it, and they rumbled off down the cobbled street.

Carmen couldn't wait to tell him the good news.

'Papá's alive! Mamá suddenly got a letter saying he might turn up in a couple of weeks.' She remembered her mother saying how embarrassed she was that Alfonso had to read it to her, although that was quickly overcome by her immense relief and joy.

'Apparently he's been stuck in an awful camp where a lot of people died of pneumonia. He's really lucky to have made it. Mamá's been going frantic waiting for him. We all have, but it's been even worse for her, especially as she can't speak French – well, only a few words – so it's hard for her to talk to anyone and make friends.'

'That's marvellous news! I look forward to meeting him. That's if he'd like to meet me.' He was suddenly apprehensive. Another person to convince about his gentlemanly intentions, and a father would be even more protective than an uncle. He told himself not to be so selfish.

He drove under the railway viaduct and along the river, but then the road began to climb. Carmen told him she was amazed that the woods were so dense and so green, being used to Spain; much more arid in winter, let alone in the scorching heat of summer.

'We have the highest rainfall crammed into the shortest time here in the Cévennes than anywhere else in France,' explained Pierre above the noise of the engine, 'and it often comes all at once. We've had some terrible floods – 'flash floods' they call them. And they sometimes come in the summer when the ground's bone dry, which makes them even worse. But it's great for our vegetable business, all that water.'

As they climbed steadily, changing gear to zigzag up the hillside, Pierre pointed at the occasional isolated stone houses, many quite large.

'See the little windows at the top? They're not really windows. They're for the ventilation for what were called 'magnaneries'. They used to be silkworm nurseries, where the worms, or 'magnans' as we call them, were reared on mulberry leaves until they made silk cocoons. It was the biggest industry here until Chinese competition killed it. Our last silk factory closed ten years ago. That's why we're all back to being poor,' he laughed. 'But you should see the size of some of the houses here which had big magnaneries. The owners must have been raking it in.'

The old truck slowly climbed and climbed until they passed a big tower.

'That was built by the Moors,' explained Pierre, 'up from Spain, like you. It shows how far they'd conquered.' Carmen was pleased how interested he was in the scenery and local history – another side of him she liked. He was clearly fond of the area and proud of it.

The truck turned up into the woods, climbing even higher. Eventually they came to a peak and Pierre pulled over. He took a big wicker basket out of the back, and led Carmen by the hand to a grassy area, laying out a picnic rug.

The view was stunning. The mountains stretched away as far as they could see, appearing to be a bluish-grey in the heat of the day, and a couple of eagles soared above them in the cloudless sky, one of them actually grasping a writhing snake in its talons, presenting it to his mate.

'Snake eagles,' said Pierre, 'they're very rare. We're lucky to see them.'

They sat on the rocks, sipping the wine he'd brought, and stared at the view in silence for a while.

Then Pierre stood up. 'Back in a moment,' he said with a smile.

Carmen assumed it was a call of nature, but not when he was gone for more than five minutes, and was greatly relieved when he returned, moreover delighted when he suddenly produced a beautiful posy of wild flowers from behind his back.

'Voila , chèrie!'

'Oh, they're lovely!' exclaimed Carmen, standing up to give him a kiss.

After that, the rest of the picnic lay uneaten.

* * *

As they drove slowly down from the mountains, Pierre suddenly decided he had to mention something. It could wait no longer.

'I don't know if you've been reading the papers, but things really don't look too good with Germany. Hitler keeps threatening Poland, something about a place called Danzig, and apparently we've got a treaty with Poland. I don't know why, but we have.

So if Germany and Poland go to war, so will France, and then I'll be called up at once.

That's bad enough. But I also know myself. I'm not sure I could kill anyone – even a bitter enemy. In fact, I *know* I couldn't. I can't even kill animals, even nuisance ones on our farm like rabbits and wild boar. And then there's my father. He went through hell in the last war. Most of his friends were killed, maimed or gassed. He gets into really dark moods and then tells me about it. So the whole idea of war sickens me to the core.'

His words hit Carmen like a thunderbolt, instantly ruining the day. Not *more* war, and more loved ones taken away! The prospect of that was unbearable. She put her hand on his knee, unable to say a thing.

* * *

'The Germans have attacked Poland!' Alfonso had been listening to the radio upstairs, and burst into the kitchen where Maria and the girls were having breakfast.

Carmen's first reaction of horror was made even worse by what Pierre had told her. *If Poland was attacked, France would go to war*, and he would definitely be called up and have to fight. Her worst fears were confirmed as Alfonso continued.

'And Édouard Daladier, the Prime Minister, is bound to declare war on Germany. He *has* to. The French have a treaty with Poland. The British, too.'

Only the two youngest girls were unable to comprehend the immediate and horrifying implications. For Carmen and her mother, it was inconceivable. Scarcely had they escaped the horrors of Spain and its grotesque civil war than their new country of refuge – what was supposed to be their new and *safe* home – was being sucked into a new war. It was beyond comprehension, tragic and shocking.

Carmen suddenly got up from the table. It was market day, and she was desperate to talk to Pierre. She ran to the market and there he was, busy as usual at his crowded stall, but certainly not with his usual smile. As soon as he spotted Carmen, he handed over to his assistant and took her to one side. Carmen could tell immediately from his face that he'd heard the news.

'So you know?' she asked

Pierre nodded bleakly. 'My father told me this morning. And if we *do* go to war, I'm afraid my call-up papers might come any moment. I came round to tell you as soon as I heard, but nobody answered the door.'

Carmen suddenly remembered someone knocking when Alfonso was telling them the terrible news. *'Don't answer it!'* he had told them. 'Whoever it is can wait.'

Pierre came from the back of his stall and gave her a hug. 'Look, I'll come round as soon as I close up here, and we can talk then.'

Carmen walked home, unable to keep back tears.

EIGHT

* * *

IT WAS JUST A WEEK LATER, MID-MORNING, WHEN A STRANGE WHISTLING came from outside in the Rue Pasteur. Ever curious, little Juanita ran to the open window.

'It's *Papá!*' she cried out, jumping up and down with glee.

Maria rushed to the window. A bearded man in battered clothing looked up at her, grinning. She almost didn't recognize him.

'Well, aren't you going to let me in?' he smiled.

And when he did come in, it was obvious that the war and the camp had taken their toll. Pedro was painfully thin and haggard. But his family was ecstatic, with the two youngest clinging to him, apparently oblivious to the stale smell of his skin and clothing. Maria quickly sent Otilia off to the dress shop to tell Carmen to come as soon as she could, and then started to heat water so he could have a bath, asking Alfonso if he could look for some fresh clothes for him.

Half an hour later, Pedro was clean and shaven and looked more his old self – and without the beard, looked younger at once. But the clothes hung off him, and Maria realized she'd have to do quite a lot of altering to make them fit, and that she'd certainly have to feed him up. Clearly he'd been half-starved for months.

At lunch, delighted with decent food, Pedro wolfed it down, telling them between mouthfuls of his ordeal since last seeing them, and what the general situation was. There had been some last despairing fighting, but the Nationalists had been far too strong. The Russian commissars, the 'Red Chaplains' who had been so brutal even to their own side – waging a civil war within a civil war – had suddenly vanished. So there was nobody left to stop the army melting away, which it duly did. Some, like remnants of the International Brigades, had actually marched with flying colours across the border. Others thought that they would be able to go by boat down to Valencia to carry on the fight. But most had thrown away their rifles and joined the last miserable flood of refugees across the mountains – taking their chances.

He had followed the same route as his own family, but certainly did not get the same friendly welcome. Rather, the men were disarmed and separated from the women and he was trucked off to an internment camp. It was by the sea, but in winter that made it windy, damp and horribly cold. They had to sleep on the ground with no blankets and there were no latrines at first. Disease spread rapidly and many of the men became sick and died. Nobody was allowed to leave unless they went back to Spain, very risky, or could prove they had somewhere to go in France, which is why he had written to Maria, trusting that Alfonso would read his letter to her. He had also lost his address book and other papers in the fighting, which was why he had mistakenly transposed the number for Alfonso's house.

But the official letter from the Mayor had worked perfectly, and at last they had let him out – and quickly to make his way to Saint-Hippolyte, and almost certainly for less than humanitarian reasons. One less mouth to feed.

'I can't tell you how happy I am to be here with you all. What's been happening?'

'The girls got into school here,' said Maria. 'And Carmen's now left and is working in a dress shop. Ah, here she is!' Carmen rushed to embrace her father.

'*And* she's got a boyfriend! *And* she's got a boyfriend!' sung out Otilia teasingly, spinning around.

Carmen blushed. 'Well, a *sort* of boyfriend. But not one I can see for much longer, he's just been called up.' Carmen turned and looked bleakly at her father. 'You know about the threat of war here?'

'I'm afraid I have, or rumours of it. That's why I think a lot of us were let out.'

Alfonso explained. 'France has just mobilised, because Germany attacked Poland on Friday, and we've got a treaty with Poland. So after two days France and Britain declared war. That's why Carmen's lad's been called up, poor boy, and is due to leave at any minute.'

'Por Dios!' sighed Pedro, shaking his head in disbelief. 'It's terrible that we just got out of *one* war only to be plunged straight back into another? Will people *never* learn?'

* * *

After Maria and Carmen had gone to bed, Alfonso poured a cognac and passed it to Pedro. 'So, what was it *really* like in the camp?'

Pedro smiled, realizing his cousin hadn't wanted to distress the women by telling them quite how wretched it really was.

'As terrible as you can imagine. We thought that Daladier's Socialist government might have some fraternal sympathy. But we were wrong, very wrong. I suppose, to be fair, they were just swamped with so many people and very, very suddenly. Half a million, it's said. Must be one of the greatest movements of people in history. But still, considering we were only internees, not prisoners, our treatment was absolutely inhumane.

The camp was just the long beach at Argelès-sur-Mer. Probably very nice in summer for a Perpignan family having a day's outing by the sea. But this was February, winter, with an icy wind off the sea. We were all fenced in by barbed wire. There was no shelter at all, and we had to scrape holes in the sand just to avoid that freezing blast. And there weren't even any latrines. So unless you went in the sea, you had to crap in the sand. There were seventy thousand of us, pretty much living in our own shit.'

He paused as Alfonso topped up his glass.

'We were also starving. After a couple of days, some trucks turned up with some bread and water, but men started to die quite quickly. And then we were tormented by lice, and many of us came down with scabies and dysentery. We even used to put the lice in a little circle in the sand and bet on which one left first – you could win a cigarette that way – well, until they ran out too.' He laughed sardonically.

'After a while, some tents and building material arrived and we were able at least to build some shelter for ourselves. Then, to relieve the overcrowding I suppose, some men were shipped out to other camps – 'concentration camps' as the French call them. Gradually the food started to get vaguely organised. But many of us died, some from pneumonia. Terrible!

Ironically, the recent threat of France at war with Germany was, strangely enough, the best thing that could happen to us. With two million Frenchmen being called up to fight, France suddenly needed men to work in the mines and the fields. One local even turned up and took away twenty former pilots to work his vineyard. God knows why he wanted *pilots*. Anyway, shortly after that, I was lucky to be let out.'

He smiled grimly. 'And thank God, they'd at last installed a de-lousing station, just in time. I don't think even *you* would have been pleased to see me here three weeks ago!'

* * *

Five days before he was due to leave to join the army, and to cheer themselves up, Carmen and Pierre had decided to go to Saint-Hippolyte's little cinema to see *Fric-Frac*, the latest Fernandel comedy. They settled in their seats as the lights went down, holding hands.

But they'd forgotten that after the 'Jean Mineur Publicité' reel of commercials, there would be Pathé News. Up to date as always, it suddenly featured Germany's blitzkrieg attack on Poland. For Carmen, the first couple of minutes were testing enough, watching the German tanks and artillery in action, but when the Stuka dive-bombers were shown toppling into their dives, punctuated with the howl of their sirens, her nails suddenly stabbed into Pierre's hand.

'I'm sorry, I can't watch this. I have to go.' She got up and stumbled past the people in their row, with Pierre following, whispering apologies. Outside he found Carmen shaking and crying, and put his arms around her.

'I'm sorry, but I've seen all that happening – *for real*,' she said between her tears. 'I can't bear it. I really can't. Not all over again. And now with you going away and everything, well, it's all too much.' She suddenly burst into a fresh flood of tears.

He nodded, full of concern. 'Don't worry. I feel the same. You know my *own* attitude to war. Let's get out of here, and go round to the café and cheer ourselves up.'

With a drink in front of them, Carmen told him of three years of war back in Spain and her own experience of bombing, including the headless mother at Igualada and the slaughterhouse scene of the shelter at Figueras station. Only now was Pierre beginning to take in quite what she had gone through in her homeland, and when escaping from it. And just as bad, what he might probably now go through himself.

As they continued to talk over more glasses of wine, Carmen gradually recovered her composure, and eventually Pierre walked her home. She paused at the door.

'I forgot to tell you. My parents would really like you to come round to supper tomorrow.'

'What, as a farewell?'

'No, as an au revoir.'

'I'd be delighted,' he smiled, and kissed her goodnight.

* * *

Trying out his very basic French, Pedro turned to Pierre as they sat down to supper. 'Carmen tells me you know a lot about the local history and wildlife.'

'Well, not a lot. There's still masses I don't know. But I've always been interested, and there's far more to see here than most people think. Most people consider it a bit of a backwater. But it isn't if you're interested in things like history and nature.'

'She really loved your trip up into the mountains. Made me want to go too, but it sounds a bit of a hike without a car or truck.'

'I won't need mine soon.'

That was the only awkward moment of the evening.

Pedro was beginning to like this boy. Evidently kind, and also well-mannered, not sitting down until everyone else did, and also happy to sit with Otilia and Juanita before supper and do a splendid drawing of an eagle for them. And it was touching the way he looked at Carmen, clearly deeply fond of her – and probably in love. It was nice, too, that he'd brought a bunch of wild flowers for Maria together with an illustrated pocket book so she could find out which ones they were, that's if she ever got around to learning French, something that was now beginning to worry him.

At no point during supper did anybody mention the war – on strict orders from Maria, and it was a happy occasion despite the gathering storm clouds.

When they moved to the salon to have coffee, Pierre turned to Pedro.

'Carmen tells me that you were once in the vegetable business, like me.'

'Yes, in the south of Spain and then again when we moved to Igualada. Well, before the trouble started.'

'I've been thinking. I'm going off to the army any day now, and my father's getting too frail to keep the business going. Would you be interested in helping him?'

Pedro paused. 'Well, goodness, that's quite a thought. Why don't you drive me to your farm after the market tomorrow and we can talk about it?'

While very relieved that he might have unexpectedly found a job, Pedro wished it hadn't been in these circumstances.

Soon after, Pierre excused himself, thanking the family but explaining he had to be up early for the market – maybe for the last time.

Carmen saw him to the door and it was some time before they heard her come in again and go straight up to bed.

After Pierre had gone home and Maria and Carmen had turned in for the night, Alfonso and Pedro poured themselves some cognac and lit their pipes.

'A very nice boy, that Pierre. Carmen could do a lot worse,' said Pedro.

'Yes, I like him too. A lot. A real shame he's got to go.'

'What do you think is going to happen?'

'To be honest, I don't know. We don't seem to be doing anything to help the Poles, and neither are the British. If you ask me, there's not much point having a treaty if we're not going to do anything. But short of attacking Germany properly and at once, there isn't much we *can* do. And we're certainly not ready to do that.'

'I certainly don't like the news coming from Poland' said Pedro, refilling their glasses, and remembering what he had read in the papers and heard on the radio. 'It looks as if the Germans are slicing through them. The Poles didn't seem to have many planes and I've heard most of them are destroyed already. So the Fritzes can bomb the shit out of what's left of them. I've even heard the Polish cavalry actually charged the *tanks*. What a bloody mess.' He paused and looked at his cousin.

'Well, if we assume the Germans win, then what about France?'

'God knows. We may be okay. After all, we've got the Maginot Line. They'd never get through that.'

'They might not bother, Alfonso. They'll just go round it. After all, they're quite ruthless enough just to go south through Switzerland, neutral or not, or more likely, north through Belgium – difficult or not. I've seen them in action in Spain with their tanks and planes working together. They don't play games with war, believe me.'

'But surely we'll have forces to counter-attack?'

'Don't count on it, cousin. Frankly, I don't think the French army is what it once was. And from what I've heard, the French parcel out their tanks to help the infantry. The Germans are far more clever. They group them all in divisions, called Panzer divisions, and aim to punch through the enemy's lines and encircle them from behind. Wait a couple more days and listen to the news from Poland. I think you'll see I'm right.'

'I sincerely hope not. You're pretty pessimistic.'

Pedro reached for the bottle. 'If you'd seen what I have, so would you be.'

* * *

Next morning Pedro was drinking a much-needed coffee in the kitchen and reading a newspaper which reported that Polish armies were indeed being encircled, just as he had so gloomily predicted the night before.

Carmen came in, ready for work, and sat down beside him. She looked very pretty, but far from happy.

Pedro quickly put the paper away. 'Carmen, I've got something for you, or rather something to give your nice boyfriend.'

She looked at him with sad eyes, not asking what.

Pedro took a tiny horseshoe out of his pocket. 'I carried this with me all through the civil war and when I was interned, and it brought me luck. I'd like him to have it. I've had my luck. I don't need any more, but you two do. Here…' He passed it over the table.

'But *your* luck might run out,' said Carmen, looking at the horseshoe.

'As I just said, I've been lucky enough. Please take it, and give it to Pierre.'

'Thanks, Papa.'

It was the first time he'd seen her smile in several days.

NINE

* * *

IT WAS A VERY SAD DAY FOR THE WHOLE TOWN, MADE WORSE BY THE steady rain falling from grey skies, almost like tears. Few people could escape the analogy of the bleak weather with the threatening circumstances and the imminent departure of loved ones. Nobody spoke much. Most had heads bowed. Even neighbours did not exchange the usual greetings, let alone the triple kisses of the region, instead nodding to people they knew and then looking away. It was only September, usually sunny and warm, but not on that day.

There were about twenty young men going off to join the army, but there was no euphoria, no pleasure or false glory in it. A little military band of old men was trying to play rousing patriotic tunes, but it didn't really work.

Everyone had climbed or driven up the hill to the station – young men with their parents, families, wives and girlfriends, and were now standing around outside the railway station, talking in subdued tones, if talking at all. There was none of the usual foolhardy mention of 'home by Christmas', and many of the older women wore black – mothers who had lost husbands in the last war. They remembered that over a million men had gone off from railway stations just like this – and never returned. And that many more had come back blinded, maimed and crippled.

Carmen was waiting with her whole family. They had become fond of Pierre and hated to see him go. She was trying to keep back the tears.

The old Citroen pick-up came to a stop, and Pierre got out, as did his elderly father – looking grim-faced, and everyone exchanged greetings and handshakes, and moreover, reassuring pats on the back – far less usual.

Pierre led Carmen a little way away.

'I'm sure I'll be alright. Try not to worry too much.'

Carmen knew that would be impossible.

She looked up at him. 'Do you have the little horseshoe?'

'Of course.' He tapped his pocket.

'Keep it close, Pierre.'

Suddenly there was a whistle, and a plume of white smoke and steam rose beyond the trees against the dark mountains. The local train came puffing round the corner from the long viaduct leading from the next town of Ganges.

Everyone crowded on to the platform. Now there was a hubbub of noise as families said goodbye to their young men.

Pierre hugged his pale and stricken father, and then turned to embrace Carmen. 'I love you,' he whispered. 'And I'll write as soon as I can.'

All too soon there was a hiss, and the train began to move.

* * *

'I think there's something very wrong with this place,' said Alfonso before going off to his garage. He and Pedro were sitting in the corner of the Café de la Bourse, away from the other customers – almost all men of their age or older, and mostly chatting loudly or playing their game of Belote – though with a few buried in the local paper.

Pedro looked round the café, puzzled.

'No, not this café, and not Hippo,' laughed Alfonso. 'They're pretty much OK. I mean the whole country, France.'

Pedro had been so glad to get out of the firing line of a brutal civil war that he had not had the time, nor even the inclination to study his new country to any great extent, and certainly not with a critical eye.

'Wrong? Why do you say that?'

'Well, I'm sure you've got no time for that bastard Mussolini, but he may have been on the right track when he said that France was crippled with bad journalism, syphilis and drink. I really can't vouch for journalism because I don't read the national papers that much, but I *have* read that an extraordinary number have syphilis. Would you believe it?'

Pedro looked aghast, and almost spilled his coffee. 'No, I wouldn't. Good God.'

'And I've just read a Government health bulletin that says that the French drink about two hundred litres of wine a head each year. Assume that women drink much less and children hardly at all, that probably means men must get through over four hundred litres of wine per head each year. And there's a bar here for every eighty-four people, five times the number of bars the British have, apparently. And look around you.'

Pedro did, for the first time noticing the number of glasses on the tables quite early in the morning, most likely of cognac or pastis. But then, he thought, there's a war on. And few of the men were of fighting age anyway.

'Does it really matter? I'd say they need cheering up.'

'I think it *does*. It means most of them must be half-drunk, or hung over much of the time. And I think it shows that this country has never really recovered from the Great War – with many of their best people killed. Over a million, I've heard.' He sipped at his coffee.

'There's a whole generation now that will do absolutely *anything* to avoid another war, even if it's drinking themselves to death. Look what happened during the Munich crisis, all of those people running away in their cars from Paris – what they called 'the stampede of the well-to-do' or 'the blue funk'. Not much of the old courageous Verdun spirit there.'

'But the French army, it's surely far more disciplined,' said Pedro.

'Don't count on it. The French even have a word for muddling through – *débrouillage* – and they're probably doing a lot of that even in the armed forces. For instance, putting a mountain of money into that Maginot Line and probably not nearly enough into planes and tanks. That wouldn't surprise me one bit.'

'Let's hope you're wrong. Although if it's anything like Spain was, you probably aren't. Even so, I don't think you need to be so hard on the French or quite so pessimistic. After all, at least they've given us a home.'

'I agree there, but I still think it's a mess,' sighed Alfonso, 'even *without* the army. You only have to look at the papers to see the social problems piling up every day. Strikes, tax revolts, riots – oh, and the usual Jew-bashing. And not just rioting and looting their shops, poor souls – but even bashing them in Parliament.' He leaned forward, lowering his voice. 'Would you believe, a Deputy in the Assembly in Paris actually shouted 'Jews to the gallows!' the other day, and was even *cheered*?'

Pedro was visibly shocked. 'No, I wouldn't.'

'Well, it's one more sign that in spite of all the glitz of the Paris Exposition two years ago, this is in many ways a very divided and backward country. And at worst, a frighteningly ignorant, biased and self-deluding one. Although, as you say, they've taken us in. We have to be grateful for that. *Only a bit*, thought Pedro, *remembering his French concentration camp.*

'Do you know that a few years back there was so much hatred in France that Georges Simenon, the writer who created that detective fellow, Maigret, got so incensed that he created a movement with people wearing badges saying 'SANS HAINE' – 'without hate'. And he was *Belgian*, for God's sake!

And in spite of the fact that our Daladier was fully part of the Munich disgrace, the French are blaming the British again. They're even calling Mister Chamberlain '*Monsieur J'aime Berlin*'. And nobody's buying silly umbrellas like his as they did just after Munich.'

Alfonso was clearly about to launch into another tirade, but Pedro put up his hand to stop him. It wasn't like his cousin to rant on like this. 'I have to say, Alfonso, I think you're being a bit unfair. You seem to forget what the French went through in the last war. I suggest you look at the village memorial some time.'

'I walk past it every morning on the way to work.'

'Precisely. You walk *past* it. Next time, stop and take a damned good look. So many names, and so many from the same families. And, as I said, France *is* our host country. We've got a lot to be thankful for. And there are plenty of decent people in this place. And, what's more, a lot of them who've seen too much like we have. It's no wonder they're demoralised, but that doesn't mean they're utterly disorganised too.'

'I'm not so sure,' said Alfonso. He pointed out of the window. 'It's bad enough here in Hippo, a town of four thousand. For God's sake, we don't even have *mains water* yet, and we have to go to the fountains. And half the houses have no electricity. We're quite literally in the dark ages. And the houses that *do* have electricity only have a few pathetic 40 watt bulbs, so we have to stumble around in the dark – as you know only too well.' He tipped back the last of his coffee. 'Frankly, for all the bombast, the parades, the boastful propaganda and all the rest, I have to say I'm fearing the worst.' He clunked the cup back on to its saucer.

Pedro studied his grim face. 'On that note, I'm afraid I'm going to have a stiff drink.'

To his relief, Alfonso smiled. 'Me, too.'

* * *

It was the fifth letter from Pierre that Carmen had received since he had left. The others had told her about arriving in the training camp, the shouting sergeants, the drill, the rifle shooting, the inspections, the route marches and the rather skimpy tactical training.

They were also full of his feelings, of his loneliness, home-sickness and, above all, of his love for her.

This new letter was different. First, it was written in pencil, which seemed rather strange. Then, it revealed that Pierre had now been moved to be stationed somewhere in the Maginot Line, although he was not allowed to reveal exactly where. Carmen, not being French, had no real idea what the legendary Maginot Line was, or even what it was meant to do. Keep the Germans out, yes. But how?

> *My Darling,*
>
> *I miss you terribly and long to be with you again. There may be good news on that, because I'll be allowed one week's leave in about a month's time.*
>
> *We're now sitting in one of the big forts in the Maginot Line. I'm not allowed to tell you where, or anything about our armament, or else this letter would be censored by my Lieutenant or you wouldn't get it.*
>
> *But as it's all being filmed for the newsreels, it doesn't seem to be entirely secret and I can tell you that it's pretty amazing. The big guns are on the top, in huge revolving steel and concrete cupolas. Then everything else is underground. We're on the first floor down, to be able to rush upstairs to man the machine-guns. But then there are elevators going down six floors – to mess rooms, kitchens, a hospital, military telephone exchanges, a gymnasium, a cinema and even an underground railway system linking us to the other forts in the Line. God knows what it all cost!*

There's even a sun-room where they give us ultra-violet sessions to keep us healthy, although it hasn't kept up the tan I got from working on the farm. In fact, I think I look pasty white!

The whole thing is powered by big diesel engines that throb away all the time. They're meant to provide the light and the ventilation. But that doesn't seem to work very well, as the whole place smells of sewage and cooking and it's always very humid in here. That's why I'm writing with a pencil. Ink seems to splodge and run on the damp paper.

It's not dangerous here, it's just very boring with nothing happening. We call it 'drôle de guerre'. Apparently the British, who are to the north of us, call it the 'Phoney War'. The Fritzes call it 'Sitzkrieg' or 'sitting war'– although I've no sympathy for them. After all, they started the damned thing.

Some of us are a bit worried about this whole Maginot Line project. It may be very impressive and even impregnable. But I overheard some of our officers arguing about it, and they were saying that the Fritzes could just avoid it, go round the southern end through Switzerland or, more likely, the northern end in Belgium. It's all a bit of a worry. In many ways, I'd rather they did go round it because, as I've told you, the very thought of actually shooting at someone to kill them fills me with dread, even if he's a Fritz. You know my attitude about all that. Just as long as someone else is there to stop them.

Anyway, my darling, I must go now to catch the post before going up on sentry watch.

I'll write again in a couple of days, or as soon as I can.

All my love.

Pierre xx

TEN

* * *

CARMEN LOOKED UP FROM THE LETTER SHE HAD BEEN READING AND RE-reading, hugely relieved that Pierre was safe for the moment – stationed somewhere on the Maginot Line, hundreds of kilometres of underground fortifications stretching down through France, all the way from Belgium to Switzerland. Telling herself that if she read it again she'd be late for work, she tucked it into her pocket and hurried to the shop.

Her first customer, a tall red-haired girl of about the same age as her, came in shortly afterwards. It was the third time that week that Carmen had seen her in the shop, and once again she was looking at the same dress. It was one of Carmen's favourites, and one she'd loved to have bought herself if she could afford it. But it was way beyond her salary, and she knew at once it would look wonderful on this potential buyer.

'One of my favourites,' she said as the girl took out the hanger and held the dress against herself. The girl smiled back. 'I can see why,' she replied, looking around for a mirror.

'If you'd like to try it on, there's a changing room down there,' said Carmen, pointing to the end of the shop.

'Thanks.' The girl disappeared for a few minutes and came back in the dress, which fitted perfectly as Carmen knew it would. 'What do you think?' she asked Carmen tentatively.

'It's perfect. Looks really good on you.'

'Honestly?'

'Honestly. You're the perfect height for it. And it really suits your hair.'

'Well, I think I'll buy it. It'll my birthday present from Mamá. I'm eighteen in a few days time and she told me to choose something I really liked.'

'Happy birthday in advance!' smiled Carmen.

'Thanks.'

While Carmen was busy wrapping the dress in tissue, the girl started chatting.

'Do you live here in town?'

'Yes, just down the road. We came here from Spain about six months ago.'

'Over the mountains?'

Carmen nodded.

'Heavens, that must have been tough.'

'It was, but not as horrific as staying there.'

The girl thought for a moment. 'I can imagine. My family are always having to get out of places. First we got out of Poland, and then Germany and – now out of Paris. Everywhere we go, it seems we have to move on. My father thinks that if the Germans ever get to Paris, we'll be much safer down here with all the woods and mountains and places to hide. Jews like us are always having to hide.'

Why? wondered Carmen. She knew nothing about why Jews felt forced to hide, but was soon to find out more.

'Things are really terrible for our people in Poland, and lots of our family are stuck there. The Germans are rounding them all up and putting them in ghettos, sealed-off areas, and we've no idea what's happening to them. We keep sending them letters, but there's never a reply. My parents are growing frantic. In fact, I'm quite surprised they're giving me a party at all with everything that's going on. I suppose they think an eighteenth birthday is a sort of milestone.'

'It is,' smiled Carmen, once again wishing she knew more about what was happening.

'Anyway, my name's Sarah Levy. It's been very nice talking. I hardly know anyone here, and all my best friends are back in Paris.'

She turned to go, but suddenly turned back. 'Tell you what, I've just had a thought. If you're not doing anything on Thursday lunchtime, why not come to the party? We don't live far from here, just on the outside of town. And as I said, I hardly know anyone of my age here. I know my parents wouldn't mind. In fact, they'd be pleased. And if you tell me your name and address, I can drop in an invitation with a map of where our house is.'

Carmen was surprised, but delighted. She seemed such a nice girl.

'Well, if you're sure.'

'I *am* sure.'

Carmen smiled, jotting down her name and address. 'I'll see you then. Thanks!'

The girl waved through the window and disappeared, leaving Carmen wondering whether to go, and, if so, what to wear. Would the dress Madame Puget had made for the dance be alright? Perhaps not. But what else was there in her wardrobe? For a split second she wondered about borrowing a dress from the shop, but quickly decided against that. She could ill afford to lose Madame Puget's trust, especially after she had been so kind.

* * *

At mid-day Carmen started to walk the kilometre to Sarah's house, a little nervous about what to expect, but at least reasonably confident about what she was wearing. Her mother had been able to adapt the dress she had worn to the dance to make it a little more formal and less floaty, lending her a light shawl to cover her bare arms. Madame Puget had told her 'the secret is not to show too much flesh, even at your age; that's if you're meeting people's parents.' And though Carmen had found the advice somewhat prudish, despite having Spanish parents,she had decided to follow it.

Following the map on the invitation, she was soon outside the biggest house she had ever seen, with several very smart cars in the tree-lined drive, astonished by the huge wrought-iron gates leading to a beautiful garden, where dozens of people were sitting at tables drinking wine. Not recognizing anyone, her confidence suddenly vanished, but then she spotted Sarah hurrying towards her. 'Carmen! Great to see you! I'm *so* glad you came.'

'Happy birthday!' said Carmen, giving her the customary three kisses, then handing over a little posy of flowers.

'Oh, it's lovely!' said Sarah, taking the posy, although Carmen was slightly embarrassed that there were lots of other and far bigger arrangements dotted all down the tables. Sarah looked around, as if reading her thoughts. 'Tell you what, I'll put this in my buttonhole,' which she immediately did. 'Perfect! Now if you follow me, I'll introduce you to a few people, though most of them are my parents' new friends and I know I'll forget their names. And then I'll introduce you to Maman and Papa later.'

Carmen was delighted to be taken to a 'young table' where three boys were sitting, all around the same age as her, and two other girls Carmen had occasionally seen in the town.

Leon, Tobias and Benjamin were all chatty and easy to be with, as were the two girls, although Leon suddenly started to show a bit too much interest in her as time progressed and the wine kept coming. She decided not to tell him about Pierre. For now, she could put up with the occasional flirtation, rather too-long eye contact and the occasional hand on her knee. But it was rather a relief when Sarah suddenly whisked her away to meet her father and mother at another table.

An hour later, with the speeches made and an enormous birthday cake now reduced to a small pile of crumbs, Carmen decided to find the washroom and then slip quietly away. Thankfully, there was a sign to it inside the door, to the side of an enormous and high-ceilinged hall, hung everywhere with beautiful paintings. Carmen paused to look at them. She had never seen masterpieces like this in her life, at least not for real, only in her father's art books. There were about thirty in all, including majestic landscapes, hunting scenes, portraits of people in amazing clothes and some beautiful pictures of someone's garden. And a small painting she was particularly drawn to – of a mother cradling her baby.

'Ah, I see you like my wife's favourite.'

She turned around to see the elegant and grey-haired figure of Sarah's father.

She looked at the painting again, feeling slightly shy.

'Yes, it's wonderful, amazing. So tender.'

'The painter was known for that, Berthe Morisot. It was her hallmark, really tender paintings of mothers and infants. We used to have more of her work, but now we only have this one.'

He sighed, looking around the room. 'In fact, there's a sad story behind these paintings. They used to be part of a much bigger collection when we were back in Germany. My late father became a well-known art dealer in

Berlin, but he decided to leave Germany just too late. By that time Hitler was firmly in power and the new laws restricting Jews like us meant that he had to hand over ninety per cent of everything he owned before he could leave, including almost all of his paintings. They all belong to Nazis now, including that terrible man, the fat, grasping Goering. We're lucky to have these few left, but it's tragic we lost so many. In fact, I think that's what killed my father, the shock of it all.'

'That's really sad.'

'Would you like me to show you around?'

'I'd love it. But right now, I'm sorry to say I have to get back to work. I've got a job in the dress shop in the centre of town. That's where I met Sarah. But I'd *love* to see them another day, and thank you for having me. It's been lovely.'

'Our pleasure.'

Carmen sought out Sarah and her mother to thank them too, and then reluctantly set off on her walk into town. She had been amazed by the size of the gathering. Even the town's Mayor had been there, whom she had recognized from local events. She'd found out that Sarah's father had been an eminent doctor in Paris. *But why would an eminent doctor need to escape to St-Hippolyte?* Surely not just because he was Jewish? And what did *that* mean? A race? A nationality? A religion?

But one thing explained the number of people. Everyone in town wanted to know a really good doctor. But the rest of it didn't quite make sense.

ELEVEN

* * *

PEDRO WAS SURPRISED BY HOW QUIET CARMEN WAS THAT EVENING, AS if she hadn't been to a party at all. But perhaps she was thinking about Pierre. Nevertheless, he decided to ask her how it all went.

'Good party?'

'Lovely, Papá. Amazing. I've never seen such a big house in all my life. More of a château, really. Apparently, Sarah's father was a famous doctor in Paris, but he didn't feel safe there, so he's come down here. She told me there was a lot of anti-Jewish feeling growing all around them. Did I tell you her family was Jewish?'

Pedro nodded.

'But surely everyone wants a really good doctor, whether they're Jewish or not. And who cares if people are Jewish, anyway?'

'Unfortunately the Germans *do*, and they're not alone. The Jews are extremely hard-working, successful people. All through history that's made people jealous. Threatened even, fearful they might take over. Time after time, they've been driven out of countries – even Spain, where people thought they did too well. In fact, the Spanish Jews – 'Sephardics' as they were called – endured decades of persecution. That's one of the reasons the Inquisition was created – something we should be truly ashamed of. We got rid of them in droves. One reason Jews are now scattered all over the world is that they've always been driven out by their success. In fact, in the fifteenth century, Spain expelled about a hundred and fifty thousand of them. Now there are about one and a half million refugees spread out all over the world, and half of them still speak Spanish.'

Carmen was quiet for a moment, picturing a vast exodus.

'Sarah told me they'd had to get out of Poland, then Germany, and now Paris. And they're still worried down here, even in sleepy little Hippo. And she also said that their friends and family in Poland were all being rounded up and sealed off in ghettos, and they can't get in touch with them. Nobody's answering letters or anything.'

Pedro puffed on his pipe for a moment. 'I'd like to talk to your new friend's father about that. He'll know a lot more than I will, coming from Paris. It's different down here, and I'd far prefer to know what's happening first-hand. The worst thing is not *really* knowing. You say he's probably rich?'

'Looks it, from the size of their house and their paintings.'

'That makes people even more jealous. They think that Jews are taking away money that is rightfully theirs. Taking over, intruding, changing societies and customs. Spoiling everything. And sticking together too much, and being too successful.'

'I don't understand.'

'Neither do I. As I said, think it's jealousy.'

There was a sudden call from the kitchen.

'You'd better go, Carmen. Your mother needs you. We'll talk later.'

* * *

'I don't quite understand why you had to get out of Paris,' said Carmen to Sarah, 'although I'm very glad you did.' They had decided to take a walk along the River Vidourle that ran through the village. It was a few days after Sarah's party, since when Carmen had become more and more curious about why Sarah's family had felt forced to move so far south. And to such a quiet little town after living in a bustling capital city.

'Well, as I told you, my father was getting more and more worried about what might happen to us if we stayed in the north. In Germany, there are what's called the 'Nuremberg Laws' which first made it illegal for Jewish doctors to treat non-Jews, and then anyone at all. Thank God we got out of there before all that was in place.

Anyway, he thought it might all happen in France if the Germans get the upper hand here and manage to take over the north, and it's one big reason he moved us south. He says this area is famous for its resistance to outside authority.

But it seems that everywhere we go, people hate us or are scared of us. Anti-Semitism is always just below the surface, and it'll probably be the same here. After all, shops belonging to Jews have already been looted in several French towns, and even people in Parliament have shouted things like *'Jews to the scaffold'!'*

Carmen winced, deeply shocked. 'That's disgraceful.'

'And when people find out about us here, they'll probably be jealous of Papa's art collection too. Not that it's what it was. The damned Germans stole most of it. It all came from his father, who was a pretty well-known art dealer. He thinks there's a real chance of the Germans looting any valuables belonging to Jewish families, just as they did in Germany. And that would break his heart. His collection is the love of his life – after my mother, me and medicine. And it's certainly not love of money why he buys paintings. It's love of art.'

Carmen could at least understand that, remembering the beautiful paintings in the house, and picturing them being looted by marauding Germans.

'Incidentally, talking about art, Papa told me he'd love to show you the paintings – oh, and meet your family if they'd like to come round.'

'I'm sure they would,' said Carmen. 'and especially my Papa. Back in Spain he was always looking at art books, especially ones on Goya and a new painter called Picasso.'

'Picasso? I think I've heard of him.'

Sarah looked at her new friend, wondering what it must be like to leave virtually *everything* behind, and for a moment feeling slightly embarrassed by her family's château, and the art collection – even though it was a shadow of its former self.

They walked along in silence for a few minutes, only broken by the sound of a waterfall, and both leaned over a moss-covered stone wall to look at it.

Carmen turned to Sarah, talking a little louder over the sound of the rushing water. 'I can't believe the Germans would kick doctors out of their jobs. It beggars belief.'

'They didn't at first. They just didn't allow anyone Jewish to treat anyone who *wasn't*. But then, after that, worse – nobody at all.'

'Even more unbelievable, and what a waste of all that training. And if you're going to start a war, you'd think they'd need as many doctors and surgeons as they could get.'

'It didn't even stop there,' said Sarah. 'Suddenly Jews couldn't even work as vets, or auctioneers, or estate agents, or even university professors. There were loads and loads of things that no Jews were allowed to do, like own a car or buy a lottery ticket. Or, would you believe it, even use a telephone. We even had to have a big red J stamped on our passports, and a yellow star on our clothes. About two thirds of all Jewish businesses in Germany were wiped out, including most of the department stores, and the rest stolen. Thank God, thank God, we got out in time.

And it's probably a very good thing we're out of Paris too, although I miss the buzz. Another reason we're here is that my dream is to be a pharmacist. Papa says that Montpellier is a good place to study pharmacology, but that we'll have to see what happens first.'

'What does he think might happen?'

'I'm not sure, but having seen what the Germans can do, I know he's really worried. He says they're so well organised. Completely different from the French. They don't have the humour that the French do, or the joie de vivre. But they're far more used to discipline, and take orders so much better. And they're frighteningly efficient about carrying them out, however cruel and unfair those orders are, especially when it comes to attacking innocent civilians from what I've heard.'

Both fell into silence for a while as Carmen tried to picture the Germans, with no real idea of even what they looked like, except perhaps taller and bigger than the Spanish and French.

A few minutes later, her thoughts turned to Pierre, as they walked across the road and up the mountain where he had taken her. 'My boyfriend took me up here for a picnic. It's really beautiful at the top. Fantastic views, but a bit of a hike.'

'I'm on for it,' smiled Sarah.

'Good. Me, too.'

'By the way, have you heard from Pierre again?' Sarah remembered the photo of the handsome dark man Carmen had shown her in the dress shop the last time she had popped in.

'Yes, I got another letter yesterday, written in pencil. He told me it was so damp where he is that the ink always runs.'

'Gosh, in *this* weather?'

'Apparently.'

'God knows what it will be like in winter, then.' As soon as the words were out of her mouth, Sarah wished she hadn't said them. But thankfully the sight of two eagles above them stole Carmen's attention, reminding her of the picnic where she'd first seen them, perhaps the same pair.

'Snake eagles,' said Carmen. 'They're very rare. We're lucky to see them.'

Pierre's exact words. He was never far from her thoughts.

* * *

Carmen and her parents had been invited to go round to Sarah's parents' château, and now she and her father were looking at the paintings. Maria had decided not to come, nervous about talking in French, as she always was. As the rest of the family gradually became more proficient, she was now becoming more and more isolated, and Carmen was sad to see her duck out of any social occasions. It was an added shame, she thought, that she wasn't here today, looking at the masterpieces all around them. Nobody needed to speak French to see the beauty of them.

They were mostly landscapes, but with the odd domestic portrait – including the one of a mother with her baby sitting in a garden, by a painter called Berthe Morisot – Carmen's favourite – and another of a lily pond by an artist called Claude Monet.

'It's lucky Monet won the French lottery,' said Sarah's father, Isaac, 'otherwise the world may never have seen his paintings. He used the money to buy a beautiful house and garden in Giverny up in the north and devote his life to art. I once took my wife Véronique there. He even diverted the local river to make the pond in that painting.'

'Carmen tells me you're a doctor,' said Pedro. 'Are you practising here?'

'Not yet. But I'm hoping to, and if not here in St-Hippolyte, then somewhere not too far away. I'm actually a heart surgeon, but I'm happy to return to general practice.'

He turned to Pedro. 'And you?'

'I used to run a vegetable garden out in Spain, well, before the troubles started, and I'd like to do that again. My daughter's boyfriend is a vegetable farmer too, but he's just been called up, so I'm hoping to be able to help his father while he's away.'

'Ah, here's my wife, Véronique.' A beautiful red-haired woman of about forty came into the hall, carrying an enormous bunch of lilies. She smiled warmly at Pedro.

'Sorry I'm a bit late. I hope my husband hasn't bored you too much about all this stuff.' She looked around the hall. 'We love it, but I always tell him you shouldn't expect other people to do the same.'

We certainly do,' smiled Pedro. 'Back in Spain I had quite a lot of art books. Have you heard of Picasso?

Isaac nodded. 'A remarkable painter. Though I'm not sure his style would fit in with what we have here. That's if I could even afford it. I've heard his prices are going through the roof, especially for the paintings in his blue period.'

Sarah's father was suddenly embarrassed by mentioning money. After all, he was looking at a man who'd left behind everything. He immediately decided to change the subject.

'Would you like to stay for lunch?'

'No thank you, another time perhaps,' said Pedro. 'I need to get back. One or two things to sort out. But I'd love my wife to see these paintings one day, although she's a bit shy, hesitant about speaking French.'

'Would she like some lessons?' suddenly asked Véronique. 'I've got a Spanish maid, Gabriella, who speaks French really well, and she's looking for extra work around here. I'm sure she'd be interested in teaching your wife. And teaching French would be far more fun than cleaning.'

Quickly realizing, like her husband, that their guests had been forced out of Spain and might be very short of money, she added that she was certain it wouldn't cost too much.

'Well, it would be great if you can ask her,' said Pedro, 'but well, as I said, my wife's very nervous. Coming over from Spain has been a huge upheaval, and it's none too easy for her in a strange country.'

He suspected immediately that Maria might decline the offer, hugely embarrassed by her illiteracy which would make teaching her French even more of an uphill struggle.

Véronique noticed the look of concern on his face.

'I completely understand if she wants to settle in for a bit first,' smiled Véronique. 'Frankly, I've had a few upheavals in life myself.'

* * *

By now, Pedro had put back on all the weight and muscle he had lost in the internment camp, and was hugely relieved to be back to his old self, not least so that he could help out in Pierre's father's surprisingly big vegetable garden. It was a couple of kilometres away in the valley near La Cadière, where he now bicycled most days, and it was arduous work, especially in the scorching heat of summer.

He had gone to the farm shortly after Pierre's departure to talk to his father, Auguste, immediately working out why he needed help. He noticed that he was limping around the vegetable gardens with some difficulty, apparently wounded at the battle of Verdun.

Now, after several weeks, Pedro was really beginning to enjoy the job – and the company of his employer – who always asked him into the old farmhouse for a glass of cognac before he set off home. It was a pleasant ritual.

Loading up the truck on Tuesdays and Fridays and running the market stall was the other part of his job, and one he also enjoyed as he began to recognize more faces in the town. Auguste had told him that his vegetable stall was the most successful one there, and that he wanted it to stay that way, and Pedro did everything he could to ensure that, not only because of Auguste but also because of Pierre and Carmen. He knew that with him working there – and working hard – it would be a huge weight off her boyfriend's mind.

Auguste had given him all sorts of tips on running a successful stall. Being more friendly than the other stall-holders. Occasionally giving shoppers a little present like a bunch of mint or an extra apple, or offering the ladies a flower. Apologising if the queue was long. Having regular price offers. Suggesting recipes or ideas. And above all, having a blaze of colour to greet them.

'Always put the fruit on the front stalls and the vegetables on the back ones.' Auguste had told him. 'And polish the fruit up so that it looks really shiny. That *really* pulls people in!'

Auguste had been right. The only problem with the job was the truck that had a nasty habit of breaking down. But at least that was a problem that could usually be solved quickly, thanks to Alfonso's repair garage in town – another blessing.

What pleased and surprised him most of all was Maria eventually agreeing to learn French with Gabriella, and her recent offer to help him out in the market on Fridays.

'Gabriella's taught me some of the names for the fruit and vegetables, and I think I've got the hang of the francs. Anyway, I'll give it a try, as long as you don't leave me on my own. *Not even for a minute.* The thought of people jabbering away at me in French still scares me rigid, I'd feel such a fool. But I'll try. And if it doesn't work out, I'll have a few more lessons and then try again.' He was really proud of her.

But at the same time he was worrying about Carmen. She had told him that her employer, Madame Puget, now had four of her five sons called up and that she was leaning more and more on Carmen to cheer her up. Whilst really liking her, Carmen was finding it increasingly difficult to know what to say, especially as with so many boys going off, fewer girls were bothering with pretty dresses and they had long periods on their own in the shop. On top of that there had been the first mention of clothes rationing, which could spell the end of the business.

* * *

Helping out Pedro at the market had started out well for Maria. It was true that she had learned some words for the fruit and vegetables, though by no means all – or even half – but anyway the customers filled the paper bags themselves, only coming to the cash box to pay. Furthermore, Pedro had put a chart with pictures of the vegetables and fruit by the money-box and weighing scales with their names and prices, so all had gone smoothly for the first half hour.

It was only when Pedro had gone off to relieve himself at the nearby pissoire that customers started chatting casually and asking her questions, and she was now at a total loss for words, feeling terribly foolish and utterly alone in this strange foreign town. It was one thing to have learned the names of several types of fruit and vegetables, but quite another to cope with the local badinage, especially with the speed of it and the strong Languedoc accent.

Suddenly panicking, she left the busy stall unattended, running towards the pissoire and furious to see Pedro chatting casually to someone outside. Running back with her to the stall and trying to calm her down, Pedro was shocked to see the townspeople, obviously hungry because of rationing, liberally helping themselves to things in their absence.

He realized in a flash that the incident was a bitter blow to his wife's new-found and fragile confidence, and one from which she might not easily recover.

But he needn't have worried about lost earnings. The man from the next stall quickly came over to say he'd collected their money.

* * *

Alfonso came into the house with a cluster of newspapers under his arm. He looked grim but said nothing, waiting until after supper until the two younger girls had gone to bed.

'Pedro, I've been collecting the newspapers in my garage because I wanted to show you quite what some people think of us Spanish. I know you don't read French very well yet, so let me translate some of the stuff in the right-wing ones – and not just from up north, but right here.' He opened up some of the them.

'Just look at the headlines. *'FRANCE IS INVADED'*. And here, *'THE ARMY OF CRIME IN FRANCE'*, and look at *Le Roussillon*, this one, a local paper. It says, 'Send back all the refugees. As for the 50,000 dangerous individuals we should say to the 'sister democracies' that we've done all we can and this rabble should be delivered at once to the justice of Franco.' *The justice of Franco*? Ha! It's almost unbelievable.'

He looked up. 'You begin to see what I mean?' Alfonso picked up yet another paper. 'Here's *La Democratie*. It says 'The dangerous Hidalgos present a real peril. The southern ports are open, the Sahara beckons.' So that's one more paper that wants us Spanish to get out. And this one, the *Flambeau du Midi*, even talks of us as 'criminals' and 'pillagers' and urges locals to avoid what they call 'contamination'.

It goes on and on. And last week I even read one left-wing paper, more on our side, complaining there was 'a wave of xenophobia which has never been seen in France.'

And just look at this.' He showed Pedro a cartoon of a fat Spaniard with a greedy expression, wearing a helmet with a red cross. Pictured walking past a sign into FRANCIA, the man was carrying a rifle and revolver, and a huge sack full of booty like jewel-encrusted crosses. The caption read *'I'm now going to 'work' in France.'*

'It's terrible stuff. Shocking.'

Alfonso tossed it to the floor and sat back in disgust.

'You see the problem, and the danger to people like us. With their young men being called up, they may *need* us Spaniards to fill their places – to work in industry, in the mines, and in the fields. But that doesn't mean they'll *like* us. Lots of them, of course, have been perfectly kind. But others? We've all heard them call us '*dirty* Spanish', and as you know only too well, your girls have been insulted at school. So please, I beg all of you, do nothing to make it worse. Absolutely *no* political gestures. Let's keep our heads down.'

* * *

Carmen was thrilled to have received a letter from Pierre, telling her that he had a week's leave and would be coming home on Tuesday.

Now she was waiting at the station with Auguste and her father who had driven his employer into town. She was hugely excited but also anxious about why the train was late. But at last they heard a distant whistle and then the chuffing of the engine, and in a few moments it was there with men piling off the train.

But where was Pierre? Carmen had a moment of panic. But suddenly she spotted him down the platform in the milling throng.

'There he is!' she exclaimed and ran off excitedly to greet him.

Pierre embraced her, almost swinging her off her feet, wishing that he didn't have to tell her that he should really spend the first day with his father. But thankfully, she didn't protest when he did. They quickly agreed to meet early the next morning and then plan for the next few days.

But when he arrived at the house, she was shocked to see that he was not in anything like the jubilant mood of his arrival, and certainly not sweeping her up in his arms as he had at the station.

'Pierre, what's wrong?'

'I've just been sent a telegram. It came just after we got to the farm. I've been ordered to go back in two day's time. Something's going on in the north.'

'What?'

'I don't know. It didn't say. And I won't know 'til I get there.'

Carmen's face fell. 'So we've only got today?'

He nodded.

Carmen found it impossible to keep back tears.

TWELVE

※ ※ ※

CARMEN'S DISTRESS ABOUT PIERRE'S DEPARTURE WAS ABRUPTLY overshadowed by much wider events.

On April 9th, the people in Saint-Hippolyte heard the shattering news that the Germans had invaded neutral Denmark and Norway, and over the next few days they listened to their radios with increasing dread. Denmark had been overwhelmed in just six hours. The Norwegians had fought as hard as they could and the Germans had suffered surprisingly heavy losses of ships and men, but in spite of an Anglo-French force landing in Norway, they were undoubtedly winning. It was only by luck that the Norwegian Royal family and Government had managed to escape to the north. Once again, it seemed that airpower had been decisive – together with German energy and boldness.

Carmen's family did their best to act normally. The girls went to school, Carmen to the dress shop, Pedro to the farm and Alfonso to his garage. And for most people in the Languedoc, the battles all seemed far away.

But it didn't take long for the majority to work out that France might be next, and almost certainly *would* be. In the cafés, some optimists comforted themselves with the thought that maybe the 'Boches' had bitten off more than they could chew. Certainly, according to the BBC French service, which they trusted, the Germans had lost half their navy. But others quickly pointed out that they wouldn't need a navy against France. Pedro, as usual, was among the most pessimistic. He had seen just a tiny part of Germany's dynamic army and air force in action in Spain, but enough to have few illusions about what they could achieve.

As the days passed the news grew worse, with rumours that the British and French might be forced to evacuate Norway, and that a British aircraft-carrier had been sunk. It was officially announced that the Norwegian Royal Family and Government had made it to England, and that a Norwegian called Quisling had been put in charge of their now surrendered and occupied country.

In France, all leave was cancelled and the last young men left Saint-Hippolyte. Some old soldiers in the cafés were all for taking the opportunity to attack while the Germans were pre-occupied in the north. 'Why don't we bomb the shit out of them *now*?' But they knew only too well that their overly-cautious leaders would sit paralysed in Paris. They had not lifted a finger to help Poland, so why would they make a move for Norway?

A few days later the options became irrelevant when Germany invaded neutral Holland and Belgium.

* * *

For the locals in the town, it was extremely difficult to grasp what was happening in the war that was almost certainly about to engulf France. The radio and the newspapers told of the bombing of Rotterdam and the quick surrender of Holland. They also hinted at the German successes in beating the Belgian forts in order to cross the Meuse, but described much more enthusiastically – and at length – the confident and planned advance of the French and British into Belgium to meet the 'main German threat'.

But then things seemed to change. The newspapers began to talk of the Ardennes forest, and of Germans suddenly arriving at towns on the Meuse like Dinant and Monthermé. And then at a place that all Frenchmen *already* associated closely with disaster – Sedan.

'My God, Sedan! That's where we lost the war with the Prussians in 1870,' someone in the café blurted out, 'where Napoleon and 80,000 men surrendered to the Kaiser and Bismarck.'

Now, at that same Sedan, a German General called Rommel had apparently been able to cross the river with just a few tanks, and a French panic and appalling collapse had set in.

In the café someone had put up a big map on the wall to try and help the customers understand the military situation. Now something had been drawn on it that shook them to the core – a big red arrow representing a torrent of German tanks that seemed to be sweeping west straight across France – as if it had no opposition whatsoever.

'Where's the counter-attack?' asked old soldiers, crowding round the map. 'What's being done? Where are *our* tanks?' They saw that French countryside that had been bravely and stubbornly held for four long horrific years in the last war seemed to have been given up in hours. It was *unbelievable*. The German tanks didn't even seem to need to do the normal thing, to stop and wait for their infantry or their artillery to catch up. It looked as if they had just pressed on – through the open, undefended landscape. One newspaper even reported that the Germans didn't even wait for their own fuel trucks – simply filling up from the hoses of abandoned French petrol stations – and rushing on. In just ten days the Germans had reached the sea, completely cutting off the British, French and Belgian armies in the north from the rest of France.

Pedro had to carefully restrain himself from reminding the miserable Alfonso that once again his predictions about German tactics had come only too true.

Worse news followed swiftly. As the British and French were squeezed up against the coast, the Belgian King suddenly surrendered his army. Some of the veterans in the cafés were openly weeping with shame. It seemed that *nothing* could stop the same fate befalling the British and the French who appeared to be at the mercy of the unstoppable Germans.

But then something extraordinary was reported. The British navy, together with civilian boats of all sizes, had come over the Channel to rescue their forces from a port called Dunkerque. In spite of the fury of the attacks by German planes, which the BBC admitted had sunk dozens of vessels, each day tens of thousands of British and French troops had been successfully lifted from the port and even from the open beaches. While Boulogne and Calais fell, Dunkerque, it was said, had held out just long enough for 338,000 men, 120,000 of them French, to escape to England. It was something of a morale-booster, but not much.

And for Carmen, there was one slight mercy in the deluge of bad news. Most of the Maginot Line seemed not to have been touched, its defenders presumably waiting for attacks that never came. That meant, she thought with relief, that Pierre was probably safe, having not even fired a shot – but now becoming a prisoner of war. When would she ever see him again? However, her personal feelings, though deeply troubling, were then overshadowed by fresh disasters for France. Scarcely pausing for breath, the Germans had now turned south, battering the French armies in front of them. This time there was nothing like the miraculous 'Battle of the Marne' that had turned the tide in 1914. On June 14th, just ten days after Dunkerque, Paris fell, with the Government fleeing down to Bordeaux. Within three days of that, all of France was conquered and the aged Marshal Philippe Pétain, the one-time hero of the 1916 battle of Verdun and now the Premier, broadcast to the nation.

'I give to France the gift of my person to alleviate her misfortunes. With a heavy heart I tell you that the fighting must stop. We are defeated and will accept an Armistice.'

The people of Saint-Hippolyte were no different from those in the rest of the country, in deep shock and overwhelmed by shame. They had readily believed their own country's confident propaganda that the French army was the most powerful in the world. Men and women, totally confused, cried openly in the streets.

However, the very next day, on June 18th, something strange happened. People who listened to the BBC's French programmes said they had just heard a very different broadcast coming from London – by an obscure, junior French General called Charles de Gaulle. He appealed to his countrymen in sonorous and eloquent tones to go on fighting,

'Must we abandon all hope? Is our defeat final and irremediable? No, we are not defeated – this is the first battle in a world war, which we *can* win.'

Very few people had actually caught the programme, but news of it spread like wildfire. Here at least was a glimmer of hope in the black gloom that had descended on the entire country. Now it would depend on Britain. Could she hold off the Germans, as no other country had been able to do? After all, the French General Weygand had pessimistically predicted that 'In three weeks England will have her neck wrung like a chicken'.

But the BBC reported that Prime Minister Winston Churchill had defiantly retorted, 'Some chicken, some neck!'

Opinions in France were split. The morale of many was so shattered that they were prepared to follow the Marshal. After all, he was a hero of France. 'A safe pair of hands – perhaps he knows best?'

But the little Spanish family was firmly on the side of defiance. It had not escaped one defeat in Spain to accept another in France.

But for Carmen, there was personal grief. Without any news from Pierre, she had to assume that he was on his way to a prisoner of war camp in Germany.

* * *

When they read them in the newspapers, the French were shocked to see that the Armistice terms were far harsher than those imposed on Germany in 1918.

The Germans would occupy three-fifths of France, the North and the whole of the coast – obviously to control all French Channel and Atlantic ports. An unoccupied zone in the south, the 'Zone Libre', was to be governed by a rump administration based in Vichy, previously only known for its spa and water. Saint-Hippolyte would be controlled from there.

Mussolini's Italians, once they thought that Hitler might win, had declared war on France, a 'stab in the back'. The French had easily beaten off the invading Italian troops, but with the Armistice, the Italians had still ended up controlling part of south-eastern France.

All the costs of the occupation were to be borne by France, to the tune of a stupefying four hundred million francs a day. The nearly two million French soldiers would remain prisoners of war in Germany 'until the cessation of all hostilities'. Carmen realized at once that this meant that Pierre might not return – *unless* Britain stopped fighting.

There were some even more sinister clauses in the terms too. Anyone who had been granted political asylum had to be arrested. Did that mean *her* family?

The French state was also instructed to hand over any German nationals. That meant political refugees, and of course, German Jews. So, almost certainly, Sarah's family.

The French Navy was to be 'disarmed, but not surrendered', probably to avoid pushing the French so far that they might go on fighting from their colonial empire.

In the town, everyone speculated. Surely the town halls, the civil servants and the Gendarmes wouldn't treat their own people as badly as that? Or *would* they?

THIRTEEN

* * *

'LES SALAUDS! LES SALAUDS!' MICHEL MORELLI, ONE OF THE town's postmen, had burst into the café, waving a newspaper.

'The bastard English have attacked our fleet in Mers-el Kebir! They've sunk some of our ships and killed a thousand of our sailors! *And sitting in harbour, too!*' He sat down at a table that Pedro and Alfonso had begun to realize was always full of Pétainists, for whom the Marshal could do no wrong. Michel ranted on about the cruel behaviour of France's former ally, how the English could never be trusted and why *'Perfide Albion'* was such a telling insult.

Pedro and Alfonso were sitting as far away they could from the table where Morelli normally sat.

'He obviously doesn't know the other side of the story,' muttered Alfonso in Spanish. 'although I'm very sad about those poor sailors. I listened to the BBC. Apparently, the French were given several alternatives and still got up steam to fight. The British had no choice. They couldn't allow the *slightest* chance of that part of the French fleet falling into the hands of the Germans. Apparently Churchill was actually seen to be *weeping* when he announced it. Even de Gaulle, while calling it *'déplorable et* détestable', admitted that it was better than the ships joining the enemy.

However, you can bet the Marshal and his pals will latch on to this to stoke more anti-British fervour. And he'll be egged on by that awful Admiral Darlan, who apparently also hates the British, and was probably always jealous of their navy.'

'Ssshh. I think we should keep our views a bit quiet,' whispered Pedro, glancing around him. Luckily, nobody seemed to be listening in.

'Quite right,' said Alfonso, dropping his voice. 'Can you imagine how touchy the French must be feeling? Their supposedly great army beaten in weeks, and now with their navy destroyed? You can almost *feel* their shame and bitterness. *And* they're blaming the British for Dunkerque as well, saying that they ran away leaving France in the lurch while it was plainly *French* incompetence that brought on the disaster.

But I think we won't mention *that* either. At least, not in French. And not *to* anyone French.'

* * *

It didn't take long for the pro-Pétain and anti-British people in the town to start feeling that they were on the right side.

Soon the news was that the German air force was beginning to attack British ships in the Channel.

'Now they'll *really* get it in the neck,' Michel Morelli could be heard gloating at the top of his voice. 'They'll bomb them to bits and *then* invade. Just you wait and see!'

Alfonso and the Casales family couldn't help feeling gloomy. Perhaps the Germans *were* going to win – and really easily again?

But Pedro, especially, was not so sure. The Channel had always seemed to be a problem for foreigners trying to attack Britain. For the Spanish, the destruction of the Armada centuries ago had been a reminder of that. While for the French, their brilliant master on land – Napoleon – had also been defeated by that little strip of water. So Pedro was convinced that nothing was inevitable – and that anything might happen.

* * *

However, a few days later, his relative confidence was shaken by new events in France.

'I can't believe what I'm reading,' said Alfonso, who had gone out to get the paper having heard something about 'denaturalisation' on the radio. 'It's not as if we're at war with Germany as much as war with *ourselves*. It beggars belief what Pétain's doing now. Going for Jews, Freemasons,

Communists, Romany gypsies, homosexuals, left wingers, and now even us – immigrants from other Mediterranean countries. What's he got against everybody? And it's only three weeks since the bloody Armistice, for God's sake!'

He pushed the paper across the table with disgust, but knew that Pedro wouldn't be able to read anything very complex in French. However, Carmen would, and he decided to give it to her to read later, giving Pedro the basic news.

'Well, in a nutshell, Pétain's enacted what they call a Denaturalisation Law. Vichy are going to review the status of all the people who've been given citizenship in France in the last twenty years – about half a million it says here. They're probably mainly going for the Jewish refugees from Germany, not us.

But this régime doesn't seem to like *us* much either. Coming from Republican Spain, they regard us as Communists, their greatest enemy. So we may be in just as much danger as Sarah's poor family. We'll have to keep a low profile. Luckily, I've got a good relationship with the Mayor. I look after his car. And his people are pretty decent – for the moment at least. But we can't trust the out-of-town Gendarmes. They'll do exactly what Vichy tells them.

'At least there's beginning to be some resistance in the north. I heard someone in the café say that in Paris travellers on the Metro are deliberately directing Germans to stations miles out of their way, and that bus conductors skip stops where Germans want to get off. And people are leaving cafés if Germans come in, and don't patronise shops with signs saying 'German spoken here'. But frankly, it's all pretty feeble stuff, and would you believe that the Paris Opera and the Comédie Française are now playing to stalls packed with German officers in full dress uniforms, with *French* women beside them?'

'No, I wouldn't.' He remembered being told that before. 'Although I might, on second thoughts. Seems to me that money buys you anything.'

'What gets to me even more is that we're actually *paying* for them to be here – to the tune of a staggering 400 million francs a day – while they're about to strip our labour force. And, even worse, there are lots of other northerners *welcoming* them. Did you read that bit in the paper about that woman north of Bordeaux actually *eulogising* about them?'

'No.'

'She literally said, and I remember this word for word, or almost, *'The population gave the victors a hearty welcome, the girls waving their handkerchiefs and scarves at the athletic young men on motorcycles; handsome as gods with laughter in their eyes.'*

'Good God!' Pedro again shook his head in disbelief.

'And it gets worse. I've even heard of shopkeepers letting their regulars and relatives go without milk, butter and eggs so that they can sell to the Germans at a higher price.'

Alfonso sighed. 'Anyway, let's listen to the radio. Could you close the shutters, please? Which reminds me; we ought to find a better place to hide the radio – and sooner rather than later. It's bad enough knowing what's going on, but *not* knowing would be even worse.'

They clustered round the old radio as Alfonso adjusted the dial. At ten o'clock the BBC French service broadcast the news, revealing that German aircraft had begun to bomb Britain's coastal towns. But there, it seemed they were facing fierce resistance. Many German planes seemed to have been shot down.

Maybe things might not go quite so well for Germany as they had recently?

* * *

'Cheer up, cara.' Pedro patted Maria's hand, noticing how downcast she seemed. 'I know things are very tough here, but they *could* be a hell of a lot worse. At least you're not working in a ghastly munitions factory like so many women in England. I've just heard on the BBC that one poor girl was dragged on to a conveyor belt in one of them by her long hair and crushed to death by the machinery, so all of the women have now been urged to cut their hair into bobs.'

'Do I have to hear that?' Maria winced, imagining the victim's abject terror and that of her own daughters in the same situation, instinctively running her hands through her hardly ever-cut hair.

'Yes, I think you do. I think it's our duty to know – and to count ourselves lucky. And at least we're not being bombed to smithereens and blitzed night after night like they are in London, and having to sleep in underground metro stations with the kids night after night – and probably after a hard day's work. Or sending our children off to live with people in the countryside that we don't even know, and not knowing when they'll ever return – or even if we'll ever see them again.'

Maria shuddered, imagining the fear of young children herded to stations and unknown destinations and foster parents, not knowing when they would ever go back to their families; that's if there was anyone left to go back to.

'Apparently, they herd the children off the trains into the nearest field, and the locals pick the child they want – or don't really want with their own to feed. Anyone looking Jewish or disabled or sickly is left 'til last. Can you imagine that?'

'No.' Maria shook her head in disbelief.

'And the biggest blessing of all here is that *we're* not Jewish,' added Pedro. 'Would you believe, the Germans aren't really putting any pressure on us here to clamp down on Jews, but the Vichy government is doing that anyway, no doubt trying to get better terms out of the Armistice. You know – the deal they imposed on us.'

Maria again looked baffled and confused, but Pedro, for once, decided to persevere.

'Jews are being hounded out from any public office or Government jobs, shut out of universities, and strictly registered as Jewish so everyone knows who they are. And what makes it all even worse is that so many of them were *already* refugees from pre-war persecution in the countries they fled from, like Sarah's family.'

Maria looked at him in amazement. 'Pedro, how do you *know* all this?'

'Because I make it my business to know. And Vichy aren't exactly hiding it, sucking up to the Germans again. Would you believe, they're not even covering up what's happening to *foreign-born* Jews, rounding them up and sending them off to camps. And there are dreadful rumours about how many will ever return.'

Maria shook her head again, putting her hand up for him to stop. 'Pedro, that's *enough*. I don't think I can face any more.'

Pedro sighed, suddenly irritated. 'That's what too many people are saying. They're turning a blind eye and a deaf ear to everything. They just don't want to know. All they want is to get on with their lives, however ghastly other people's are.' He paused. 'Or deaths, come to that. And I don't want you to be one of them.'

Maria dropped her knife and fork on her plate with a clatter. 'Pedro, can't we just have a decent lunch for *once* without you going on and on about the war? It's rare enough we have lunch together, without all this.'

For the first time in their twenty-year marriage, Pedro was suddenly truly exasperated with her.

'No, Maria, we *can't*. It's our duty to *know* what's happening, even if we can't do anything about it. And I don't want to live with an ostrich – someone who puts their head in the sand – however much I love you.'

Maria suddenly burst into tears.

Pedro immediately regretted his words, but at the same time was relieved that he had finally said them. Protecting women was deep within his Spanish nature, but protecting them from the truth was not.

FOURTEEN

* * *

S ARAH'S FATHER ISAAC HAD ASKED ALFONSO IF THEY COULD POSSIBLY meet at mid-day, preferably at his home, saying he had something truly important to ask him. Now Alfonso was walking up to the front door of the house – or rather, château. Every time he had visited, and it was several times now, he had always marvelled at the size and beauty of it. And though there was always a warm welcome, he wondered why Isaac hadn't suggested meeting somewhere in town.

Sitting in the kitchen of the château over a glass of wine a few minutes later, he discovered why.

Isaac was pale, and there was something of a haunted look in his eyes.

'Thanks for coming,' he said. 'I didn't want to meet you in the café, because you never know who's listening these days. And you often can't hear yourself speak anyway. I wanted to ask you something important.'

Alfonso waited for him to continue for several seconds.

'Of course you know my family is Jewish.'

Alfonso nodded.

'And of course you know the whole of the north and the coast is occupied by the Germans.'

Alfonso nodded again.

'And that Pétain's Vichy government started anti-Jewish laws even *before* the Germans asked them to?'

Another nod.

'Well, I'm getting increasingly worried about my family. I'm very much afraid that with Pétain in Germany's pocket, he may soon start expelling the Jews. I've seen the terrible things that happened to Jews in Germany. That's why we got out of there, and then out of Paris. It was perhaps foolish of me to hope that we'd ever be safe down here. After all, France has been riddled with anti-Semitism for years. They hardly need any lessons from the Germans on that score. We should remember what happened to Dreyfus. You know, the Jewish officer who was falsely accused of treason.'

Alfonso, being Spanish, could *not* remember the Dreyfus affair, but nodded again anyway.

'The one person I'm *really* worried about is Sarah. She's the last female in my family, and the women in Jewish families carry the blood-line. If anything happened to her, it would be a double tragedy, and it would kill my wife.' He paused for a while. 'And me. That's if we're not dead already.

I don't expect you to say yes, but I want to ask you a favour. If things *do* get worse, and they start to hunt down Jews, I'd like to think she has a safe place to go to, or at least a safer one than this. The château will tell the Germans we've got money, so they may come for us early. She needs to be somewhere safer, less conspicuous. Perhaps we were mad to have bought it, but we never thought there'd be *another* war and that the Germans would win.'

'My house?' asked Alfonso.

Isaac hesitated. 'I know it's an enormous amount to ask, but I don't know what else to do, or who else to turn to. Everyone's deserting us, now Pétain's in charge. Only a few months ago, this place was packed with so-called 'friends' on Sarah's birthday, but where are they all now? We hardly ever see them. There's always some excuse. Only a few have stayed loyal. The reason I'm turning to you is because your niece and Sarah are now such close friends. I wouldn't be asking at all if I had any alternative, and without making an offer.'

An offer? Did Isaac mean money? Alfonso was startled. Liking Sarah a great deal, money was the last thing on his mind. What worried him was the instant thought of Carmen sharing the same tiny bedroom with Isaac's daughter, although his niece almost certainly wouldn't mind, given the potential gravity of her friend's circumstances. But would Sarah be safe in the centre of town?

'I wouldn't want money,' said Alfonso.

'What I propose is this,' said Isaac, 'giving you custody of my paintings, and then complete ownership if anything happens to me and my wife. It would help you look after our daughter, and perhaps to extend your house to accommodate her – or even help her buy a little place of her own. If you could store my collection, perhaps in your garage, and then keep it for good if anything happens to us, then we'd sleep a lot easier.

By the way, they wouldn't take up too much space. I can take the canvasses out of the frames and roll them up, sealing them against damp and damage. God knows, I've had to do it before.'

Alfonso was overwhelmed, shocked by Isaac's predicament and guessing the value of the collection he was prepared to give away.

'I couldn't possibly accept all your paintings.'

There was a long pause.

'And we couldn't accept it if anything happened to our daughter.'

Both of them thought for a while in silence.

'Do you *really* think the Germans could start deporting Jews?' asked Alfonso.

'Yes, I do. It's happened too many times before, starting in Poland where we used to live. We've never heard what happened to our friends and relations there after we left and they got rounded up and herded into ghettos. There's been absolute silence, but terrible rumours. And in Germany most of us got ruined and had to leave. It could happen here. I know what Germans can do, and better than most. Believe me.'

'But couldn't you escape somewhere?'

'Where to? The Boches are everywhere, or at least their Vichy lackeys are. And we've run three times already. We're exhausted by it. We haven't got what it takes to move yet again. And where would we move to? Everywhere we go, we're hunted down.'

Alfonso thought for a moment. 'Then the answer is yes. We'll take Sarah in.'

Relief flooded Isaac's face. 'I don't know how to thank you, I really don't. And it'll be a *vast* relief for Véronique. She's been worried sick. At least let me start by re-filling your glass. And this time I'll join you. And I'll fetch my wife. She hiding upstairs, terrified you might have said no.'

* * *

The BBC news the previous evening had been bleak. The Germans had bombed London by day and night and its docks had been badly damaged with fires raging all over the city.

Alfonso and Pedro were sitting in a different café. They couldn't bear to hear what Postman Morelli would say about London. At least Alfonso wasn't, as usual, complaining that the French drank too much, now that rationing had hit alcohol and the custom of having a mid-afternoon aperitif had been strictly outlawed. But his mood was nevertheless dark, as was that of everyone else there, mostly sitting in silence or talking in subdued tones.

'I'm not sure how long I can keep the garage going,' said Alfonso. 'Not enough people will soon be able to afford to run cars or vans with the price and rationing of fuel.'

'Don't tell me,' replied Pedro. 'It may not be long before I can't drive to the market either. Auguste and I will have to buy a horse and cart or go under. But a horse will be another mouth to feed. And it's tough enough already feeding the family. And I'd have to find a stable, or build one. But what with? Money doesn't grow on trees.'

Alfonso leaned forward. 'Perhaps I should sell one of Isaac's pictures while I've still got the car. I could drive it to Nîmes or Arles and see if anyone's interested. Probably not with everything else going on. Anyway, it would make me feel really guilty if I did.'

'At least we're better off than some,' said Pedro, trying to lighten the mood. 'And not just the Jews. Thank God, we grow *edible* crops to sell, not just useless vines. I'm also really sorry for all our cattle farmers with all their animals sent off to be eaten by the Germans.'

Both men fell into dismal silence for a while.

Alfonso looked round the café and continued in Spanish. 'At least we're not as obsessed with food as the French are. Eating really is their theme song. They don't eat to live, they live to *eat*. Frankly, I just don't see how they're going to live with rationing, especially when the rations are so terribly mean. No wonder people are forging ration cards and tickets. And I've even heard that some people are reading the obituaries in the paper and then disguising themselves as police officers and stealing ration cards from the relatives of the dead. Would you *believe* it?'

'Nothing surprises me these days.'

'Incidentally,' continued Alfonso, 'I think you'll have to be really careful bringing us that many fruits and vegetables from the farm. If you get found out, we'll all be in big trouble.'

'I know. I've been thinking about that. I guess it isn't worth the risk, but I hate to see the kids going hungry.'

Both men sipped at their coffee, but with neither enjoying it without any sugar, and both disliking the taste of saccharine. But at least it *was* coffee, rather than the more usual substitute – bitter-tasting toasted barley mixed with chicory.

'By the way,' said Alfonso, I'm getting more and more worried about Sarah's family, ever since the Jews have been banned from everything – even making films, for God's sake. That's alarming enough, and I really fear that's only the start of it. And, as Isaac told me, that huge château won't help if people start resenting the Jews. In fact, that's already happening.

Come to think of it, if we ever *do* want to sell a painting, it might be better to do it now, so we can afford to build another bedroom for Sarah. That's if we can get the building materials. It's not fair to Carmen to expect her to share that tiny box-room. But in any case we'll have to take the poor girl in. From what she said about what the Germans did to the Jews in Germany, there's no knowing *what* will happen here. And it looks as if the Vichy government is completely in the Germans' pockets.'

'I know, it's really worrying.'

'And as for that new stall in the market right beside yours, it made me want to throw up. All that propaganda about how marvellous Pétain is, and those ghastly little pictures and busts of him. I can't believe anyone would want that rubbish, let alone read that terrible leaflet. What was the title? Oh yes, 'The most touching reasons why you love your Marshal Pétain'. What self-regarding crap!'

'I know. I'm rather worried that some of my customers will start going to the other vegetable stall by the church just to avoid seeing all that trash. In fact, as his stall's right next to mine, I got chatting to the fellow selling the Pétain stuff and asked him where it all came from. And would you *believe*, he told me that Pétain's actually set up a factory to produce it all, called 'Art Maréchal'. He even got Rodin's student, Léon Drivier, to create the bust of him – and he's churned out tens of thousands of them. And made some top artist paint an official portrait which they've put on everything – Sèvres vases, Baccarat crystal, medallions, ashtrays, pens, cups, paperweights, posters, calendars – you name it. And, of course, his stupid face is on all our postage stamps. The man even showed me pictures of tapestries from another factory called 'Atelier Maréchal', with his picture and sayings woven into them. It's almost as if Petain's proclaiming himself to be a saint.

Actually, I think the stall-holder is slightly embarrassed by the whole thing. He probably couldn't get any other job. In fact, he was quite funny. He even joked that the dinner plates were nice, but that it's a pity we don't have enough food to put on them.'

Alfonso didn't laugh. 'Pétain's clearly trying to fool people with his dignified, grandfatherly image, but he must have an ego as big as a house.'

Pedro glanced at his watch. 'Anyway, better get going, unless we've got anything more cheerful to talk about.'

* * *

'Do anything nice at school today?' Maria asked her two youngest, both busy drawing at the kitchen table.

'You mean after having to sing that silly song, 'Maréchal, here we are?' Maria sighed. 'Yes, after that.'

'We had to write about our families,' said Juanita.

A chill ran through Maria. In any other circumstances that would have been utterly normal. But these days, it was different. Surely this wasn't another ethnic inquisition, and surreptitiously, through people's children while at school? It was bad enough finding out from Pedro what was in the papers, but unthinkable that the authorities and Petain's henchmen – or even women – might be trying to extract information from the very young.

'Write what, exactly?' she asked.

'Well, where we lived. What we do at home. Whether we've always been here. What we like to do most.'

'And what did you both say?' asked Maria, trying to look interested rather than worried.

'Not much,' said Juanita. 'I don't like writing compositions, and I didn't say we came from Spain because Uncle Fon told us not to last week if we were ever asked. He said it was nobody else's business.'

'It isn't.' said Maria. 'Your uncle's right. And you remember that.'

Both girls nodded.

'And I just said I like drawing and drew a picture of the forest,' said Otilia. 'Madame Lafont was very cross about that. She said that it wasn't an art class, and I got a bad mark for being naughty.'

'But you get a good mark from me,' smiled Maria, wondering if even a schoolteacher could be an informant for the Vichy Government. The thought was horrifying.

Later that night she discussed the conversation with Pedro and Alfonso round the fire.

'Probably quite harmless,' said Alfonso. 'It's normal to ask kids about family life; that's pretty much all they know. But I do agree, I don't much like the sound of teachers asking kids where they come from. That said, it could be that they're aware that some of the kids might need protection – if not now, then later on. Let's hope there nothing more sinister than that.

But I'm worried about something else. I've heard they're now recruiting schoolchildren into French copies of the 'Hitler Youth'. One scheme is called Companies of France, and there's another – Youth of France Overseas. We'd better make sure the children aren't tempted to join up.'

An hour or so later, the adults once again clustered round the radio, again playing it quietly in case other ears detected that they were listening to London.

That evening the news was startling. The Germans had launched huge attacks on London, but they seemed to have been defeated, with 183 Luftwaffe planes shot down.

'It's probably exaggerated,' said Alfonso, as he got up to switch off the set. 'But even so, the Germans seem to be getting nowhere. According to the French, by now the British should hardly have any fighter planes left. But they obviously *have*.'

'Good to hear it, said Pedro. 'Nice to know the Fritzes aren't having it all their own way as they usually do. The British must not only have good planes and pilots, but some kind of much better system. They seem to be mincing the Nazis, and at least *that's* good news. I was on the receiving end of those German planes a couple of years ago. I'm really glad someone's shooting back at them.

Incidentally, isn't it incredible – the difference between the English and French news? I bet all *our* papers are putting a Nazi slant on the news for fat German subsidies, toadying up to the Fritzes. Thank God we know what's *really* going on. But it's dreadful to think how many people don't.'

* * *

'Carmen, my dear, if you don't mind my saying so, you're getting too thin,' said Elaine Puget. 'Those trousers are hanging off you.'

Carmen looked down at them knowing her employer was right. 'I know,' she sighed. 'It's just because the food's so awful, and there's never enough of it. The bread we get now is so revolting, it doesn't taste of anything. That's if we can get any bread at all. And I'm sick and tired of eating cold hard-boiled chestnuts. And now Papa has really been forced to cut down on what he brings us from the farm, because with the Germans taking it, there's hardly enough for his stall. So there's even *less* to eat. And what there is, is so expensive.'

'Well, *you* be careful. I can't have the best girl I've ever had fading to nothing.' Elaine Puget rummaged in her pocket and pulled out a small box of chocolates.

'Here.' She handed it to Carmen. 'I've had them for ages, so they've probably gone stale, but maybe they'll still be edible. And the last thing I need is chocolate. I'm probably the only person in town who's *glad* to be losing weight!'

Carmen laughed and took the box. 'Thanks. I can hardly even remember the taste of chocolate!'

'Well, have one now.'

Carmen did. Even though it *was* stale, it was total luxury to enjoy something sweet now that sugar was so drastically rationed.

'Delicious!' she beamed.

Elaine looked at her kindly. 'Have you heard anything more from your young man?'

'Yes, but he's not allowed to say anything, I guess like your boys. He can only fill in a gap on a pre-printed card saying '*I am in*, then there's a space with dots, *health*. What if he were ill? He wouldn't even be able to say so.'

'It's the same with my lot.'

They both sat in silence for a while. Five young men, now all in camps like thousands of other prisoners of war, and not knowing when and if they would ever get back.

'And how's Sarah?' asked Elaine, wanting to change the subject. 'She doesn't seem to have been in for a while.'

'She's not too good. Her parents are very worried about all the restrictions being put on the Jews. In fact, she may have to come and live with us if things get worse.'

'Let's pray they don't get worse,' said Elaine, patting Carmen's hand. 'Things are quite bad enough already without trying to find another enemy in our midst. It's very worrying. Do you know, I even heard a rumour that they might start *christening* Jewish children here to try and protect them?'

Carmen was shocked. 'I can't *believe* it could come to that.'

'Nor can I,' said her employer. 'But these days I can believe almost anything.'

* * *

If Carmen had lost too much weight, Sarah had lost even more, and Carmen was getting desperately worried about her. No longer did she have the energy or enthusiasm to walk up the mountain regularly as they used to, or even come to town much. And though her small box room now had another bed and was ready for her friend to move into, Sarah was still delaying the day to do so.

By now Carmen almost always went to Sarah's parents' château rather than Sarah coming to Alfonso's house, and was always saddened when entering the hall with all those stunning pictures gone, now replaced by boring and rather bad local landscapes almost certainly bought in the market. The family had probably been depressed by the sight of bare walls, or more likely, worried that anyone searching the house might realize that something valuable was missing. The cheap replacements were an instant reminder of the growing anti-Semitism that was sweeping France. And for some months now, she always had to ring the courtyard bell in a special code as the family was becoming afraid of visitors. And even then, she was always asked who she was before the gates were unlocked.

Moreover, the garden was now getting sadly overgrown, as if Sarah's mother no longer had the heart to do any gardening, or was even afraid of going outside. It was all so different from how it had looked on Sarah's birthday a year ago, and it was very unlikely there would be another kind of celebration for her this year, and definitely not *en plein air*.

The last time Carmen had visited the château, Sarah's father had given her a key to the gate.

Now, as she turned it in the padlock, she felt a wave of fear for her best friend and her family.

* * *

Two weeks later, Carmen's fears turned out to be only too well-founded. Just before she was due to go off to the shop, she heard a frantic banging on the door and the bell ringing. It was Sarah, absolutely distraught. She had been in the market, trying to buy food, when Gabriella, the Spanish maid from the château, had rushed up to her, crying. She had led Sarah to the corner of the square and told her a terrible story.

At six in the morning, a police Citroen had turned up with a man in plain clothes and two armed Gendarmes. They had wrenched open the gates and the front door. Gabriella had quickly hidden in her bedroom cupboard, knowing her own precarious status as a foreigner. Sarah's parents had also tried to hide but were quickly discovered. They were then given a few minutes to gather some clothes, as the leader of the group strolled around the house. Then, as they left, she had heard him ask 'Is there anyone else here, Bollon?' and another man say, 'There's usually the young Jewish slut, but she doesn't seem to be here.' The terrified maid had no idea where Sarah's parents had been taken. Perhaps the railway station? Sarah was deeply shocked, but even in her traumatized state realized that she could never go back to the château and had to move in with Carmen's family at once.

* * *

As much as Carmen had disliked the Fascists enough back in Spain, now she hated the Germans, or the Nazis, even more, shocked beyond belief at what she was hearing.

How could they have attacked so many countries for no reason she could see? Poland, Norway, Denmark, Holland, Belgium, France – and now Britain. And what kind of perverted people could drag Sarah's parents away like that? The Germans were obviously behind that too, or their wretched collaborators. And they'd taken away Pierre, and like two million others he would have to stay imprisoned in Germany 'until hostilities ceased'. Well, that could take years.

All that misery, suffering and death for what? To create a master race more powerful than the world had ever seen? And in order to do that, destroy people like a gentle middle-aged heart surgeon and his wife? And, of course, millions of others?

Nothing she had read or heard from anyone explained such savagery, or even began to provide any motive.

There was one thing she knew: that she couldn't stand back and do nothing about it, as a lot of other people around seemed prepared to do. She had considerable sympathy for her father not doing so after three years of the fighting and horrors back in Spain. And also for Uncle Fon, who clearly felt he was too old to fight, but not for thousands of perfectly healthy others who seemed prepared to sit back and hope it would all blow over in due course. Every ounce of her conscience told her she couldn't do that, or if she did, there would be a time when she bitterly regretted it – and for the rest of her life.

In the meantime, she resolved to do something practical – to find out the names, and if she could, the home addresses of the police team who had taken Sarah's parents away. One day they might be brought to justice.

* * *

It was going to be a hugely difficult conversation with Sarah, still constantly tearful two days after she had moved in with the family, but Carmen knew it had to be said. And that she was the only one in the family who could say it. And now was the best time to do so, early in the dawn hours in her tiny box-room with no-one else around.

'Sarah, are you awake?'

'Yes.'

'Look, I absolutely *hate* to say this, but I think we ought to do something about your hair.'

There was no response from Sarah. Had she heard? She didn't seem to have done.

Carmen paused, but persevered. It was no time for cowardice, and if she didn't tell Sarah now, she probably never would.

'It really makes you stand out. Red hair is so rare around here. And the people who took away your parents may well know about you or recognize you, or put two and two together with your Mamá red-haired. That makes it even *more* dangerous for you.'

Sarah said nothing, but Carmen was certain she was at least grasping things now.

'Look, I know my mother dyes her hair, or at least used to before all this happened. And I also know she's got some hair dye left. I found it yesterday in the bathroom. If we dye your hair black, you'll be far more difficult to recognize.'

Sarah still said nothing.

Carmen summoned up the bravery to go on, 'And if we cut it short too, you'll be even safer.'

She looked over to the other bed – in the early morning light – suddenly noticing tears rolling down Sarah's cheeks. But to her vast relief, Sarah nodded.

Carmen wondered if she should mention anything else to persuade her, quickly deciding she had to. There was no choice.

'And all of *us* will be safer, too.'

* * *

'Coming to help me in the market today?' Pedro asked Sarah a couple of weeks later. 'It might do you good,' he added. 'You haven't been out for ages.'

'If you don't mind, I think I'll stay here,' said Sarah. 'The last time I helped you, someone asked me my name. Someone I don't know, and it scared me stiff. Even though I'd changed my hair by then. *And* he was looking at me in a strange way.'

'And what did you say?' asked Pedro.

'I told him I was called Sabine, as you told me to if anyone ever asked.'

'Good girl. In fact, I've started thinking we should use that name for you in the house. Then you'll really get used to it, and so will we. Anyway, he was probably just an agricultural worker, and quite harmless. Or maybe he liked the look of you. You do look very good with your hair like that.'

'Thanks. Although I feel a bit guilty about nicking all Maria's hair dye.'

'Don't be. Who cares about things like hair dye in a war like this?'

'Me,' smiled Sarah.

Pedro suddenly turned more serious.

'Sarah, I think you should know you're not alone in being hidden and protected by people around here. I've heard rumours that several people are doing that. We think it's got a lot to do with the past history of this region – the religious persecution for centuries and all that suppression of the Protestants – the killings, the destruction of the Temples, the hanging of the Pastors, and so on. So the Protestant French *really* know what it's like to be to be mistreated and bullied as a minority. I've heard that all over the Cèvennes they're now hiding Jews, at great risk – and even baptising Jewish children as Christians to save them.

In fact, for the same reasons, they were equally understanding to us Spaniards, as outsiders, when we first arrived. Surprisingly so.'

Pedro could see that Sarah understood, and was perhaps partly relieved, but knew she could only be thinking of her parents, who'd been too late for such life-saving help.

'Well, I'd better be off,' Pedro said, now feeling uncomfortable. 'Have a nice morning.'

As soon as the words were out of his mouth, he felt stupid. How *could* you have a 'nice morning' when you were worried sick about your mother and father, probably fearing you would never see them again, and frightened yourself about going out at all?

FIFTEEN

* * *

JEAN BOLLON AND PHILIPPE LAPORTE BARELY SAID A WORD ON THE hour's journey to Nîmes, hugely excited about what was behind them in the truck and dreaming about what they would do with the fortune it would fetch – almost certainly hundreds of thousands of francs. Girls, drink – that would be just the start of it.

This was their second visit to Nîmes in a week, the first one simply to drive around and check out what seemed to be the smartest fine art and antiques dealer in the city. Neither of them would have dared to ask anyone in Saint-Hippolyte about art dealers for fear of arousing suspicion. After all, why would people like *them* be asking? They had eventually found a street near the arena in which there were several art and furniture galleries and went to look around. They quickly decided not to try any shops with a Jewish-sounding name. They might just know the origins of their haul, and they might not be in business for much longer anyway, not with all the recent restrictions on Jews.

Both of them agreed that one gallery seemed to be the smartest of all. It was rather empty, as were many of the galleries, and for a moment they wondered if anyone sold valuable items with a war going on, or if they did, it was only at reduced prices. But with such a big collection to sell, they assured themselves that it would hardly matter.

Now they were parked just down the street from their chosen gallery.

'I'll go in first and see if anyone's interested,' said Jean. 'You stay here and guard the truck. I don't trust that lock in the back, not with a fortune behind us.'

'Bonjour,' said the small bespectacled man in the gallery, getting up from his desk just inside the door. 'May I help you?'

'I hope so,' said Jean. 'I have a van outside full of fine furniture and paintings, just inherited from my father. I have nowhere to put them, so I've decided to sell. There are so many hungry people in St-Hippolyte-du-Fort where we live, and if I can sell the collection for a reasonable price, I could help to feed them and the poorest to survive.'

'A noble gesture,' said the man. 'I am the owner of this gallery, Xavier Donnadieu, and I don't think I've ever heard of someone selling for such a humanitarian reason.' He smiled warmly at Jean.

'Well, if you'd like to bring it in, a little at a time, I can certainly put a value on it. I'm sure you'll be aware that fine art and antiques aren't picking up the prices they used to before the war, but there are still buyers – especially if items are exceptional. There's always a market for those, albeit reduced, especially from Paris.'

Jean went back to the truck and he and Philippe started bringing in the chairs and tables and clocks, and several beautiful vases. To their delight, the gallery owner seemed interested, even excited.

'These are fine items. Very fine. In fact, exceptional. Your father, I have to say, had truly excellent taste. As I said, I can't sell at the same prices I used to, but I'd certainly be interested in selling these.'

One hour later, Xavier's spare space in the gallery was almost full of the items he had decided to buy, and that was before they'd even brought in the paintings.

Now, as Jean went to fetch the ornately-framed pictures, he was wondering what he would do with the money, his mood jubilant. But he reminded himself that he and Philippe would have to be extremely careful. If they lorded it around Saint-Hippolyte, or Sauve where he actually lived, it would soon get noticed. And it worried him that Philippe was even more partial to drink than he was, and a loud mouth on top of that. He tried to put the thought to the back of his mind while carrying the first of the pictures out of the truck.

Half an hour later, all of them were placed around the gallery. But each time one was brought in, Xavier Donnadieu seemed to look puzzled, scratching and shaking his head from time to time and muttering 'This is strange, most strange.'

At last he had finished his inspection. 'I'm afraid to say that these paintings are worth nothing. Well, just a few francs apiece. They're done by local painters, certainly amateurs, and were most likely bought by your father in local markets.'

He picked one of them up. 'This, for example, is one of Sauve, and I think that one is of Durfort. I'm afraid, as I said, they have virtually no value.'

He walked around the collection again.

'But what *does* interest me is the frames, they're quite beautiful. It's almost as if they once held truly valuable paintings and someone has taken them out for safe-keeping.'

A stab of fury ran through Jean and Philippe. So that damned old Jew had fooled them both, and hidden the only *really* valuable things in his house – his art collection.

Xavier turned to Jean, frowning, 'Did you never see more beautiful paintings in these frames? They certainly would have contained them once. There's no doubt of that. Nobody would bother to put daubs in such wonderful frames. Surely you must have seen lovelier ones when you were growing up?'

Jean shook his head. 'No. Well, I don't really notice things like paintings, and ...'

Xavier interrupted. 'You *would* have done if my thinking is right. They would have been *masterpieces* with these sorts of frames. Unforgettable, even to an amateur eye.'

For the first time Xavier Donnadieu doubted these two customers, and wondered if the whole haul was perhaps stolen property. Moreover, now he thought about it, the sort of person who had the eye to buy such furniture and own such frames was hardly likely to be the father of one of them. Both seemed unsophisticated country people, and as far as he could tell, not that educated. There was now something truly suspicious about it all. At almost the same moment, he decided to reduce the price he would offer for the furniture and frames by at least half, guiltily knowing that with such strong doubts about their ownership, he shouldn't really be offering them anything at all.

But there was one last question he wanted to ask. He turned to Jean.

'Do you have any proof of ownership for all this? Perhaps your father's will?'

Jean thought quickly. 'I'm afraid not. His will was lost when we recently moved house.'

'That is most unfortunate. We art dealers are not normally permitted to sell without such proof, or buy for that matter. And anybody around here would tell you exactly the same thing.'

The price in his mind had reduced again. It was almost certainly stolen property.

Ten minutes later, Jean and Philippe were back in the empty truck, even more silent than they were when going there. Each of them was now a few thousand francs richer than before, but nothing like as rich as they had hoped to be.

That damned Jew had swindled them out of a fortune. So had that wretched art dealer. And so had the person who had the paintings now.

SIXTEEN

* * *

THE TOWN WAS BUZZING WITH SPECULATION. WORKMEN WERE RUSHING to renovate the old and rather elegant central building of the former Military Preparatory School. And more intriguing were the four sentry boxes and the barbed wire blocking the road on the north side. What on earth could be going on?

The answer came quickly in the form of about three hundred men, all in civilian clothes, who were marched up from the railway station singing some song about 'Tipperary', much to the amusement of the locals. It turned out they were English, or rather British, because many of them were apparently Scottish. They quickly settled into the old barracks and then strolled out and into the town, seemingly allowed out from after lunchtime until six in the evening. Extraordinary. But then, they were legally 'internees', not prisoners of war – with a lot more privileges. And that same General Weygand who had predicted that 'England would have its neck wrung like a chicken' seemed to have become more charitable towards his former allies. He had specified that they should 'be treated like gentlemen' – and instituted a régime called '*Liberté Surveillée*', whereby they were allowed into town and on their honour not to escape. In Marseille, in the Italian control zone, this had apparently not worked too well, and over two hundred had absconded. So the French had been ordered by the Italians and Germans to find somewhere more secure – further from the sea and boats.

Carmen met some of them the following day. One of them was an officer, a pilot, a smiling fellow who had a little bit of French – enough to ask her to join him and his friends for a drink. He revealed that some of them, especially the airmen, had no intention of sitting around and that escape plans were already in preparation. The Commandant in charge of the barracks was apparently a nice old French reserve officer, a Capitaine Leblon, who appeared to have a rather relaxed attitude towards the security of his charges, who seemed to be called 'Détachement W'. The pilot even told her that they were going to be allowed to build a swimming pool over by the old Fort.

Their attitude, Carmen thought, was amazingly positive. Many of them had been captured during the defeat in the north, or more recently shot down, and they had all gone to great lengths to reach the so-called 'Free Zone', only to be captured and interned. But there was none of the morose local defeatism that she was used to, and hearteningly the British seemed not to consider anything but ultimate victory. With people like this around, she felt that maybe there was some hope at last.

* * *

Two days later she was walking towards the dress shop in an even better mood. Sarah seemed to be recovering a little, and the BBC news last night seemed to be proving that the British might be right to be optimistic. There had hardly been any more German bombing raids in daylight, although the night-time ones must have been horrible for the civilians. But Pedro had pointed out that it might also mean that there would be no actual *invasion* of Britain – at least for the moment. After all, the Germans had not beaten the RAF, let alone destroy it, clearly their first real setback.

'Excuse me.' Carmen felt a tap on her shoulder.

She spun round to see a small, smiling figure, remembering him at once from the dance evening with Pierre – Maurice Bertrand, the trumpeter from the local jazz band.

'Can you ride a bicycle?' he asked.

Carmen was surprised. 'Yes, I can ride a bike. Why?'

Maurice fell into step beside her. 'I think I can trust you,' he said quietly. 'I know you're Spanish, and that your father was fighting the Fascists. And that you helped your Jewish friend.'

Carmen was shocked. If he knew so much, who else did? But Maurice Bertrand continued calmly.

'You know those British fellows, the internees? Well, we need to help them escape, especially the flyers. Lots of them got out from their fort in Marseille, and they want to do the same here. But, of course, they're now miles away from the sea or from neutral Spain. So anything we can do to make the journey less hard is a big help. That's where the bicycles come in. We're collecting them from all over the countryside, however decrepit, then repairing them so the men can escape along deserted country roads into the Pyrenees. We've got other methods of escape of course, but the first couple got away on bikes last night.'

Carmen listened in astonishment.

'Amazingly, old Capitaine Leblon is almost *encouraging* us. Would you believe what he told the Senior British Officer when they arrived? 'If there's anyone missing from roll-call, perhaps there's no need to report it for twenty-four hours'. They'd nearly be back in Marseille or in the Pyrenees by then!'

Carmen had to laugh.

'So what I'm asking you is this, would you help collecting the bikes? I'll give you the addresses of the folk who've agreed to donate them and your job would be to get them to the cycle workshop of Pierre Trabuc, down near the Protestant Temple. We think the flics are much less likely to be suspicious of a girl.'

'Are you in the Résistance?' asked Carmen, before answering him.

'Well, the first beginnings of it, I suppose. We've got together a group, but we realize there's absolutely no point shooting at people for the moment. It would do no good and just lead to reprisals, maybe for the whole town.

However, 'Détachement W' being brought here is a real opportunity to do something. If we can help people escape who *can* shoot at Germans, especially the flyers, that's much more valuable than any acts of local sabotage, assassination or whatever.'

Carmen thought for a moment.

'I'll do it, but on one condition. I want to borrow a pistol. Not to fire it, I wouldn't know how to anyway – just to threaten someone. Make them back off.'

Bertrand looked shocked. 'But as I just told you, we don't want problems here. And I'm certainly not happy with the idea of a girl with a gun.'

'I understand that, and I promise I won't do anything stupid, especially here in Saint-Hippolyte. It's just that there's one thing I need to do.'

He paused for a moment.

'Well, I'm not sure about that. Though I suppose I could lend you an empty one.'

* * *

Gendarme Jean Bollon was pedalling very slowly on his brand-new bicycle, thinking that in spite of its modern gears, his hangover – even worse than usual – would make the seven kilometres to work in Saint-Hippolyte feel more like seventeen. He really must try to cut down on the drinking, he told himself. But it was very difficult *not* to over-indulge when the bars of his home village of Sauve always insisted on giving him drinks in exchange for certain 'favours' – knowing he would usually turn a blind eye to rationing infringements.

As he cycled on to the long bridge across the deep, rocky gorge leaving Sauve, he saw two girls with bicycles standing near the middle of it, just near a gap in the parapet and the pile of stones where a truck had hit it two weeks ago. Getting closer, he noticed that one of them was extremely pretty, and though he couldn't see the other one as clearly because of her beret and dark glasses, she certainly had an amazing figure. He was a bit too old for them, but with so many men away as prisoners, he suddenly wondered if he had a chance there – especially when they smiled and waved at him unexpectedly. He immediately stopped, pausing for a motorcycle to go past and went up to them, propping his shiny new bicycle against the bridge.

'Bonjour!' said the pretty one with the long hair, giving him a lovely smile. 'One of my wheels has jammed. Do you think you could help?'

She pointed at her front wheel, and as he bent over to look at it, she swung the gun.

Leaning over, he suddenly felt a sharp blow to the back of his head as if he had been hit by a piece of lead, and falling to the ground, hit his head again. When he turned to face her, dazed and raising his arm to protect himself, she struck him again on his shoulder. Screaming with pain, he stifled his cries when spotting the gun in her hand.

The taller girl with the beret and dark glasses now bent over him.

'What happened to the Levys when you took them from the château?'

His eyes widened visibly with fear.

'I don't know. I was only doing what I was told to. We just took them to the station and another man from Nîmes took them off on the train.'

'Where to?'

'I don't know.'

'You *must* know.'

'Probably the camp at Gurs.'

'Where's Gurs?'

'Somewhere in the north. I don't know.'

'Then what?'

'Don't ask me. I've no idea. All I was doing was following orders.' He moaned with pain.

'Just following orders? Did they include going back and looting the place? Don't lie to me! That was my *parents'* house. *And* our maid saw you packing a van.'

The man said nothing.

'And who were the two other men?'

When he hesitated, Carmen stepped forward and shoved the barrel of the gun into his cheek. 'Five seconds,' she whispered.

That was enough to make him tell her.

Sarah now reached in her pocket and pulled out a half bottle of cognac, which she emptied over him, as he spluttered with the vapour and stink. Whoever found him would now think he had fallen off his bike, dead drunk. Then she took off her dark glasses and glared at him.

'I'm the 'Jewish slut' you were looking for. Now you've found me!'

Bollon stared at her, wide-eyed again, now attempting to get up, and almost toppling headlong over Carmen. Now falling over herself, she gave him a violent shove. Bollon swayed on his feet and suddenly fell backwards through the hole in the parapet, falling about eighty feet on to the rocks below.

Sarah and Carmen stared down at the body in deep shock. Neither spoke for a good minute, until they realized that they must absolutely not be seen there and had to get away fast. They left his bicycle, but on its side as if its owner had fallen off, together with the cognac bottle, and cycled towards Saint-Hippolyte, neither of them speaking. For Sarah, it was especially traumatic. She knew that Bollon had ruined the lives of her parents – and perhaps even worse, had played a role in ending them. Nevertheless, war or no war, she knew she could never kill intentionally, and that the screams of the falling Gendarme would stay with her forever.

Twenty minutes later, just before Saint-Hippolyte, she was forced to stop – overcome by a wave of nausea – and was violently sick on the side of the road.

Later that week the local newspaper *Midi-Libre* reported that *Jean Bollon, 42, resident of Sauve, had died after a traffic accident, after twenty years valuable service to the state in the Gendarmerie.*

* * *

Sarah was sitting in the back pew of the local church in Saint-Hippolyte, not caring that it was not a synagogue. For her, it was a sanctuary, a place where she could come and hide if anyone in the street looked at her a bit too long, which men often did. It never struck her that anyone might be looking at her a bit too long because she was striking, and always there was that frisson of fear. And not only fear for herself, but for Carmen's family.

And she found it soothing to light candles for her parents there, and saying prayers for them with the little Hebrew that she remembered while thinking back to happier times with them. Were they still alive? She could only pray for that now.

Her thoughts wandered to the château and the day of her eighteenth birthday, just after she'd met Carmen. It seemed years ago now, like another world, as indeed it was, although it was only eighteen months.

Suddenly she noticed a man who had tried to talk to her twice in the village walking past her pew. He smiled as he passed, but didn't attempt to talk to her, going to sit a little further down the aisle. But again she felt uneasy. Had he noticed her coming in earlier and decided to follow her? She felt her pulse racing, and wondered if she would be safer outside in the throng of the market. But suddenly the man got up and walked down to the altar and bowed in front of the effigy of Jesus on the cross. He then turned and walked back past her pew, giving her a smile and a polite nod.

At that precise moment she decided she would have to get out of the town and escape in the hills somewhere. If she couldn't even trust someone in a church, who *could* she ever trust except for Carmen and her family? Not being able to talk to anyone else was becoming more and more of a prison, and one she could no longer bear.

Leaving a few minutes later through the first door out of the church she was horrified to find the man waiting inside the porch.

'Will you talk to me this time, Sabine? And maybe have a coffee with me?'

'I'm sorry,' said Sarah, 'but I don't much like being followed. And especially not in here. And I'm supposed to be on an errand, and expected home.'

'I wasn't following you. These days I often come here when I've got the time to say a prayer for my mother. She died a few months ago.'

Was he telling the truth? Probably.

'I'm sorry,' said Sarah.

'Thanks.'

To her shock, the man suddenly started weeping and wiping his eyes. 'Forgive me,' he said, embarrassed. 'Pathetic of me. A grown man bursting into tears.'

All Sarah's instincts were to offer him words of comfort, but she didn't want to talk to this stranger, or any other stranger, let alone go with one to a café.

Any doubt about getting out of town and into a 'safe house' vanished at that precise moment. Suddenly she knew she had no alternative, no alternative at all.

'Well, au revoir then,' said the man. 'Hopefully we'll meet again.'

* * *

'I've seen that man again, the one who asked my name in the market a couple of weeks ago. He was in the church and he suddenly greeted me with the name I gave him – you know, Sabine – and asked me if I'd like to go to the café.'

'And did you?' asked Carmen.

'No, of course not. I didn't dare. I said I was about to run an errand and expected home in a few minutes. And he looked disappointed and said he hoped to see me again.'

'He might be totally harmless.'

'I know, but it still scares me rigid when strangers talk to me. In fact, I've been thinking. I don't think I can bear being frightened any more, day after day, scared of anyone even glancing at me. I can't stay here any more. And when *you* go, I'll have no-one to talk to, or at least talk to in the same way. And it isn't fair to your family either to put them in danger after all they've done for me.'

'So you're thinking of going into hiding?' asked Carmen, feeling a guilty flood of relief mixed with sadness.

'Yes, and sooner rather than later. Anyway,' she continued, ruffling her short dark hair, 'I've got no choice. Your mother's hair dye has just run out. I used the last of it this morning, and she's told me there isn't any more in the pharmacy. Women probably can't be bothered with their appearance these days, especially if their men aren't around. So I *have* to go into hiding, if not with the Résistance, then somewhere else.'

'The trouble is,' said Carmen, 'as I understand it, there *is* no Résistance as such – not yet. No bands of armed men in the woods in tents or safe houses, or anything like that. People are just carrying on with their lives, as best they can, while quietly preparing and doing whatever they can without attracting attention. The people I'm dealing with think the immediate need is to help the internees get back to Britain to continue the fight. So I'm not sure where *anywhere* you'd be going would be any safer than here. However, there's no doubt about one thing. You staying in a place known to be lived in by Republican Spaniards is dangerous enough and getting more so. We're bound to be checked out more than French people.

Anyway, I've got a meeting with Maurice and some of his companions tomorrow. I'll ask them about you, and see what they can do.'

* * *

Carmen had been asked by Maurice Bertrand to go to a house called La Bastide on the outskirts of town on the road to Monoblet. It was set back from the road, and Carmen put her bicycle behind the wall near the gate. The meeting was to talk about her possible role in the Résistance, but Carmen was determined to bring up the subject of Sarah, whose position was increasingly precarious as she had been told last night.

After introductions by Maurice to the four other men, they all sat down, but the atmosphere was not completely friendly. The reason became quickly apparent.

A local Gendarme called Bouisseau, who had secretly joined the Résistance, was the first to speak.

'Last week, on Tuesday, one of my Gendarmerie colleagues, Jean Bollon – albeit a greedy, crooked, Pétainist bastard – fell off the Sauve bridge and was killed. A friend of mine happened to be driving past on his motorcycle that morning and saw him talking to two girls with bicycles.' He stared at Carmen. 'I think one of them was you. You also borrowed a pistol from Maurice two days before and returned it two days later – unfired – but probably something to do with Bollon's fate.' His eyes bored into her.

Carmen felt her face flush. 'I didn't kill him, I promise. And neither did my friend. But we *did* see him fall over the bridge.'

'And how did *that* happen, exactly? With a little bit of help?'

Carmen said nothing, knowing that it was useless to insist that his death was entirely accidental. Her very presence at the scene was incriminating enough.

Paul Roux, a man she knew was often driving British internees off to the Pyrenees in a taxi, now leaned forward. But to Carmen's huge relief, his face appeared sympathetic.

'We think we know why you were there. That Bollon fellow took part in the Levy raid and then the looting of the château. So you probably wanted to help your friend to get revenge. As she certainly did. And you got away with it.'

'He fell, I promise.'

'But I somehow don't think he would have done without you two there.'

Maurice now spoke out. 'Anyway, changing the subject, you're doing a great job collecting bicycles, but as I explained to you when I first talked to you, we *must* confine ourselves to things like that. You may think the situation's bad here, but it would be much, much worse if Hitler thought that Pétain couldn't control things and took over the South.'

'And,' Paul Roux added, 'the Germans, in spite of their failure to invade Britain, are still far too powerful to fool with. We think they'll be on the move again soon, and if there's trouble here they could come back and crush us like bugs.

Half this country actually *likes* Pétain, for God's sake, and goes along with the occupation. And you should hear what's going on in Paris. Loads of smart women have taken up with German officers, '*collaboratrices horizontales*' as they call them. And the vast majority have a 'wait and see' attitude – largely put out by the Pétain Government. Nobody wants to do anything, unless they absolutely have to. Frankly, they just don't want to get involved.

But wait. As rationing gets more brutal and more and more of our food is seen to go to the Germans, and our two million prisoners of war *still* don't get returned, and above all when the Boches get under *real* military pressure, then we'll *really* start a fighting war.

And one *good* thing about this area is all our wooded mountains. They've helped us resist our enemies for years – centuries, even. Religious wars, Protestants, Camisards. And most of the time we've been resisting enemies from Paris – so I don't think we'll hesitate with people from Berlin!'

Gendarme Bouisseau now interjected. 'In the meantime, we have to wait. So you absolutely must *not* get involved in private feuds, however justified they may seem to you.' He stared hard at Carmen. 'And if you can't promise to do that, forget about joining us – and forget about your friend. If she wants to track down anyone else involved with taking away her parents away, she can't do it now. She'll have to wait, and do it in the future – until it won't harm whatever else we're doing. Or for that matter, accidentally end up betraying us all. *Do you hear me?*'

Carmen nodded, hugely relieved that she hadn't been rejected from the group.

'Fine, said Maurice. 'We'll leave it at that. Now, let's have a glass of wine and get back to the subject of bicycles.'

Carmen immediately realized she couldn't bring up the subject of a safe house for Sarah – at least not for the moment. But she also knew it couldn't wait long.

* * *

The dress shop was only two hundred metres or so from Alfonso's house and Carmen had now walked past three 'MISSING CAT' posters on the way, all with photographs of the lost pets and their names, and heart-rending messages from their owners. She shivered at the thought of what may have happened to them and wondered if their owners had guessed their probable fate, or were in deep denial at what may have befallen them.

It was perhaps understandable now that food was so drastically rationed or prohibitively expensive, but still unthinkable and deeply depressing. As was the prospect of walking past the posters every day as they faded in the summer sunshine, along with any hope that their owners may have had about seeing their cherished pets again.

'Are you alright?' asked Elaine Puget as she entered the shop, noticing Carmen's sad expression.

'I'm fine. It's just those cat posters. There's another one up today.'

'I know,' said Elaine. 'I've just seen it, too.' She thought it better not to suggest the cats had probably strayed. Carmen was no fool.

'Best not to think about it,' was all she could think of saying, patting Carmen on the shoulder while desperately hoping that there wouldn't be more posters on the trees in the weeks to come.

Unfortunately there were, and several in the coming days. Posters all the way down the main street warning people about the health danger of eating stewed cats.

SEVENTEEN

* * *

I T WAS ABOUT THREE IN THE MORNING IN CARMEN'S TINY BEDROOM.
'Are you awake? she asked.

'Yes,' replied Sarah.

'Thought you were. I've just had an idea. Do you mind me talking?'

'Not at all. Couldn't sleep anyway.'

'Look, I've been lying awake wondering if you could go to Pierre's father's farm. You'd be a lot safer out there than here, and he really needs someone to keep an eye on him. Papa says he's getting pretty frail and rickety lately, falling over things and finding the steps and stairs harder. If you went there, I could easily see you, and so would Papa as he's working there every day. We could keep an eye on you far more easily than we can here. I really wish I could have brought up the subject of you at the meeting the other day, but after that rebuke about Bollon, it just wasn't the right time. In fact, it's very lucky we got away with that.'

Sarah thought about it.

'And you'd certainly eat a lot better,' added Carmen.' You're getting far too thin.'

'And you,' said Sarah, 'everyone is.'

'What if I mentioned it to my father?'

Sarah didn't reply at once. 'I wouldn't want to be a burden on Auguste, although I certainly don't want to be a burden on your family either.'

'You wouldn't be a burden,' said Carmen. 'You'd be the opposite. And you're not a burden on us, just a worry, and in a way that's a bigger problem. I'll really miss you here – it's lovely having a great girlfriend to talk to. But I'm scared for you, as you are about yourself. It's awful that you have to hide whenever the doorbell rings.'

There was a full minute's silence before Sarah answered.

'Do you think he'll have me? After all, I could put him at risk too.'

'Much less risk. The farm is out of town for a start. Less prying eyes and people to see you. And with food there, vegetables at least, you wouldn't even need to come to town to shop. And I'll always be around to come and see you. At least, when I can.'

'But Carmen, how can I pay him for my bed and board?'

'You wouldn't have to. First you'd be helping out, and remember, if you really need money, Uncle Fon knows where all of your parents' pictures are. So he's guarding your money, and he'd tide you over. In fact, he'd spend anything to keep you safe. Only the other day he said he'd grown really fond of you. As did Papa.'

There was another long silence while Sarah thought about it.

'Well, I'd certainly sleep easier at night. Sometimes I find it difficult to even sleep at all. The slightest noise outside freaks me out'

'I know,' said Carmen. 'Like now. That's only thunder outside, not guns.'

There was another protracted pause while both of them thought of the prospect of Sarah living with Auguste.

'You okay?' asked Carmen.

'Fine. But if I go, I'll *really* miss you.'

'I'll miss you too, but as I said, you'll only be a little way out of town. And never far from my thoughts.'

Sarah groped for Carmen's hand. 'I don't know what I'd do without you.'

'Or me, without you,' said Carmen. 'Friends for life.'

'Friends for life,' agreed Sarah. 'But do you think he'd want me there, I mean, Auguste?'

'Absolutely! A lonely man, living on his own, and worried about his son and his own failing health? Of *course* he'd want you. He'd welcome you with open arms!'

'But wouldn't Pierre think I was putting his father at risk?'

'I hardly think so. Far more likely he'll be relieved to hear there's someone keeping an eye on him. Let's talk to Papa in the morning.'

'Okay, But promise me one thing.'

'What?'

'That you won't stop trying to find out the names of the other two men who took my parents away. That's if it doesn't put *you* at risk. There must be a way. The local Gendarme may have been easy, but that man from Nîmes in plain clothes – that may be more difficult to find out.'

'Of course, I'll keep my ear to the ground. But I'm not quite sure what to do if I find him. I got into enough trouble about Bollon. It was lucky I wasn't kicked out of my resistance group.'

They lapsed into silence again, until Sarah spoke.

'I wish I wasn't Jewish.'

'Never say that,' said Carmen, sitting up. 'It would kill your parents.'

'I think my parents have been killed already. Who'd want to waste money on feeding Jews? Not Germans.'

Suddenly Carmen couldn't think what to say.

* * *

Three days later was market day and Elaine Puget's shop had a few customers in spite of the clothes rationing. She had let all the other girls go, except Carmen – her best assistant. At about 11.45, just before noon, the start of the normal French two-hour lunch break, Elaine came over to Carmen and gave her a letter.

'A Gendarme, that nice one, just came by and asked me to give you this. He said it was *very* important, and you should read it at once.'

Carmen went to the end of the shop and ripped open the envelope. The scribbled note shocked her to the core.

RAID TONIGHT. GET HER OUT!

She quickly asked Elaine if she could go off for lunch early, explaining there was a crisis at home, then put on her coat and ran as quickly as she could back to the house.

Thankfully Sarah was in the kitchen with Maria.

'Sarah, you need to come upstairs! *Now!*' As soon as they were out of Maria's earshot, Carmen spoke quickly and decisively.

'You have to go to the farm – *today!* I've been tipped off we'll be raided here tonight. Put as many clothes on as you can under your coat right now and put the rest in shopping bags. You can't be seen with a suitcase. Then Papa can bring you the rest of your stuff later in dribs and drabs.'

Sarah stared at her, wide-eyed with shock.

'And we need to get rid of any evidence you've been here. And slide your camp-bed under mine. And then scatter around any clothes you can't take. With any luck, they'll think they're mine.'

She paused, wondering what else Sarah ought to take.

'Oh , and make sure you take your forged papers – the ones calling you Sabine – and your ration tickets. In half an hour Papa and Auguste will be packing the leftover market stuff into the van. We'll stroll down, looking casual as if we've been shopping, and then get you in the van. And I'll come and see you as soon as I can.'

When Carmen came down alone to the kitchen, she explained the desperate situation to her mother and both immediately agreed to send Otilia and Juanita to families of their school-friends in Ganges, hoping fervently that it could be arranged at such short notice. Children of their age could all too easily blurt out something to the police only too easily. Thank God her mother wasn't panicking – as Carmen had anticipated.

And thank God, too, that one of the mothers at the school gates had later agreed to take her sisters in for the night, hearing there was a family crisis.

Later, when Alfonso returned from the garage, he drove them off. The children's delight at the prospect of staying with friends was in sharp contrast with the mood of the rest of the family.

* * *

At five in the morning, there was a loud banging on the front door. Alfonso went down the stairs, deliberately slowly as the banging got louder. Opening the door, three uniformed Gendarmes barged past him and then a man in a raincoat who flashed a badge, announcing he was an Inspector. The group immediately began to search the house, while Pedro, Maria and Carmen hurried down to the kitchen from upstairs.

'Who else lives here?' the Inspector barked to Alfonso.

'Just two little girls, ten and twelve. They're in Ganges tonight, staying with school friends.' He pointed to a cupboard. 'Their papers are in there, along with ours.'

'Anyone else?'

'No, nobody. Anyway, there's no room for anyone else. You can see how cramped we are already.'

The Inspector ordered one of the Gendarmes to take out and check their papers. To her huge relief, Carmen suddenly recognized the man who stepped forward – Gendarme Bouisseau – the same man she had met at the Résistance meeting. He took out the papers, put on his glasses, and appeared to inspect them carefully.

At last he looked up.

'They're all Spanish, Sir, and fully naturalised. None of them have had their naturalisation revoked. And I happen to know who they are.' He pointed to Alfonso. 'He services all our cars, including the Mayor's. The other one runs a vegetable stall, and the young lady works for Madame Puget at the dress shop. And this is her mother, Madame Casales, who occasionally helps out at the medical centre' – a fabrication that would have astounded Maria if she had been able to understand him properly.

'All their papers are completely in order.' He looked up, and out of sight of the Inspector, winked at Carmen.

'Must have been a false lead,' grunted the Inspector, obviously very annoyed, before turning to his men. 'Okay, you lot, let's get out of here.' There was no apology to the family.

Carmen closed the door on the last of them to leave – Gendarme Bouisseau – who surreptitously turned to smile at her before catching up with the group.

* * *

It was just getting light as Pedro pedalled up to the farmhouse on his bicycle. He was soon hard at work helping Auguste load the vegetable boxes into the Citroen van.

Auguste was an old soldier, a veteran of Verdun, and was very interested to hear real news about the present war – news he certainly couldn't get from the controlled and biased French media – but that Pedro could get from the more honest BBC. However, he did seem to have trouble taking it in.

Pedro was in a good mood as he lugged the boxes.

'Do you know Auguste, that the Italians – those cowardly, bullying bastards I know so well from Spain – attacked Greece two weeks ago? God knows why. Maybe Musso wants to show off to Hitler that he can win wars too. Or maybe he wanted to score off him. But, anyway, guess what? The Greeks are *really* fighting back. And they're actually *beating* the spaghetti-eaters, even though they're hugely outnumbered. They're even advancing into Albania. Mussolini must be feeling a complete fool. And the British beat him in the desert too. Seems he can't do *anything* right!'

They were interrupted by Sarah coming down from the farmhouse.

'Would you two like breakfast?'

They both nodded with pleasure as Pedro secured the last box. In the house, he washed and dried his hands and then fished a piece of paper out of his pocket. While Auguste was focussing on his rather skimpy breakfast, Pedro signalled to Sarah and passed her the note. It was from Carmen.

Cherie,

I thought you might like to know that Philippe Laporte, the other Gendarme who came to your house, died in Durfort two nights ago, hit by a bus, outside a bar.

They say he was completely drunk, buying drinks all night for his pals, apparently flush with money, but upset about his best friend, Jean Bollon .

That leaves the third man. I think I've tracked him down –

Jean-Francois Veziers, from the Commissariat Général aux Questions Juives.

It's at 18, Rue de l'Arène in NIMES.

Remember, sit tight. And don't do anything silly. See you Thursday.

Cx

EIGHTEEN

✵ ✵ ✵

IT WAS A BEAUTIFUL SUNNY MORNING AS THE NÎMES TRAIN PULLED INTO Saint-Hippolyte.

Albert Salles, even after many hours on trains, was really looking forward to this assignment. He was a senior official in the new 'Commissariat Général aux Questions Juives' in Paris, charged with the seizure of Jewish assets. It was not often that anyone in his job was asked to search a property of the size and grandeur of the one he would apparently see today. He knew it was the largest house in Saint-Hippolyte, and from what he had heard, more of a château, and he had been reliably informed that it would be full of priceless objects, and especially paintings, in which those important men of the 'Bureau Otto' – Hermann 'Otto' Brandl and Dr Eric Gritzbach – working for *Reichsmarschall* Goering – seemed to have a special interest.

He had been instructed to record them all, and then prepare them to be sent to Paris, complying with the orders of Otto Abetz, the German Ambassador, who was in charge of the art programme. Salles knew a good result would certainly boost his career.

On the platform at Saint-Hippolyte he was met by Jean-Francois Veziers, an official from Nîmes. He was a nervous little man, who had apparently been in charge of the arrest of the Jewish owners, picked up early because of their obvious wealth and art collection. They drove the short distance to the château, with Albert Salles in pleasurable anticipation of what to expect.

They unlocked the outer gate and walked through the garden – an untidy wilderness, neglected of course. Salles pictured the haul inside.

Most of the places he visited were pretty ordinary houses – as were the objects inside, some of them hardly worth taking at all. But this would be decidedly different, a château that really made his job worthwhile.

Veziers fiddled with the stolen front door keys, and finally they were inside. But then they stopped and stared around in shock.

There was nothing there, or almost nothing.

Hardly a stick of furniture. Only cobwebs everywhere, and not a single painting. Only darker patches on the walls where they had clearly been.

'What the hell *is* this?' he snarled at Veziers. 'I've come *fifteen* hours from Paris. For *this?*'

Veziers seemed to be equally shocked. 'It was all here when *I* came last time. I can't believe it!'

'Well, it's not here now, is it?'

Without saying another word, Salles walked quickly up the graceful stone staircase, followed by the nervous Veziers. There was nothing upstairs either, except big wrought-iron beds and unexceptional furniture. And again, none of the paintings Salles had been told to expect. Coming downstairs again, now livid with fury, he wondered if there were any outbuildings where they could be hidden – or maybe a cellar. But there was no cellar.

Now, walking into the garden, they found an annexe, but the door wasn't even locked – and inside were only old brushes, rakes and firewood. The building had clearly only been used as a garden shed.

He turned on Veziers. 'Someone has quite clearly stripped the place. Why the *hell* wasn't it properly secured? What kind of country idiots are you? You realize there'll have to be an investigation? And a thorough one?'

Veziers looked sheepishly at the ground.

Driving back to the station, Salles knew that they could probably sell the building, but it was scant comfort with property prices at rock bottom. Not worth the effort. What a wasted trip! And he remembered with a shudder that Dr Eric Gritzbach was also an SS Führer, and well-known for being irascible. As they got to the station, he turned and snarled, 'I expect *you* to find who did this, Veziers, and also get the stuff back. *You hear me?*'

Veziers gave him an abject nod, relieved to hear the whistle of the approaching train.

* * *

Carmen had elected to meet some of the British officers of 'Détachement W' in the Café de la Bourse, just down from the barracks where they were housed. She was thankful that the odious little Pétainist Morelli was not there in the afternoons. He would have loudly revelled in the news she brought to the British. The Détachement's radio had been temporarily confiscated as a reprisal for the many escapes, so the internees were eager to hear the latest news.

Consulting her notes on last night's BBC broadcast, Carmen spoke to the British pilot, Flight Lieutenant Will Ewbank, who understood French, while he translated for his colleagues. She had to tell him that, unusually, the French newspapers and the BBC had agreed on something – that for the British, things had gone very badly in Greece.

It seemed that Hitler had chosen to come to the rescue of his hapless ally, Mussolini, who was getting nowhere against the plucky Greeks. So Germany had first attacked Yugoslavia and bombed the completely unprotected capital Belgrade – and that for once, everyone believed the horrific toll of 17,000 civilians dead there.

She went on to reveal that when Greece was then invaded by the Germans, the British had sent troops they could ill afford to spare from the desert. But in Greece they had been forced to retreat in the face of overwhelming ground and air attacks, evacuating most of their forces to Crete. And that nobody knew what might happen next.

The British crouched over their beers, listening intently to Carmen's quiet voice.

After she and Ewbank had finished, one of them said to his friends in English, 'You have to hand it to the Krauts, they never stop for anything.'

Carmen's pilot friend shot him a disapproving look before turning to her and speaking in French. 'Thanks for telling us. We'll pass it on. It's certainly bad news, but I'm afraid it's not surprising. With France gone, it's going to take an awful long time if Britain has to fight all alone. We need someone bigger on our side, but America still wants to keep out of things. Mind you, we've got a couple of volunteer American pilots here. *They* may now wish they'd kept out too!' He laughed bitterly.

'Anyway, there's absolutely no reason *not* to go on escaping. The Résistance people here have been incredibly helpful to us, fantastic. We must have got nearly eighty out already. So if *I* get out, I'll be saying this is one of the best places to get arms to.'

Two days later, Carmen was delighted to hear that Will Ewbank had done exactly that, getting out and escaping towards Spain in Paul Roux's ambulance.

* * *

Back in Nîmes, Jean-Francois Veziers had not slept well for two nights, knowing he was in deep trouble. The visit from that man Albert Salles had terrified him. Who on earth had the paintings now? They must be exceptionally valuable for someone like that to come all the way from Paris to see them, and if even that Reichsmarschall Goering was interested.

He was already shaken enough to discover that the two Gendarmes he had taken on the original raid were now both dead. And that both had been found to have an unusual and suspicious amount of money on them. It looked as if they were almost certainly the thieves who had emptied the château. And when he had checked the local antique dealers, he had questioned one called Xavier Donnadieu in Nîmes, who readily admitted buying a number of valuables from two men, but no art masterpieces. In fact, Donnadieu had told him that the paintings offered to him were 'rubbish', not even worth the price of the paint. And he had quickly proved he was telling the truth when readily showing them what remained of the collection. While no art expert, Veziers could see at once that they were amateur, local daubs, albeit extremely attractively framed.

Donnadieu had gone on to say that, in his view, the expensive frames had almost certainly once contained something very valuable, at which point Veziers had begun to realize that someone else had removed the original works of art.

He decided to call his informants and get them to sniff around in the local area. Almost immediately two names had cropped up as local friends of the Levys – a garagiste called Alfonso Dubois and his cousin Pedro Casalès. Could it be that *they* had been entrusted with the paintings as close non-Jewish friends of the family? It was certainly a possibility. He had been told that they had already been searched for the missing Levy girl, but that their house was 'clean', and she may well have escaped from the château and gone to Spain in the flood of humanity going the opposite way to the 1939 exodus out of that country.

He felt a frisson of relief to have turned up two possible suspects already, and ordered immediate searches of both the house where they lived and also the garage. Indeed, he had decided to go himself. The last thing he wanted was any more slip-ups.

That night Alfonso was surprised to hear banging on the door, and to open it to some uniformed Gendarmes led by a little man in plain clothes. 'I have orders to search this house,' he said waving a piece of paper. 'I have reason to believe you're hiding a collection of valuable paintings, now the property of the state. It might be easier for you just to tell us where they are.'

'What paintings?' asked Alfonso. 'There are certainly no valuable paintings here.'

'I'm not sure I believe you,' the man said, pushing past Alfonso and turning to his men. 'Right you lot, tear the place apart!'

Two hours later, sitting in the shambles of their home and with Maria and the two youngest children in tears, the family watched the evidently angry and disappointed leader of the group coming down the stairs. He left one Gendarme outside to prevent anyone leaving, and then, taking Alfonso's keys, he turned to his men. 'Right, we'll do the other place now.'

As they left, and the tearful Maria went off to find some coffee in the mess of the kitchen, Pedro turned to Alfonso with a look of despair.

'We're in *real* trouble now.'

To his astonishment, Alfonso smiled. 'No, we're not. They'll trash the garage of course, but that will be it.'

Pedro looked puzzled. 'Why?'

'Because they won't find a thing. As I always say, it's a good idea to stay one step ahead of those bastards.'

NINETEEN

* * *

THE NEWS FROM THE WAR CONTINUED TO BE DEPRESSING FOR THE Gaullists. Having evacuated Greece, the British had been overwhelmed on the island of Crete, losing several ships from air attack and tragically being forced to leave many men behind as prisoners when they left. And in North Africa, a dynamic new German General called Rommel had appeared and taken the initiative.

At least there was good news from Carmen's friends in 'Détachement W'. No less than sixty-three internees had managed to escape in April alone. She wondered how long this splendid defiance of the authorities could go on, and for how long the friendly and clearly indulgent Captain Leblon could keep his job. She had heard it was the Italians who were meant to be supervising the Détachement. Surely, she thought, they must be losing patience.

One afternoon, among a group of officers, she met a rather mysterious new arrival. He seemed to be called 'Pat O'Leary', but did not appear to be either British or Irish. And he spoke French perfectly, in fact better than Carmen, albeit with a slight accent – perhaps Belgian. He had just been captured on the coast with two others, which seemed a bit unusual. However, she never had a chance to talk to him again, hearing that all three of them escaped almost immediately.

Only days later, she was introduced to another man whom she heard was famous. Her British friends explained that he was American and rich, celebrated in both British and American 'society' for being a playboy racing-driver. Apparently, he had volunteered to fly in Britain's Royal Air

Force, but had then been shot down and interned. She was told that he too was using a false name, and as 'Captain Willard', briefly became the 'Senior British Officer' in charge of the barracks. Again she never got to know him, or his real name, hearing that he had been repatriated on medical grounds as part of the agreement with the French.

At the end of June, with the weather hot and the Détachement men marching every day down to the old Fort to enjoy the swimming pool they had created, the relatively relaxed atmosphere was suddenly broken by the news that the Germans were on the move again. Now Carmen had good reasons for remembering her pilot friend's words about 'Britain needing someone bigger as an ally', although it turned out that it was not America as Will Ewbank had hoped, but the Soviet Union.

The BBC, and also the French media, announced that the Germans had callously attacked their supposed Russian 'ally', pouring across a 1,400 kilometre front with nearly four million men and thousands of tanks. Once again they appeared unstoppable, and soon Pedro was gloomily pointing out that they were now closing gigantic pincers behind the Russians, and this time not trapping just thousands, but tens of thousands or even hundreds of thousands.

However, for the Communists in France, a huge dilemma had been removed. They had been totally confused and dismayed by the unexpected and cynical Non-Aggression Pact in August 1939 between two sworn ideological enemies, Hitler and Stalin. This was especially true of the Spaniards, who had, after all, been in a long fighting war with the Nationalists – proxies for German interests.

Now everything would be much simpler, with the Communists allowed to fight Fascists again. And it did not take long for this new change to register itself in Saint-Hippolyte. Late one Saturday morning, Carmen was approached in a shop by a woman she vaguely recognized, who asked to speak to her. Going outside, the stranger quietly told her, 'My husband would like to meet you and your father – today if possible.'

Carmen was surprised and slightly worried. Could she trust her? She seemed pleasant enough. Maybe it was worth the risk. One couldn't go around not trusting *anyone*.

'Tell him to wait until just after twelve and then come to our house. It's number 36, Rue Pasteur.'

Carmen had just enough time to find her father, who luckily wasn't working at the farm that day, and quickly brief him on her conversation. Then there was a knock on the door. Their visitor turned out to be about sixty, short, thick-set and barrel-chested. Carmen brought him into the kitchen.

'Bonjour. Thank you for seeing me. My name's Pascal Lagarde.'

Pedro shook his hand and offered him a glass of wine. They all sat down round the kitchen table.

'Let me tell you a little about myself. I used to be a coal miner both in Alès and La Grande Combe – before my lungs started giving out. I'm retired here now, and I'm the leader of the local Communist party. As you can imagine, since Pétain took power, we've had a pretty rough time. We've had a lot of Spaniards assigned to the mines. I've come to you because I know you fought the Fascists in Spain, which is what we want to do now, but here in France.'

He paused and sipped his drink.

'Two years ago we were totally amazed that Stalin and Hitler signed that Non-Aggression Pact, though we knew soon enough that it was mainly to carve up Poland. Maybe Stalin was also trying to buy some time. Probably Hitler, too. Who knows? But we were really confused. We knew, or thought we knew, that the Fascists and Nazis were our enemies. But suddenly they seemed to be sort of friends. And that made it extremely difficult for us to know how to deal with Pétain and his regime. Our hands were tied.

But now, with the attack on Russia, everything's changed. We *know* who our enemies are again. And we want to help, get going, and find arms. We're hoping that you might act as a go-between with the Résistance people here. They're likely to be very suspicious of a direct approach from me.'

Pedro nodded and thought carefully before responding.

'Two things. First, as a known Spanish Republican, I'm under suspicion, so for the sake of my family, I personally have to keep out of things, so I don't really know the people you're talking about. But my daughter Carmen here *might*. She's the one to help you.

But second, she'll tell you that the Résistance people are being really careful not to act prematurely.'

'That sounds like the usual pathetic lack of aggression,' sighed Lagarde, turning to Carmen.

'No, not at all,' she replied calmly. 'They think that currently *any* acts of aggression, killing or sabotage, will do no real good and risk reprisals that the countryside – suffering enough, just can't afford. What they *are* doing is helping the 'Détachement W' people to escape. Sixty-three of them in April alone. And that's risky enough, and can't last much longer. In fact, I'm sure there'll be some arrests among our friends pretty soon.'

Carmen looked very serious when she continued.

'I know the other thing they're afraid of, apart from the usual brutal reprisals, is the Germans coming in and taking over the Free Zone. *Anything* showing the Germans that Pétain isn't on top of things might trigger that.'

'I don't think that's much of a threat right now,' said Pascal. 'Hitler must have his hands pretty full in Russia.'

'Well, I'm happy to introduce you to my colleagues, but I warn you that they're *very* serious about not starting things that aren't going to do any good, in fact, anything that may be counter-productive.'

Pouring him some more wine, she decided to change the subject, 'Incidentally, what have you heard about Russia?'

'Terrible, a real disaster! The Soviets seemed completely unprepared, as if they couldn't believe it would ever happen. They lost 1,500 planes destroyed *on the ground* during the very first day alone. How on earth did *that* happen? The Germans have advanced three hundred kilometres in three weeks and seem to have surrounded whole armies, taking literally hundreds of thousands of prisoners. Stalin may be lucky to survive – the way things are going. I just hope things improve. Mind you, Napoleon got screwed by Russia, so maybe Hitler will too. And probably by the weather. Anybody can drive a tank across a dusty plain – it's different when first the mud and then the snow turn up.'

Lagarde didn't stay long, realizing he was getting nowhere. He got to his feet to go, thanked them for the wine and handed over a piece of paper.

'Anyway, here's where you can reach me. I'll wait for you to tell me when and where we can meet. And *do* something. It's so frustrating, sitting back.'

When he had gone, Pedro looked very worried.

'Let's hope they don't cause trouble. I'm not entirely sure about him.'

* * *

'How are you?' asked Carmen, relieved to see that she needn't have asked. Sarah looked good – visibly less stressed and clearly putting on a bit of much-needed weight, even in the two weeks since she'd seen her last.

'Fine, but I do miss the buzz of your place. You know, the children and things. And us being able to talk. It's pretty quiet here, as you can imagine. But Auguste is sweet to me, and I can't complain. And I have to admit I *do* feel safer out of town without all those prying eyes, and that man who tried to talk to me – you know, the one that came into the church. It was really beginning to get to me.

By the way, thanks for your note about that other Gendarme and the Jewish affairs fellow. I thought about that today. I was looking down on the road and watching the bus from Le Vigan really struggling get up the hill, obviously just been converted to charcoal and hopelessly slow. I suddenly thought that our thieving Gendarme Laporte might still be alive if the bus that hit him had been a charcoal one. Lucky for us that it was one of the last of the petrol ones, and not going at a snail's pace. Otherwise he'd still be with us.'

There was a long pause.

'Carmen, do you mind if I ask you something?'

'Not at all.'

'Do you ever feel terrible about that man on the bridge?'

Carmen paused. 'Bollon? If I'm honest, yes, sometimes.'

'Me, too, in spite of what he did to my parents. I keep seeing him in my mind, falling on to the rocks.'

'It was an accident.'

'Yes, but one that needn't have happened. I wonder if we should really have gone after him.'

Carmen paused before answering.

'We had to. Remember, he knew about you. So you were in danger, too. And we didn't *mean* to kill him.'

There was a long silence.

'Friends?' suddenly asked Sarah, touching Carmen's hand.

Carmen nodded. 'Friends for life.'

'Changing the subject, Sarah, you know about that raid on our house the other night? And the search afterwards in Alfonso's garage?'

'Yes. Very clever of your uncle to bring the paintings up here before it happened.'

Carmen was astonished. 'Alfonso brought them *here?*'

'Yes, and where nobody will ever find them in a million years. Buried under the floor of one of the old outhouses in a steel box and covered over with concrete, and even a load of chicken manure on top of that. It's so smelly, nobody would even want to go in there. Alfonso told me the other day. He thought I ought to know. I wondered what on earth he was doing in there all week .'

She smiled at Carmen's surprise.

'Your uncle even darkened the concrete and distressed it to make it look old, although I'd have thought the manure would do that.'

Carmen suddenly remembered Alfonso coming back to the house stinking and covered in grey dust, much to her house-proud mother's distress. He had always claimed that the dust was from the garage.

'So that's one more problem out of the way.'

Sarah nodded. 'Thankfully – although, quite frankly, the last thing on my mind is paintings.'

Understanding immediately, and feeling at a loss for what to say, Carmen changed the subject. 'And how's Auguste?'

'To be honest, not brilliant. I think his memory's going a bit. And I'm having to help him quite a lot when your father isn't here. For instance, when writing letters to Pierre. His hands are getting more and more arthritic, though he never complains. And his legs aren't too good either. If ever there was a parcel at the door, I don't think he could get there quick enough, and I'm certainly not showing myself to the postman. But I think he really enjoys a bit of company – as I would if I were stuck out here alone. It must have been very lonely for him once Pierre had gone and when your Papa wasn't here.'

Carmen changed the subject again, worried about her young friend compelled to become a frail man's companion, however delightful he was.

'Does he still hear from Pierre?'

'Yes, like you do. But only on those awful pre-printed cards like you get – you know – with only one word allowed in a slot.'

'Don't tell me,' said Carmen. 'It's so cruel. And if they're cruel about things like that, what *else* are they cruel about?' She suddenly flinched, remembering Sarah's parents being taken away.

* * *

For Carmen, one of the few pleasant parts of her routine was removed. The French military authorities, urged on no doubt by the Italians and the Germans, had withdrawn *Liberté Surveillée,* the privilege the British had to wander round the town. They could still march down to their swimming pool by the old Fort, properly supervised by armed guards, but there was no more meeting in the cafés or playing football and boules with the locals. And the barracks had become much more like a proper prison. And Captain Leblon was almost on probation. This meant that the British no longer knew what was going on in the war, and the only news about 'Détachement W' now had to come via the Résistance people when they helped one of the escapers.

However, that didn't mean that escapes had stopped, far from it. The locals only heard later that a major one was only foiled by Captain Leblon being alert for once. He had noticed a curious light coming up from the ground one night. It turned out that a team of internees led by a coal miner had laboriously dug a fifty-metre tunnel reaching nearly as far as the local Catholic cemetery, and only days from a planned mass escape.

The locals also saw a French General inspecting the barracks one day, almost certainly intending to put a stop to the escapes. And no doubt he would quickly notice other things: that the first-floor windows had no bars, the busy streets were too close, the guards were elderly and not very fit, and that Captain Leblon was far too friendly. Many in the town could now work out that the Détachement might be moved soon. It would be sadly missed.

Soon after, parcels from England – with the popular magazine *Picture Post* – revealed to the delighted inmates that the formerly unknown Saint-Hippolyte had suddenly became famous with the British public. In August, a Swiss photographer, Thérèse Bonney, had heard of the camp and obtained permission from Leblon to visit and take photographs. These included ones of the roll calls – the men in the barracks, the swimming pool and even Captain Leblon cosily taking tea with British officers. Many of the men asked her to photograph them during her short stay, so she had told them to gather into groups, like 'the boys from London', 'the boys from the Highlands' and so on. The internees were thrilled by their unexpected fame.

However, such publicity of the relaxed regime in the barracks was not likely to make Captain Leblon more popular with his superiors.

* * *

That summer and autumn of 1941, there was no campaign map in the café to show the progress of the gigantic war in Russia. There was discussion about it certainly, and it was sharply divided. The Pétainists like Morelli were full of themselves, with a tedious 'I told you so' response to each new German victory. The Gaullists were gloomy enough, but it was even worse for the Communists. All their illusions were being shattered.

Anyone reading the papers or listening to the radio was stupefied by the very scale of the operation – four million German attackers, four thousand tanks, three thousand aircraft and even, rather strangely, 650,000 horses. Huge encirclements seemed to be capturing literally millions of Russian soldiers. The local French had never even *heard* of most of the places that were being over-run, such as Minsk, Smolensk, Viazma and Kharkov.

But there seemed to be no doubt that the Germans seemed to be winning, moreover in rapid and spectacular style. Indeed, they were fast approaching Moscow and Leningrad. Perhaps Russia would just collapse, most thought.

Others were not too sure. Most people in France, and even children, knew the story that going into Russia had been Napoleon's greatest moment of false pride and his greatest failure. And anyone familiar with the poignant paintings of his Grande Armée in pathetic retreat through the snow also remembered the weather. For a start, every autumn in Russia it rained ceaselessly, turning everything into impassable deep mud – including the unpaved roads. And then it would freeze and start snowing and Russia's traditional military ally would arrive – 'General Winter'. And by October that indeed seemed to have happened, with the German armies at an unexpected standstill.

Then the BBC reported something spectacular. Apparently from out of nowhere, and with whole new armies, the Russians had suddenly struck back, first in front of Moscow and then all along the front. The Germans, frozen in the snow, were actually reeling back. At last in St Hippolyte it was the time for the Pétainists to fall silent and the Gaullists to start hoping.

* * *

The members of the Résistance group in the Menviel house were crouched over the radio for the BBC news. As it was now forbidden to listen to the BBC, like many radios it was hidden or disguised, in this case as a Singer sewing machine box. Everyone was waiting to hear more about Russia's possible successes in the snows in front of Moscow when something even more dramatic was announced. Without any warning, Japanese aircraft had attacked somewhere called Pearl Harbor, sinking several American battleships. And the Japanese army and navy had started advancing into the British and Dutch possessions in the Far East. What is more, they seemed to be winning. The group was stunned. Paul Roux broke the silence.

'I've never met anyone Japanese, but I certainly don't like the sound of them. Look what they've been doing in China. Remember Nanking a couple of years ago? Literally thousands of civilians killed, shot or bayonetted. And thousands of women raped – and *then* killed, for God's sake.'

Maurice nodded in agreement. 'And you'll notice our spineless Vichy government has simply let them take over our colonies in French Indo-China. So we're no longer an imperial power. Mind you, I've always wondered how small European countries can go on ruling huge bits of the world if they don't want to be ruled.

Anyway, we'd better get word to our British friends in the barracks that something big and pretty bad is happening to their empire. I think there are a couple of Dutch fellows in there too. They'll all be worried about their people out there.'

Paul interjected a more cheerful thought.

'There *is* one good thing. The Americans are now in the war, at least partly. I wonder if they'll help in Europe? But perhaps all they'll care about is Japan. We'll have to pray they get around to fighting the Germans. That's going to be our only salvation here in France.'

Within hours, their prayers were answered. Hitler had, very foolishly, made the mistake of declaring war on America.

TWENTY

* * *

'ANYTHING ELSE YOU WANT TO SAY?' ASKED SARAH.
'Nothing I can think of,' replied Auguste.

Sarah was helping him write another letter to Pierre, now that the arthritis in his right hand was getting even worse. It was a weekly ritual that she now had to remind him about. 'What if we were to tell him that the Russians are now fighting on *our* side and that could be a real turning point in the war?'

'Have they?'

Sarah didn't tell him she'd told him several times already. He was really beginning to forget things lately. Only the day before he'd forgotten there was a pan of cabbage soup on the stove until the kitchen was full of black smoke. If she hadn't noticed it swirling through the open windows into the garden where she was picking flowers, the whole farmhouse could have gone up in flames, and him as well.

'Thankfully, they have. And that could change things a lot, hopefully to our advantage. Carmen told me it's certainly led to a big boost in morale.'

'By the way, how is she, and the family?'

It was as if he hadn't taken in the news about the Russians at all. She decided it might be a waste of time telling him about the Japanese.

'To be honest, I don't know,' replied Sarah. 'She's been too busy in the Résistance – you know, collecting bicycles. By the way, haven't you got an old one she could have in the outhouse? I'm sure I saw one when Alfonso was working out there.'

'Don't know. Have I?'

Clearly, his memory was going. Not senile dementia – he was under fifty, more likely the devastating effect of gas in the trenches in the last war.

'So,' said Sarah, 'shall I finish it?'

'Finish what?'

'This letter,' she said, lifting it up and smiling. 'To Pierre.'

'Oh, yes. Sorry, I forgot we were writing it. To my son, isn't it?'

'Yes, your son, Pierre.'

Suddenly Sarah was getting really worried. What if his memory went completely and he could never be left alone, or if he fell and she wasn't able to lift him? Or if Pierre ever got home, and his father didn't know who he was? That was an unbearable thought.

If only Carmen weren't so busy. Sarah was desperate for someone to talk to.

And she would have to get Pedro to take him to to the local doctor, Pibarot. The risk of her going with him was far too great. On the only times she'd been to the surgery before, the waiting room had been packed. And who knows might be sitting among them? Probably someone who would recognize her. And know she was a Jew.

* * *

The winter of 1941 was particularly harsh, and adding to the miseries of the unexpected snow and ice, the population of St-Hippolyte was rife with flu, made worse when people were already affected by malnutrition caused by the feeble rations.

With her entire family now stricken and in bed day and night, Carmen was run off her feet trying to look after them all and coping at the same time with her Résistance duties. She was extremely relieved that Elaine Puget had temporarily closed the dress shop, being ill herself – although Carmen missed her company – and, she had to admit, her salary.

The house was now freezing cold inside and she was forced to ration what little firewood was left in the shed. Being unable to drive, she had no means of bringing more to the house, and these days it was so chilly that she could even see her own breath inside it. It was hardly the best place to treat flu patients.

Adding to the daily misery was the constant sound of church bells from down the road, most likely for another funeral, although Carmen tried to keep that thought out of her mind, and though not as depressing, the sight of the normally bustling café – the heart of the town – virtually empty day after day. The market was a shadow of its former size, and many of the shops were shut like the dress shop. Nobody wanted to take the risk of picking up the current influenza virus in public places.

At least she was pleased that Sarah was now out of the village and protected from the epidemic that was ravaging the local population.

Increasingly she wondered if there was a God at all. First there were the horrors they had left behind in Spain, the families bombed in the shelter, and that appalling trek across the mountains. After that, there was this whole wretched new war and Pierre being taken away, the fate of Sarah's parents and then Sarah being forced to leave the house. And on top of all that, she hadn't heard from Pierre for weeks now. Had his prison camp also gone down with influenza? And if so, would anybody really care what happened to the prisoners? She tried to put that thought out of her mind, instead concentrating on looking after her family as best as she could.

But it was an enormous strain trying to keep everything together and stay smiling and cheerful, or be in any way optimistic with all the bad news constantly pouring in. At times she felt ten years older than her nineteen years.

* * *

Christmas Eve was very strange. They had tried to make it fun, especially for the two younger children, but it was hard to pull it off. To be sure, Pedro had achieved a brilliant coup by bartering some vegetables for two scrawny chickens. And they had saved up and pooled their ration tickets for the rest of the meal. But it was all a shadow of what it should have been.

Pedro had driven Auguste and Sarah down from the farm. In the case of Sarah, there was a risk. But they couldn't believe that anyone would be fanatical enough go Jew-hunting that day. Or indeed, that night, when she slept on the sofa.

They were all sad to see that Auguste seemed to have deteriorated so quickly. He could hardly walk, and as Carmen had warned them, his memory had gone. He could just about recognize some of them, but did not seem to know what Christmas was. But he seemed very pleased to be there, smoking his pipe and nodding as they chatted – and happy to stay overnight in a makeshift camp bed.

There was no Christmas tree, no presents, no decorations around the house, but nobody, even the children, now expected them. But then, they had never experienced a Christmas like that – born in wartime, and still in wartime. Such frivolities were, sadly, already totally alien to them. This was just the day when Christ had been born, and they now had little reason to have faith in him.

During the next afternoon they suddenly heard singing, realizing that it was the British in the barracks also celebrating their Christmas. Presumably they had hoarded some beer and wine since the days of *Liberté Surveillée* when they were allowed into town, and had probably received some Red Cross parcels.

They might not have sounded so happy if some other depressing news of that Christmas Day had filtered through to them.

On the other side of the world, the Japanese had taken Hong Kong.

* * *

After the meagre celebrations of Christmas were all over, and for the Casales family, the just as meagre Spanish 'Los Reyes' festival celebrating the Three Kings, the town was bleak and empty and the café noticeably quieter. It was evident that the customers no longer entirely trusted whom they were talking to, and keeping their opinions to themselves. Gone was the vociferous debate of even a few months ago, and gone too, were the little huddles of people in the market chatting to each other about what was happening.

It was as if the whole community was falling apart along with the rest of the country.

Fear about different opinions stopped people mixing, and the ever more severe rationing also stopped them buying, almost as much as the poor quality of the food they were still able to get. With the market now a shadow of its former self, Carmen's father was even considering giving up trading, although panicking about what else he could do.

And to Carmen's distress, Elaine Puget had told her she was thinking of closing down. 'Nobody wants to buy pretty clothes any more, or even dull ones. Day after day we sit here and hardly anyone comes in. I may have to pack up.'

It was the same story in the flower shop. A 'CLOSED DOWN' sign had recently gone up, as it had at the local grocer, once a really popular place in the town. It was as if the whole town was dying on its feet, becoming a graveyard.

Carmen suddenly remembered the place as it used to be, when they had first arrived from Spain: the fairs and fairgrounds, the buzzing market, the running of the bulls in the town and the happy throngs of parents and children. This was like another world, and one to which she could see no end.

* * *

The Communist Pascal Lagarde arrived with two companions. One was a rather quiet man called Pierre and the other a woman of about thirty called Myriam. Over cups of weak coffee, Maurice started proceedings by asking if Lagarde had any fresh news about Russia. Apparently, things had stalled, with the Germans pulling back from Moscow, but with the Russian counter-offensives petering out.

'When can we get arms?' Lagarde asked.

'To do what?' countered Maurice.

'Well, to start killing Pétainists and anybody helping them.'

Maurice sighed.

'We thought we'd made it *very* clear that we think there's no point in that at all. All it would do is to provoke a reaction.'

'Well, *we* think that's just being cowardly,' said Myriam, banging her hand on the table in frustration.

'You may think that,' said Maurice, trying to keep his temper. He had been risking his life for months, while the Communists dithered safely. 'There are plenty of people in *our* group who have every reason to hate the Vichy regime and their supporters. Not least Spaniards, who've been fighting them for years, and Jews who've already lost loved ones and are certainly under dire threat themselves. We've even had to stop our *own* people carrying out revenge killings. In fact, I think we've done a damned good job helping the British to get home and start fighting again, especially the airmen.'

'Who cares about *them*? We want to start hurting the *Pétainists*, and as soon as possible.'

Paul Roux raised his hand and slid a copy of a Paris newspaper across the table.

'If you read this, you'll understand the risks of killing the Germans and their supporters. At first the reprisals meant just heavy fines for the communities near an attack. Then it got serious. Look at this here – the announcement by General Stülpnagel, France's military governor, after your Communist comrades killed a Fritz official in Nantes. *Fifty* hostages shot, and *another* fifty when they could make no arrests. A hundred French martyrs for just one unimportant German.

The very next day, a *hundred* were shot in Bordeaux, after another *single* German was killed. And these hostages, these martyrs, are not *your* people. They're just ordinary citizens, picked off the street. We *absolutely* don't want that happening here.'

The meeting deteriorated into an ugly squabble, with neither side understanding the position of the other.

Eventually Paul Roux intervened, raising his hand and almost shouting to get heard.

'STOP! SHUT UP, EVERYONE!'

Thankfully, the room fell silent enough for him to continue.

'Look, all this in-fighting is getting us nowhere. If you want to start knocking people off, I suggest you do it on your *own* patch and nowhere near Saint-Hippolyte. Or team up with the Spanish groups working in the mines in Alès and La Grande Combe, and we won't interfere. But *don't* come anywhere near here.

We should keep contact to a minimum, so above all, we can't betray each other to the regime. And by the way everyone, remember *we* don't have arms, nobody does – just a few old hunting rifles and shotguns. We'll have to capture some, or wait for the British to work out a way to get them to us.

And another thing. Half this country is still resigned to Pétain or even thinks he's doing a good job. But as the food situation gets worse, the mood will change and then we'll get more support from the locals, either to hide us or fight with us.'

The Communist group plainly did not agree, and after much shaking of heads and curt handshakes, left the meeting – clearly frustrated and irritated.

* * *

'*Eat!*' said Maria to Otilia. She was sick and tired of watching her middle daughter push her food round her plate yet again.

'I can't,' said Otilia. 'It's disgusting. What is it?'

'Swede,' said her father. 'And it's not disgusting, and if you don't eat, you'll starve. Think yourself lucky I can even *get* swedes. Lots of people out there don't have any food at all.'

'Lucky them,' said Otilia, dropping her fork on to the plate, 'that's if it tastes at all like this.'

'That's enough!' snapped Maria. 'If you don't eat, you'll have no strength to walk up the mountain tomorrow. You'll have to stay here, and not go on that school expedition.'

'I don't want to go anyway,' grumped Otilia. 'Who wants to go on a boring bark-rubbing expedition and learn the bloody names of trees and flowers?'

Neither of her parents had ever heard either of their daughters swear before.

'Go and wash your mouth out!' said Pedro. I will absolutely *not* have you swearing, especially in front of your mother. While you're at school, she's slugging her guts out to get food around the table, and …'

Otilia suddenly burst into tears.

Maria put her hand on Pedro's. 'Leave her alone, caro. It's tough enough on them.'

'It's tough on *all* of us,' said Pedro, 'and they've got to learn.' There was only the clatter of cutlery for the next few minutes, until Maria broke the uncomfortable atmosphere.

'Anyway, I think it'll be rather fun going on a bark-rubbing expedition. I've never done that before. At least it's a trip out, something different, away from the classroom.'

'It might have been if you'd remembered to get us a packed lunch,' grumbled Otilia.

Pedro was beginning to fume. 'I've already told you. Your Mamá is going out first thing tomorrow to get you one. She's had a heck of a lot to do today. You don't seem to realize who tidies up after you, fetches water from the fountain, washes your clothes in the river, cleans your room, makes your beds, gets food on the table, and …'

Otilia interrupted. 'And brings us to another *maldito país de mierda* where's there's a war on.'

Pedro was stunned.

'GO TO BED!' he shouted. 'NOW! And if you don't apologise to your mother when she comes up to tuck you in, you're *not* going on that school trip at all!'

'Don't want to go anyway,' repeated Otilia, sullenly.

Their middle daughter flounced out of the room.

Suddenly Juanita started to cry and ran after her sister, leaving the stunned adults in the kitchen. 'Hormones,' said Alfonso to Pedro. 'They're growing up. And they've never grown up in anything but wartime. In a way, I don't blame Oti for swearing.'

Pedro put his hand on Maria's and looked at him sadly. 'To be honest, neither do we.'

* * *

Pedro was enjoying cycling to the farm in the crisp spring sunshine that was lighting the new green leaves on the trees. At times, sights like that were some relief from the grey monotony of life in wartime. He thought back to the time when the sheep used to be herded back up into the mountains with their wool dyed in bright colours and wearing clanking bells round their necks – part of the past now, like so many things. But he did not allow that memory to spoil his mood that morning.

He was surprised that Sarah did not respond as he opened the door to the farmhouse with a merry 'Bonjour!', wondering if she was out in the garden. But suddenly he noticed a huddled figure through the open kitchen door, still in a dressing gown and shivering despite the warm weather.

He guessed what might have happened at once.

She turned to him from where was been sitting at the table, red-eyed.

'Sarah, what is it?'

'It's Auguste,' she said, bursting into tears. 'I think he's dead.'

A wave of shock ran through Pedro, despite him having feared the worst was coming for some time.

'I went into his room this morning when he didn't get up, and found him in bed. And he was completely cold. And I've checked several times since and there's been no difference.'

Pedro glanced upstairs, thinking quickly.

'Look, you stay here and keep warm, and I'll go up there.'

Sarah nodded, her face drained and colourless.

Gingerly entering Auguste's bedroom, it was immediately clear that Auguste was not simply asleep. His face was deathly pale, and his mouth was hanging open. And touching him, his body was completely cold as Sarah had told him. But just as a precaution Pedro checked his pulse, as he had done so many times in Spain for fallen comrades. Nothing.

With a wave of sadness, he tenderly pulled the coverlet over his friend's face, tried to compose himself for a minute, and then taking a deep breath, returned downstairs.

Sarah looked up at him stricken.

'I'm really sorry,' said Pedro. 'You're right. He's gone.' Sarah burst into tears.

He went over to the back of her chair and put his arms round her, rocking her gently and thinking rapidly. Right now there was nothing he could do but take the van and go and tell Alfonso what had happened, and then ask him to come back to the farm and help take away the body as soon as possible. But where could Sarah go now?

'Look Sarah, you stay here and I'll take the van and get Alfonso. We'll be back as soon as we can. You stay here in the kitchen, is that okay?'

Sarah nodded, trying to keep back more tears.

About five kilometres away Alfonso was busy finishing clearing up the garage, a job he had already delayed for far too long since it had been ransacked to find the Levy paintings. Now he was actually finding the job quite agreeable, delighted that he had found the good sense to hide them in Auguste's farm in time. It was extremely satisfying to think how disappointed the potential thieves must be. And, he told himself, it was high time he had a good clear-out anyway. Adding to his upbeat mood was the chance discovery of a small wooden box he had completely forgotten about, containing photographs of his wife. He suddenly remembered that ages back he had wanted to frame them, but had never got round to it like so many jobs. Well, he would now, he decided.

Suddenly Pedro was outside, parking the van. And Alfonso noted, grim-faced. He immediately guessed what might have happened from Pedro's expression before he even climbed out of the cab, and his unusually upbeat mood disappeared in a flash.

They had both talked about the possibility of it happening for some time. And exactly like Pedro, he wondered where Sarah could go now. The authorities might just check over the farm. Sarah couldn't possibly live there any more – even if she wanted to live in such a place alone.

TWENTY-ONE

*** * * ***

THERE WAS A SOMBRE MOOD IN THE CAFÉ ON THAT COLD FEBRUARY morning. The news had come that Britain's great fortress in the Far East, Singapore, had fallen. And, trying to save it, that two of her most famous battleships had been swiftly sunk by Japanese aircraft.

The atmosphere was curious. Even the most ardent Pétainists no longer seemed quite so enthusiastic about the humiliation of France's old ally. It might have been easy enough for French newspaper readers to gloat over the pictures of those British Generals shamefacedly carrying flags of surrender, especially in those long baggy short trousers, which were almost as symbolic of a fading old order as Chamberlain's much-mocked umbrella.

But few of them were gloating now. There were now too many stories filtering out about the brutality of both the Germans and Japanese – not only to vanquished soldiers, but to civilians as well. Everyone was now realizing that they didn't seem to fight wars like other people.

And every day it became clearer that Germany was *not* going to return France's prisoners of war, nearly two million loved ones, but *was* going to methodically loot France of its raw materials and food until the already prostrate country was starving.

Perhaps the 'beloved' Marshal was not the 'saviour of France' after all?

* * *

There was news, too, from the barracks. According to friendly French guards, the Italians and Germans had finally lost patience with the French handling of 'Détachement W'. A Polish pilot had applied for a medical appointment, but had actually gone to the cinema and then disappeared – no doubt halfway to Spain on one of Carmen's bicycles. It was the last straw.

Nice, easy-going, pro-British Captain Leblon had suddenly been dismissed and put into detention himself for a week. He had been replaced as Commandant by a hard-faced Pétainist called Captain Digoine who had clamped down on any remaining privileges and tightened supervision, prior to Détachement W being moved away completely to somewhere 'more secure'.

* * *

Sarah was now back on the camp-bed in Carmen's tiny bedroom. It was well after midnight, but Carmen knew she was still wide-awake, as she herself was.

'Sarah, you'll have to go into hiding up in the mountains. And the sooner the better. You can't go back to the farm, let alone stay there. People have only got to see a lamp on to know someone's there. And if that someone's Jewish, I don't have to tell you what could happen. You'd be in real trouble.

I'll talk to Maurice Bertrand first thing in the morning, as soon as I can. He's bound to know about a safe house, somewhere you can go.'

'I know,' said Sarah. 'And I can't be a drain on you any longer. You've done enough for me. And the last thing I want to do is put you all in danger, any more than I have already. It's not fair to you or your family.'

'But you can't just wander off and try and find somewhere yourself. I'd be worried sick about you. We *all* would.'

There was a long silence from the next bed.

Carmen reached for Sarah's hand, worrying about whether she was sounding too harsh, especially after the day's traumatic events. She decided to soften her tone.

'Look Sarah, we'll get through this. I'll find a way.'

Sarah squeezed her hand. 'I don't know what I'd do without you.'

Carmen thought quickly, wondering whether she could say what was on her mind, suddenly deciding it was worth the risk.

'*I* do. You'd probably wander off alone, and get yourself killed.'

* * *

Carmen was just back from work, and arriving in the kitchen, still in her coat, had noticed that Sarah wasn't there with the rest of the family.

'Where is she?'

'Upstairs,' said her mother, glancing upwards, 'where she's been most of the day, poor child, although I've tried to get her down. Maybe you could pop up and tell her that supper's almost ready. That's if she'll eat.'

'I can tell her something even better,' smiled Carmen, 'Maurice Bertrand – you know – my contact in the Résistance – has somewhere she can go.'

'Oh, that's *wonderful!*' Maria clasped her hands together beaming, hugely relieved both for Sarah and the entire family.

'Where?' she asked excitedly.

'In Cros, up the mountain, about four kilometres from here. One of our Résistance people, Charles, has a house up there. His wife Marianne is German, but very much on our side. And she's really lonely up there all by herself. Charles told Maurice that the neighbours don't want to talk to her any more. She's desperate for company and really wants Sarah to go there.'

Maria frowned. 'A German? I don't much like the sound of that. And nor, I'm sure, will Sarah. I …'

Carmen interrupted. 'She'll have to. Look, Mamá, as I said, Charles's wife is on *our* side. And if she's married to a Résistance member, I can assure you she'd have been thoroughly checked out, or her husband wouldn't have been able to join us. Not for a minute. And I'll tell you something else. She comes from a place called Alsace-Lorraine, right up in the North East. After the last war, lots of Germans were kicked out of there and she *chose* to stay in France, not go back to Germany, though she could easily have done that. Do you honestly think I'd put Sarah at risk?'

'No, of course not. But couldn't you find someone French?'

'Mamá, we haven't got time. Not if you want to keep us all safe. Every day counts. And we may not get another offer.'

An hour later, both girls came downstairs while Maria was still clearing up. She was vastly relieved to see that though Sarah had clearly been crying, she now appeared composed and calm.

* * *

Pedro was deeply saddened by Auguste's death, being immensely fond of him, and also knowing that he also owed him a great debt. Without the fruit and vegetables that Auguste had given him from the farm, he knew that his family would have been in far worse straits. And being able to able to barter produce for other things had been a huge help.

Now, sitting in the church with his family, he bowed his head to the coffin as it was borne down the aisle, wishing that Sarah had been able to join them in their last respects.

The evening before had been enough of a trauma helping Carmen to write to Pierre with the sad news about his father. It had taken them both hours to find the words, but neither could bear the thought of more of his postcards arriving at the farm with him left in ignorance about what had happened.

Pedro placed his hand on Juanita's who was sitting beside him. It was the first funeral the children had attended, but as long as this wretched war went on, he knew it wouldn't be the last.

Up in the mountain at Cros, Sarah was sitting with her new friend, Marianne, reading prayers for Auguste. One of them, that Sarah had written herself, was for thanking Auguste for helping her to save her life.

It ended with a 'thank you' for Marianne too.

* * *

In the prisoner of war camp near Cologne, Pierre had received the letter from Carmen, and was devastated to hear of his father's death. What reason was there to go back to Saint-Hippolyte now? And even to Carmen, who had probably pretty well forgotten him and was maybe only writing out of a sense of duty. It was so long since they'd seen each other.

Now, in the food line as usual, he felt a sense of despair. Not of danger – the guards were strict, but behaved correctly. It was the kind of despair that comes of not knowing when it would ever end, and *if* it would ever end, and no longer dreaming of what he might become.

'*Eat!* You need to.' The young soldier behind him tapped him on the back, noticing he'd only taken a tiny helping. Pierre took another portion of potatoes, knowing he wouldn't touch them, only to please his friend.

* * *

Halfway through March came another day of farewell for the town. There was great activity around the barracks, and word soon spread that the British internees of 'Détachement W' were leaving for another 'more secure' location.

And that morning, it happened. There was the sound of marching and everyone rushed out from the shops and cafés to see what was going on. With a sullen-faced Captain Digoine at its head, the column of men set off for the station. They were guarded by many extra guards, fully-armed, who seemed to have been drafted in from Nîmes or somewhere. Even in civilian clothes the British marched with discipline and style, with a burly man with a white armband, probably a Sergeant-Major, occasionally growling something at them.

Some of the women in the crowd were in tears, while others waved handkerchiefs. The men of the town's little Résistance group also watched with regret. Now there would be no more bicycles to collect, and no more men piling into Paul Roux's ambulance behind Madame Roudier's house. But the Résistance group thought with some satisfaction that it had been able to achieve something unique in a highly unusual situation. Thanks to its members, nearly a hundred and seventy men, many of them valuable pilots, had managed to reach England and re-join the war.

One of the soldiers tapped on a little drum as the column climbed the Anduze road towards the station. Maurice Bertrand smiled as he briefly thought that it would have been nice if he and his 'La Parisiana Jazz Band' had been able to lead the column, playing something jaunty like 'South Rampart Street Parade' or maybe a fast 'Saint Louis Blues'.

But, he realized, that *might* have drawn a bit too much attention to their excellent relationship with the British.

* * *

In fact, this was the last time Maurice Bertrand would smile for a while.

Someone had apparently betrayed him, because shortly after arriving at home after the British departure, there was a knock at his door, and he opened it to find four Gendarmes outside.

His horrified neighbours saw him arrested and bundled into a car, and it would be some time before anyone could find out his whereabouts.

TWENTY-TWO

✳ ✳ ✳

'IT'S OFF, ROTTEN!' SHOUTED OTILIA, SWIPING HER SPOON ACROSS THE boiled egg which sent both the egg and its cup crashing to the floor. Maria sighed inwardly. Her middle daughter was becoming more and more difficult. But she had some sympathy. The family was supposed to get an egg or two for each of them a month, but rarely did. For months they would go without any, and then suddenly be told, perhaps in March, that the previous November ones were now available. The egg that Otilia had sent flying was obviously in that category.

Maria was at least one of the luckier mothers in town she told herself, married to someone who could bring home things like carrots, turnips and Jerusalem artichokes. Almost everyone else had to queue for ages to get what little there was, and getting drenched in the rainy season. And many of them were forced into some kind of dishonest practice to obtain enough food – and in full view of their children who would then grow up to think such dishonesty was the norm.

It seemed that however much France produced, her people were never going to receive more than starvation rations. It was nearly all going to the Germans.

'Clear that up!' she barked to Otilia, pointing to the egg running all over the floor. 'Go and get a cloth, and then eat *my* egg.'

'I can't. I feel sick. And yours is probably off too.'

'If you don't, you won't get your packed lunch tomorrow. And I *mean* it!'

'Do as your mother says,' said Pedro. 'Now!'

He too, was getting increasingly worried about Otilia, and more so as she grew prettier as the years went by.

He dreaded the days when boyfriends would be on the scene. However, there was one ray of sunshine. It was becoming ever more apparent that she had an astonishing talent for painting, and had even managed to sell a few paintings in the town, a real feat with almost everyone in dire financial straits.

He pictured her some years down the line, sitting in her own studio and happy at last, perhaps even famous, his reverie spoiled by the very real possibility that even supplies of paint would soon dry up. It was hard enough to get it as it was.

Suddenly Otilia was back and cleaning up the mess on the tiled floor. On impulse, he reached down and stroked her hair.

Her tear-stained face looked up at him. But to his relief, she smiled.

* * *

'Do you think we've got a traitor?' asked Paul Roux.

The group was still trying to absorb the shattering news of Maurice Bertrand's arrest.

'Very unlikely,' replied Louis Gireaud. 'We're a very small team, mostly friends, and I can't see any of us betraying the others. And if someone had, surely they'd have picked *everyone* up by now.'

The others nodded in agreement.

'I think it's much more likely that we helped the British escapers for so long, over a year, and someone was just bound to notice all the activity after a while.'

'Do we know where Maurice has ended up?' asked Jean de la Olla.

'No, but it's quite likely to be the Central Prison at Eysses, in the Lot. I know that's where a lot of Résistants have ended up. I suppose we'll eventually get word.'

'So now the British have gone, to a fort near Nice we think, what do you think our group should do? I think we all agree that attacking Gendarmes or civil servants isn't going to do any good.'

They all nodded.

'Let's hope those over-enthusiastic Communists don't do anything rash, or if they do, hopefully do it a long way away.'

'I think we could help to hide the Jews,' volunteered Charles Menviel. 'There must be quite a few left, and I have a very nasty feeling that Pétain and Laval will start handing them over to the Germans wholesale. When they went for individuals like the Levys, they were just after their money. In fact, I think some of our local women have the idea of baptising the children at least, to make them look like Christians. What if we help them, or perhaps get some of the kids out?'

* * *

Pedro was working at the farm when a stranger came in from the road, younger than himself and dark-skinned with a moustache. Even before he spoke, Pedro could tell at once that he was Spanish.

'Hola! Señor Casales? I'm Miguel.' He didn't offer a second name.

Pedro took him into the house and offered him a drink of water, which the stranger politely declined.

'I believe you were in the Republican army – an officer, a Captain?'

Pedro hesitated, suspicious, cautious.

The stranger smiled. 'There are loads of us here like you and me – thousands. When we got out of those appalling camps, many left for places like Mexico, Argentina and Chile. Some, foolishly, tried to get back to Spain. But many of us, like you, stayed and went to work for the French. As you probably know, Spaniards have gone all over France to work in factories and build fortifications, or stayed down here to work as 'travailleurs étrangers' in the mines over in Alès and in La Grande Combe, or else in agriculture.

But I'm sure you know all that. What I'm here to tell you is that we Spanish are now organised into groups of *guérilleros* and we'll start to sabotage and fight in due course.'

Pedro studied him, guessing what was coming.

'Needless to say, Señor, an experienced officer like you would be very valuable. We'd very much like you to join us. You wouldn't have to leave your work here – just give up some time.'

Pedro looked at the young man thoughtfully, beginning to like him and also admiring what he was trying to do.

'What you're doing is commendable, and also brave. But for the moment, I have to refuse.'

He smiled at Miguel. 'Are many of you married?'

Miguel shook his head. 'No, very few.'

'Well, you see, I *am*. With a wife who still barely speaks French, and three daughters, one only ten, and a cousin. You probably know him, Alfonso the garagiste. I can't risk endangering a whole Spanish family, already likely to be under suspicion as Red Republicans.'

'But...'

Pedro held up his hand.

'I'm sorry. For the moment my mind's made up. However, I may change it in time, depending on what happens. But even then I'd need to join one of your groups further away. Do you have people over beyond Le Vigan and Mont Aiguoal?'

'Yes, as a matter of fact, we do. '

'Then let me know how I could contact you.'

'I can do that right now.' Miguel took a piece of paper out of his pocket and handed it over. They shook hands.

* * *

'I'm so glad you're up here,' said Marianne, looking at Sarah over her glasses. They were sitting around a cosy log fire as Carmen helped her sort out a basket of skeins of yarn. 'It was getting so lonely, really depressing with Charles away so much and with nobody to talk to. Hardly anyone wants to fraternize with Germans like me any more, or even be neighbourly. It's amazing how people you thought were really good friends can suddenly turn on you – and even the best of them back off. I was beginning to feel like a real pariah. I guess it doesn't help that I *look* so German with my blonde hair, pretty rare around here.

'Better than having red hair like mine,' smiled Sarah, running her hand through her now fast-growing mane. That means you *really* stand out, the last thing you need if you're Jewish. I dyed mine for months until Carmen's mother's dye ran out, and then the pharmacy didn't have any more. In fact, I hardly dared to go out at all.'

They sat in silence for a minute, lost in their own thoughts.

'But it worries me you'll get bored up here,' said Marianne. 'It's so quiet now, especially as nobody pops round any more. And it's not fair at your age. What are you? Twenty?'

'Yes, nearly twenty-one.'

Marianne thought for a minute.

'Too young to be stuck up a mountain with me. But if you like, and *only* if you like, I can teach you how to weave to fill in the time a bit.'

Sarah smiled. 'I'd like that.' By now she had often seen Marianne at her loom and was fascinated by her skills and dexterity, and above all, realized that she needed something to do.

'And I can probably teach you a few other things,' smiled Marianne. 'That Germans aren't *all* bad. That some, like me, are really ashamed of what's happening, and would do anything we could to turn the clock back. Lots of us are horrified, and especially by that terrible man, Hitler. He often makes me ashamed I'm German at all. In a way, I'm not surprised that nobody here wants to talk to me any more if they think that kind of cruelty runs in the German blood.'

There was a pause for a minute while Marianne riffled through her basket of skeins, wondering how much Sarah actually knew, appalling things that Charles had told her, and even then, probably edited.

Marianne picked up a skein of yarn. 'Do you like this one?'

'Yes, it's lovely.'

'Tell you what, why don't I make you a shawl out of this colour?'

Sarah thought for a moment. 'But I wouldn't want to put you to any trouble, not after what you've done for me.'

Marianne shrugged, smiling. 'It's no trouble, and we could start today if you like. That's if we both don't freeze to death making it! Remind me to ask Charles to get in more firewood. That's one thing we *do* have enough of up here. In fact, storms bring down the trees all the time. We can't get rid of wood fast enough.'

'Thank you,' said Sarah, suddenly feeling glad she was with a German – and someone who might better understand what her parents had been through, someone now ashamed of her race and what was happening. But there were still doubts about whether she was *really* welcome, about to be allayed.

Marianne smiled. 'You'll be the daughter I never had. I couldn't have children, sadly, or not safely. We lost two babies, and the doctors said it would happen again. I couldn't bear the risk, and neither could Charles.'

* * *

'An amazing thing happened to me today,' said Maria when Pedro came home that evening. 'You know our butcher, Yves?'

Pedro nodded.

'Well, I was in there this morning, and I was just about to pay for our pathetic ration of meat when he suddenly asked if we'd like a leg of mutton. A *leg* of mutton, would you believe? A bit different to a few pathetic grams of meat per head each week. Anyway, he was about to take if off the hook behind him when he suddenly stopped as if he'd changed his mind. Goodness, I was disappointed. And a bit mystified, too. So I went back an hour later, and he told me he'd spotted a plain-clothes policeman coming into the shop. You know, one of those Pétainist sneaks. Apparently, they're all over the place. The great news is that Yves kept the leg of mutton for me and we're eating it tonight.'

'Marvellous!' Pedro beamed. 'But I do worry about the shopkeepers doing us favours. God knows what would happen if they get found out. It's bad enough as it is with nobody knowing who's a Pétainist or a Gaullist. Like a sort of war within a war.'

'That reminds me,' said Maria, 'the girls were actually asked to write a letter to Pétain in school today and draw his portrait, so we certainly know which side the teachers are on.'

'And did they?'

'What?'

'Do a letter and a portrait?'

'Yes, and Otilia said she made the portrait the worst one she'd ever done on purpose. And that made the teacher very cross. Well, you know how good she is at art.'

'Perhaps we'd better tell her not to do that again.'

* * *

Carmen had decided she couldn't wait any longer to tell Elaine Puget of her decision to join the Résistance. She had delayed doing so for months, too long already. It had to be *today* she told herself as she walked to the shop, and as soon as Elaine arrived, before they started chatting about the usual day-to-day things. *Girls joining the Résistance? The idea would be unthinkable, ridiculous. Elaine's life – and business – had been dedicated to making girls look prettier to attract men, not just to feel better about themselves. Decent clothes were a passport to marriage – sadly, the only ambition of too many girls.*

Now, walking down the street, she was dreading the moment and Elaine's reaction. How would she take it? Carmen suspected she would be very shocked and upset, although with four of her sons interned she would probably understand better than most.

Waiting at the shop a few moments later for Elaine to arrive, she rehearsed what she would say in her mind for the umpteenth time, feeling her heart rate rise as she did so, and once again fearful of losing her courage at the last moment. Elaine had been so kind to her, almost like a second mother, and kind to Sarah too – even giving her a whole lot of clothes when she had first come to her uncle's house when told that she could never again return home and only had the dress she stood up in.

'Bonjour, cherie!' Elaine breezed into the shop in an unusually sunny mood. Carmen almost lost her nerve, but knew she had to get the words out and not delay yet again. If she hadn't even got the courage to do that, how would she ever have the courage to be a Résistance fighter?

In the event, Elaine took it remarkably well, far more worried about Carmen's safety than she was about losing a loyal and long-standing assistant. But one of the reasons for her calm acceptance was her surprise announcement that she was finally thinking of packing it all in herself.

She even gave Carmen a long and affectionate embrace when the shop closed for the day, thanking her for her support and good service.

TWENTY-THREE

* * *

'CORREGIDOR? THAT'S WHAT WE USED TO CALL A SHERIFF OR MAGISTRATE, isn't it? asked Alfonso.

'Si. Why do you ask?' said Pedro.

'Because the Americans now seem to have surrendered a place with that name.'

'Good Lord! Here, pass me the paper.'

For those in France who were looking to America to save the world, April and May had been terrible months. The devastating destruction at Pearl Harbor back in December had been bad enough – but there was some excuse – after all, the Japanese had attacked completely without warning or declaring war.

But the Philippines seemed to be something else. Just as they did against the British, the Japanese were winning, albeit more slowly. For weeks the newspapers had been reporting – and the BBC admitting – that they were pushing down towards Manila, though an American General, MacArthur, had vowed to hold a peninsular called Bataan, and boasting publicly, 'We've inflicted heavy casualties on their troops, and tomorrow we'll drive them into the sea.'

But it seemed that it was only the *Japanese* who were doing any driving, and confirming this, it was soon reported that 76,000 Americans and Filipinos had surrendered in Bataan. The Americans had ended up in a concrete fortress in Manila Bay called 'The Rock of Corregidor'. And there MacArthur had left them – and after days of bombing, the Japanese had attacked and the surviving Americans and Filipinos had surrendered.

'They seem to have fought a bit better than the British, but it's still a humiliating defeat,' said Alfonso miserably. 'It looks as if the Germans and Japanese just can't be beaten.'

'I'm not so sure, especially about the Japanese,' said Pedro thoughtfully. 'They're thousands of kilometres from America, there are three times more Americans, and the Americans *produce* ten times more. And they're now very angry. Let's wait and see.'

* * *

Otilia was in a jubilant mood, coming home from school and later on at supper. She had just been awarded the art prize for her painting of 'My family', which was now being displayed in the church. Tomorrow night half the town would be able to see it, as her parents and sisters would – at an exhibition of the winning exhibits.

And her mood was made even better by the fact that Uncle Fon had found a whole lot of paints in the garage. 'My wife used to paint, but not as well as you. She did the one in the kitchen of the irises, though as you know, it's not very good. Although I happen to love it.'

To his relief his niece wasn't rude about it. These days she could be horribly blunt in her opinions, and sometimes he felt quite sorry for her parents.

* * *

'Did you hear that?'

Alfonso looked up from reading his book.

'No, Pedro, I don't listen to the BBC *every* night. The news is usually so gloomy.'

'But this is *good* news. The British have just bombed Cologne with a *thousand* bombers. A thousand! Can you imagine? Back in Spain, we'd count a dozen planes as a big raid. But a thousand? It's unbelievable! They must be bombing the shit out of the Germans, and nearly every night.'

'Yes, but when Carmen comes in, don't go on about it.'

'Why ever not?'

'Well, she's pretty sure Pierre's prison camp is somewhere near Cologne.'

'Oh God, I'd forgotten that. Thanks for reminding me.'

They sipped their beer in silence for a while.

'There's another thing. The Germans are demanding French workers to go to Germany to work. And they've cooked up a scheme so that three volunteer workers get one of our prisoners of war released. So if they don't go, they'll feel guilty.

But, when you think about it, who'd ever want to go to Germany if they think they're going to be mistreated by the Germans *and* bombed to bits by the British? And I'll bet the Americans will start bombing soon as well. They'll never get enough Frenchmen to volunteer. So they may make it compulsory, and then things will *really* change.'

* * *

It was only a week later that aircraft featured in another BBC news report. In the Pacific there had been a naval battle between the Americans and the Japanese. It appeared that naval battles out there were not like in the old days, between battleships and their big guns. Now they seemed to be between aircraft-carriers and their planes. This first one, in the Coral Sea, seemed to have been a draw.

But only days later, the BBC reported that something really important had followed. No less than four Japanese aircraft-carriers had been sunk by the Americans who only lost one of their own. For the Japanese, it was a stunning defeat after so many runaway victories.

'I told you so,' said Pedro. 'And the Japs won't be able to replace big ships like that in a hurry – while the Americans will go on churning them out. I had a cousin living in Detroit – you know, where they build all those cars. He always said that if those huge factories turned to making planes and trucks and tanks, there would be no holding them.

And the Japs must have lost a lot of pilots with those ships sunk. I'll bet that's the end of their conquests. I tell you Alfonso, they've bitten off more than they can chew.'

* * *

However interested Pedro might be in such matters as the distant battle of Midway, the fact was that locally he was something of an exception. The basic problems of just getting by from day to day had begun to dominate life in the little town and overshadow any news from abroad or the wider war.

So the fact that the British had been forced to retreat from Burma now hardly registered. Nor did the German General Rommel's advance in the desert. And nobody bothered to put maps on the café wall any more, let alone find out the locations of Derna, Gazala or even Tobruk, which Rommel had apparently just captured.

For that matter, nobody except the Communists even seemed to care about the much bigger places overrun in huge battles by the Germans that summer in Russia – Kharkov, Rostov, Sevastopol, and a new name just beginning to be mentioned in the bulletins – Stalingrad.

Much more important and alarming to the locals was the announcement of a new Vichy law changing the STO, the *Service du Travail Obligatoire*. Up until then, a system called 'La Réleve had been tried, whereby one French prisoner of war would be released for every three volunteer workers. But such German efforts to get sufficient Frenchmen to volunteer to work in Germany were failing – not surprisingly with German cities and factories being steadily and increasingly bombed. So being taken off to work in Germany was now going to become compulsory, a really worrying prospect.

* * *

Alfonso and Pedro were extremely surprised when Michel Morelli, one of the village postmen, came up to their table in the café. They had always hated his strong Pétainist views, and Morelli knew that only too well. Indeed, if he were ever in the café and the two turned up, he had noticed that they always chose the furthest table away from him.

'Do you mind if I talk to you?' he asked the surprised men. Neither of them looked too pleased, and at first neither answered.

'Well, not if you're going to go on with your Pétainist rants,' said Alfonso.

'The *last* thing I want to do,' said Morelli, immediately noticing their surprise. 'That's why I want to talk.'

'Okay, take a chair.'

Morelli sat down, looked at the two men, and took a deep breath. 'Look, you know I've always been a big supporter of Pétain. At least, I was until now. I thought he was doing a reasonable enough job in pretty difficult circumstances. But now a number of things have changed my mind. And one in particular that I've just heard, something truly horrific – and which you may not know about.

My brother's a prisoner of war, and according to the Armistice, he should have been let out ages ago. I didn't like the English. At first, because they left us at Dunkirk, then because of the sinking of our fleet at Mers-el-Kebir. Then it was because I thought that by keeping fighting they were stopping my brother being released. However, I've changed my mind about all that.' He paused and sighed.

'My family's starving, as nearly everyone is, and the Vichy government has done absolutely *nothing* about so much of our food going to Germany. And now, with the enforced STO, they're going to take people off to be bombed there. And that may include my son. So I was getting disillusioned anyway. But now I've heard something so utterly appalling that I can't support Pétain for a moment longer.'

He had lowered his voice, clearly shocked to the core about what he was about to divulge, and now looked around the café – as if concerned that he might be overheard.

'I've just got a letter from a cousin of mine who lives in a Paris suburb called Drancy. Right opposite there's a recently-completed housing development that was supposed to be peaceful and quiet called 'La Cité de la Muette', the 'City of the Dumb' – as if nobody ever talks there. Well, they certainly do *now*.

Her house is about fifty metres from the gates. She's a pretty girl, and the other day she got chatted up by two guards, the gendarmes outside. Apparently, and they openly admitted this, and without any shame, that trainloads of Jews have been taken there – thousands and thousands of them – to a place meant for only hundreds. And they also told her that just as many trainloads were now being taken *out* of there – and sent to Poland – including, according to the guards, about four thousand children.

And when she asked what would happen to them, they openly admitted – and without any shame – that scores of them wouldn't even *survive* the journey, because there wouldn't be any food or water for them on board.'

Morelli paused for a moment, looking cautiously around the café again.

'And it gets worse, much worse. The guards also said the camps were almost certainly not work camps, they seemed designed to kill people.

After all, they reasoned, if that many people died on the trains, who'd care about those who'd survived the journey?'

He took another deep breath.

'My cousin felt she ought to tell me. She felt I should know. And not just *me*. *Everyone* who supports Pétain, or at least as many as we can tell safely. And now every last gram of respect I ever had for him and his Vichy set-up has gone out of the window. Clearly, all that resettlement talk is rubbish. They're just wiping the Jews out.'

'Why doesn't anybody know about this?' asked Pedro, shocked to the core.

'I think the Germans are being horribly clever, masking the truth and pretending the Jews are just being resettled in the east and put to work. After all, if *you* knew you and your family were doomed, you'd *surely* resist and there'd be full-scale fights all over the place.'

'But why would those guards tell your cousin such a dreadful thing?' asked Alfonso.

'Probably because they're *proud* of what they're doing. And because there's so much anti-Semitism around, casually assume that most other people would go along with it.'

All three men sat in appalled silence for a while, picturing terrified Jewish families packed into crowded trains, probably going to their deaths.

Michel Morelli broke the silence. 'So now I'm firmly on your side.'

Alfonso proffered his hand. 'I'm relieved to hear it. And on that note, may I offer you a brandy?'

'I think that honour should be mine,' said Morelli getting up to go to the bar.

As he left the table, Pedro turned to Alfonso, worried.

'That sounds pretty horrific for Sarah's parents.'

'I know.'

* * *

Otilia was unusually quiet during supper as if something was on her mind, and with the meal almost over, Pedro was to discover what it was when she suddenly turned to him, frowning.

'Papa, what are the Germans like? *Really* like? We know a bit about them from school, but not much. And I don't think the nuns really know. It's weird being at war with people I can't visualise, see in my head.'

Pedro paused, not sure how to answer.

'Well, for a start, they're extremely efficient people. Far more organised than the French or Spanish. And far more obedient. They do as they're told – if I may say so, unlike you! And they're capable of being extremely cruel, as you know they are to the Jews like Sarah. They're basically a nation of fighters whereas France is a nation of farmers, and completely under the grip of their leader.'

'Hitler,' said Otilia.

'Yes, Hitler. A terrifying man, if there ever was one.'

'But what do the Germans *look* like? I don't even know that.'

'Well, they're fairer than us, living in a cooler country. They mostly wouldn't have dark hair like ours. And they're usually bigger and taller, because they're better-fed than we are. Especially now, while they're stealing all our food.'

Otilia thought for a moment.

'But why do they want to come here?'

'To finish off a war they'd started twenty years ago, and fifty years before that. And grab our land, our food and our resources. And make our people work for them, and turn them into the most powerful nation on earth.

Here in France, most people simply get on with their lives, farming mostly – at least, around here. And we're pretty disorganised, what the French would call 'laissez faire.' The Germans are exactly the opposite, more like organised machines. They salute authority, and they even do *that* in a terrifying way.'

'How?' asked Juanita, rapt with attention.

Pedro got to his feet and mimicked a Nazi salute, suddenly stretching his right arm above him in the air. 'HEIL HITLER!'

Maria was horrified as both children immediately leapt to their feet and copied their father.

'HEIL HITLER!'

'HEIL HITLER!'

'SIT DOWN! shouted Maria, 'I will *not* have those words said in this house!'

'But it's funny!' said Juanita, laughing as she sat down.

'It's *not* funny,' snapped her mother. 'Not funny at all. Imagine if you were up north and a Jew like Sarah and had to hide away for fear of your life. Or wear a yellow star to tell everyone you were Jewish. And if you weren't even allowed to queue for food if you were wearing one – or had to go right to the back of it.'

Juanita frowned. 'Well, how do Jews eat?'

'With great difficulty. And tremendous danger.'

'Well, why don't they simply take off their yellow stars?' asked Juanita.

'They can't,' said Maria, 'because the German authorities know exactly who they are anyway. And they watch them all the time. And the poor Jews are terrified of being dragged away, including children your age. And what if they come here and started dragging people away, as they may well do? And not just Jews. Any boy who's old enough to go and work for them, and like a slave. If I had sons rather than daughters, I'd be terrified.'

Both children fell silent, as did Pedro, pleased that Maria was really beginning to take things in. None of them had ever heard her speak out so vociferously before.

* * *

'Do you want to hear something rather amusing?' asked Alfonso.

'What?' Pedro certainly felt he could do with some good news.

'I've just heard the latest gossip about our British friends in 'Détachement W'. As you know, they were packed off to Nice because, theoretically, it would be more secure than here. They had their *Liberté Surveillée* revoked and now were made to wear uniforms. But it *still* didn't work!'

'How do you mean?'

'They dug a tunnel through a wall – incredibly, with knives, forks and spoons – and fifty-eight of them went through it and escaped. Some *were* recaptured, but it looks as if something like twenty-five will have made it back to England. Amazing! And that sour-faced Capitaine Digoine has been court-martialled and kicked out of the French army, and the General in charge has been retired, and they may even have to move the Détachement yet again. The Germans and Italians are really angry!'

'That's wonderful news!'

'And you remember that fellow who spoke perfect French, but with a bit of an accent? Well, he turned out to be a Belgian medical officer who joined the British. And after he escaped from here, he deliberately stayed on in France to set up escape lines. His nickname's 'Patrick O'Leary', and one of the lines is now even called the 'Pat Line'.

It was him who organised that mass escape – so he has a huge price on his head. Let's hope they never catch him – he deserves to be famous one day.'

'He certainly does. At least he's tried to do something useful. I've heard from French friends in Paris and from the papers that the French seem to have just rolled over and accepted occupation, and that the theatres and nightclubs are booming. People like Sacha Guitry, Maurice Chevalier and Fernandel are apparently seen partying every night with the Germans, who seem to regard France as one big holiday camp. And with the artificial exchange rate, the bastards can buy up everything.'

* * *

The Germans, at least in Africa, now appeared to be in trouble. There had been a huge battle at a place called El Alamein which the British had won and who were now advancing steadily. And soon came much more important news for the French – that the Americans and British had landed in French Morocco, Algeria and Tunisia. Sadly, at first there had been fighting with local Vichy French forces in some of the places, but that had luckily died down, although only after a thousand Frenchmen had died. A deal had then been struck between the American General Eisenhower and Admiral Darlan, who had changed sides.

Of course, the Pétainists in the town had jumped on this invasion to blame Britain yet again, and even, ridiculously, to claim that the British were even trying to steal their colonies.

There was a much more serious and immediate result for the people of Saint-Hippolyte. The Germans quickly invaded the Free Zone to occupy southern France. Such an operation had obviously been planned for years, in case Germany was suddenly faced with danger from the south, so it took only days for German tanks to reach the Mediterranean.

However, one thing seemed to go seriously wrong. Once again, it was the BBC that reported that the Germans had rushed specially to Toulon to capture the powerful French fleet.But they were too late. As it had *always* promised, the French Navy resisted, buying enough time to scuttle all the ships, seventy-seven in all, including the battleship *Strasbourg* that had managed to escape from the British bombardment of Mers-el-Kebir.

Apparently, the German tank crews were then forced to sit on the dock in fury watching the capsized, sunken ships burning for days on end.

It was a thought that Pedro particularly relished, as was the revelation that some of the submarines had been able to submerge and set off to join the Free French in North Africa.

But after this scant good news, now all the people in the town could do was wait for the arrival of the first Germans – and guess what that might mean.

TWENTY-FOUR

* * *

THE VERY FIRST GERMANS THE VILLAGERS SAW IN SAINT-HIPPOLYTE CAME UP the road one Tuesday from Nîmes and then drove slowly round the town in a little convoy of grey vehicles, led by a police Citroen. Some people, including Maria, stayed indoors, but most of the locals were too curious not to come out and look at them, not quite sure what to expect.

Pedro, for one, thought they looked surprisingly unimpressive. He noticed that two of the trucks were old Simca French army ones, with black crosses painted on the doors. The soldiers, looking out cautiously, seemed mostly very young. He also noticed that there were only about thirty or forty of them – probably, he thought, reflecting Saint-Hippolyte's low priority as a security risk. After all, it was often described as a 'sleepy little town'.

Few of the villagers spoke as the convoy disappeared into the old Fort, apprehensive about how these newcomers would alter their lives.

They were soon to discover starting the next day, when the soldiers started coming into the centre of town, mostly in pairs and wearing soft forage caps rather than the steel helmets Pedro would have expected. Probably, he reckoned, because they wanted to look less intimidating. They all carried rifles, but loosely slung over their shoulders. And all of them seemed perfectly friendly and polite.

After a couple of weeks, they seemed relaxed enough to begin buying things and chatting in the shops – some of them speaking a little French – explaining that they had previously been stationed for some months in Saumur, on the Loire, about four hundred kilometres to the north. Soon they also started to frequent the bars and the café.

Pedro and Alfonso kept their distance, but other locals were more forthcoming, and it was from them that they discovered more, while rather alarmed by the goodwill the new arrivals seemed to be attracting.

It appeared that they were from an old infantry regiment, mostly recruited near a German town called Mannheim. They had admitted that they were only too delighted to be staying in the comparative comfort of France, spared the horrors going on in Russia and terrified they might be ordered back there. In that last winter in the snow outside Moscow, they even ruefully admitted that their regiment had lost half its strength, not just from battle but also from frostbite and disease.

If other villagers were sympathetic to these stories, Pedro and Alfonso were decidedly more cautious, even when, after a few drinks – and when their officers weren't listening – the German soldiers had begun to reveal their gloomy disillusionment with the war and with their leaders, and their real fears of the retribution that might come from those whom Germany had mistreated. They had seen things done in Russia, they admitted, that made them really ashamed.

To the disbelief of the locals, they also grumbled that their own families in Germany were scarcely better fed than those in France, and that everyone was terrified and exhausted by the constant bombing by the British at night and the Americans by day, and which their own much-vaunted air force seemed totally unable to counter. Apparently, some cities were in ruins already, and they were beginning to dread letters from home – or indeed the lack of them. Remembering the terrible ordeals of Spain, Pedro was less than sympathetic.

Everybody agreed that the ordinary soldiers seemed fine, at least acceptable, but the people in the town did not like the look of one or two others who had been spotted arriving later, also stationed at the Fort. They were dressed in civilian clothes and travelled in a black Citroen, and there were alarming rumours that they were from the dreaded Gestapo, the secret police. As such, they would be actively looking out for anyone who might resist the now discredited Vichy regime in its efforts to track down Jews, as well as members of the Résistance and the growing number of men hiding to evade the STO – compulsory work in Germany.

* * *

Almost as soon as they'd arrived, the mood of the young German soldiers changed and they started to look anxious and pre-occupied. It turned out to have nothing to do with the pleasant little French town, and all to do with a Russian city thousands of kilometres away – Stalingrad. And Pedro, with access to the mostly truthful BBC news bulletins, could guess why, as could the Résistance group in the Menviel house.

Since the summer they had listened to reports of the attempts by the Germans to smash their way through a town that used to be called Volgagrad, because it straddled the Volga River. But under its new name of Stalingrad, it was not hard for the French to guess that it had become a symbol for both leaders. Stalin could scarcely afford to lose a city with *his* name attached to it. And Hitler could not refrain from trying to take it at all costs.

It gradually appeared that this dreary industrial town perfectly suited the strengths of its dogged Russian defenders – brutal close-quarter fighting. There was no more scope for dramatic sweeping panzer advances and imaginative flanking movements. For the Germans, this was just trying to batter a way to the Volga through smashed, burning buildings and smoking rubble. And it went on for weeks and weeks, metre by metre – with vast loss of life.

And suddenly the BBC had announced a spectacular change. Huge new Russian armies had apparently emerged and had broken through on both flanks, encircling the Germans completely. So now *they* were the besieged, not the besiegers. A quarter of a million men appeared to be trapped. Aircraft could not supply them enough, no breakout had occurred and an attempted rescue offensive had been beaten back.

On Christmas Eve, the Germans had been summoned by their officers to the Fort to listen to a special broadcast. They later revealed that it was linked to no less than thirty transmitters all over Europe – one even in a plane and another in a U-boat. A highlight of the messages was the apparently calm and confident 'Here is Stalingrad. Here is the front on the Volga', followed by the singing of 'Silent Night' and other hymns.

Some of the soldiers came back to the café, nearly in tears. They plainly did not believe the propaganda – and suspected the worst. 'We've got a sister battalion of our regiment in there,' Pedro heard one say in anguish. 'My brother's in it. God knows what'll happen.'

Everyone would know soon enough. At the end of January, the German survivors in Stalingrad surrendered – although apparently their

High Command had tried to pretend that they had 'fought to the last man and the last bullet'.

'It's really quite hard to hide a Field-Marshal and ninety thousand men surrendering,' mused Pedro with a grin as he listened to the BBC.

* * *

'Oh Sarah, it's gorgeous!' Marianne had just unwrapped her birthday present, the blue woollen skirt that Sarah had spent weeks weaving on the old loom.

Marianne studied it for a moment, amazed by the quality of her handiwork. 'You're as good as me now, probably even better! It's beautifully done. And I love the colour. Thank you!' She stood up and draped it the garment in front of her, but suddenly noticed that Sarah was looking a little downcast. Surely not about her reaction to the skirt?

'Is anything the matter?'

'As a matter of fact, there is. I was drawing back the curtains upstairs in my bedroom an hour or so ago, and I saw that man again outside. And he saw *me*. And he was really staring. So I immediately came down here.'

Marianne thought for a moment. 'Probably nothing sinister.'

'I rather fear it is. It's not normal to stare at people's bedroom windows at seven o'clock in the morning. Not normal at all. To be honest, Marianne, I'm beginning to think I'm in real danger – and *you* as well, and that both of us might be safer if I got out and went into a proper safe house. And as soon as possible. That's if they'd have me. It's simply not fair on you for me to stay here any more.'

Marianne was about to protest, but stopped herself, knowing Sarah was right.

'I'll really miss you,' she said, tears filling her eyes. 'The daughter I never had. I'll talk to Charles this evening. And if this is to be our last day together, let's make it as happy as we can.' She patted Sarah's knee. 'And I suppose you'd be happier if we cancelled our picnic?'

'If you don't mind,' said Sarah. 'Or we can have it on the terrace here. Thankfully, he can't see us there with your high wall.'

* * *

'Are you alright?' Maria was concerned. Pedro, normally with a smile for her and the girls as he returned from work, looked decidedly grim-faced as he hung up his coat.

'No, quite the opposite. In fact, I'm *livid.*'

'What's up?'

'Tell you in a minute. Quite frankly, I'm too angry to even speak.'

He turned to Maria. 'Have you got any of that old bottle of brandy left?'

That wasn't like Pedro either.

'I'll look,' said Carmen, and hurried off to check whether there was any left, wondering what on earth had happened. Something to do with Sarah?

She returned empty-handed. 'Sorry, we must have drunk it.'

'Mierda!' said Pedro.

Maria frowned. That wasn't like him either. 'Whatever's the matter, Pedro? Tell me.'

'In a minute. Give me a moment to calm down.'

Twenty minutes later, sitting around the fire, he apologised for being so offhand and explained the reason.

'You know I told you that all of us farmers had to go to a meeting at the Town Hall?'

Maria and Carmen nodded.

'Well, the meeting was today. The Mayor was there, a nice enough chap, but looking very sheepish. And he was flanked by two French Vichy people, from Nîmes I suppose – and a German. And they announced that a *third* of what we produce will have to go straight to Germany, and even worse, paid for by those ridiculously under-valued 'Invasion Marks'. First of all, it's impossible to do while feeding ourselves and making enough to live on. Second, now the town won't even get its most *basic* rations. And third, the black market prices will now go right through the roof. Frankly, I may have to pull out altogether. It's just not worth going on.'

'Good God!' exclaimed Carmen. 'What on earth are you going to do?'

'Nothing much I *can* do. If I refuse to give it to them, I'll be in real trouble. And so will all of us. In fact, they said they'd even *fine* the town if we don't produce their quota. And they pretty well know how much I'm producing at the moment, and they'll be checking up on me all the time from now on. You can be sure of that. There'll be snoops all over the place.'

Maria shook her head in disbelief. 'But they can't just have *one third* of everything we're growing. That's an *amazing* amount.'

'Certainly is. It's ludicrous. And most of us are already struggling. After all, they took away most of the horses and mules a few months ago so farming is even harder. *And* there's no fuel for tractors. Even fertilizer's a thing of the past. Output's plummeting anyway, half of what we used to produce.'

All three of them knew they were luckier than most, getting fresh fruit and vegetables, although even for them it wasn't enough. The idea of a third of it disappearing was terrible.

Carmen suddenly got up and put on her coat, stony-faced. 'I'll be back in a moment.' Her mind was made up. A few minutes later she knocked on the door of Paul Roux.

'I want a *proper* role in the Résistance, Paul. It was fine rounding up bicycles for the British when they were here, and passing messages. But we're going to have to fight these people soon, and I want to do that with the rest. And believe me, I'm tough enough to do it.'

Paul studied her face, knowing she was right. Like many of his male friends, he was wary of forthright, opinionated and strong women, but Carmen was different. Extremely attractive, but with an attitude much more like a man. He could see her working in the Résistance, but still baulked at the idea of a woman being armed. And willing to fire. Would she be able to kill?

Then he suddenly remembered Gendarme Bollon's death on the bridge. Was she responsible for that, despite her denial? Possibly.

'I'll see what I can do. But I think you should join a Spanish group. They're very well-organised and very motivated. Don't leave home just yet, and *whatever* you do, don't draw attention to yourself. Keep your head down. You hear me?'

Carmen nodded.

* * *

Sarah was up in the mountains, freezing cold, in an old stone cottage long abandoned by its owners and now a safe-house for both her and those desperate to avoid the STO – the compulsory work service for young French men in Germany. This was the third 'safe' house they had moved to, and Sarah knew it probably wouldn't be the last. At least it was high up enough for anyone to want to avoid the arduous climb to reach it, and across broken rocks, tough enough for any climber, let alone anyone carrying a heavy gun and pack.

She listened to the nightly 'peep, peep' of a Scops Owl somewhere above the cottage, a sound she used to love, although she was now fearful that even a noise like that might be imitated as a signal by anyone hunting for them.

Alexandre, one of the young men in the safe house, placed a hand on hers, obviously sensing her fear and the particular reason behind it.

'I don't think even the Boches can replicate a sound like that.'

She smiled at him, yet another young man who was afraid of being dragged off and made to work in Germany, probably only to be bombed as soon as he got there. This was the third safe house they had shared.

'Let's hope not,' said Sarah, putting her other hand on top of his.

'Merde! Your hands are *freezing*,' exclaimed Alexandre, and standing up, he took off his coat and wrapped it around Sarah's shoulders.

That small kind gesture suddenly made Sarah burst into tears, pent up for months.

'Sorry,' she said wiping her eyes.

'Don't be,' said Alexandre. 'Frankly, I sometimes feel like crying too, with all the mess the world's got itself into.'

She looked up at him. 'You know I'm Jewish?'

'Yes, but who cares? I certainly don't. Except that it puts you more at risk.' Someone had told him what had happened to her parents, although she'd never spoken about it.

'In fact, without you lot, there wouldn't be nearly enough people in the Résistance. I've heard about twenty per cent of those who've joined are Jews, even though they're only one per cent of the population.'

'Twenty per cent? I didn't know that, but I'm not surprised. They've got far more motivation. Nowhere to go, on the run, and far stronger reasons for revenge. At least we're lucky to have somewhere to hide in this part of France. Hills, forests and mountains like here. God knows what it's like in flat places like Holland, with no shared border with a neutral country.

Do you know Jews in Holland are now called 'divers', because they literally have to dive under the surface of society, hiding in cellars?'

'No I didn't,' said Alexandre, picturing their plight.

Two hours later she was asleep beside him, on a damp rug on what was left of the old and battered and rough-tiled floor.

Alexandre was still wide-awake, and wondering if he was beginning to fall in love.

* * *

'That awful boy Gérard has just joined the Milice.' Carmen was reporting the latest gossip from the town to her mother. 'You know, the one that was always trying to make a pass at me.'

'What's the Milice?' asked Maria, puzzled. She had never heard the word.

'It's a new kind of police force that Vichy, no doubt pushed by the Germans, have just cooked up to do its dirty work. The kind of work that the regular police and Gendarmes are beginning to shy away from because it's making them so hated by the locals. Frankly, they're a load of Fascist thugs and released jailbirds. Not to mention Jew-bashers. A thoroughly nasty lot. Not remotely fussed about oppressing their own countrymen. And would you believe, lots of them are convicted rapists, crooks and even murderers – freed by the Vichy courts to enlist?'

Maria was shocked. 'But why would anyone *want* to join?'

'That's easy, Mamá. They may have been far right in the first place – you know, people like 'Action Française' – or anti-Jewish. Or there might be much more basic reasons. Money, for one. They get quite good pay, and I hear much better food than us. And of course by joining the Milice they get let off the STO, being shipped off to work in Germany. All pretty selfish motives. I know one other fellow who's joined up, and his personality doesn't surprise me, either.'

'Will they be a problem for you?'

'Who? The Milice? Yes, I think they will. And a big one. Unlike the Germans, they speak perfect French, and can understand the Occitane accent around here. And they know the people and the places. In fact, I think they could be *really* big trouble once they get going.'

She paused to give herself another sip of rather unpleasant chicory coffee.

'But they aren't as bad as the 'Carlingue' – the other lot.'

Once again, Maria hadn't ever heard the word. 'Who on earth are *they*?'

'Well, sort of French auxiliaries who, believe it or not, work for the German Gestapo. My maquis friends say they're led by a crooked ex-policeman called Pierre Bonny, and his men are all really well-known criminals.'

'These days I'd believe anything.'

'The whole group's full of gangsters, cheating officials and informers. Sometimes people just refer to it as the 'Bonny-LaFont Gang'. It's as if the American President Roosevelt had hired Al Capone to do his dirty work. It's just another lot that will harass the Résistance, and they don't even wear uniforms. That makes them even more dangerous.

But they're all getting really hated, even more than the Germans. I wouldn't want to be one of them if the Germans end up losing and leave them behind.'

Maria thought for a moment, utterly confused by all these new names and worried about her daughter. It was so abnormal for a girl to be involved in such things.

'Carmen, do you *really* think it's a good idea getting into this Résistance thing?'

'Yes, I do,' said Carmen, but deciding to change the subject fast.

'By the way, Mamá, I've heard that people around here have been doing something wonderful. They've been taking in Jewish children and getting them baptised as Christians. I don't think it's happened here in Hippo, because as far as I know we don't have any Jews – except for poor Sarah. But over in Lasalle and Soudorgues and other small villages they've pulled it off. It's really good that they've outwitted those racist bastards.'

Maria flinched to hear her daughter swear, something she knew she would never get used to. Like everything else, her daughter appeared to be changing too fast.

'And another bit of good news. We've heard that after a long fight the Americans have beaten the Japanese on some island called Guadalcanal. Funny name – sounds Spanish, doesn't it? Anyway, it does no harm, even here, for all *three* of the Axis powers to appear not to be winning any more.'

Axis? Maria nodded, though confused again.

* * *

That night she barely slept at all.

While the world was at war, she was fighting another battle – within herself – ashamed by her lack of understanding about what was going on, and torn between simply wanting to be a good wife and mother and the need to be a far better-educated confidante.

Half the conversations in the house in the house were now in French, especially when they had visitors, and half of them, certainly among the adults, were about the war and world events – to her, a maelstrom of constant confusion.

Was love possible without respect? Did people look down on her, or pity her, because she'd never learned the language properly? And think of her as a second-class citizen? Was it her own fault she felt increasingly cut off, isolated? These days, everybody jabbered away in French, usually becoming frustrated when they had to translate for her, which held everything up, almost to the point she didn't dare ask them to help. Or, like Otilia, groaning inwardly – or even outwardly – when she did.

Despite Pedro lying curled beside her with his arm companionably over her back, she felt frighteningly alone.

TWENTY-FIVE

* * *

I N FEBRUARY, PEOPLE IN THE TOWN WERE SHOCKED TO SEE NOTICES
going up everywhere, extending the *Service du travail obligatoire.* They
knew the original September order, signed by Marshal Pétain himself, had
required 'all able-bodied men aged 18 to 50 and single women aged 21 to
35 be subject to do any work that the Government deems necessary'. Not
much had happened in the area since then. But now all men over twenty
were called up for the STO. And it looked as if it were going to be properly
enforced, and this time not just by the Germans but by the already-hated
Milice – with their far better knowledge of the local people and their
language.

The young men were meant to report to the Town Hall where any
exemptions were noted, like being a student or (with luck) a farm worker.
The rest of the men would be shipped straight out to Germany. Vichy
seemed to have hesitated about including young women, because the
churches, both Catholic and Protestant, were hardening their disapproval
about conscripting females, but for the men it was a nightmare.

Nobody, absolutely nobody, wanted to go to Germany. They had
heard quite enough about the unpleasant, indeed appalling conditions the
millions of foreign workers were already enduring. And the bombs.

Any illusions had been swept aside by the underground magazine,
L'Insurgé, which reported: *'Journey: long, little food, under German
supervision. On arrival: camps where workers treated like cattle. Later:
sleeping in barracks, herded together. Work: twelve hours a day. Wages:
enormous taxes and fines. Cost of living: higher than France. Food: not*

even enough for Italians used to low subsistence. Freedom: nil. Conclusion: prisoner status. Thousands of workers killed by bombing.'

Everyone now knew that the bombing by the British and Americans was becoming both devastating and round the clock. Indeed, even the Germans in the Fort had confirmed the pervasive fear among civilians back in their own country.

That same week Pedro was approached in the café by Michel Morelli, looking very agitated. Sitting in a corner, the postman spoke in a low voice.

'Pedro, I wonder if you can help? I mentioned to you last time that I've got a son, just twenty. So this STO law is going to catch him. Some of his friends have already gone – they've just disappeared, and I'm not sure where, but I can guess.'

'So?' asked Pedro.

'I wondered if you have any connections – you know, with the people up in the hills.' He whispered, 'in the Résistance.'

'I'm not saying I do, and I'm not saying I don't,' said Pedro guardedly. 'I'm not involved in anything like that. Frankly, I saw too much of that back in Spain. But I may know someone who could help. Write down your address, and I'll try and get someone to visit you.'

'Can it be quick?'

Pedro paused. 'As quick as I can make it.'

* * *

Maria was amazed to see her middle daughter, Otilia, walk into the kitchen. Gone was her long mane of black hair, now replaced by a short bob.

'Por Dios! What made you do that?'

'Boredom,' replied Otilia, patting her hair. 'I was fed up with having it so long. Such a bore to wash. And I saw a great picture of someone called Coco Chanel in Uncle Fon's paper. I liked her hair. Really chic. And cooler in summer. It's so fucking hot here.'

'Don't swear. It doesn't suit you. I've told you before, and so has your father.'

Otilia groaned. 'Okay, it's *bloody* hot, then.'

'That's not much better.'

Maria surveyed her daughter, once again regretting she was often so aggressive, but deciding to be kind. 'Actually, it looks quite good.' She smiled. 'A bit of a shock, that's all. But don't go putting ideas in Juanita's head. I'd like one of you to stay with long hair.'

'Honestly, Mamá, you never want to see *anything* changed. You're so old-fashioned.'

'Not true,' said Maria. 'But I've seen enough changes in the last few years to last me a lifetime. Anyway, sit down and eat your breakfast. And if you don't mind, I'd like you to bring down all that hair from the bedroom *before* you go to school. I guess it's all over the floor, and I've got enough to do already without clearing it up.'

Otilia sighed. 'Oh, Mamá, why do you always have to do *everything* at once?'

'Because if they're not done at once, they *never* get done. Not unless *I* do them. Now, eat your breakfast, and I'll fetch the brush and dustpan.'

She suddenly turned at the door. 'Oh, and by the way, I wouldn't mention Coco Chanel at school. You know she's a Nazi sympathiser?'

'No, how would I?'

'Well, you do now. Your father told me the other day.'

* * *

Pedro met Alfonso in the café with some startling news. Squeezed between the British advancing from Egypt and the Americans from Algeria, all the Germans and Italians in North Africa had just surrendered.

'Two hundred and forty *thousand*?' Pedro exclaimed.' Good God, I expect that most of them were Italians, but that's still a *huge* defeat for Hitler. He didn't seem to pay much attention to Africa – until he sent some last-minute reinforcements. So that just meant he swelled the bag of prisoners.'

'It's weird how things are going,' added Alfonso. 'Have you noticed we've not heard much from Franco recently, have we? I'll bet he's glad he didn't throw in his lot with Hitler and Mussolini two years ago. Apparently he asked for so much food and material in return for letting the Germans through to attack Gibraltar that any deal fell through.'

Pedro nodded in agreement. 'It's hardly surprising. Judging by the amount of food the Germans are stealing from us, they can't even feed *themselves*, let alone give anything to Spain. And they can't run their factories either without using foreigners as slave workers – hence the STO.

You *really* shouldn't wage war unless you're rich. And if you're doing it to *get* rich, you'd better make it a short one. I'm sure the Japs are beginning to learn that lesson too.'

'I'll tell you something else,' said Alfonso. 'Franco's hands are tied, because the British and their navy are the ones to decide if Spain's going to get any fuel and food from America. And I'll bet they'll let just enough in to keep him dangling, with a half-starved backward country.'

'And, Alfonso, you know that token force Franco gave to Hitler to show some solidarity, the Blue Division?'

'Yes, I remember.'

'Well, I've heard it's going to be pulled out of Russia soon. Too many people in Spain think they can detect a lost cause.'

'I'm beginning to enjoy this conversation, Pedro. In fact, I think I'll have a cognac!'

* * *

Juanita was up in the mountain at Valatougès foraging for edible fungi, and mushrooms if she could find them. Ever since her father had been ordered to give away one third of the produce on Auguste's farm there had been even less on the table, and her mother had begged her to make the trip, arduous though she knew it was with such a rocky climb. But Juanita's bag, even though small, was still barely a quarter full. Obviously, everybody else was doing the same thing, and even the fruit-bearing trees on her way, which should have been laden at this time of year, had all been stripped.

Suddenly, she spotted a dead snake on the path. Could that be eaten, she wondered? She picked it up, smelling its flesh. There was no rancid odour, and at least it was meat, rare enough these days. It could probably make another meal, she thought, adding it to her too-empty bag and wondering how much further she could walk. She was exhausted from climbing – all the more so from knowing it was hardly worth the effort.

Depressed, and passing a meadow on the way down the mountain, she suddenly spotted a mass of wild flowers. On impulse, she went into the field to pick some, knowing her mother would love a bunch. It was so long since there had been any colour in the house. But without scissors, most refused to be picked or were too difficult to be pulled up. Résistance fighters, she thought, just like her eldest sister.

* * *

Carmen was led up into the woods by a young Spaniard who had been sent to collect her. She was quite nervous as they walked through the trees to a dilapidated wooden house, long since abandoned by its owners.

But she was greeted by the group inside in a friendly and cautiously correct manner. Even in the gloom she could see that the walls were covered in rifles and sub-machine guns hanging from hooks and nails.

'Good afternoon, Señorita,' said a young thin-faced man who appeared to be the leader. 'I'm Cristino Garcia and I command all our forces in the hills here – about seven hundred men and a few women at the moment. These are my comrades.' He pointed to each one on turn. 'First, Gabriel Perez – he commands the 21st brigade. Then over there is Joachin Arasanz, code name 'Villacampa', our political Commissar.' Carmen was reminded that many of them were Communists.

'Then, Julian Hernandez.' A young man raised his hand. 'Julian's just done something amazing. He was bound up, about to be shot by a firing squad of Germans, when he freed one hand, grabbed a sub-machine-gun, shot five of the guards, freed the other hand and then knocked over the officer and ran away – *and* with a bullet in his leg.' Cristino went on round the room while Carmen hoped she could remember all the names, before he then got down to real business. She'd certainly remember Julian.

He now turned to her. 'And then, there's Carmen. We know of your father, so your credentials as a Republican we can accept straight away. But I'd like to know why you *want* to join us. And how you think you can help.'

Carmen drew a deep breath. 'I had good enough reasons to hate the Fascists back in Spain, and I now I've got even better ones to hate the Germans and their Vichy lackeys.'

'And what, precisely, do you want to do?'

'I've played my part passing messages, collecting bicycles and smuggling things for the British in Saint-Hippolyte. But now I want to fight. *Really* fight. *And* fire a gun, if I'm allowed to.' She heard someone laugh, and noticed Cristino raising an eyebrow.

'You don't have to worry that I haven't the guts to pull a trigger. I just need one to pull, and the training to make me shoot straight.' She looked at him straight in the eye.

Cristino thought for a moment, surprised, not least by her un-female attitude. 'Well, we *do* have women fighters. But very few. Most women do more ordinary things like washing and cooking for the men. But if you can keep up with us in training, I'd be prepared to give you a chance, as I think all of us would.' He looked round the room to gauge the reaction of the others, none of them objecting – at the moment.

Carmen was relieved to see most of them nodding.

* * *

Carmen turned out to be very good as a soldier. She was intelligent and watchful, so she learned quickly, and could soon strip and re-assemble weapons as fast or even faster than her male colleagues. And when they were allowed to, really deep in the hills, she sometimes outshot them too.

Cristino Garcia also noticed that she seemed to be surprisingly strong – fully able to carry her share of weapons, ammunition and equipment. And of course, as a girl, she was soon adopted as some sort of mascot. Only one person, a slightly older Sergeant called Gonzalez, seemed to resent her. But she shrugged off such sour grapes.

She was very soon rushed off her feet. The principal role of her Résistance group was dealing with the rapidly rising number of men who were trying to evade work in Germany. They needed safe houses for secure shelter, food of course, and also false papers that had to be carefully forged. She had the advantage of being a girl, and a very pretty one at that. It meant – with luck – that the German soldiers, the Milice and Gendarmes, would all be too busy trying to flirt with her rather than being properly suspicious of her movements.

It was not the most exciting work, but one morning that changed when Alvaro arrived with a small party of strangers. One was introduced as a British officer. He had a French Sergeant with him. Both were disguised and dressed like local Frenchmen, with moustaches, long hair and scruffy working clothes. *Goodness knows how the British man had got here* thought Carmen, *either from England or North Africa, presumably through Spain on foot. Surely it was still too far to fly and parachute in.*

Captain 'Felix', as he introduced himself, brought interesting news and equally interesting weapons. He spoke in good French, with only a slight accent. *Not English. Perhaps Belgian,* Carmen wondered. He revealed that the British 'Special Operations Executive' or S.O.E. had heard about the effective Spanish resistants in the Cèvennes and also about Saint-Hippolyte from the internees who had escaped from 'Détachement W', and were more than grateful for the efforts of the local Résistance in helping them to get away. So the British were going to supply arms and support to them in the near future. But he had some serious words of warning.

'The invasion *will* come for sure, next year, in 1944. And it'll need your help, because it's going to be tough. They'll want you to harass the Germans at every turn, to cut their communications – whether road, rail or telephone. And stop their reinforcements, or at least slow them down. But it *must* be timed cleverly. There's absolutely no point going out before that and attacking the enemy, not if there's no immediate tactical purpose.

If we do that, I can promise you that all that will happen is that they'll take reprisals on innocent people that you'll be powerless to prevent. In many parts of Europe, if a German's killed, they just round up and shoot ten local hostages, including blameless civilians – men, women and even children. Sometimes, it's fifty. In Russia, it can be a hundred. And in places like Hungary and Rumania, the S.O.E., our Special Operations Executive, just had to pull out. We'd have got too many innocent local people killed.

So you *must* try to stop any premature, ill-thought out action.'

'We may have a problem there,' said Juan Perez. 'Some of the other Communist groups are fanatics, keen to hit the Germans fast and whenever they can. We've managed to hold them back so far. But only just.'

'Good,' nodded Captain 'Felix'. 'We've had exactly that problem further north. It just causes trouble to no effect – or actually much worse than that. It makes the locals hate us so much that they prefer to betray us, rather than support us.' He paused and lit a cigarette.

'Anyway, let me show you the kind of weapons we're going to get to you. They'll come by parachute when we get close enough.'

He turned to the table and pulled away a blanket, revealing a machine-gun with a bipod and a smaller sub-machine-gun and some magazines.

'This first weapon is a Bren light machine-gun. It was designed and built by the Czechs in a place called Brno and the British in Enfield – hence the name Bren. It's a simple gas-operated weapon, very reliable and not too heavy. It has nothing like the rate of fire of the German guns, but at two or three hundred metres, or even further, it can be as accurate as a rifle. You can even hit the enemy at a thousand.'

Cristino couldn't contain his curiosity.

'However did you get it here?'

'We actually took it off the Milice over beyond Beziers. You know your own slogan – '*Each weapon should bring in at least one new weapon in a week.*' 'Felix' smiled. 'The Milice were issued with them – captured ones from Dunkirk. But you'll get brand new ones, straight from Enfield.'

'Felix' picked up the Bren, placed it on the floor and lay down behind it. The French Sergeant lay down on the left of the gun.

'Now, I'm called the 'Number One'. *I* fire the gun. The second operator is called the 'Number Two' – in my case, Pierre here. He passes me the magazines, adjusts the gas regulator if it fouls and changes the barrel when it gets too hot. Though I doubt if we can get you any spare barrels at the moment.

This gun is very reliable. There are only two likely reasons why it'll ever stop firing. That's why we have automatic drills that we call IAs, 'Immediate Actions'. The 'First IA' is used because *this* magazine, on top of the gun, has simply just run out of ammunition. It only contains twenty-eight rounds, so it runs out fast, and often, in battle.

So the 'First IA' is, cock the weapon, like this, and remove the magazine, then replace the magazine and continue firing.' He looked up at the group to see that it had understood. Carmen had been quietly translating for some of the Spanish boys whose French was still skimpy, and the British officer seemed to be noticing this tall, confident and pretty girl for the first time.

'Then there's the 'Second IA'. As we shout out in our training drills, 'GUN FIRES ONE OR TWO ROUNDS, AND STOPS AGAIN!'

Again Carmen quickly translated his French.

'Almost certainly the regulator valve that sends the gas back to work the reloading mechanism has fouled up with gunshot residue. Number One cocks the gun, removes the magazine, pulls the trigger, cocks the gun again, and removes the barrel. Number Two reaches forward and turns this regulator, here, to open up the gas passage. Then, barrel on, magazine on, you start firing. It has to be quick and automatic, otherwise I'm afraid to say you might be dead.'

He got up and dusted himself off. 'Would you like to try them?'

The young Spanish men all tried their hands at the drills. Then Carmen, to the surprise of the British officer, lay down behind the gun.

She more than held her own, learning to act without hesitation. 'Felix' looked astonished, but impressed, and then turned to the other weapon he had come to show them.

'Then we have this, the Sten gun. I don't know why it's called that. It's a simple, cheap submachine-gun, firing nine-millimetre ammunition that we can get pretty well anywhere. We'll be getting you these, the Brens, ammunition, and also things like explosives to blow railway tracks and bridges.'

'When you get them, you'll need to practise – up here in the hills – and I hope we can get you some instructors. But you *must* not, I repeat, *must not* fire them on automatic. It's one thing for the Milice or the Germans to hear the odd shot, maybe thinking it's from a hunter, but quite another to hear a *burst* of fire. Sometimes you *may* be able to fire bursts, but only when you're *really* isolated. We can leave one Bren and a Sten, with some ammunition to practise with. And then we'll get you more later.

Well, my friends, I have to move on now to talk to other groups. I think things will start to hot up soon. Good luck.' He looked around, his gaze lingering on Carmen.

* * *

At first Carmen's proficiency with their precious Bren gun caused some problems within the Spanish group, probably due to the normal 'macho' attitude of Spanish boys. But when they went off deep into the hills and Carmen actually *fired* the gun, and moreover, and very surprisingly, was one of the best shots with it, their respect rapidly increased. Only one of them, Felipe Gonzalez, maintained a surly resentment.

The others began to accept that she could have the gun as long as *she* carried it and didn't expect one of *them* to do so. It might be called a *light* machine-gun but it was still much heavier than a rifle, and in these rugged hills, they were only too happy to see a girl lugging it about. This Carmen did without complaining and seemingly without getting tired. But then, she was tall and very fit, hardly ever drinking or smoking as they did.

A boy from Valencia called Sebastian soon ensured that he became her Number Two – and to the amusement of the others, the two of them often went off and diligently spent time practicing the AI drills. It was only natural for some of them to start being a bit jealous of him.

* * *

'I wish we lived in Paris,' sighed Otilia, picturing dance halls and lively cafés, and women dressed in pretty clothes. And, above all, handsome young men.

She and Juanita were in their bedroom, still chatting well after eleven o'clock.

'At least there would be more boys there.'

'There are loads of them here,' said Juanita. 'Half the school are boys.'

'Yeah, but boring ones. Country boys, not city ones.'

'What's wrong with that?'

'They don't know anything. Well, only things like farming.'

'And football,' chuckled her sister.

There was a long silence while Otilia dreamed about Paris again, comparing it with the dreariness and monotony of daily life in Saint-Hippolyte.

'Are you asleep?' asked her sister.

'No. Just dreaming.'

'Then you *must* be asleep,' giggled Juanita.

Otilia laughed, but bitterly. 'You don't have to be asleep to dream. I was thinking of all the shops and galleries, and the nice places to go. And all the street painters. Apparently there are loads of them there. And all the fun people have.'

'Except the Jews,' added Juanita. 'That's if there are any of them left.'

Otilia ignored her sister's riposte.

'If only the bloody English hadn't gone on with the war, if only they'd given up, we'd have all our decent boys back by now. You know, like Pierre. They've just made life worse for us, and even more dreary. And I don't think I can stand it for ever. Anyway, as soon as I can, I'm going to try and get out of here.'

Juanita was shocked.

'What, this house?'

'Yes. And St. Hippolyte. And go to Paris, and have a bit of fun at last.'

'But where would you go? You don't know anyone there. And who would look after you?'

'Me. I'd get by. I'm tough. Or if I can't afford to go to Paris, then Lyons. Anywhere bigger and more fun than it is here. *And* I could earn my way. I got twenty francs just from my last exhibition here – you know, the one in the church – although Mamá immediately stole a quarter of it.'

Juanita was even more shocked. 'She didn't *steal* it. She needed it to feed us.'

'I guess so,' sighed Otilia. 'But it's really depressing when you slog your guts out, and then Mamá takes the money.'

'A quarter of it,' her sister corrected her.'

'Well, whatever it was.'

There was a sudden loud banging on the bedroom door, as if someone was hitting it with a sharp object.

'Go to sleep, you two! You've got school tomorrow!'

'Worst luck,' muttered Otilia under her breath.

Ten minutes later, Juanita was still awake, quietly weeping. She couldn't believe what her sister had said, or bear the thought of her leaving.

Pierre, gone. Sarah, gone. Carmen, gone – or mostly not there. Auguste, gone. Even the nice British men in the barracks, gone, who had sometimes given her sweets. And now *Otilia* was thinking of going too. It was all too much.

She turned over her pillow, wet with tears.

* * *

Maria looked up from Alfonso's album of faded black and white photographs.

'Pedro, why don't we take the kids to the Camargue on Juanita's birthday? From these photos it looks fantastic. Full of wild white horses and flamingos, and gorgeous lakes.'

'And mosquitoes from what I've heard,' interrupted Pedro.

Maria frowned. 'Why do you always have to put a dampener on everything these days?'

'I don't. It's just that I'm worried sick about the farm.'

'I know,' said Maria. 'But I do think the kids need a bit of a break. And it would be lovely for them to go to the seaside. Or even ride a horse.'

'And who's going to pay for *that*?'

Maria sighed. 'Look, Pedro, I know things are tough, but we all need a bit of a treat, or a day out together. I can't even remember the last time we had one as a family. We could even make it a two-day trip and sleep in the van. I know it'll cost money, petrol and all that. But surely we can sell something?' She looked at her left hand. 'In fact, if it wouldn't upset you, I've been thinking about selling my wedding ring.'

Pedro was suddenly guilty. 'No, don't do that. That *would* upset me.'

'Well then, we could probably pawn it. And hope we can get the money to buy it back some day.'

'No, I'll work out something. Remind me, what day is Juanita's birthday?'

'Pedro. Honestly, you're losing your marbles. Can't you even remember that?'

'Not at the moment. Too much on my mind.'

'June the twelfth, three weeks away.'

'Oh yes, of course. He patted her on the hand. Look, I'll see what I can do.'

'Promise?'

'Promise.'

Maria went back to the album, and the beautiful photographs of white horses galloping in the surf.

A day or two out would so relieve the day-to-day monotony. But where was the money? Perhaps, she thought, she could offer to wash other people's laundry. But it was a horrendous load already.

She could only hope that Pedro would keep his word.

Two days later, she was over the moon when he came home.

'I think I can do it,' he said, giving her a hug.

'Do what?'

'Manage a couple of days in the Camargue. I worked it out today. I've got just enough petrol rations. And if we sleep in the van, we won't need anywhere to stay.'

Maria beamed. 'Oh, that's wonderful! I can't wait to tell the kids.'

* * *

The family trip to the Camargue region – around four hours' drive south from St. Hippolyte – had been a huge success, despite the heat inside the van from the boiling summer sun and the tremendous number of mosquitoes attracted to this region of vast inland lakes. Everyone had been bitten, but not badly enough to spoil an otherwise perfect outing in an area so very different from the mountainous region where they lived. For kilometre after kilometre, the children stared out of the back windows, entranced by the many wild grey horses as they galloped through the endless shallow waters, until they reached a little seaside village called Saintes-Maries-de-la-Mer.

Going to the beach – which seemed to stretch for miles on either side – Maria watched the family happily swimming for the first time in the sea under the supervision of Pedro, regretting that she had never had the opportunity to learn to swim as her daughters had, but delighted to be able to talk to another Spanish family there – and in their native language. It turned out that they too had made the same treacherous journey over the Pyrenees and had now settled in the little village behind them. Maria chatted to the mother for a good hour while Pedro and the children built a huge sandcastle, and was handed her address, though Maria doubted they would ever meet again. Nobody could really make plans in wartime.

'I wish we could live there,' said Otilia on the way home. 'It's so much more fun than Hippo, with the sea. And easier to wash. Not having to fetch endless water from the cursed fountains every day.'

This time, Maria chose not to chide her daughter for swearing, deciding not to spoil the day. And, like her daughter, she too had dreamed of living by the sea that afternoon. Perhaps that might be possible when the war was over, she thought, *if* it were ever over. The concept of it lasting right through to the end of all her daughters' childhoods was more than she could bear.

'You okay?' Pedro turned to her from the driver's seat, noticing that she had been silent for some time.

'Fine. Just daydreaming.'

'About what? Getting a place down there?'

How well he knows me, mused Maria. 'Yes, among other things.'

Pedro didn't ask her what the other things were, deciding to change the subject. 'I think we should do this again one day, even if we can't afford it.'

'So do I,' agreed Maria. 'It's just a shame Carmen couldn't join us.'

'I know,' Pedro replied. 'But I think things are hotting up.'

* * *

'I see the spaghetti-eaters have packed it in!' Pedro had just returned, and Alfonso was talking with some satisfaction about the news that, while Pedro had been away, the Italians had signed an Armistice.

He had also read that Mussolini had been arrested by his King, and the radio had reported that the Allies had landed at Salerno.

'Excellent!' exclaimed Pedro, with equal relish. 'The Italians were always quite good at attacking civilians, and bombing cities – as they did in Spain of course – but their army and navy were always bluff. Look how they performed in the desert against the British. Ridiculo! They're actually quite gentle, sweet people. They really shouldn't have gone to war at all, and they certainly should *never* have listened to that Musso's crap.

But look how quickly the Germans have reacted! They've just *poured* in to Italy, with no hesitation. I'll bet there'll be a long war there. Never under-estimate the Germans, I say. Hate them as I do, I admit in warfare I'd prefer them to be on my side than against it.'

TWENTY-SIX

* * *

OTILIA HAD JUST HELPED HER MOTHER LUG ANOTHER HUGE BAG OF dirty clothes to be washed in the Vidourle, the river than ran through Saint-Hippolyte. In the heat of summer, and with the water retreating, the job was getting even harder, but at least she hadn't been asked to do it, as yet. But she knew that would change when she left school in a few months. Already she was dreading the words, 'All hands to the pump', or in this case, 'river', when she'd become a drudge like her mother, forever cleaning or washing – unless she could find a means to escape that, perhaps with a career as an artist. And hopefully *not*, she thought yet again, in this backward and unexciting country town.

As she leaned over the bridge, she watched her mother laboriously washing clothes in between wiping the sweat from her brow, with plenty of her neighbours doing the same. 'It's where I get most of the gossip in town,' her mother had told her. 'That lightens the load a bit.'

Now, thought Otilia, that gossip would be all about the Germans who'd recently come to town, although they seemed pleasant enough, not at all like the monsters everyone had been led to expect. She had even noticed them exchanging a few words with the locals in the café, if not exactly sitting at the same tables, and one of them, she had heard, had so taken to the town that he wanted to set up as a tailor one day, and in the very shop where her sister once worked – now closed down and derelict, like most of the others.

However, she and her sister had the strictest instructions not to 'consort' with the Germans or talk to them at any time – as their former enemy in Spain. This had been drummed into them so many times that Otilia now groaned inwardly, and sometimes even outwardly when the subject was brought up yet again.

She had noticed one young German in particular on her trips to carry the washing to the bridge where she was standing now – a very tall and unusually good-looking boy who had always glanced at her before proceeding up the hill, obviously on patrol.

Now, leaning over the bridge, she was suddenly aware of someone standing behind her, and turned to see the very same young man.

'Bonjour, Mam'selle.' He took off his cap, revealing his almost white blond hair, and gave her a little nod, clicking his heels together.

'Bonjour.' Otilia was shocked, her mind suddenly in a turmoil, but had returned the greeting instinctively. It suddenly seemed so rude not to, and anyway her parents weren't there to hear. She glanced down at her mother, still busy washing and with another whole load to go, calculating that she'd be at least another half hour there, time to have a harmless chat if that's what this pleasant-looking boy wanted. And there was nobody else on the bridge to see them and report her to her parents. She knew what trouble would lie ahead if *that* happened. Spanish girls, she reflected, weren't even allowed to go out with *any* boys unless they had a chaperone to escort them, although her sister *had* been allowed to go to that dance with Pierre unescorted – and to that picnic up the mountain. Life was changing, she told herself. And this boy seemed so very different from the ogres her parents had always painted the Germans – with his friendly blue eyes and kindly expression.

He was dressed in a grey-green uniform, with a rifle slung over his right shoulder, but Otilia wasn't in the least alarmed by the gun – he looked the very last person who would ever use it.

'Do you live in town?' he asked, with a surprisingly guttural accent.

'Yes,' replied Otilia. She pointed down the street to the left. 'Just down there, about two hundred metres away. I'm here to do the washing. ' She glanced over the bridge. 'At least, my Mamá is. She's down there now.'

The boy frowned. 'And you're not helping her?'

Otilia felt a stab of irritation mixed with guilt. The first time she had ever met the enemy, and he was actually criticising *her*.

The boy looked down over the bridge at the long line of women in the shallow water, mopping their brows in the heat as they washed and wrung the wet clothes, doing the latter in pairs to make the job easier.

'I wouldn't want to do that job week after week.'

'Nor me. And my Mamá doesn't want me to do it until I leave school. I just help her here with the bags and taking them back. She says we all deserve a childhood.'

The boy looked her up and down for a moment, bemused. 'A childhood? How old are you?'

'Sixteen, nearly seventeen.'

He smiled, surveying her again. 'Almost the same age as me. And from what I can see, hardly a child.' He grinned. 'Certainly old enough to go out with boys.'

Was that a pass, Otilia wondered? She was suddenly flattered. He certainly looked interested in her, studying her face, and far more closely than was normal for a stranger.

'Frankly, there aren't any boys here I'd want to go out with, even if I were allowed to. All obsessed with football.'

'The boy laughed. 'I'm not. Though it's the same in Germany. We're not so different.'

They leaned against the bridge companionably for a while, until Otilia broke the silence. 'How do you speak French so well? Did you learn it at school?'

'A bit. But I really learned it at Saumur, in the north of France, where we were stationed before here. We stayed there for months, and it's not that difficult a language.'

'I don't speak a word of German,' smiled Otilia.

'No need to,' replied Hans. 'At least, not with me. That's if we meet again.

Perhaps we could have a coffee sometime? It's pretty boring being billeted here. Maybe we could go to the café. The one by the fountain.'

'No, *anywhere* but the café,' laughed Otilia, before suddenly realizing with embarrassment that she'd virtually agreed to a date.

'Well, anywhere else you suggest.'

'Here, when I come to lug the washing every bloody Saturday.'

He laughed. 'That's not very romantic.'

Now Otilia laughed too. 'Well, to be honest,' she continued, 'I'm not allowed to talk to Germans, let alone go out with one. No girls are, especially Spanish ones. If my Mamá saw me talking to you, she'd kill me. Remember it was *your* planes bombing us back in Spain. And now you've done it in France. We're always being told not to fraternise with the enemy.'

Hans sighed. 'I don't feel like an enemy. And we're not all animals, you know. And some of us, including me, actually *hate* what's going on. I never wanted to join the army in the first place, and I certainly don't like the Führer – you know, Hitler – our leader. Far too aggressive and over-confident, and even frightening at times. He can't even protect us in *Germany*, for God's sake. My mother says streams of bombers go over her house in Mannheim every night. I'm scared stiff all the time that one night they *won't* go over, and bombs will come crashing down on her.'

Listening to this, Otilia suddenly warmed to him a little more. She had never before seen things from the other side. 'Well, maybe if you could get some time off, we could walk up the mountain, or better still, meet up there, so no-one sees us together. If anyone did, I'd be in *real* trouble. It's a risk enough here.'

'For me, too. I'm supposed to be patrolling up here, not talking to a pretty girl.'

Otilia felt a flush of pleasure at the compliment, and looking over the bridge, was glad to see her mother still washing.

'What's your name?' she asked.

'Hans. Hans Pieter,' he replied. 'And yours?'

'Otilia Casales. As I said, I'm Spanish. We escaped here over the Pyrenees at the end of the Civil War.'

'God. That can't have been easy.'

Otilia was pleased that he knew something about it. 'It wasn't. It was hell. And then we got out of that war only to be plunged into this one.'

Both leaned against the wall for a while in silence, with Otilia greatly relieved that no-one had passed them, but knowing someone might do so at any moment. It was now or never, she decided. *Why shouldn't she see this nice boy again?*

'What if we meet on the mountain road at the fork to Valatougès?' she asked him, hoping she wasn't sounding too forward, or doing something truly foolhardy, but telling herself she needed and deserved a life. Anyway, he seemed so pleasant. Not at all like her parents had described the Germans.

'Fine. I know it well,' said Hans.

They arranged to meet the following Saturday afternoon, half an hour after his duties ended.

With that agreed, Hans looked at his watch. 'Well, I'd better be going. Nice to meet you.'

'You, too.' Otilia smiled, before glancing over the bridge yet again. 'I guess I'd better go too, and help my Mamá haul up all that washing.'

'Good girl,' smiled Hans, patting her hand. 'See you next Saturday, then.' He stood up and gave her a little bow, clicking his boots together. 'Au revoir, Senorita.'

She smiled at his touch of Spanish, and watched him march up the hill without looking back, as if in professional military mode.

At last she and her mother were back on the bridge, covered with perspiration and weighed down by a heavy damp bundle, which they dumped on the pavement. Maria was now amazed by how cheerfully Otilia then picked it up and carried it home without a single grumble. Although she was soon to discover, and to her annoyance, it was the last time she would ever help with the never-ending laundry load.

* * *

Otto Heinz, an eighteen-year-old German soldier, looked around the café for the umpteenth time, after several months still astonished by French customs and traditions. He leaned over to his friend Gustav Mueller, cupping his hand to his mouth to be better heard above the din.

'It's incredible the French ever get around to doing anything with all the time they spend kissing and embracing each other.'

Gustav glanced around him. 'I agree. But I think it's rather nice. And they probably think we're pretty cold fish for *not* doing it.'

'I wonder when it all started,' mused Otto, looking at yet another group of locals exchanging embraces.

'Oh, probably at the French court on the order of one of their mad kings – or queens. But three kisses, I agree, *is* a bit over the top. And wasn't it just two when we were back in Saumur?'

'Can't remember,' said Otto, 'but I seem to remember it was. And even two is one too many. And they all *talk* so loudly, far louder than we do. It's as if they're totally deaf as well as sentimental. And they all talk so *much*. Do you know, I've even heard people from other towns call them 'Cigalois'

– from the French word 'cigales' for crickets – because they chatter all the time. And that they're actually *proud* of that.'

'Ah, so *that's* why they've all got china crickets nailed to their houses?'

'Yes, and cricket-shaped door knockers. It's a sort of local symbol.'

'Funny people,' smiled Gustav, shaking his head. 'Sentimental, over-loquacious, clearly deaf…'

'And rather nice,' Otto chipped in. 'Rather nicer than we'd be if they occupied *our* towns. In fact, I feel quite sorry for them having us lot here, effectively robbing them of everything if you think about it. Food, self-respect, men – and even women.' He leaned forward to Gustav. 'Which reminds me, my friend. I think you should be pretty careful sleeping with local girls. You never know what they might have got if they're having it off with other men.'

'But we can't live like monks for years on end. And anyway, I'm not that stupid, even if those Vulcan Sanex condoms we're given are awful.'

'Glad to hear you're using them. Better than dying of syphilis, my friend.'

Gustav tipped back his head to drain the last of his coffee. 'And on that pleasant note, would you like another coffee? If you can call this chicory stuff that.'

'What?' asked Otto, cupping his hand to his ear again, once again struggling to hear his friend above the babble.

Gustav pointed to Otto's empty cup. 'DO YOU WANT ANY MORE?'

Otto nodded. Even the word 'Ja' was likely to be lost in the cacophony of the café.

TWENTY-SEVEN

* * *

'THANKS FOR COMING.'

Michel Morelli got up to shake Pedro's hand as he arrived in the café, and Pedro noticed that he was far from smiling. In fact, he looked grim-faced. Maybe it was even more bad news about the war. He was soon to discover that it was in many ways worse than even that, at least on a personal level.

'Look, I'm really sorry to tell you this, Pedro, but I've just heard on good authority that your daughter Otilia has been seen out with a German. One of our postmen, André Lebrun, spotted her up at Valatougès the other day, walking hand in hand with a very tall blond man – certainly not one of us. André knows all the locals, and says that he's definitely not from here.'

Pedro was appalled. *Hand in hand with a boy and out on her own? And worse still, probably with a German?*

'There must be some mistake. It *can't* have been her!'

'Well, André said it was. He was pretty sure. And I thought you ought to know.'

Pedro nodded, but still in disbelief. 'If it *was* her, which I very much doubt, he might not be a German. And it isn't *that* unusual to be blond.'

'But it is to be so tall around here. And anyway, I'm sorry Pedro, but André saw the same boy again in town – in German uniform. I felt I'd better warn you, because I really fear there'll be reprisals, if we ever win this war, on girls who've been seen out with the enemy'.

Pedro's mind was reeling. So *that* was why Otilia had been so much happier and more helpful lately? It had nothing to do with simply 'growing up' Pedro realized, dreading having to tell Maria. Maybe, he decided, it was better not to. Only if Otilia refused to listen to him, and it needed two of them to make her see sense.

The whole idea of his daughter consorting with a German was utterly repellent – as was the sudden thought of her having a half-German baby. That would kill Maria, indeed them both. The shame would be unbearable.

He pushed away his coffee and got up, tossing some coins on the table.

'Sorry, we'll talk about this later. I think I'm about to be sick. But thanks for telling me. That's if it *was* Otilia, though I still can't believe that.'

'Good luck, my friend. You're probably going to need it. If there's anything I can do, let me know. After all, I owe you a huge favour. I can never thank you enough for saving my son from the Service Obligatoire.'

* * *

'What have you said to Otilia?' asked Juanita accusingly the next morning. 'She's been crying all night. And she wouldn't tell me why.'

'Something she needed to know. And that you *don't* need to know.'

'Why? She's my sister, and I don't like to see her crying.'

'Do you think *I* do?' asked Pedro, patting her hand. 'I simply told her something for her own good.'

He decided to change the subject, though worrying that Otilia might confide in her sister, and that Juanita would then blurt things out to Maria.

'Doing anything nice at school today?'

'Not nice enough to forget about Otilia,' Juanita replied, still wanting a proper answer.

Pedro sighed inwardly. If it were hard enough to have daughters at all, it was even more difficult in wartime. But he had never for a minute envisaged a crisis like this.

It was painful to see Otilia that evening, still looking so stricken, probably thinking she was in love, and being forced not to see her boyfriend again. She'd probably try to, Pedro knew. But hopefully, he told himself, if only to tell him what might happen to her when and if the war were ever over, if their relationship continued. If he knew that there might be severe reprisals for local girls consorting with the German occupiers, he might just back off.

Maybe, Pedro decided, if he could get his name out of Otilia or the postman, or someone in the Résistance, he could tell the boy himself.

And with luck, he thought to himself, his superiors might reprimand him – that's if they found out about the relationship. Surely they'd have some code about local behaviour? Or maybe not. They probably wouldn't give a damn about the fate of local girls.

* * *

Hans couldn't sleep. It wasn't the stifling hot night that was keeping him awake, or the pervading smell in the barracks – though both were bad enough – or even worries about his mother's house being bombed in Mannheim.

It was Otilia.

He thought back to the first time he had met her. He knew that he shouldn't have talked to her while on duty, let alone for so long. But he had to: she was so beautiful, so vital-looking, and so full of life. And he was certain that she was equally interested in him.

But now she had suddenly disappeared. For the last five Saturdays he had patrolled the bridge hoping to see her, but she had never turned up, although he always spotted her mother washing clothes below in the river. Somebody or something must have warned her off.

He thought back to that magical first kiss up the mountain road, six Saturdays ago, shortly after that yellow postal van had passed them. It seemed like years ago. Possibly someone who knew her had spotted them together and reported it to her parents – maybe even that postman – and she had been gated to her home.

It wasn't young people who created war, he thought to himself bitterly, it was much older ones – so unfair on the next generation who only wanted to live in peace, not interested in the land and riches they could plunder from other countries. Like most of his friends in the billet, he no longer really knew what the war was about other than enriching Germany and making it the world's most productive machine, as well as the most Aryan one in the world.

Suddenly there was a cough from the next-door bed.

'Rudi – are you awake?'

Silence.

Maybe a good thing, thought Hans. Despite Rudi being his best friend, he'd probably tell him he'd been a bloody fool getting involved with a local girl. It wasn't exactly forbidden, but certainly not encouraged.

And from today, he wouldn't even be patrolling the bridge any more, with new instructions to guard the main road coming into town instead, almost as if his Commanding Officer *knew* he had been consorting with a village girl while on duty.

* * *

'How's Sarah?' Pedro asked Carmen, on one of her rare nightime visits from the hills. He realized he hadn't enquired after her for a while.

'As safe as we can make her,' replied Carmen, 'though it isn't easy with those Gestapo creeps around. We have to keep moving her all the time to stay ahead of the game.'

'I can imagine.'

'And these days, you can't even trust the *locals*. They're getting on a bit too well with the Germans.'

Pedro flinched, thinking about Otilia. 'Don't tell me. Some of them in the café seem like real buddies with the Boches. Makes Alsonso and me feel quite sick at times, especially when people buy them drinks.'

'Of course,' Carmen continued, 'I can't tell you where Sarah actually is. The fact is, I don't know. Only that she's up in the woods. And from the latest reports, okay.'

'I understand.'

'And how's Otilia?'

'Better. But a big worry. I can't make her a prisoner, but I really fear for her if she sees that young German again.'

'Me, too. There'll probably be dreadful reprisals against local girls who consort with Germans; that's if this war ever ends in our favour.'

'Sssh!' said Pedro, suddenly putting his finger to his lips, noticing Maria at the sitting room door.

Carmen nodded. These days, she had to keep quiet about so many things that one more wasn't a burden. And if her mother ever guessed what might happen to Otilia if the war went in the Allies' favour, she knew she would immediately go to pieces. Even as it was, she was ageing too fast, looking greyer and more frail on the rare times Carmen returned home.

'Lovely seeing you,' said Maria, embracing her before wearily sitting down in an armchair. 'We've missed you.'

'Missed you, too.'

'And I'm really sorry you can't stay.'

'Me, too. But let's at least enjoy dinner and not talk about the damned war.'

Carmen got up from her chair. 'Shall I go and fetch Otilia?'

'If you would. Thanks. That's if she'll come down. She's terribly moody these days.'

Carmen was suddenly even more worried about her sister. The world at war was bad enough. Another war within a family would make things ten times worse.

* * *

'Had a good day?' Pedro was often irritated when Maria asked that when he got home, although knowing it was force of habit and always well-intentioned. But today her question was particularly annoying.

'The *last* thing it was,' he replied. 'I had a Milice guy snooping around the farm for hours. And he brought a huge and clearly very well-fed Alsatian dog. That *really* irritated me – probably where lots of our food is going. And he spent ages looking around Auguste's kitchen to see if I'd hidden anything there.'

'Had you?'

'Luckily, no. Anyway, as he was bending over to look in one of the cupboards, I had an overwhelming desire to hit him on the back of the head with an iron skillet. I think it was only the thought of the dog attacking me that stopped me.'

Maria was shocked. 'For God's sake, Pedro. You've got to keep calm or you'll put the whole lot of us in danger.'

'I know. I will. But it infuriates me that so many boys in the town have joined the Milice and are spying on their own people. God knows what their parents and neighbours must think, seeing them strut around like that in the Germans' pockets. The shame would *kill* me.'

'Me too,' said Maria. 'I can't understand why any of them *would* want to join.'

Pedro laughed bitterly. 'That's easy enough to work out. *Money*. And more of it than they'd get doing anything else. Juanita told me the other day that several boys in her form are openly talking about joining them as soon as they leave school, and far from being ashamed, they're actually *crowing* about it.'

Maria sighed as she bent down to pick up the basket he'd brought home. To her dismay it was swedes yet again – what used to be given to only starving cattle before the war. 'Oh, Pedro, I can't *bear* it. Not *more* swedes. Is that all you've got?'

'Sorry, it's pretty well all I dared get with that wretched snoop there.'

Maria shook her head. 'Otilia will *kill* us.'

'No, she won't.' Pedro rummaged around in his coat pocket, and brought out a bag of strawberries. 'These'll keep her happy!'

* * *

'You okay?' Pedro had walked into the kitchen to see Juanita chewing on a pencil, obviously struggling with her homework.

'No,' said Juanita, looking up. 'I can't think what to say. And I've got to do this before tomorrow morning.'

Pedro picked up the sheet of paper in front of her, instantly disgusted. On top of the page were the words; 'TEN REASONS I LOVE PETAIN', with the numbers one to ten below, with lines to fill in.

'I think I can help you with that,' he said.

'But you *don't* love Pétain,' replied Juanita.

'No, I certainly don't, but I can still think of something.'

'And hopefully fast,' chipped in Maria. 'Supper's almost ready.'

For once, Pedro was vaguely irritated by his wife, now getting so like the French. Everything seemed to revolve around food, mostly paltry as it was. He decided not to complain, looking at the homework again.

'A PRIZE FOR THE BEST ENTRY – A STATUETTE OF PETAIN FOR YOU TO KEEP!'

Pedro knew his daughter wouldn't win that, but his contribution would at least keep her out of trouble. 'Here, give me that pencil.'

Ten minutes later he had completed the ten reasons, by now rather proud of himself, although wishing that Maria would also see the funny side of his answers as Juanita read them out, or even understood them dictated in French.

'1. Because I rather like his fantastic moustache 2. Because we get sweets on his birthday. 3.Because he looks like a grandfather I never met, because both of them died before I was born. 4. Because he won in the last war. 5. Because we get a 'Petain Day' off school every year. 6. Because he's easy to draw. 7. Because we're not Jews. 8. Because he's not General Franco. 9. Because he wears a nice uniform. 10. Because this is easy homework.'

'Right.' Pedro looked up at Maria. 'Homework finished!'

'And dinner coming up,' smiled Maria, stirring a large casserole.

Pedro winked at Otilia. 'Happy with that?'

Otilia giggled. 'It's absolutely brilliant! And do you want to hear my war poem? It's tomorrow night's homework but I thought I'd get it done. It's only short, Mamá.'

'Fine, go ahead.' Maria sighed inwardly, knowing it would be in French again.

'The bombs are falling, it's all appalling,
and all the men in the danger zone
all want to go home, all want to go home.
The German horses, the Allied forces
all fighting, lots dying in this terrible war,
with all of us asking, with all of us asking
what's it about, and what's it all for?
A war never-ending, a war with no glory.
And that is the end of my sad poem story.'

Pedro was suddenly as depressed as he was impressed, seeing the war through the eyes of a child, but decided to hide that.

'It's wonderful, Juanita! Really good. Goodness, a poet in the family as well as an artist! Well, I never!'

TWENTY-EIGHT

* * *

'TAKE CARE, AND I DON'T WANT YOU BACK TOO LATE. *NO LATER THAN eight-thirty.* Do you hear me?'

Juanita groaned. 'Oh Mamá, you worry too much! I'll be fine. *Honestly.*'

Maria was not so sure she *would* be fine. Lately, her youngest daughter had made a regular habit of joining her school-friends in the slightly rough Pradet area of town in the early evening. And Maria was afraid of what she was hearing, not from Juanita, but from Gabriella who had come round to warn her, as had other mothers in the town.

Apparently the kids listened surreptitiously to American swing music on prohibited radios, humming along with it, and frequently talked about the mysterious Allies over the Channel who would one day come to liberate them. There was a bit of flirtation, Juanita readily admitted, but she reassured her mother that it was all quite harmless.

Maria remained wary. Like other mothers in town, she greatly feared there would be young Milice working in the crowd, ready to report even former school-friends – and particularly if they were heard denouncing Pétain or laughing about him.

Only a week before, her daughter had told her about an alarming incident at school. Apparently, the pupils had been forced to sing Pétain's song for his birthday and learn extracts from his speeches off by heart. But when the teacher was absent, three girls, with the tacit approval of their classmates, had torn up Pétain's portrait looming over them in the classroom, then stamped on it and thrown it into an old stove. A little American flag had then been placed where the portrait had been.

Returning to the classroom, the teacher had exploded in incandescent fury and gone off to fetch his sinister colleague, a part-time member of the Milice – a man called Daudet. Three girls were then suspended from the school for eight days. 'My friends Monique, Janine and Suzette!' Juanita had told her mother proudly.

'Well, that's all very funny. But you listen to me, Juanita. *They're all French*. Please make sure you do nothing *ever* to draw attention to yourself. You'd put our whole family in danger if you do. Pétain and Vichy regard us all of us Spanish as dangerous Communists and the slightest thing could get us all into trouble. *Do you hear me?*' she asked again.

* * *

Sarah was watching Alexandre carve a little Scops owl out of wood by the light of an oil lamp, the bird whose constant 'peep, peep' she used to fear at night. Now she was no longer afraid of it – thinking it might be imitated by the Milice as a signal – and was fascinated by Alexandre's patience and skill.

'Wherever did you learn to carve like that?'

'My father taught me. I've got lots of things I carved at home. Probably all in the attic by now. My mother was always complaining they were cluttering up the place.'

'That's a shame,' said Sarah, watching him polishing the little figurine with a rag soaked in olive oil and turning it round to inspect his handiwork. 'That's if they were as good as that one is. You could easily be a professional carver.'

'Probably, but I'd rather keep it as a hobby. What I *really* want to do is something in maths. That was the only thing I was really good at in school. It was my dream to study it at university before the war broke out, and then be a maths teacher.'

'It could still be your dream.'

'It is, but my dream right now is just to escape going to Germany to work and then getting bombed.'

Sarah watched him for a while, wondering if she could ask him about something he'd mentioned once or twice but had never explained, suddenly plucking up the courage.

'Alexandre, what made your parents so anti-Semitic?'

He shook his head. 'I don't really know. Just ignorance, if you ask me. They don't even *know* any Jews. There aren't any in Hippo, or at least none that I know of. Your family was probably the first Jewish one to settle there. And from what little I know about Jews, I don't think you're farming types. But I'm probably wrong.'

'No, you're right.' said Sarah. 'We were never allowed to stay anywhere long enough to farm, always being moved on, shunted off somewhere else. And in most countries we were only allowed to be tailors or money-lenders. Also it's very difficult to live on a farm out of town if you're at all Orthodox, because you have to walk to a synagogue. You're not allowed to use a car on the Sabbath. That's why we're mostly city people.'

'But coming back to my parents,' said Alexandre, 'I think the real reason they don't like Jews is a form of jealousy. They see you as being too clever by half, too successful, taking things over – oh, and sticking together too much.'

Sarah laughed bitterly. 'All stories I've heard before.'

'Well, not ones *I* believe in.'

'I know, thank God.'

'Here.' He handed her the polished figurine. 'I'm a bit wiser than my parents, especially since knowing you.'

'Like this owl,' she smiled, holding it up to the light.

Alexandre chuckled. 'Perhaps not *that* wise!'

The oil lamp suddenly spluttered out leaving them in total darkness.

'Damn,' said Alexandre. 'That's the last of the oil.' He felt for her hand. 'Well, nothing for it but to turn in.'

'I don't mind.'

Alexandre laughed, pulling her up from her chair. 'Neither do I.'

'Are you awake?' asked Alexandre, five hours later, feeling Sarah stir beside him.

'Yes.'

'Something's worrying me a bit. In fact, a lot.'

'What?'

'Do you think I should have joined the Résistance, rather than just gone into hiding?'

'No,' said Sarah. 'You can't *all* join the Résistance, there aren't nearly enough guns to go round from what's Carmen's told me. And on top of that, I don't really see you as the killing type. Any more than I am.'

Once again she remembered watching Gendarme Bollon falling to his death from that bridge – something she had never told Alexandre about, and probably never would, even when he woke her from nightmares and asked her what she'd been dreaming about.

'Anyway,' she continued, 'far more people are hiding rather than actively resisting. Most are just trying to avoid the S.T.O. like you. You're in the vast majority, not the minority.'

'Well, if you ever think I *should* do something more active, I'd like you to tell me, and tell me at once. Promise me you will. I'd hate you to lose your respect for me.'

'I promise,' said Sarah squeezing his hand.

'But you're hardly a coward sleeping with a Jew, specially after what you told me about your parents.'

* * *

It was the autumn in the forests of the Cévennes, and although the days were warm, at night it was beginning to feel chilly. The Spanish maquis group moved often, keeping deep in the thickly-wooded mountains and getting their information from trusted scouts sent into the valley.

One morning Alvaro suddenly arrived with a small party of strangers. They turned out to be British, led by a tall young man with fair hair. Carmen at once recognized him from a few months ago – 'Felix'. He had several men with him, all very tough-looking. Everyone gathered round, and Alvaro spoke in French. 'I'm here with a message from Cristino Garcia.'

He turned to the tall man. 'You may remember this British officer, with the code-name 'Felix'. He visited us before and brought those weapons for us to practise with. He's been in the hills with the other groups for many weeks now.' He pointed at the other men. 'He's brought eight parachutists, some French, some British – and also a lot of weapons and explosives, some of which we've already distributed to other groups. Cristino's also said that 'Felix' will be in charge of us for a while.'

The tall British officer stepped forward. 'Good morning, gentlemen. And, I see, ladies!' He had immediately noticed Carmen – and another girl, Clara, on the edge of the group.

'You may remember me. I'm called 'Felix', a Captain attached to our Special Operations Executive,' he announced in surprisingly good French.

'We've heard that you Spanish are a highly-active and dedicated group. Your colleagues down in Saint-Hippolyte were also very helpful in getting so many of our soldiers and airmen back to England. One was a good friend of mine, by the way, and I'm glad to tell you he's now flying again.

I can also tell you things are going to start happening that will make you and your efforts ever more important. A few days ago I flew in from Italy with eight other men in two big bombers. We parachuted down north of Le Vigan and brought several containers of weapons and explosives.'

There was an appreciative stir in his audience.

'We've brought quite a few Brens, some Stens, Lee-Enfield rifles, PIAT anti-tank launchers and lots of demolition charges for blowing bridges and railways. We've given some of them to the other groups further west, but we've enough for you to increase your firepower a lot. It's all in a barn down in the valley, so I'm afraid we'll have to haul it up here. That'll be a hell of a job, but we absolutely can't risk a vehicle.

Within a few months the Allies will invade, and *that's* when we need to disrupt the Germans. In the meantime, you'll need to train on these weapons and without the Germans and Milice detecting you. I know people have said this before, but it's vital not to go off at half-cock, as we say. Attacking the Germans or the Milice too early is pointless, actually suicidal and really dangerous for the locals. The Germans are still too strong for us to start having pitched battles with them. It's when they're wrong-footed by invasion and over-stretched that our work should begin.'

Suddenly a small thin-faced man interrupted. It was Felipe Gonzalez, speaking with deliberate rudeness in Spanish.

'Alvaro, why are we being saddled with this foreigner? For God's sake, he doesn't even speak Spanish!'

'Felipe,' Alvaro shot back, 'Cristino was very specific and said he has his reasons. And one in particular – getting more and better training.' He turned and explained to 'Felix' in French, who nodded and stared hard at Gonzalez. Nobody really liked Felipe much, and some of them had questioned whether he'd really been a Sergeant as he claimed. And they knew they certainly didn't want *him* in charge.

After some discussion, the group sat down to eat. The British officer came up to Carmen, obviously curious about her role. 'And what do *you* do around here?'

'I'm a Number One on a Bren gun.'

The young officer looked astonished.

'At least, I *will* be,' she continued. 'We've only had that one Bren to practise with, and, as you taught us, we've only been allowed to fire single shots in case we alert the enemy. Just once, a burst or two. But I know the two 'IAs' well enough.'

She held out her hand, and he shook it warmly. 'By the way, I'm Carmen.'

He sat down beside her. 'I'm Felix. I'm sorry,' he said to her, 'that I can't use my real name yet. And I didn't realize girls could be fighters. Most of the ones I've met in the woods just do the cooking and laundry or message carrying, useful though that is.'

'Not for me!' laughed Carmen.

She explained to him why she had wanted to actually *fight*, rather than just leaving it to others, and why she felt so strongly about the 'Fascists', as she called them.

Clara brought them tin mugs of hot soup that she'd brewed up, and they sat together talking while Carmen described the terrible last few days in Spain five years before, to which he listened with rapt attention. She also mentioned how Sarah's parents had been treated in France, but instinct stopped her from describing Gendarme Bollon's fate on the Sauve bridge. Nor, suddenly, did she feel like discussing Pierre.

'Felix' did not explain his life, but he *did* describe how his colleagues had flown from a base in Italy in two four-engined Lancasters. 'And after they parachuted in, I took them to meet several maquis groups to the west of you, and gave them arms and explosives. But I wanted to meet your Spanish group and get to Saint-Hippolyte. That's from where my pilot friend escaped.'

He suddenly chuckled. 'Our operation's called 'Snow White' for some reason. But we've got *eight* men, and *none* of them are dwarves!'

Carmen found this young man very attractive. He laughed a lot and somehow made the telling of even very serious things amusing, and she was disappointed when he had to get up and crisply start instructing the members of her group about their future roles. But she listened carefully, especially when he stressed yet again that any premature action against the Germans might be worse than useless.

'It may well bring reprisals against the local population and draw attention to our presence. Our job is to wait *unseen*, to train and practise and to be ready to support the invasion when it comes. I can't tell you when and where that might be. In fact, I don't know, but I'm pretty sure it won't be much longer now.' He got to his feet.

'Okay, everyone, let's get to work!'

TWENTY-NINE

* * *

'**T**HIS IS INTOLERABLE!'

The meeting held on the 5th of February in the Gauleiter's office in the Kommandatur in Nîmes promised to be stormy.

'You mean to tell me that a handful of these Résistants broke into *your* prison, undetected, *and* in a way you can't explain? And that they freed *twenty-three* prisoners, and really important ones? And as they all left, you say you might *just* have wounded one of them?'

The Governor of the prison had stopped trying to explain. He simply nodded glumly.

The Gauleiter sat back in his chair, red-faced with anger and frustration.

'Meinen Herren, in this region we now have a situation getting completely out of control. The hills are swarming with men avoiding work in Germany. And they're backed by the Résistance – indeed many are joining it. We know that they've already got weapons, and we've also got evidence that more arms and explosives are being parachuted in by the British. We need to nip this whole thing in the bud.'

He turned to General Bittrich.

'I think you should plan a sweep through the whole area, but especially into the rat's nest of the Cévennes. I can trust *only* the SS to be vigorous enough.'

Bittrich nodded, 'Zum befehl! I started planning two days ago.'

* * *

On the night of 27th of February 1944, the prediction by the British Captain 'Felix' that 'things were going to hot up' came tragically true, but it was not the long-awaited invasion by the Allies – but a lightning and unexpected move by the Germans. At three in the morning, the inhabitants of Saint-Hippolyte heard the rumbling of vehicles, but thought it was German 'manoeuvres'. It was not until daylight that they could see what was happening, and when they did it was with considerable shock.

It was the dreaded SS that had arrived. Very different from the easy-going soldiers of the regular German regiment in the Fort, these new hard-faced men had absolutely no reason to get on well with the local population. In fact, if people had known of their brutal record in Russia they would have been even more afraid.

Part of the 9th SS Panzer Division, named *'Hohenstaufen'*, they quickly set up roadblocks and installed their headquarters in the large Château de Planque, an ancient building just by the railway viaduct, and it soon became obvious that their purpose was to hunt down the evaders of the STO and their Résistance helpers. Columns of vehicles had already spread out right through the countryside as far as Lasalle to the north and Valleraugue to the west. But the very large force that was used indicated that they had almost certainly over-estimated the number of STO evaders and both the numbers and arms of the Résistance.

Early in the morning at Driolle, they *did* succeed in surprising a handful of STO evaders, capturing them and bringing them back to the Château. But at a farmhouse near Colognac, they apparently missed the maquisards of Lasalle by two days. In fury, they then turned on a young local, Fernand Soulier, whom they had bullied into guiding them, and shot him in the back of the head.

Carmen's group had been very lucky. An alert sentry posted on a nearby hill had seen and heard the unusual vehicles in the valley below, and they had abandoned their camp just in time to go up deeper up into the hills behind them.

The SS had ended up only capturing half a dozen prisoners, now imprisoned in the Château. It seemed a rather pathetic return for the huge efforts of an élite Panzer Division, so the officers now decided to make a public example of those avoiding working in Germany.

Roger Broussoux, only twenty years old, a simple youth who had been tending goats at Le Driolle, was asked by the SS troopers why he was not working in Germany. He had apparently said, and very bravely though foolishly, 'I would rather live and die here in France'.

The cynical retort from the SS officer, clearly heard by onlookers, was horrifying. 'CHOOSE YOUR TREE!'

In fact, instead of a tree, the SS decided to put a rope around his neck and hang him from the railway viaduct in full view of the appalled townspeople.

One horrified onlooker was Madame Ordinez, dragged up to a window of the château with her head yanked up by a German so she was cruelly forced to look up and watch the hanging. Even worse, her husband and son were among the prisoners, so she was almost certainly terrified that they would later suffer the same fate.

And there Roger Broussoux swung, hanging pitifully from the viaduct for all to see until the SS had gone – two long days later.

Worse, the day he was murdered was full of other horrors. Two men were shot in the street – almost casually. And one of them was deaf, and shot in the back for failing to obey the German orders to stop that he had not even been able to hear.

The Casales family was also caught up in the horrific events of those few hours.

Two cars full of maquisards had driven into town without realizing that the SS had arrived there. In a fire-fight, several were killed, but some of the wounded escaped and were quickly hidden in local houses. The SS promptly conducted a rigorous search but found nothing. Then, in their frustration, they forced most of the locals to parade in the Place de la Canourge at gunpoint, with the men separated from the women and children.

At that critical point, Juanita nearly caused a massacre.

The little girl suddenly saw her father among the group of men and tried to run to him, 'Papa!' Instinctively her mother leapt forward and cried out to stop her. But instead of her name, Maria screamed out her nickname.

'Liberté!'

The SS swung their guns towards the group, who had appeared to shout out in defiance. Only the lightning action of the Mayor, Albert Monpeyssen, succeeded in calming the situation. He explained the nickname quickly to the Germans, avoiding another tragedy.

A shocked and sullen crowd finally dispersed to their houses. Early the next morning the SS left – a long column, heading east, and loaded with booty. It was only a couple of days later that the townspeople heard with horror that all the seventeen prisoners had been hung in Nîmes – guilty of nothing. These included two of the desperately wounded maquisards from St Hippolyte, who had been successfully smuggled to hospital in Nîmes, but then betrayed – and worse, by French collaborators.

It was all too much for Pedro. That night, he talked to Alfonso late into the night.

'I know I always said I'd never go back to fighting after Spain. But this is *too* much. Here I am, about the only trained and experienced infantry officer around, and I'm doing nothing. If the Résistance is going to start relying on people like my own daughter to try and win fire-fights with the Germans, I just can't stand back and do nothing any more. But first I had to talk to you. What worries me is Maria, and how she'll get through it without me. And how you'll cope with her if I go.'

* * *

As expected, Maria had put up fierce resistance to the idea of Pedro leaving and joining up, and the ironic thought went through his head that this was in many ways worse than any battle he might face in the Résistance itself.

'But you *can't* just leave us and go off into the mountains, and so far away! And what if anything happened to you? Pedro, *honestly*, you seem to be forgetting I've gone through all this before in Spain, and that was horrific enough. I just can't be expected to go through it all over again. In fact, I can't *believe* you'd ask me to!'

'Look, Maria. I was a Captain in the army back in Spain. Here, they simply don't have enough properly-trained men like me. And if I don't do anything, after what we've just seen from the SS Fascists, I won't be able to live with myself.'

'But how am I supposed to live without *you*? I still get completely lost when people jabber away in French, and with that local accent. And I don't even understand the children half the time. And I need you here to control Otilia. These days she hardly ever does anything I tell her to do.

She only does when *you're* here to back me up. And how are we even going to *eat* without you at the farm? We get little enough as it is.'

'Alfonso will help you. I've talked to him.'

'So you've talked to him before even talking to me? I can't believe you'd do that behind my back!'

'I had to, to be sure he could help you. Bring you food and things, and look after you all.'

Pedro saw that she was about to cry, but he knew he had to persevere.

'I'm really, really sorry, cara, but my mind's made up. It hasn't been an easy decision, I can tell you. But I know deep down it's the right thing to do. The honourable thing.'

'For you maybe, not for me.'

The tears suddenly came, and Pedro took her in his arms knowing there was nothing he could do or say to comfort her, but hugely relieved that Alfonso had supported him and would be there for *her* support. Of course, if it weren't for Alfonso, he knew that he could never have joined up.

Alfonso had promised to look after Maria as much as he could, but with both of them knowing that it would be far from easy if she didn't improve her French and mix more with the locals. She had never really recovered from her panic attack in the market when Pedro had left her alone at the stall, and was clearly afraid of her daughters assimilating when she couldn't.

'I'm sure she'll be alright,' were Alfonso's last words as they went upstairs to bed, although he had strong doubts that she would be.

That would be *his* battle, but one he was fully prepared to take on, hoping that one day the French would actually *realize* what the Spanish were doing to help them, not least the maquisards' wives who had been left behind. All the talk was of the *French* Résistance, he thought ruefully, as if the Spanish were doing absolutely nothing.

* * *

'GET OUT, GET OUT OF HERE, NOW!' Captain Felix had burst into the house.

'*Take anything you can, but you've only got five minutes.*'

His comrades stared at him with incredulity.

'NOW!' he repeated.

They scrambled up the hillside for about three hundred metres and lay down behind the rocks. There they unslung their rifles, and Carmen and Sebastian flattened themselves behind the Bren.

Half an hour passed, and some of the group became restless.

'Wait,' whispered Felix, looking down through his field glasses at the little stone house, its chimney still smoking. Suddenly he saw them. Dozens of grey figures converging on the house. There was a burst of firing and then silence. Then a small group advanced, and he could just make out the stick grenades they were obviously preparing to throw. But with continual silence from the house, they paused. Eventually a group of three rushed forward and kicked in the door. After a while the rest followed, presumably to search inside. Eventually, an officer emerged and slowly scanned the hillsides with binoculars. He then went back in, and soon he could see that the building was on fire.

The German officer came out and looked around again, then led his men off down the hillside, all moving cautiously and well spaced out. They had obviously realized that they'd lost any element of surprise, and were now in danger themselves from a possible ambush in the woods.

'Let's wait here for a while,' said Felix, 'and then give them time to get well away.'

After half an hour, he got up and walked over to where Felipe Gonzalez was sitting smoking.

'Eres un cabron, Felipe! UN TRIADOR!'

Carmen and everybody else were astonished that he had suddenly spoken in excellent Spanish. 'You're faithless, Felipe! A traitor!' And then shocked to the core by what he did next.

He drew his revolver, cocked it and calmly shot Felipe in the chest, then shot him again as he toppled backwards.

He turned to the wide-eyed and open-mouthed group, his revolver still smoking in his hand, and continued to speak in Spanish.

'I know you think I've just done something terrible, but let me explain. I've been suspicious of someone here for days. The Milice and the Germans seemed to know far too much about our movements. So I asked two of you, and only *you* know who you are, to watch out. And you saw Felipe down on the road talking to a Milice Sergeant and pointing up at the hills to the house. Only I and Felipe knew which safe house we'd use today.

I repeat, *only* me and him. So Felipe was *clearly* the traitor. There's no doubt about it. None at all.'

And we don't have time for trials, and I couldn't ask you lot to make up a firing squad to shoot a Spanish comrade. So *that's* why I did it. I *had* to. There was no choice. It was either him – or all of us.'

He looked at his stunned group. 'Anyway, we'll have to go further up the valley in a minute.'

As they muttered among themselves, he went and sat down next to Carmen and lit a cigarette. Only she could see that his hand was shaking.

She didn't ask about Felipe Gonzalez. She already had her own strong suspicions, but questions too. 'Where on earth did you learn to speak Spanish like that?'

'Cacarés.'

'Yes, but why? How?'

'Well, first of all Carmen, you should know I'm not actually English. I'm Irish. Never mind the 'Felix' code-name. My real name's Sean O'Neill.'

Carmen was puzzled, not really understanding about foreign names. But one thing she *did* know was that Cacarés, in the west of Spain, had been behind Nationalist lines from almost the very start of the Civil War.

'I'll have to explain later. It's a long story, and right now we've got to get moving. I don't trust those Germans not to come back. I'll talk to you when I can.'

He got to his feet. 'And Carmen, I'm sorry you had to see that.'

* * *

Many hours later, Carmen and 'Felix' were sitting in the dark together, some way from the others, and he at last had time to explain.

'You'll understand in a moment why I didn't reveal I spoke Spanish, and why I'm familiar with Spain. One reason, of course, was to do with what you just saw. It was helpful to let the others talk in Spanish, thinking I didn't understand it. However, the other reason's related to *you*. At least, your country.'

Carmen began to feel nervous.

He continued, 'My name is actually Sean O'Neill, I'm Irish, not English. Well, half-Irish because my father's Belgian, from Charleroi, hence my proficiency with French. Like many others, including some

Germans, my father was recruited by the Irish government to work on engineering projects when the British left. That's the first thing.

Next thing; when your civil war started and all those priests and nuns were murdered, there was a huge movement in Ireland to intervene. It was the Catholic Church, of course, that was behind it, led by a Cardinal Macrory. They were approached by the pretty extreme Catholic Spanish Carlists for help in what was called an 'Anti-Red Crusade'. And then a politician called Eoin O'Duffy – a hero of our war against the British – volunteered to take a force of fighters to Spain.

Because of my mother, I was a fervent Catholic then, but very young. And every day my mother went on and on saying 'something should be done'. Then, there were loads of recruiting advertisements in the papers. So, without telling my parents, I sneaked off and volunteered. O'Duffy actually raised seven thousand men, but the Irish government was dead against the whole thing, especially as it would annoy the British who were trying to enforce *non*-intervention in Spain. But O'Duffy *did* get seven hundred men together and we ended up with a whole lot of priests and people singing hymns on the dock at a place called Galway. And then we sailed off and went to Ferrol on a German ship that O'Duffy had chartered. I'd left a goodbye letter behind, and I later discovered – with some pain – that my mother was incredibly upset I'd taken her so literally.'

'So *that's* why you went to Spain?'

'Yes. And in Cacarés, we were attached, as the Fifteenth Bandera, to the Spanish Foreign Legion, whose boss unfortunately *loathed* O'Duffy on sight, which didn't help. We trained there and I made sure I learned Spanish. Most of the others seemed to have joined just to avoid the Depression and unemployment back in Ireland. And they made a real nuisance of themselves, constantly complaining about the food and *always* getting drunk. So the people in Cacarés didn't like us much either.

Then the only fight we got into turned into a bloody farce. At the battle of the Jarama, some new Nationalist troops from the Canary Islands mistook our uniforms for Republicans, so we even had an hour's battle with our *own* side, for God's sake! Four of our lot were killed. Then, O'Duffy – who used to be a good commander – took to the drink, I'm afraid.

By then Franco was winning and had the Carlists firmly on his side, so he didn't really need us nuisance Irish any more. So we were shipped off home. You won't understand this in English, but we lost so much respect for O'Duffy that we began to call him 'O'Scruffy or 'Old John Bollocks'. A typical *Irish* war, I'd say.' He laughed rather bitterly.

'Anyway, I didn't kill anybody on *your* side. I wanted you to know that.'

Carmen didn't know what to say, except to mutter a 'thank you'.

'Then I *did* join a proper army, the British Army. It was after Dunkirk. Many of my Irish friends had been killed, or else captured at Boulogne, and I felt I had to do something. So I went up to Belfast and enlisted. Because of my languages, they put me in the Intelligence Corps. And because I seemed to know something about soldiering, eventually I became an officer. The Special Operations Executive, the S.O.E., was advertising for volunteers and I met a fellow called Peter Kemp who'd been very involved with Spain. After my S.O.E. training, parachuting and everything, I hung about for months getting a bit bored, until they began to realize how valuable the Spanish Republican fighters here could be. So they sent me off to find out. And that's why I'm here.'

Carmen knew she'd have to think about these startling revelations, some of which she really didn't understand, and her shock that he had once been on the hated *other* side in Spain was mixed with her affection for him.

She decided to sleep on it before coming to any conclusions.

* * *

'You amaze me, Carmen. You're not like any other girl I've ever met.' Sean shook his head, studying her. 'More like a man in some ways.'

Carmen laughed. 'Oh dear! That doesn't sound much of a compliment!'

'It's meant to be.'

She and Sean were in a hut up in the mountains, talking late at night when everyone else had turned in.

He looked at her again in the dim lamplight, so female with her long black hair, full lips and curvaceous figure, but with so many attributes he'd never come across in a woman before. Seemingly able to take anything in her stride, and not just the rigorous training, even keeping her end up in a comradely way when the men were being pretty vulgar, which they often were. And not for the first time did he wonder how she could carry and work the heavy Bren so well, and how she could – almost miraculously in his eyes – somehow hold on to her femininity in such a deeply male environment, where sweat, stink and deprivation were the norm.

'Carmen, what made you *really* join the Résistance? It's very strange for a girl to want to fight. Your parents surely can't have liked the idea. In fact, I'm amazed that they ever allowed you to come here. They must have known you'd be thrown in with a whole lot of men, so you'd probably be facing a lot more difficult situations than just war ones. It's hard to see any parents of daughters accepting that.'

Carmen thought for a while.

'I guess it was my friend Sarah – you know, the Jewish girl I told you about – the one whose parents were dragged away. I couldn't just sit back and do nothing while that kind of thing was going on, and anyway, I guess I'm a bit different from most girls. For instance, I've known for ages that I'd never become a typical Spanish housewife like my mother, always stuck in the kitchen and pandering to men.

And on top of that, I think the world's changing. I'm sure that after this war, if it ever ends, there'll be a whole lot more girls like me. Ones who'll want to be more equal with men. And I'm not that tough. I even know two girls who are brave enough to *sleep* with the Milice, to get information out of them, even though if the war ends in our favour, there might be terrible reprisals for them from people who don't know any better. You may think *I'm* tough, but they're a hell of a lot tougher. That's a job I could never have done in a million years.'

'But do you ever think of, well, female things like getting married, having children – that sort of thing?'

Carmen smiled, 'Not often, and certainly not now. Probably one day. To be honest, I really don't know what I think, except I'm glad I joined up.'

'Me, too.'

Carmen paused for a moment, aware that he was certainly showing more than a flicker of interest in her.

'You know I have a boyfriend, don't you?'

'Yes, you told me about him the other day. A farmer.'

'And if he knew I was up here, he'd be horrified. And being with a whole lot of men, with only one other girl.'

'But surely he'd admire your guts.'

'Probably, but he'd still be pretty disturbed. He'd think the whole thing was most strange, very un-female.'

Sean tried to picture Carmen's boyfriend – clearly a lot more traditional and strait-laced than himself – and not seeing him as a match for Carmen at all, but at the same time respecting her loyalty.

'Well, it's a pity you've got a boyfriend. Because I have to admit that I volunteered specially for this mission. And it wasn't entirely about being grateful for the help with 'Détachement W'. To be honest, I wanted to see you again.'

Carmen was glad that the darkness would hide her blush.

He patted her on the shoulder. 'Well, I guess we'd better turn in. Big day tomorrow.'

THIRTY

* * *

OBERGRUPPENFÜHRER WILHELM BITTRICH WAS NOT A VERY PATIENT man at the best of times – even for an SS General. And now he was incandescent.

'Unmoeglich! Impossible! I send three thousand of you into that rat's nest of the Cévennes, and what have you got to show for it?'

His officers, standing to attention – all hardened men – quailed from his enraged voice.

'You shot a few people, hardly any of them really Résistants, and one who was wandering along who turned out to be deaf and couldn't even *hear* you. *And* you hung a harmless goat-herd. And I know you stole a whole lot of stuff, not for the Reich, but for yourselves. And you then bring back a *tiny* handful of prisoners to hang. Frankly, it was hardly worth the precious fuel you used up.

I'll remind you that this division was created from two of the finest in the Waffen SS – *Leibstandarte* – the oldest and Hitler's original bodyguard, and *Das Reich*, my own division and the one I was once proud to lead. You've had a good rest here in the south. I just hope that when the Allies come, *and* they will, you and your men will do a more efficient job.

And another thing. Without orders from me, in Nîmes you hung the people you brought back, while knowing that hardly any of them were Résistance fighters. So all you've done is create a whole bunch of martyrs. It's just stupid! The next time there will be Court Martials in the field.'

He paused, his anger seemed to abate, and he smiled.

'At ease!' He moved to his desk.

'Meinen Herren, let's put this ridiculous little incident behind us. We've received urgent orders to go back to the Ukraine, and quickly. We've got troops trapped in Ternopol, and, as usual, it's our job to rescue them. And with *proper* SS fighting.

By the way, Transport Officers, please remember *before* you put the vehicles on the trains, to fill their engines with the right anti-freeze levels for Russia and *not* for France. I don't want any more engine blocks cracked by frost. *That* will be a Court Martial offence.

Dismiss!'

* * *

'Good work, you two!' Gendarme Bouisseau was sitting at this desk in the Préfecture, the local police headquarters in Saint Hippolyte, looking at two of his brightest young recruits across his desk – Corine Leboyer and Julie Lafont – both only eighteen but unusually level-headed for their years. He knew, looking at them with admiration, that if he had ever had daughters, he would have hated them being involved in such dangerous work.

'Not just good work, *excellent* work,' he continued. 'We managed to evacuate that safe house just in time – with only hours to go. Ten good men saved. Well done!'

Corine and Julie smiled at their boss, a man in his forties. It was always good to hear that their efforts had paid off, in fact the only part of the job they enjoyed, even though they were proud to be doing it. Most of the rest of it was risky, dangerous, and at worst highly degrading – having to cultivate relationships with the Milice to extort information from them, and at worst have sex with them in order to do so. Working in the Préfecture gave them a certain respectability among the very few who knew their role and an excellent cover, but the job certainly came with extreme downsides. And both knew that if the war ever ended in the Allies' favour, there could well be reprisals against girls known for having consorted with Milice men, and also at times Germans when necessary, by people who had no idea of their secret job.

Bouisseau studied them for a moment: Corine, with her slight build and attractively gamine face, and Julie, with her unruly black hair now tied up in a topknot. They were clearly pleased that their efforts had paid off again – and deservedly. Three safe houses had been moved on in as many weeks thanks to their information.

'How are the relationships with your partners going?' It was something he hated asking, but was compelled to do for their safety.

'I don't think mine suspects anything,' said Julie. 'He just thinks I've got a boring secretarial job with the police, and I'm doing my best to keep it that way. I simply tell him I spend all day typing and filing, and then say I'd rather hear what *he's* been up to. He usually complies – the sort to enjoy talking about himself.'

'Good. Keep it that way. And if the relationship becomes too difficult for you, report to me at once.'

Julie nodded.

'And you, Corine? How's it going with *your* partner?'

'Well, from a work point of view, really well. Like Julie's target, he's a talker, and I'm certain he hasn't cottoned on. Although, like her, I find the rest of it a nightmare.'

Bouisseau nodded. 'Tell me immediately if it becomes too much. That goes for both of you. There's only a limited time that any young girl can do this job without breaking. And I need to know at once before you reach that point, to give you further instructions – not least on how to exit your relationships safely. Do you hear me?'

Both girls nodded.

'Good', said Bouisseau. 'And now I think I'll reward you with a decent cup of coffee for once, not that awful chicory stuff. My wife found an old pack of real coffee beans in our kitchen this morning, and I told her that two of my staff really deserved it more than us.'

With their coffee finished, both girls knew what was coming next. By now they were used to it, and knew the rigmarole off by heart.

'Finally,' said Bouisseau, 'may I ask you to recite the ten golden rules? I know it's boring for you to do it again, but they're essential for your safety. Please repeat them to me in turn.'

'One,' said Corine, 'never push for information. Instead, allow it to come out.'

'Two,' continued Julie, 'never touch alcohol. But turn a blind eye if the Milice do.

'Three,' Corine took over, 'flatter, but only believably.'

'Four,' Julie followed, 'never speak to anyone of our real work except you. Only talk of our general police duties.'

'Five,' they both chimed in together, 'if we have any suspicion whatsoever that our partners suspect us, report to you at once.'

'Six,' Julie followed again, 'appear to be great supporters of Pétain. Say flattering things about him at every opportunity, but only if we sound entirely believable.'

Bouisseau listened with pleasure, unable not to congratulate himself for choosing these recruits and the strict training he had given them.

'Seven, never drop our guard, even when at home with our families and with those we most trust.'

'Eight,' said Julie, suddenly forgetting to her horror what Rule Eight was.

Her friend came to the rescue. 'Inform you at any time, day or night, if we feel we can't go on for whatever reason.'

'Nine,' followed Julie, relieved she had not been reprimanded for forgetting Rule Eight. 'Never ever have unprotected sex.'

'And ten,' they both said in unison, 'never ever take any paperwork out of this building.'

'Well done!' smiled Bouisseau, again mentally patting himself on the back for hiring them. 'I'm proud of you both. More coffee, either of you?'

He paused for a moment.

'Incidentally, I feel I need to say something else; something I've said many times before, but probably not forcibly enough. If this wretched war goes in our favour, there could be terrible reprisals against women people see as collaborators, *collaboratrices horizonales*, as they're called. Or even *field mattresses*. I just hope I can protect you if that time comes, and I can only promise to do my best.'

* * *

Pedro had some difficulty keeping up with young Miguel as they scrambled up through the rocks and deep into the wooded hills far from home. He had been so shocked by the brutal behaviour of the S.S. in the town that he felt he could no longer sit back, and had got in touch with the young man who had visited him at the farm. Of course, he was now risking the safety of his family, and would also have to neglect the farm.

But he knew he was making an honourable decision, despite Maria's wrath and anguish.

About two kilometres from where they had left the road and headed up into the woods, there was a low whistle from ahead of them.

Miguel stopped. There was nothing to be seen in the dense foliage.

'Hola, Miguel!' came a voice.

'Hola, Enrique!' replied Miguel, obviously recognizing it, and not surprisingly. Moments later Miguel was embracing his brother. Then he headed on, indicating to Pedro to follow.

The camp consisted of an old, dilapidated forester's hut and a couple of tents camouflaged with foliage. About eight young men were clustered round a small fire. Others were on the perimeter, acting as sentries.

The leader, Cristino, leapt to his feet and came over, smiling with his hand outstretched.

'I'm really glad you decided to join us. Bienvenido!' Everyone started to speak in Spanish. He quickly introduced Pedro to all his team, explaining their roles and expertise, before sitting down with them to drink the usual hot chestnut soup with bread.

'You were a Captain once, weren't you?' asked Cristino.

'Yes. I ended up commanding a Company of infantry back in Spain, although by then a pretty depleted one.'

Cristino laughed, but not with mirth. 'Well, as you can see, we haven't even *got* a company up here – depleted or not.'

'Don't worry, I'm happy to act as an ordinary soldier.'

Cristino shook his head, with a smile. 'That would be a waste of your experience. I can ask you to at least to command a Section, and hopefully later, a Peleton.'

'I'd be honoured.' Pedro paused to drink some soup. 'What kind of weapons do you have?'

'Well, after starting with just sporting guns, we graduated to French Army rifles. But now we've captured some decent German stuff, and recently the British have parachuted in Bren light machine-guns, British rifles, Stens, some anti-tank PIATs, and almost more important – radios. You won't believe it, but we used to have to walk down to a call box and hope the old lady on the village switchboard wasn't a Milice spy! At least we don't have to do *that* any more.

Generally, because we've got people who came from fighting in the Civil War, we're a bit older and more experienced than most of our French friends. You won't have to teach them weapon training, for instance – they're past that. But we *do* have to work on tactics, guerrilla tactics. We always have to stop our boys trying to take on Germans at their own game. If we get into pitched battles, we won't have a hope in hell.

So we'll have to wait. I'm sure the invasion is coming soon, and when it does, we'll be able to show people what we can *really* do.'

He paused.

'By the way, Carmen – she's your daughter, isn't she?'

'Yes, and I'm proud to say that.'

'You should be. Not many of the women we get actually want to fight. Or *could*, even if they wanted to.'

'She has her reasons.'

'So I gathered. And she's just as good as the men. I put her in another group further west. But you'll probably meet up with her sometime.'

THIRTY-ONE

* * *

H ANS PIETER WAS AT BREAKFAST WITH HIS COMRADES IN THE BARRACKS in Saint-Hippolyte, surprised and rather worried to be told by a Sergeant that their Commanding Officer wanted to see him.

'Good luck,' said Rudi between mouthfuls. 'See you in a minute. Or, if he wants to punish you, I'll watch out for you on the parade ground a bit later. It's not the worst crime, gambling with the Sergeants, and he'll probably only dock a bit of your wages, the bit he thinks you nicked from them.'

Hans smiled. 'I didn't nick it, I *won* it fair and square. They're useless at poker. Anyway, I'd better go, or I'll be in even worse trouble.'

'Good luck.'

A few minutes later, Hans could see only too easily from the face of his Commanding Officer, the middle-aged Major Schmidt, that it was nothing to do with a game of cards.

'Sit down, Corporal.' The Major's face was full of compassion, not anger.

Hans felt a rush of fear.

'Look,' said Major Schmidt, 'I'm really sorry to tell you, but I've just had bad news. There was a bombing raid over Mannheim a couple of nights ago.' He paused. 'I'm afraid we've just heard your mother died. Her house was flattened by the Allies in the middle of the night.'

'Oh, God!'

Schmidt looked at the evidently stricken young boy in front of him, the same age as his own son fighting in Russia, fervently wishing that this wasn't part of his job.

'I'm terribly sorry. You have my deepest sympathies.'

Hans was dumbstruck, to the point where his Commanding Officer desperately wanted to breach military rules and give him comfort, perhaps by putting his hand on his shoulder, but knowing that human contact with his men, even in these circumstances, was not permitted. 'Again, my condolences, Gefreiter Pieter.'

He waited for a response, but not expecting one, noticing that the boy was struggling not to cry.

'You may have the rest of today off. You are relieved of any military duties.'

Hans looked up, wide-eyed and stricken, pulling himself out of his chair. He saluted and left the room, desperate to hold back his tears until then, and equally desperate to see Rudi – *anyone* to talk to – swamped in a whirlwind of emotion, and suddenly feeling totally alone in a war that he'd never understood or wanted to get into in the first place.

Stumbling into the barracks' breakfast room, he was hugely relieved to see Rudi still there, and alone, but getting up to leave. His face obviously told Rudi to sit down again, which he promptly did, clearly fearing the worst.

'It's my Mutti,' said Hans. 'I've just heard. She's dead.'

Rudi said nothing, deeply shocked.

'A bomb on her house.' Tears streamed down his face.

This time there *was* a comforting hand on his shoulder.

* * *

Otilia was sitting on a boulder outside the Protestant church, looking down at her sketch pad, when she was suddenly aware of someone in front of her blocking out the light. She looked up to see Hans, shocked by his miserable face.

He, too, was shocked to see her, noting that she had lost a considerable amount of weight since he had last seen her. 'Oti, how have you been?'

'I'm sorry, but I'm not allowed to speak to you, or be seen with you. Or my parents will kill me. You'd better go. I'm sorry, but it's better for both of us, ever since what happened to Roger Broussoux and the others.' She looked down at her drawing.

'You *know* we're not all like those SS bastards. And I *have* to speak to you,' said Hans miserably, and looking up at him, Otilia noticed how wretched he looked, and red-eyed as if he had been crying. Surely not because of her? It was weeks now since they had last seen each other, and she even admitted to herself that it was now less painful.

'Oti, I have to speak to you. *Please.*'

'Okay, but you'll have to keep it quick. Someone could see us at any moment. And they're all sneaks round here, particularly my Papa's friends. You've no idea what trouble I got into when they found out we were seeing each other. It's not that bad for the French girls, but it is for us Spanish. My parents will never forget what the Germans did to us in Spain.'

Hans pleaded with Oti to listen. 'I'm desperate. My mother's just died. I heard just now from my Commanding Officer, and he gave me the day off. If I don't talk to you, I think I'll go mad.'

Otilia looked up from her drawing, horrified, and for a moment she was speechless. 'I'm terribly sorry.' Her immediate instinct was to stand up and give him a hug, but she was instantly afraid to do so in a public place. She glanced behind her. 'Look, let's go into the church for a bit. It's not safe here.'

Minutes later, they were in the empty church, with Otilia's hand on his, as he told her all about his mother; only forty years old, and a 'kindergarten' teacher, a word Hans had to explain was a children's school. The church was relatively warm, but his hand was not, and Otilia could not help but console him in his extreme distress – thinking to herself that her parents would surely forgive her for talking to him at a time like this. It was next to inhumane, she told herself, if she refused to listen and console him.

'Please see me again,' said Hans, after a protracted silence. 'I've got good friends in the barracks, but they're all terrified about their own parents, and I can't talk to them. And anyway, I'm in love with you. For weeks, I've been going out of my mind not seeing you, though it's obviously not the same for you.'

'Who says it isn't?' asked Otilia. 'It's been hell for me, too,' suddenly flattered by the idea of a young man in love with her, particularly one this handsome. She squeezed his hand, thinking for a moment. 'Maybe if we're really, really careful, we could meet up the mountain again so you can tell me more about your mother, and more about what it's like in Germany. I don't really know anything about it. But if my parents ever found out, there'd be hell to pay.'

'No worse hell than it is at the moment,' replied Hans. 'And probably for both of us.'

* * *

'Going painting again?' asked Maria, now used to Otilia's regular painting trips up the mountain each Saturday.

'Yes, if that's okay.'

'It's fine. There's less work here now with only four of us. But I'd love to see some of your paintings one day.'

'You will. But it's much easier to keep them up there in the hut rather than lugging them up and down the mountain every time.'

'But a scroll is hardly heavy,' protested Maria, baffled. 'And won't they get damp up there?'

'No. The hut's made of stone. And pretty watertight.'

Maria gave up. 'Okay then, off you go. And take something to eat with you if you won't be back for lunch.'

'I'll see you around four then.'

Maria watched her daughter as she sliced some bread and tossed it into her knapsack, noticing how striking she was becoming. She wondered when she'd ever see the paintings, and how many there would be – quite a few she imagined after such regular expeditions – probably enough to have another exhibition.

She felt a flush of pride in having such a talented daughter and one who had become noticeably less headstrong over the past few months, in fact ever since Pedro had left to join the Résistance up in Mont Aigoual.

If was somewhat strange that she never ever brought her paintings home – but certainly not worth arguing about. And it was bliss these days, not having anything else to argue about either. Otilia in many ways, was a completely changed child.

* * *

Carmen's group was picking its way carefully through the thick woods up in the mountains. Their information was that something was happening up in the north. It could be the invasion, they had been told – or perhaps a diversion. But in any event, things were certainly hotting up.

Below her was an old stone hut, and as Carmen checked it out through her binoculars, she suddenly she saw a movement at the doorway. And focussing her glasses, she was dumbfounded to see who it was. Her sister, Otilia.

But perhaps she had come up to paint? She remembered her mother mentioning something about that the last time she had gone down to visit. She looked through the binoculars again, now even more shocked to see another figure come out of the house – and a German almost certainly, with that blond-white hair. Exactly like the boy her father, or rather Morelli, had described. So Otilia was *still* seeing him, having sworn not to. The *stupid, stupid, girl.*

Perhaps she should warn her father? But how in hell to do that, both of them stuck up different mountains, and on the move? And it was hardly something she could confide to anyone else, even if there were anyone else to confide in. She suddenly felt terribly alone.

'Anything down there, Carmen?' came the quiet voice of Sean, slightly further up the trail.

'No, nothing.'

'Okay, keep moving along this hillside.'

She hoped it was the last time she would ever have to lie to him.

* * *

It was a few days after Carmen's disturbing sighting of Otilia and it was very hot, surprisingly so for early May. Carmen and Sean were taking a break under an oak tree a little away from the group, who had now fully accepted that they had become close, though how close they didn't know. Both were fanning their faces with their caps, and almost deafened by the millions of 'cigale' crickets.

She turned to Sean. 'Do you know what I'd like more than anything else?'

'Apart from the end of the war?'

'Yes. Right now there's something I'd give *anything* for. A damned good bath and somewhere I could wash my hair. It's horribly matted and tangly. And boiling hot. Quite frankly, I'm thinking of chopping the whole lot off.'

Sean looked at her thick black hair, falling halfway down her back.

'Don't you dare. It's one of the things I most like about you!'

Carmen laughed. 'You're not the one who's putting up with it. It's horrific in this heat. The next time we see a stream, at least let me stop and wash it.'

'Okay, promise.'

'Thanks. Anyway, changing the subject, I want to ask you something. Something that's really bothering me, and probably the others too.'

'Go ahead.'

'What do you *really* think the chances are for the invasion?'

'Pretty good, I'd say. I've seen something of the early build-up in Britain. It's just huge. They joke that the island will sink under the weight of the Americans there.'

'But the Germans are so *good*. Look what they did to France in a few weeks!'

'Sure. But the French were ruined by old thinking. They thought of their Maginot Line as a stronger, concrete version of the trenches in the last war. And they never imagined that the Germans would simply go around it. And the Germans use their tanks like cavalry and their planes like artillery, so they don't have to wait ages for the rest of their army to catch up. That's worked again and again in this war until they came up against real, organised opposition – as in the Battle of Britain. In fact, an awful lot of their success can be put down to sheer energy, boldness – and frankly, I'd say, bluff.'

'Bluff?'

'Yes, bluff. It's so easy to be tricked into thinking they're all-powerful, invincible. But a lot of it's hot air. Britain alone, believe it or not, produces more planes and tanks than they do, let alone the Americans and the Russians. The Germans have created some great weapons, like their Tiger tanks, but then managed to build them in pathetic numbers. As for all the 'Blitz' talk, they only used about two hundred light bombers against London, while we use a nearly *thousand* heavy ones against them – *and* night after night.

And they must be incredibly overstretched – our strongest card of all. Most of their troops have to be in Russia where they're outnumbered three to one. In fact, German tank *divisions* are now facing whole Russian tank *armies*. On top of that, they've left a quarter of a million men in Norway; they're having to fight tooth and nail in Italy – and now they have to cover France as well, in the north and now the south too. Just look what happened to those SS bastards who swept in and killed your neighbours around here. Even *they* could stay only a few days, luckily, before being rushed off to Russia to avert some disaster. That's typical of what's happening all the time. And underestimated.'

Carmen suddenly felt more optimistic.

'I reckon their air force is in even worse shape,' continued Sean. 'It's having to support ground wars on every front, at the same time trying to defend Germany against air raids every day and night. And, apart from their U-boats, they've got no navy. It must be a nightmare in Hitler's headquarters, although I've hardly any sympathy for them.

So, yes, I *do* think the invasion will work. And I think we'll win. And if I didn't, I don't think I'd be here.'

Carmen thought for a moment.

'Sean, I think it would be a really good idea to tell the others all of that. Fighting is bad enough. But when you're fighting pessimism as well, it's even tougher.'

Sean nodded.

'Probably not a bad idea.'

* * *

Carmen was feeling immensely guilty thinking about Pierre, and wondering if she'd been a fool, but at the same time not regretting last night. For the last three months the electricity between her and Sean had been constantly growing, and it had become impossible to ignore it any more, or the fact that their love-making had been such a pleasure, and on top of that, an incredible release after holding back for so long. And it was all the more relaxing and releasing because Sean had a pack of condoms. At first, she didn't like the idea of that, because it was almost as if he was *expecting* to make love with her, but Sean had gently explained that was not the case at all, and that in no way was she under any pressure.

She reminded herself that Pierre had been away four years, and would almost certainly have changed like her – that's if he were still alive, and comforted herself with the thought that her enforced lack of letters since she joined the Résistance might have told him that the relationship was over, and that too much time had passed to consider there was still a relationship at all. She could only hope so, though she hated the idea of him feeling abandoned.

'You okay?' She felt Sean's hand stroking hers.

'Fine. Really happy.'

It wasn't entirely true.

* * *

'Do you think we ought to tell Alfonso?' Michel Morelli asked.

'I'm not sure. He's probably got enough to cope with looking after Maria and the girls and keeping the garage going. And he must be worried sick about Pedro and his older niece in the hills. It's probably better to keep it to ourselves.'

Michel Morelli was in the café with his postman friend, André Lebrun. He had just heard that André had seen the younger Casales girl out with the German again, indeed not once but several times, and worse, that other people must have seen them together because word was now beginning to spread around the town.

'What makes it all the more horrifying is that her family's Spanish, and Spanish girls aren't meant to go out with *any* boys unescorted. Back home they'd have needed a chaperone. They're far more strictly brought up than our girls are, which makes it even more of a scandal. And a pretty public one it seems. I even heard the butcher's wife openly complaining about it the other day. If Maria knew people were gossiping like that about her daughter, it would kill her. It's a damned good thing she understands so little French.'

'I suppose that's one blessing.'

Morelli stirred his coffee, wondering what to do. 'What if *I* had a word with her?'

'Who, Maria?'

'No, André, of course not. I meant Otilia.'

'Well, you certainly know where to find her. Always in the same place every Saturday, or at least pretty well every Saturday I've done the post run to Valatougès. She waits for him on the corner where an old track goes up from the road. In fact, she's getting pretty brazen about it. She's even waved at me a couple of times recently, as bold as brass. I suppose she thinks I won't talk. And I haven't, except to you.'

'Good God!'

'Probably with her father away, she feels free to do what she likes, as do lots of other girls here. She's certainly not the only one consorting with the Boches. Although you'd think that with their fathers and brothers fighting them or working for them, they'd think twice.'

'Perhaps not if there aren't any French boys around, all in hiding or prisoners or working in Germany. You're incredibly lucky your son escaped the S.T.O.'

'I know, just in time, and thanks to Pedro. That's why I feel I ought to do something. I owe him a hell of a debt for keeping my boy safe. Perhaps I should try to talk to the girl next time I see her.'

'Perhaps, but in town, if I were you. Not up the mountain. You wouldn't want to come to blows with a boy that big.'

André drank the last of his cup. 'Anyway, time for another coffee?'

'In a minute, thanks. But I want to ask you something. If this war ever ends, what do you think *will* happen to girls who get off with the Germans?'

'I hate to think. But one thing I know is that women can be much crueller than men. And if they *do* take it out on *collaboratrices,* you can't really blame them. After all, many have had their menfolk taken away either as prisoners of war or as workers in Germany. So they're lonely *and* angry. And they'll immediately assume that someone like Otilia is getting more rations because she's with a German – and not only of food, if you know what I mean.

Believe me, if this war's ever over, they'll *really* take their revenge. And it won't be pleasant.'

* * *

'Juani, what do you want to do on your birthday?' asked Maria, patting her daughter's hand at supper. 'I thought it would be rather fun to go up the mountain at last, and have a picnic.' She glanced at her elder daughter. 'And then we could see your paintings, Oti.'

Otilia was instantly horrified, knowing she had to think of an excuse fast. 'What a boring birthday, Mamá. I'm sure Juanita's school-friends don't want an hour's trek up there and back – or even more if they live out of town. Especially if it's raining.'

'Raining? Don't be silly, cara,' laughed Maria. 'It's midsummer! And Alfonso could easily drive us all up there in his van.'

'*All* of us, including half her form?' retorted Otilia. 'That would take at least three trips there and back. What a hassle! Far better to do something here.'

Alfonso knew all too well why his niece was objecting. There wouldn't be any paintings up there, or at best, only one or two. He tried not to picture what she was doing up there; it was all too abhorrent. 'Actually, the van's not working very well, and I don't think I can get it fixed on time for Saturday.' He turned to Juanita. 'What about a picnic by the river instead and then a game of boules in the square?'

'B-o-r-i-n-g,' said Juanita, shaking her head. 'That's what old men play. All I'd like is a party here with some decent food for once.'

Maria flinched. 'Okay, cara, I'll try and make a cake if I can get the ingredients, and we can play some games here – hide and seek, or something, or blind man's buff.'

Juanita let out a petulant sigh. 'Mamá, I'm going to be *twelve* years old. We don't play games like that any more in case you haven't noticed.'

'Juanita, don't be rude to your mother,' said Alfonso. 'She's trying to do her best. And as you know all too well, it isn't easy planning anything, especially now the invasion's coming. Nobody knows what that means, except that it'll almost certainly be all the more difficult to get decent food in.'

'I know! How about face painting?' Juanita piped up.

'What with?' retorted Otilia, sullenly, 'These days it's almost impossible to get paints.'

She suddenly realized she'd landed herself in it, but luckily nobody seemed to notice or ask what she was doing up the mountain every weekend *if paints were so scarce.*

'Well, if it's all that difficult, I don't want a party at all,' mumbled Juanita.

'Of course you do, cara,' replied Alfonso, patting her hand, determined to do something nice to mark the occasion. Birthdays were always so important to children. But what could they really do? All the local musicians had been called up, except the much older ones who wouldn't play the sort of music that youngsters now enjoyed. Taking the kids to a film would be too expensive, and any films they might see could be interrupted by horrific newsreels about the war. But perhaps there was a conjuror someone knew in town? It wouldn't matter how old he or she was. Magic was magic, and God knows, three was little enough of it these days. He suddenly remembered seeing a conjuror in his childhood magically producing a rabbit out a hat, wondering if the very name 'Abracadabra' was Spanish.

Later on, when Maria was seeing Juanita to bed, Alfonso decided to confront Otilia.

'I know *exactly* why you don't want to go up the mountain with us. And much, much worse, so do other people in the town. As it happens, my van's working perfectly – as you probably realized. But I'm certainly *not* driving it up there so your Mamá sees there *aren't* any paintings. As you said yourself, it's hard enough to buy paints anyway.'

Otilia hung her head.

'If we ever win this war,' continued Alfonso, 'there'll be terrible reprisals against girls who consort with Germans. It's got to stop, Otilia, and *stop right* now before everyone knows what you're up to, and before *all* our names – as well as yours – are dragged into the mud.' He sighed deeply, shaking his head. 'I beg you, Oti, see sense.'

Otilia suddenly burst into tears. 'But they're not like the people everyone thinks they are. He's really kind, really nice, and he doesn't like this war any more than we do. In fact, he *hates* it. And he's just lost his mamá in a bombing raid in Germany, so he needs me now more than ever. I just can't walk away from him, and if you can't understand that, I'm going to bed.'

She was about to get up when Alfonso grabbed her hand on the table to stop her, and more roughly than he had intended.

'Oti, you think of him as a nice, handsome young man. But you don't seem to have realized that people regard the Germans more and more as bitter enemies. They beat the French humiliatingly fast, they've kept two million of their boys as prisoners of war, they forced thousands more into the STO and worse, they're sending thousands of Jews off to God knows where, like Sarah's parents – and almost certainly to their deaths. And you remember when the SS came here, hanging that poor young shepherd Broussoux from the viaduct and nearly shooting your own sister in the square. *And* the Germans are stealing most of our food. Haven't you noticed how hard it is to find anything for the table? And, above all, haven't you guessed if news *really* gets out about what you're up to, what might happen to you?'

He saw tears welling up again in Otilia's eyes, and to his despair, she shook off his hand forcibly and went up to bed. Suddenly, he wished he had nephews, not nieces, although immediately realizing they would have been called up for the hated Service Obligatoire, or kept in captivity like Pierre.

Lock up his niece on Saturdays? Confront the boy himself, or with other locals who'd got wind of it? Try as he might to think of a solution, he was at a loss what to do. About all he *could* do was dock Otilia's already meagre pocket money, but even then she could borrow from her boyfriend – as she probably was already. He'd noticed that she was wearing a new dress yesterday, as had Maria, although Otilia had assured them that it came from someone in her school who'd grown out of it. Was that true? Now, he wasn't sure.

And what to do about a present for her sister?

The kitten she wanted? Out of the question. Yet another mouth to feed. It would have to be something from the flea market like a little ornament or a brooch or bracelet. That was a possibility. People were selling everything these days just to keep going – and so desperate to sell that prices were now at rock bottom. Half an acre in the town was flooded every Saturday with everything from clogs to cutlery, clothes to bric-a-brac, vinyl records and old gramophones to stamp albums, and pots and pans to old wine glasses – anything to raise a franc or two. And there were countless decanters now that no-one was tending the local vineyards, and wine production had all but dried up. But with any luck, Alfonso thought, someone might at last be selling a fishing rod. It was infuriating to see all those trout in the river Vidourle in town without any means of catching them.

And even more annoying was that nobody would lend people rods or nets in case they weren't returned, so they lost out on a valuable source of free food. If he could only get one, feeding a kitten would be no problem.

And if he couldn't, it was *nothing* compared with the looming crisis of Otilia. What on earth was he to do, if he couldn't make her see sense?

* * *

Otilia was now frantic with worry, at least four days after she should have started her period. What a fool she'd been that day up the mountain! Hans had said he knew what he was doing. But how could he, if it was also the first time for him? And what if that contraceptive hadn't worked?

And what could she do if the worst came to the worst? Her parents would be utterly appalled, all the more so being Spanish. And so would everyone else. And word would spread like wildfire in a place like Hippo – full of gossips – and, of course, people who hated Germans. Alfonso's warning rang in her ears.

She would have to leave home, but where could she go? And Hans probably wouldn't be able to help, especially now – with Germany apparently starting to lose. He could be sent off anywhere – even Russia. He'd already warned her about that.

Wasn't there a way of getting rid of an unwanted baby? The thought was repellent, and who to ask? She didn't dare to confide in the local doctor, or indeed anyone. Even Hans.

Going out in the town was now a nightmare. Suddenly there seemed to be women pushing prams everywhere, heightening her fear. All she could do was pray fervently that she wasn't pregnant, but would God listen? She was too afraid to even go inside the church, and worse, right next to it was a baby clothes shop.

It was another two agonizingly long days before the nightmare disappeared, by which time she vowed never to take the risk again. Unless she was married. And there was little chance of ever marrying Hans now.

THIRTY-TWO

* * *

'**U**NCLE PIERRE HAS PLANTED HIS ONIONS! THAT'S IT!'

Sean took off his headphones, which he'd been using to listen to the BBC programme 'Ici Londres', beamed to France. Carmen, for one, had no idea what he was talking about, and why anyone would care about an Uncle Pierre and his onion planting.

Sean smiled, and then hurriedly explained. 'It's one of the coded messages from London for the Résistance that we've been waiting for, to activate us.'

He looked at his notebook. 'Here are some of the others, and they all sound equally bizarre. '*Jean has a long moustache*', '*There's a fire in the insurance agency*', '*Yvette likes big carrots*', '*Giraffes don't wear collars*'. And what about this? '*Wound my heart with a monotonous languor*'. I wonder what crazy poet thought *that* one up!

But the 'Uncle Pierre' one is for us. It means we can go into action soon. But once again, we *must* wait to find out what's happening.'

The next day the BBC announced that the invasion had at last come – and not at the coast near Calais where everyone had expected, but further west, in Normandy. Sean immediately relayed the news to the excited group. 'There's been hard fighting, but they're ashore, thank God, thousands of them. The Germans will have to rush reinforcements up there. We're not close enough to be involved yet, but the maquis groups north of here *certainly* are. We'll have to wait for orders.'

Three days later Sean assembled the group, producing a sheet of paper.

'Here's a copy of an urgent cable message from the French General, Marie-Pierre Koenig, in London, who as you know, is in charge of all Résistance activities.' He held up the paper, and read out the message.

'PUT MAXIMUM BRAKE ON GUERRILLA ACTION. CURRENTLY IMPOSSIBLE TO SUPPLY ARMS AND AMMO IN SUFFICIENT QUANTITIES. WHEREVER POSSIBLE, BREAK OFF ATTACKS TO ALLOW RE-ORG. AVOID LARGE SCALE GROUPINGS. FORM SMALL ISOLATED GROUPS.'

There was grumbling of dissent among the men, who clearly thought that the message displayed cowardly vacillation. But Sean put up his hand and explained.

'I'll tell you why that message was sent out. We keep warning about premature action, until you're probably bored as hell with it. But here's why we do. Three days ago, an over-keen Communist Résistance group suddenly took over a town called Tulle up in the Lozère, and killed forty Germans and Milice and then just left, disappeared. And they left the poor town to its fate. And what happened next? I'll tell you.

The SS arrived, and rapidly retook the place – with instant reprisals. They grabbed completely innocent hostages and then methodically hung them all the way down the main street. They hung ninety-nine men in all, from lamp-posts and balconies, and only stopped because they'd run out of rope. And then they took dozens more away with them. And, only the very next day, in a place called Oradour, over two hundred men were shot, and four hundred women and children burned alive, yes *alive*, and in a church for God's sake, and by the very same division of the SS.'

The entire group stared at him in horror.

'I take no pleasure in saying I told you so. It's appalling. But the fact is that lightly-armed and poorly-trained *maquisards* are really absolutely sitting ducks for German fighting units and experienced commanders. We've got to stay small, and use hit and run tactics.

However, you'll all be pleased to hear that after your friends took over La Grande-Combe and its coalmines, there's been no reaction from the Germans or the Milice – at least, so far. We can only hope that the Germans in this part of the country are now so over-stretched that trying to get any more coal out of the mostly-disabled mines is the *least* of their problems, and that the Résistance is getting so strong that any reaction may face disaster.'

One of the young men raised his hand.

'But why, Sir, *are* we so lightly armed? Why haven't we *been* given heavier weapons?'

Sean looked at him carefully.

'Well, if it were up to me, Carlos, I would. But, to be frank, the bosses in London are *very* cautious about us. They're anxious about some of the French Communist groups who've been very noisy about how they intend to make France a Communist country when the Germans have gone. You can see de Gaulle and Churchill agreeing that they've got to be kept in check. Sadly, you Spanish have been tarred with the same brush. I'd love to have mortars, heavy machine-guns and anti-tank guns, as no doubt you would. And that nice American howitzer that arrives in bits. But I'm afraid we'll have to make do with what we've got.'

* * *

A few weeks later, Sean paraded the group to give them startling news from his wireless operator. There had been a new invasion, this time in the south of France on the Côte d'Azur, and he was pleased to announce that the Americans had got ashore without too much trouble or loss and were beginning to move north – up the Rhone valley.

Looking down at his message pad, he then became more specific.

'Intelligence in London thinks that the Germans on the coast from Bordeaux to Biarritz will be ordered by Hitler to leave – in fact to retreat. Otherwise, they'll be trapped between the two invasion forces. They'll try to avoid our planes, so with more troops retreating from Toulouse, they'll all be coming towards us down minor roads, and quickly. We've been ordered to harass them all the way – the less men and equipment that make it eastwards towards Germany, the better.'

He spread out a map.

'I know that other groups are being mobilised to the west of us, and they're going to blow bridges and tunnels wherever they can. We'll do the same, starting with the Nîmes to Le Vigan railway line, at Saint-Hippolyte. And we'll blow the track inside tunnels, so it's more difficult to repair. Manuel and Enrique, I want you to blow the line just inside the one where the track enters from the viaduct. And make damned sure you don't harm any French railway staff.

We'll take another demolition team beyond Ganges and blow some of those lines too. I've scouted the best ones.' He pointed out three places on the map.

'There, there and there. And the road bridge at Pont d'Hérault. All spots where it'll be difficult for the Germans to move, to outflank us or retreat. TEAM LEADERS – MEET ME IN TWENTY MINUTES! And the rest of you – start packing up, ready to move in an hour.'

Then he turned towards Carmen and beckoned her to come over.

'Cara, I've been ordered away – to run a special radio unit to help all the groups converging on this area, even including bringing in planes. I'm sorry I can't be with you.'

Carmen instinctively reached out and clutched his hand. Sean squeezed it.

'Please promise me, Carmen, try not to do anything too dangerous when I'm gone.'

* * *

The radio soon confirmed that various columns of Germans were indeed streaming east, obviously under orders to escape being trapped by the Allied invasions from the north – and now the south. Résistance groups started moving down from the hills towards the roads and their allotted blocking positions. It was not long before violent action was reported in Alzon and then in the streets of Le Vigan, and that another British-supported team had blown up the bridge at Pont d'Herault, forcing the German columns to split up and weaken their numbers.

And now Pedro's group was ordered to converge on Ganges, the little market town on the Hérault River, arriving in two trucks in the early morning. The men were greeted by the 'Aigoual-Cevennes' maquis, who showed them the best places to intercept, assuming that the Germans would want to take the obvious direct Saint-Hippolyte main road towards Nîmes.

Pedro placed his ten men in windows and doors overlooking the road where it turned on to a bridge across a dry river, and they settled down to wait. Some local women brought them some bread, goat's cheese and water after about an hour and then disappeared.

At about eleven o'clock came the sound of loud explosions and sustained heavy firing from the west of the town, the slow firing of the

Brens contrasting with the frighteningly faster-firing German machine-guns.

Suddenly grey vehicles burst into view, and Pedro and his men opened fire. They stopped the trucks easily enough, with several crashing, but there was an armoured car that managed to avoid a PIAT anti-tank projectile, and roared off on to the bridge and out of sight, followed by several trucks. Then, some of the German infantrymen dismounted and moved along the sides of the houses firing and throwing grenades. One of them tried to throw a grenade up into Pedro's window, but it fell short and exploded back in the street, wounding both the man who had thrown it and another German.

But nevertheless, Pedro's little group – working with the French teams – trying to fire back in the smoke and dust – didn't stand a real chance. Two more trucks and a half-track broke through, with the last infantrymen climbing aboard and disappearing. Pedro discovered that several of his men were wounded, and one killed. But they *had* succeeded up to a point, because no more vehicles or troops came through, and it became apparent that the vigorous Maquis action had persuaded the German commander to divert the rest of the column off down the Montpellier road, if only for a few kilometres. Fighting among crowded houses and from vehicles, Pedro realized, and to his relief, that it must have been very difficult for the enemy to work out just how few fighters the Résistance people actually had.

He quickly concerned himself with helping a local doctor with the Spanish as well as the German wounded. One was the German Sergeant who had tried to throw the grenade, and with fragments of it now in his own smashed-up leg. As he lay there, he heard Pedro speaking in Spanish, and puzzled, asked in broken French why a Spaniard was there.

'A long story,' replied Pedro laconically. He noticed that many of the German prisoners were either very young or, in contrast, middle-aged and rather overweight. *Too much French stolen food and comfort*, he thought, *not exactly crack troops* – perhaps, he surmised, why they couldn't throw grenades effectively, thank God.

But it was not long before fresh radio orders told them to hurry eastwards, to circle down side roads and try and get ahead of the Germans again when they would hopefully be delayed – at least for a while – by the French Maquis in Saint-Hippolyte.

* * *

Maria would have been horrified if she had known the dangers for Pedro over in Ganges, but right now Alfonso came with news of more immediate ones. The Germans were heading straight for the town and the local maquis was going to try and stop them, so there would be battles in the streets really close by.

'I want you and the two girls to stay here in the kitchen, and if you hear firing nearby, lie on the floor at once. These walls and the stove will protect you from stray bullets.' Maria looked far from reassured, as did the girls, both wide-eyed with fear.

'Don't even *think* of looking out of the windows. I heard that yesterday in Ganges several people were wounded that way. I'm told the Germans aren't trying to occupy the town or hang about fighting. They're trying to *escape* eastwards towards Nîmes, and they want minimum trouble and delay. But, if our Maquis friends succeed, there *will* be fighting nearby. So keep inside with your heads down. The word is that some of the Germans will come straight from Ganges, but others may have been diverted there and may come up from Pompignan. I'll go out and get some food now, so we can hole ourselves up tomorrow.'

The next day, very early – about three in the morning –they heard people up and about, moving around and some vehicles starting up in the dark. Alfonso rushed down the Rue Pasteur to the house of Monsieur Vessière, where he knew the defence was being co-ordinated.

'They've spotted Germans coming from Pompignan,' he said on his return, 'and the Ganges people have phoned to say they're also on the move from there.'

Sure enough, at that very moment they all heard the sound of distant firing, which went on and on. Alfonso, to calm everyone down, asked Maria to make some coffee. *A mundane task might make everything appear more normal.* Suddenly, they heard some aircraft, but they flew on. In the past few days, there had been plenty of Allied planes about.

The sound of firing continued and then got closer, so the family quickly followed Alfonso's advice and sat or laid down on the floor. Now it was very difficult to work out what was happening, because the noise of gunfire confusedly echoed round the narrow streets. The only thing that *was* certain was that gunfire was now also coming from *their* side of the town, from along the Vidourle river bank. The family sat in tense and miserable silence, thinking about its own situation, while Otilia was thinking very different thoughts. Where was Hans? Obviously in danger, somewhere out there fighting.

All at once, a loud banging on the door made everyone jolt. Then there was more banging. Alfonso hesitated, but then to his relief heard French voices outside.

He opened the door very cautiously to see three very young Frenchmen, two carrying rifles, and propping up another whose arm was covered in blood.

'Please help, he's wounded. We can't try and find a doctor because the streets are crawling with Germans.'

Alfonso immediately helped to take the weight of the wounded boy, who looked dangerously pale, calling to Maria to bring hot water so they could clean his wound. The boy appeared to have taken a bullet in a muscle on the side of his arm, but apparently without fracturing a bone or lodging in his flesh. They bandaged it as well as they could, and to their great relief noted that the bleeding soon stopped.

'There's a doctor just at the end of the street,' said Alfonso. 'and when the shooting's over, we can try and fetch him. Do you know the town?'

'No, I've only been here a couple of times, on market day. We're from Lasalle, from the maquis there. Your boys asked for our help, so we piled into a car and a bus and set off as quickly as we could. We weren't expecting to meet any Boches, but coming down the road we suddenly saw a column of them on the other side of the river on the road to Cros. God knows why they were going that way. They must have been lost.'

'They probably were,' said Alfonso. 'To confuse them, the town took down all the signposts a couple of days ago, or changed them around.'

'Then a hell of a fight started,' continued the young man, 'with both sides firing at about a hundred metres from behind those stone walls. Next minute, it was disaster. Two of our leaders came around the bend behind us. They were on noisy motor-bikes, so maybe they couldn't hear the shooting. Anyway, riding their bikes and sticking up above the low wall, they both got hit – and killed. And they were two of our best people, Jean Salazet – who we called 'Hardy' and Jean Vilaret, called 'Milette'. Then yet another of our fellows, Guy, got shot. It was tragic. Three great friends. The only good thing is that I think we were winning – even when more Germans came back down from Cros. But we couldn't wait to see what happened after that. I had to get Francis out of the battle. I should have said, he's my brother.'

Alfonso went to get a bottle of cognac, and poured three glasses. 'Should Francis have one?'

'Why not?' whispered Francis himself. 'In the old days, it was probably the only cure.'

'Thanks for your help. I'm Arnaud, by the way,' said his brother after taking a gulp of cognac. He looked at the family. 'Are you French?'

'No, Spanish. We came over at the end of the Civil War. I'm Alfonso. This is Maria and her daughters. And my cousin, Maria's husband, and their other daughter, are both fighting with the Maquis, in Spanish groups.'

Suddenly they all noticed at once that the firing had stopped. The town was silent.

'I think they've gone,' said Alfonso, opening the shutter and listening. 'It's probably safe. I'll wait a bit longer to be sure.'

He left after ten more minutes of silence and came back with Doctor Pibarot, who immediately went to work on Francis.

'Luckily, the bullet hasn't done too much damage,' the doctor announced after a few minutes. 'But I'll need to clean the wound. Madame Casales, could you boil up some water for me?'

As Maria quickly went to the kitchen, ordering the two girls to come with her, Alfonso turned to the others.

'They've definitely all gone. Someone told me on the way to the surgery that apparently some of their trucks got so lost that they even started to go back towards Ganges – exactly the wrong way. But most of them are now on the road to Anduze. And with any luck, they'll be hit again over there. And hard.'

THIRTY-THREE

⁎ ⁎ ⁎

HIS RIFLE ACROSS HIS KNEES, CORPORAL HANS PIETER WAS SITTING nervously in the back of the third truck, the last of their little detachment. Engines running, they were pulled in by the side of the road to Anduze, two kilometres from Saint-Hippolyte. Some of the men were out on the road, alert with weapons ready, staring at the trees and the rocky slopes that overlooked them.

The sudden and desperate retreat from the west was now on – to escape Allied armies from their two successful invasions, Normandy and Provence. Hans and his comrades had been given only minutes to get out. His Sergeant told them that radio orders had warned them not to try to make it out on their own through countryside now full of maquisards, advising them that they'd be much safer joining a large and strong German column that had come all the way from Toulouse.

Above the sound of their engines ticking over, they could all hear the sound of heavy firing from Saint-Hippolyte – while Hans could only think of Otilia. Was she alright? Would he ever see her again? He hadn't even been able to say goodbye. The garrison had known something was bound to happen ever since the second invasion on the Côte d'Azur, so suddenly he and his comrades had been strictly confined to barracks. With the confident maquisards pouring out of the hills, he was now all too well aware that the once calm and friendly town was suddenly a very dangerous place.

In the past hours, the radio had told them of their columns retreating from the west being under almost constant attack. Bridges had been blown up and tunnels blocked. Delays had been created by heavy battles with the Résistance in Le Vigan and then Ganges. Now it was the turn of Saint-Hippolyte.

Suddenly he saw grey vehicles coming up the road – at the front, motorcycles with sidecars, then two Kübelwagens with officers, and then trucks – dozens of them. Several of them had shattered windscreens and other battle damage, and Hans could see wounded men in two of the open trucks, heavily bandaged.

The leading Kübelwagen skidded to a halt. Hans looked round the truck's canvas cover and saw a General standing up and shouting urgently at Major Schmidt, who nodded and saluted. Hans took the opportunity to lean out from the back to ask a soldier in the truck stopped next to his what had happened. He was frankly shocked by his appearance – his face unshaven and lined with fatigue, his uniform unexpectedly filthy. Even the hand holding his cigarette was visibly shaking.

'It was very, very bad. We've come all the way from Toulouse, under attack every few miles. Blown bridges, diversions, ambushes. And then in that last damned town, they'd taken down all the road signs, so parts of our column got lost, and we were then attacked *again*. We lost vehicles, men as prisoners and quite a few killed and wounded. One old French bastard even shot several of our guys one after another with his hunting rifle, for God's sake! Let's hope we're through the worst.' He puffed at his cigarette nervously. Then his truck clunked into gear, and the soldier shouted, 'WIEDERSEHEN!' before disappearing.

Hans' own truck now inched forward. When two other trucks had rumbled past, an officer waved all three from the little garrison of Saint-Hippolyte on, to slot themselves into the column, which Hans knew was meant to be 'large and safe'. But *was* it?

Nervous enough about his own fate, Hans looked miserably back in the direction of the little town he had begun to like, and thought of the girl he had begun to love.

* * *

By mid-afternoon the heat near Anduze was almost unbearable as Carmen lay in the bushes. The racket from the millions of Cigale crickets was so loud that she nearly didn't hear the two-man German motor-cycle reconnaissance sidecar puttering under the railway bridge, presumably to be dealt with by her comrades further on. Now she was thoroughly shaken to see what was approaching, and just how big the German column was as it came towards her, its vehicles seeming to stretch back all the way back to Tornac.

'*Suicide, just suicide,*' she thought, terrified. Sebastian, her young Number Two from Valencia, was frowning, trying to appear brave and gripping the Bren magazines tightly in his big brown hands, probably to hide them shaking. She prayed fervently that the daring bluff – that they were a large force – thought up by Cristino, Miguel Arcas, Gabriel Perez and the Frenchman 'Carlo' – was really going to work.

The leading Kübelwagen was just thirty metres from the railway bridge. Suddenly Carmen was struck by noise and blast. Dynamited, the whole steel railway bridge had fallen down on to the road, blocking it completely. Chunks of metal and earth dropped around them as they crouched face down on the embankment. Then the smoke cleared.

'*Feu à volonté! VITE!*' shouted 'Carlo'.

As soon as she could see, Carmen started firing, in short five-round bursts as she had been taught, gratified to see that most of the leading Kübelwagen's crew soon seemed dead or wounded. After all, because of their secrecy in the hills, this was only the second time she had fired the Bren with anything but single shots. The rifles, the other two Brens and their single Hotchkiss machine-gun were also firing as hard as they could, not just to hit the enemy, but also to give the impression that there were hundreds of maquisards – not just a tiny handful. Carmen knew they only had thirty-two Spaniards and eight Frenchmen, whereas the enemy column looked as if it contained hundreds, its vehicles now piled up on the narrow road in a desperate traffic jam.

There was now a more distant explosion. So, Carmen told herself, the training by Cristino Garcia with the dynamite stolen from La Grande Combe's coalmines was at last paying off .The road *behind* the Germans must now be blocked, with the column trapped between the deep drainage ditches on both sides of the road. Nothing could move. And the Germans seemed unable to tell from where in the thick vegetation the deadly firing was coming.

Carmen, calming down, steadily fired off magazine after magazine. The cartridge cases piled up under the gun and the gun's barrel was getting very hot. Suddenly, it stopped firing. The gas cylinder had clearly clogged – but, just as they had been taught, Carmen slid the barrel forward so Sebastian could quickly open the gas regulator a notch. 'Mierdo!' he swore as he burned himself, but thankfully the Bren fired again.

Like their comrades, they both kept crawling to different positions in the thick bushes every few minutes to give the Germans the impression that there were many more of them. The heat, the effort and the fear bathed them all in sweat.

When she had a moment to think, Carmen became puzzled. The Germans, despite their numbers, seemed confused and indecisive, huddling near their vehicles and not fanning out into the vineyards to return fire methodically and counter-attack. So who *were* they? Conscripts? Support troops? Cooks? But Carmen had been told that even German cooks were trained to fight properly. What the *hell* was wrong with them? But, thank God, *something* was. She now swung the gun, and shot at two figures trying to get a mortar up on to its bipod plate.

Suddenly the firing stopped, and a German officer with a white flag emerged and walked forward cautiously. Why? Did he want to surrender? *Thank God they don't know how few we are,* thought Carmen. Then, after a while Carlo stood up and walked out very cautiously to meet him, but Carmen and the others could not hear what was said.

A strange silence then fell on the battlefield, but with urgent whispered instructions coming along the line from Gabriel Perez, 'Keep down! Don't show yourselves!'

After a while, two German officers disappeared with two of Carmen's comrades, Captain Capdur and Marceau Lapierre. The rather strange news now came whispered down the line that the Germans had refused to surrender to 'irregulars' – incredibly insisting on doing so to proper, uniformed French authorities. '*Typical Germans,*' smiled Carmen, when she heard. '*They always respect a uniform.*' They were then seen being driven off to the Anduze police station to surrender their huge force to a mere Gendarme! But apparently they then kept demanding 'free passage' for their column – exactly what the guérilleros were there to block.

Carmen managed to gulp a mouthful of water down, then saw them return, and found out in whispers from her friends what had happened. Another pause.

Now, just when Gabriel Perez was loudly insisting on unconditional surrender, the Germans suddenly broke the truce and started firing again, and Carmen saw one of her friends clutching his hand before he could drop down out of the line of fire.

All at once, the whole situation began to look much more dangerous. More of the Germans seemed to have been urged into action by their officers. Two of their mortars went into action, but most of the bombs luckily fell behind Carmen's position. More serious, a light anti-aircraft gun on the back of a truck then started firing, to a 'pom-pom-pom' sound as the shells started hitting the rocks below the castle – really dangerous for her comrades up there, Carmen realized. But the gun had no armoured shield, so with her Bren, at 300 metres, she managed to pick off the three men working it. For the moment, nobody seemed to want to take their places. But more worrying, much further away, she heard the louder noise of an anti-tank gun now beginning to fire at her comrades below the castle.

Carmen's Bren was now down to just four full magazines, only about a hundred rounds; the gas regulator was opened wide at maximum, and she sensed, the barrel was now red-hot. She had no replacement for it, and knew the gun could easily jam and stop firing at any moment. Others must be in the same position. She shuddered. Was their defiant and brave action about to collapse into failure, defeat and death?

And then she suddenly lifted her head. The sound of aircraft? Several aircraft!

* * *

Flying very low down the railway line, Flight Lieutenant Roy Railton eased back on the throttles for the twin Merlin engines. Even though he loved Spitfires and Seafires, he had to admit that this Mosquito was a terrific plane, incredibly fast – and in spite of its bigger dimensions, easier to land on a carrier. And with its rockets, bombs, four cannons *and* machine-guns, it carried a hell of a punch.

Someone on the ground with the Résistance, called 'Felix', had radioed and guided them to a big retreating German column, which was immobilised and under fire. It had taken them just thirty minutes to arrive.

Suddenly Roy saw the column. It stretched nearly a mile he quickly estimated, and looked like a confused jam of grey thin-skinned vehicles. Smoke and dust from the battle had been thrown into the air, but not enough to obscure the target – and *what* a target!

'See them, Jim?' His wingman was flying behind and to the left of him.

'Roger, Roy.'

'Let's come in from the rear, follow me.'

'Wilco.' The other two planes behind them also radioed their understanding.

Roy banked his plane out over the rugged hills and then came racing back over the roofs of Anduze. He flicked the switches to arm his rockets and guns.

The four planes each made two passes, firing all the way, pulling up before they reached the railway. There was no flak and the German troops seemed to have flattened themselves into the vineyards. Many of the trucks were now blazing, and one had blown up.

With the column in chaos, the British planes now turned, climbed, and headed back towards the sea, their crews jubilant.

* * *

Carmen had wanted to get up and cheer, but lay in the grass with the planes' brass empty cases showering down. As the British fighter-bombers droned away, she looked up and saw that the result of their raid had been spectacular. Many enemy vehicles were on fire, with guns smashed and men killed and wounded in the open. What was more, she realized that their maquisards' fire was now intensifying. More Frenchmen, including some Gendarmes, had arrived. Some had crawled up the embankment and lay down on either side of her. One pair was another Bren-gun team, and before opening fire, its Number Two rolled through the grass to give Sebastian a pat on the shoulder and a large bag of precious, full Bren magazines.

Down below them Carmen could see the Germans were at last trying to break out, but now there must have been over fifty invisible new guns, many automatic, firing down at them so they couldn't move. And unexpectedly, she then heard a cracking sound above her head – the bullets from another, new French machine-gun firing long bursts from way *behind* her, from the high rocks of Le Paulhan, hundreds of metres away on the other side of the river, but still able to rake bullets straight down along the paralysed line of German trucks.

And now another white flag appeared. All at once the firing petered out and stopped.

And this time the truce held, and under Gabriel Perez's eye, the Germans began throwing their weapons on to piles. At last, the maquisards on the hill and on the railway embankment were told that they could stand up, and one by one, they scrambled to their feet.

The Germans now stared up at their victors, amazed. Even with the recent reinforcements, the maquis still only numbered less than a hundred. And by now someone must have told the German General that earlier on he had been held up for hours and beaten by even fewer – just forty men and women.

A shot suddenly rang out.

The appalling shame and humiliation for a senior German officer of surrendering hundreds of men and all their equipment to a tiny irregular band had obviously overwhelmed him.

Leaving Sebastian to bring the Bren, Carmen carried the magazines and went over to inspect the area she had been covering. By the side of the road and in the vineyards, there were dozens of Germans being patched up – by their own medical orderlies and with the help of two French doctors from Anduze.

Several dead bodies had been laid out. Looking down, Carmen suddenly thought she recognized one – a very tall one. His helmet off, she could see his blond, almost white hair.

'Qui est il?' she asked the nearest wounded German, her anxiety rising.

'Gefreiter Hans Pieter,' came the mumbled and dispirited reply.

Carmen was stunned, suddenly thinking about her sister and knowing she could never tell her.

Immediately deflated and depressed, despite their astonishing victory, she quickly walked over to a group of her comrades, where Gabriel Perez, the Commander of the 21st Brigade, was sitting examining the Luger pistol and identity card of the General who had killed himself.

'Lieutenant-General Konrad. A. Nietzsche Martin,' he read out. 'Poor bastard. Just imagine his thoughts when he was told that his eight hundred had been beaten by our forty.'

He offered Carmen a cigarette.

'Well, that certainly worked out, didn't it? Although I did see a few of the bastards escape down the road towards Sauve. But we must have captured over seven hundred. The Fritzes had about ten killed and way over a hundred wounded. Amazing, and in a way almost ridiculous. And I've just been told we had just *one* man wounded, in the thumb – and *nobody* killed. Fantastic! Pity Cristino couldn't see it, still wounded from the jail raid.'

He, laughed almost in disbelief, and then looked more serious. 'Well,' he added, looking around him, 'now we've finished up here, we'll take these weapons and go off to Spain to try to get rid of Franco. I wish you'd come with us.'

Carmen shook her head. 'I can't, Gabriel. I've been telling you for weeks, but no thanks. I've got a family here and my job now is to help them – more than ever. But good luck. You're probably *really* going to need it. For God's sake, take care.'

She couldn't help thinking that for a tiny group to go back and infiltrate Spain *now* – with Franco firmly in power and plainly bent on revenge – was not only quixotic, but very risky to say the least.

A few minutes later, with a rush of surprise and pleasure, she spotted her father walking towards her. She hadn't seen him for weeks. He must have been part of the reinforcements that had suddenly arrived, and had been several hundred metres away along the ridge near the ruined castle. He had obviously been pinned down by that flak gun, and Carmen revealed that she was the one who had silenced it. They hugged each other, for much longer than usual, only too aware that either or both of them could easily have been killed.

'Let's get back to Hippo in the morning,' said Pedro. 'It's too dark now. Do you think we can get one of those German jeeps to run and get it out of the traffic jam?'

* * *

'You did WHAT?'

'I brought you some letters, Mamá,' Juanita announced proudly.

'*What* letters?'

'I went to see Carmen near Anduze on my bike, and she sent me away, but some of her friends gave me letters to give to you and other families.'

'Madness!' said Maria, immediately furious, realizing that they had the addresses of all the maquisard families.

Juanita flinched, but continued. 'And then I came back on my bike and picked up the bread you wanted in Tornac, hiding the letters under my blouse.'

'Did anybody stop you?'

'Yes, two German soldiers on bicycles.'

'Dios! What happened?'

'They looked under the bread and in my basket, and then one of them looked at me an said something like 'kleine', which I think means little, and he smiled and let me cycle on. He was nice.'

'Por Dios,' said Maria. 'If they'd found those letters, they'd have all the names of the maquisard families, and they could have killed us!'

Juanita shook her head. 'No, no, Mamá. There *aren't* any Germans now. They've gone. Masses of them went past me as I cycled back. And then I heard a lot of shooting from where Carmen was. Then it all went quiet. And when I got here, people were beginning to cheer in the streets. I don't think they'll be coming back.'

She looked around. 'Where's Otilia, Mamá?'

A lot of shooting from where Carmen was? Suddenly the letters were the last thing on Maria's mind. *Were Pedro and Carmen still alive?*

But she still responded, 'Upstairs, but not talking to us. But maybe she'll talk to you.'

* * *

Very early the very next morning Maria was shocked to be woken by someone furiously knocking on the door. Pedro? Carmen? No, they had keys. Opening it cautiously in her dressing gown, she was pushed roughly aside by a burly, unshaven stranger asking her where Otilia was. She had no time to wake Alfonso before the man leapt upstairs and returned with her screaming daughter, still in her night-dress, manhandling her roughly past her and out of the house, and hearing his last terrifying words, 'You'll find her in the square at ten, along with the other Boches-lovers!'

Boches-lovers? At least, she understood that. Clutching his coat, she was desperate to plead her daughter's innocence, but was unable to speak French well enough to do so.

Now, frozen with horror, Maria stood crushed up behind the barricades in the square with Alfonso, watching the pathetic little group of young girls and women being heckled, all of them staring at the ground while the baying mob screamed insults and threw rotten vegetables at them. On the way to the square, Alfonso had hurriedly explained that Otilia had been seen 'consorting' with a Boche. For Maria the utter shock of that was compounded by the fact that he and her husband had never told her.

But she knew that she had to come, if only to give Otilia support in this appalling ordeal. That's if Otilia would ever be able to see her at all with so many onlookers, many of them clearly relishing the prospect of seeing these so-called 'collaboratrices' publicly shamed. And even worse, shamed by having their heads shaven in public, one by one.

Not far from where she was standing was a chair on a table, towards which the terrified queue was being herded, where a woman whom she knew from the butcher's shop was gloatingly brandishing a large pair of scissors, awaiting the next victim – and with obvious relish. Another, beside her, was wielding a razor, and waving it around to the delight of the crowd. Maria immediately vowed never to speak to either of them again, though realizing that was pathetically inadequate revenge, and dreading the moment when her daughter would be at the head of the queue. Her heart rate was now soaring – as she knew Otilia's would be. She watched with misery as three more girls' heads were shaved, feeling people press against her from behind to get a better view, gloating vociferously and even cheering as their long locks fell to the ground. Worse still, when their heads were shaven, most of their clothes were torn off and the abject girls were paraded in the street under a placard saying, 'I WHORED WITH THE BOCHES.'

Suddenly there was a disturbance in the crowd and people leapt out of the way as a Kübelwagen jeep roared into the square and came to a sudden halt in front of the two women.

Out leapt Carmen with a sub-machine gun from which she fired three shots into the air. And only just in time. Otilia was now at the head of the queue.

'LET HER GO!' screamed Carmen at the top of her voice to the two women, while pointing the gun straight at them in turn, still smoking.

She then swung it round the crowd, wild-eyed with fury. 'Where were *you* lot when we were all in the hills? What have *you* got to be so proud of? What's the point of even *more* misery, attacking defenceless young girls? Haven't we all been through enough in this cursed war? STOP THIS MADNESS, NOW!'

Carmen strode to the chairs and kicked them over, and Pedro was suddenly at her side, grim-faced. He also held a gun.

'GO HOME, EVERYBODY!' he screamed. 'GO HOME *NOW!*' His voice echoed around the square.

Little by little the muttering mob began to slink away.

Pedro took Otilia's hand, noticing it was freezing cold even on a warm day. 'Time to go home, cara.' He knew she would never forget the ordeal for the rest of her life.

She clung to him sobbing as he stroked her hair. At least she had been saved the utter degradation of having it shaved off. But it was scant comfort to either of them in the face of such public shame. Nor was it going to be easy to explain to Maria why she had not been told of Otilia's relationship. That was another battle ahead.

Now, from the other side of the square there was a sudden shot. A few moments later a woman they knew passed by and muttered an explanation; 'Un milicien.'

Carmen shrugged, by now, indifferent.

* * *

Several extremely difficult days passed, much of them calming Otilia and trying to get things back to normal – or as much as they could be. But the atmosphere in the house was bleak. Then, early one morning there was a knock on the door. Carmen went down and opened it, surprised to see an American jeep, its engine still running.

And to her absolute delight there stood Sean O'Neill, now in a British Captain's uniform. He swept Carmen up in his arms and kissed her, much to the amusement of the army driver she noticed, when he finally let her go.

'Come inside!' she said, thrilled to see him.

'Sadly, I can't, I haven't got time. I'm on my way to a meeting in Montpellier and then I'm following the Americans up the Rhône valley. In fact, I'm late already. But I had to see you. And then I'll be off again somewhere – probably Italy. But I needed to tell you something before I go. I've *really* missed you. You wouldn't believe how much. I've never met anyone like you, and really want to see you again. I had to tell you myself.

Please wait for me, that's if you feel the same way. And I'll write as soon as I can.'

He kissed her again and was gone.

THIRTY-FOUR

* * *

CARMEN HAD STAYED UP THE NIGHT BEFORE UNTIL EXTREMELY LATE, sorting out her bedroom and taking an unusually long time to wash her long, thick hair, almost as if she was washing out all the horrors of the last few years. She was suddenly luxuriating in the simple pleasures of being back at home with her family, a feeling only spoiled by seeing Otilia so quiet and withdrawn. She tried desperately to keep the picture of Hans's limp and dead body out of her mind after the battle at La Madeleine, but every time she looked at her sister the memory came flooding back, and with it, guilt, completely wiping out any feeling of triumph she may have had, or the satisfaction of being told that very day that she and each one of her comrades were to be awarded a medal for bravery, the highly prestigious Croix de Guerre with the Silver Star.

She prayed that Otilia would imagine that her boyfriend had been recalled to Germany and would never know what really happened – a secret she knew she would have to keep to herself for the rest of her life. But with so much talk in the village about the battle, it was likely that Otilia would one day put two and two together, causing a possibly unsurpassable family rift. And what if Otilia asked her *outright* if she knew anything of his fate? She would have no option but to lie.

It wasn't until two a.m. that she and Alfonso and her father finally went to bed, and for once she slept soundly for a good eight hours despite her worries, only woken by someone knocking repeatedly and loudly at the front door. Perhaps it was Sean again? No, it couldn't be. He'd said he would be in the Rhone valley, and then off to Italy.

And why had nobody else answered the door? Assuming that everyone else had got up and gone out, she wrapped a dressing gown around herself and went downstairs to see who it was, still knocking impatiently.

Opening the door, for a good five seconds she didn't recognize who it was. The figure in front of her was bearded, haggard and gaunt, and the smiling eyes she once remembered were now dull and sad.

'Carmen, it's me, Pierre!'

She had envisaged this moment many, many times over the initial years of his absence, rushing into his arms and feeling the once familiar warmth and comfort. But now she was stuck to the spot as if somehow paralysed.

He held out his arms, and Carmen stepped into his embrace, deeply shocked, and moreover, unnerved, embarrassed and guilty about Sean. The glorious homecoming she had once pictured could not have been further from reality, and in all his time in captivity she had – stupidly – never imagined or planned for this, or worked out what to do if and when it ever happened. It was like embracing the past, not the future – an impossible situation.

Pierre rocked her silently for a few moments, stroking her hair. 'I'm sorry, I know I've changed. And I haven't been home yet to clean myself up. I thought I'd come straight from the station to see you, hoping that you'd be in.'

Finally releasing her, she couldn't help noticing him glancing down at her left hand, almost certainly to check there was no engagement or wedding ring, and saw his look of profound relief.

Carmen led him inside the house in a mixture of shock and panic, wishing that someone else were there for support, and telling herself to calm down. It was abundantly clear that imprisonment for so long had taken its toll. He looked at least ten years older rather than the four he'd been away. His teeth were badly stained, his once-thick hair had thinned dramatically, and it was as if the light had gone out of his eyes. And although flooded with pity, she was equally flooded with shame, unable to help thinking about Sean.

For the next hour or so, he told her about what had happened to him, first in Germany, and then at a camp at Metz in Lorraine, making ammunition for the Germans – once in a while asking her if she had missed him. Each time she nodded, but desperately wishing that someone in her family would come home and make the reunion easier.

'At least we got liberated early, because we were in France not in Germany, I suppose I've got to be thankful for that. It was the Americans who got us out. The POWs in the German camps will probably be still stuck there for months.'

He paused, looking at her dishevelled hair. 'Anyway, you probably want to get dressed. Will you be in later?'

Carmen nodded. 'Yes, I'll be here. I'm out of work now. I used to be in the Résistance until very recently, but of course that's over now.'

'The Résistance? Good God! What on earth did you do? Cooking?'

'No, I was a Number One, the shooter, on a light machine-gun.'

Pierre gaped at her, aghast. 'What? *You* on a machine-gun? And you actually *used* it?'

'Yes.' She prayed that he wouldn't ask if she had killed anyone, because she knew she had – and almost certainly wounded a lot more.

Pierre let out a low whistle, shaking his head. 'Well, things have certainly changed since *I've* been away.'

'Yes, they have,' said Carmen, relieved to bring up the subject of things not being what they were. 'The war changed everything. In fact, I don't think they'll ever be quite the same for women. Certainly not for me. We've seen and done too much.' She was desperate to put across the point that the world had moved on, but not to the point of upsetting him.

Pierre studied her face for a moment. Graver and more serious than he remembered. 'Well,' he said after a while, 'I'd better go to the farm, and maybe we could meet up later, and probably go out this evening.'

Carmen panicked, not feeling ready for a date and being alone with him too long, and guiltily picturing Sean again. 'Tell you what,' she said, thinking quickly, 'why not come here for supper and see the family again? You obviously need feeding up a bit, and they'd love to see you.'

To her profound relief, he smiled. 'I'd love to. Well, that's if they wouldn't mind.'

'Of course they wouldn't.'

'What time then?'

'About seven?'

'Perfect.' He looked down at himself, embarrassed. 'And I'll look a damned sight better when I've got cleaned up.'

Carmen got to her feet, suddenly worrying that she was appearing too brisk. 'Fine. I'll see you then.'

Embracing him before he left once more unsettled her. She knew all too well that if Pierre was still in love with her, or even imagined he was, there would be extremely difficult days ahead.

'See you at seven, then,' said Pierre at the door. She watched him until he reached the end of the street, turning around to blow her a kiss, suddenly remembering that she hadn't consoled him about his father, and that the farm would now be in a pretty neglected state with her father having also joined the Résistance. He needed to know, so that it wouldn't come as too much of a shock.

'WAIT!' She ran after him, feeling stupid in her dressing-gown, and meeting him at the corner. 'I'm really sorry about your father, and you may find the farm isn't looking too good. My father kept it going for about three years after you left, but the Boches stole more and more food, so he gradually gave up and joined the Résistance like me. When the S.S. came here, it was just too much for him. In fact, for all of us. Did you know that they actually *killed* about twenty completely innocent local people?'

'No,' said Pierre, shocked. 'What *animals*! But nothing surprises me much now. Not any more. Anyway, I'll see you around seven. He looked down at himself, embarrassed. 'And if the water's still on there, I hope I'll look better, and smell better than this.'

Turning to go back to the house, Carmen noticed her father going in. She felt desperate to talk to him, but he was an old-fashioned man at heart. He would never understand the concept of being torn between two men. That simply didn't – or couldn't – happen with Spanish daughters. Fidelity and loyalty were all.

* * *

'Sarah, are you awake?' It was about one o'clock in the morning, several weeks later, and Sarah was once more back with them.

'I am now.'

'Mind if I talk to you?'

'No.'

'It's about Pierre. It's just not the same. I *do* feel for him, but not in the way I used to. There's too much pity there, and I don't think that'll go. It's all changed. And to be blunt, I can't really face the idea of sex with him any more – or even a proper kiss. He hates the fact that I'm now so different, but *he* is too. He's still lovely, but so much of the fun seems to have drained out of him. It's sometimes as if the light has gone out of his eyes. And feeling sorry for someone isn't the same as love.'

'Hardly surprising after all those years locked up. It might change after he's been back here for a while. It's still very early days. He needs time to recover.'

'I'm not sure he ever will. I think he's been permanently damaged. And he can't cope with the fact that I've become completely different too, or accept that I became a soldier, and even trained to kill. It utterly repels him. And he absolutely *won't* talk about it, and that's another big sticking point. It's a huge gulf between us, and getting bigger all the time.'

Sarah thought for a minute, picturing them together and wondering what to say.

Carmen suddenly interrupted her thoughts. 'What I think he needs is a conformist female, a more traditional sort of woman, and I can never be that any more. I pretend I am at times to keep him happy, but I'm not. And I never will be again. And that's a terrific strain. Nor, I know now, could I ever be a farmer's wife, if that's what he has in mind. The fact is that I want to see the world, find out about it, not be tied to a farm year in year out. Every time I go there, I'm reminded that kind of life's not for me. To be blunt, I feel remorse more than love, and I'm not sure that will ever change. And, as I said, I just don't fancy him any more. The sparkle's gone. And I'm pretty sure it won't come back. In fact, I know it won't.'

'That *is* a problem.'

'Of course I listen to him, all the ghastly things he went through, and there were certainly enough of them, but I need to move on – and I don't think he can, or maybe ever will. I'm afraid he'll always be stuck there somehow, glued in a timeframe, looking backwards not forwards, unable to shed all the baggage I don't think I can cope with. And I can't ever tell him what *I've* been through. People shot right in front of me, or even with me doing the shooting. There's a huge gulf between us.

And there's something else. I've never told you this, but I think I'm probably in love with another man, an officer called Sean, more like me, someone I met in the hills.'

'Wow, that *is* a bit difficult.'

'Yes, and getting more difficult all the time.'

'What if you had a bit of a break from them both?'

'Well, I *am* having a break from Sean. He's away in Italy, fighting again. But if I don't see either of them, I don't think it'll make any difference. As I said, Pierre's changed. I think permanently. And I've changed even more. In a way, it's a miracle he still wants me, but he certainly seems to. Probably because there's nobody else he can really talk to. And I just can't see any honourable way out of it.'

'The truth. Tell him.'

Carmen paused, picturing herself doing just that.

'Do you think I should?'

'Yes. It's fairer for both of you. You can't be with someone thinking you'd be happier without him, or happier with someone else. It isn't fair on them, or you. And you were so young when you first went out with him, you couldn't have known what sort of person you'd turn into. And nor could he.'

'I know. But how can I tell him I don't think it feels right?'

'With great kindness. And saying, as you said, you've become a different person without mentioning that he has too. Or if you do, very carefully.'

There was a long silence while she waited for Carmen to answer.

'Carmen, are you still awake?'

'Yes. Thanks for being honest. I guess I'll have to summon up my courage.'

'Well, you've certainly got a lot of that.'

'Yes, but a different sort.'

* * *

'Why didn't you ever tell me about Oti?' asked Maria, her back to Pedro, peeling potatoes at the sink. 'I might have been able to do something.'

'I don't think so,' replied Pedro. 'Alfonso and I tried to do everything we could, and all of it fell on deaf ears. Oti just wouldn't listen.'

'She might have listened to me,' replied Maria. 'I can't help but feel angry you kept it from me, her own mother.'

'Believe me, cara, she wouldn't have done. We did everything humanly possible, but she was too much in love.'

He paused. 'Remember when *you* were?'

'Yes, but to be honest not right now. I don't like being kept in the dark, and certainly not by my own husband.'

Pedro paused.

'It'll never happen again, I promise. Here…'

She turned to see him stretch his arms out to her, and to his vast relief she accepted his embrace.

THIRTY-FIVE

* * *

'THANK GOD SARAH ISN'T HERE,' SAID PEDRO, DEEPLY SHOCKED. HE had taken Carmen to the cinema to see what she was really looking forward to, the much-publicized American film, 'Gone with the wind', now at last dubbed into French. But the shocking newsreel beforehand had made them both want to leave before it even started.

It showed the Soviet army in Poland over-running what had been several Nazi concentration camps – first Majdanek and then Belzec, Sobibor and Treblinka. Apparently, the SS guards had abruptly marched away the surviving inmates and then tried to hide the evidence, but had run out of time as the Soviets advanced. The camera showed the shockingly emaciated survivors, men, women and children. And they also laid bare the terrible secrets of the gas chambers and cremation ovens – shown full of skulls and bones. These were clearly *not* 'resettlement camps' or 'work camps' as the French had been led to believe, but extermination camps, killing machines. And it was reported that there were many more of them. Furthermore the newsreader, obviously now freed from German or Vichy censorship, had asked how those French officials who had set up the holding camp at Drancy and then sent thousands of Jews to the East were feeling now. He also urged that instead of wasting their anger on French *collaboratrices* and shaving their heads, the nation should vent its ire on those who had knowingly collaborated in this genocide of its own citizens.

Carmen got up to leave, so horrified that she was in no mood to watch the main film, any more than Pedro was.

Worse, returning home, they discovered that Sarah had already got wind of the rumours of the same appalling news from Poland and had gone out and bought French newspapers. Now free to tell the truth, they had also featured the same dreadful revelations.

Sarah brought up the subject, deeply shocked and subdued. She had plainly been crying.

'I don't know if my parents went to one of those camps, but I fear the worst. All I can do is hope that by some utter miracle they survived.'

* * *

'My God, I thought the Germans were finished!' Alfonso had been listening to the radio the next morning – something people no longer had to hide.

Pedro looked worried. 'So did I. As did the Americans and the British, as far as I can see. They seem to have been really caught napping.'

They were referring to the shocking news of a huge and completely unexpected German offensive. The world had assumed that the squeeze on Germany from both west and east was inexorable and that the end was coming soon. But suddenly the Germans had created flying bombs, and now Hitler seemed to have secretly massed reserves of men and tanks and hurled them towards the recently re-opened and crucial port of Antwerp. They had punched through the snowy forests of the Ardennes, the same scene of the German dramatic breakthrough of 1941. And there were reports that inexperienced American soldiers had fallen back in disorder.

'I can't believe the bastards are going to start winning *again*,' said Alfonso, almost in despair.

'I don't think they can, they've just got so much up against them. And you notice they've done it in fog and snow. If the weather clears, Allied airpower will stop them.'

Indeed, it soon turned out that the Germans were critically short of supplies, desperate to capture them from the Americans and British, and unlike in 1940, there were no convenient filling-stations where the German tanks could refuel.

After several days, Pedro heard on the news of the response of an American General to German calls for surrender. 'Nuts!'

Pedro looked up the word in a French-English dictionary from his daughters' school.

'Les noisettes,' he said, puzzled. 'That's a funny thing to say!'

He might not have understood the General's slang, but Pedro was certainly proved right in his view about the outcome of the offensive – the 'Battle of The Bulge' as the Americans apparently called it. The Germans *were* halted, their objectives never reached, with the skies now cleared and Allied fighter-bombers taking their dreadful toll.

Within days, it was obvious to all that the German gamble had failed. All Hitler had done was to waste the lives of tens of thousands *more* of his men, and almost certainly more serious to him, lose hundreds of irreplaceable tanks and aircraft.

'I think that's it,' said Pedro. 'Millions of Russians will close in now, he'll have nothing to stop them, and that will soon be the end of it.'

He was right again.

* * *

'I'm sorry,' said Sarah watching Carmen tidy up their cramped shared bedroom and getting out of bed to help. 'Tidiness was never one of my great virtues.'

'Nor mine,' smiled Carmen, hanging up a couple of pairs of trousers. 'But if we're going to share this bedroom again, I think both of us will have to learn. It's getting impossible in here. I can never find anything. Look at it!' She kicked a pair of shoes under Sarah's bed.

Carmen was really irritable, and Sarah knew she had a point. Furthermore, she had been thinking long and hard about a solution. Not for a moment did she want to go back to the château, but now she was the sole owner and knew who her parents' solicitor was in town – presumably in possession of the deeds – she was in a position to sell it. And not only could she move out, but also buy a place of her own and help Carmen's family financially. At the same time she had also given a lot of thought to the paintings, wondering if it was now a good time to sell them – that's if they had survived being buried out at the farm for so long. With luck, she thought they might still be in a good enough condition to fetch a reasonable price.

'Damn!' Carmen was now trying to stuff things into a drawer which had completely jammed.

'Carmen, stop that for a moment. I've got an idea.'

'Well, make it quick. I can't face this shit heap any longer. It's not a bedroom, it's a junk heap.' She slumped down on the bed. 'Okay, fire ahead.'

'I think it's time for me to move on,' said Sarah. 'You and your family have been marvellous to me, but now I'm in a position – at long last – to fend for myself. In fact, I'm thinking of selling the château and the paintings. That way I can move out and help everyone. You, your family, Uncle Fon, Pierre and also me and Alexandre if we get married.'

'I'm sorry,' said Carmen. 'I didn't mean to be so irritable. And I don't expect you to go. In fact, I…'

Sarah put up her hand. 'No, it all makes sense. There's no point sitting on money if it can help everyone. I've thought everything through, and it all makes perfect sense. My mind's made up.'

'But where would you go?' Sarah asked. 'I'd really miss you if you moved out of town.'

'I've no intention of doing that, at least not yet. I could get a place here to start with and then see how it works out for a while. And then, if the paintings sell well and haven't gone all rotten, I could think again about all of us. And with any luck, Alexandre.' She looked up at Carmen. 'Did you know he wanted to study maths at university before all this happened?'

'No.'

'Well, that's still his dream. So if we *do* get married, we'd have to live near a university city like Montpellier to make travel easier.'

Sarah sat down on the bed beside her. 'Do you think his parents will try and stop you? I mean, getting married?'

'Yes. I'm sure they will. But he's always telling me it won't make any difference. Although I'm frightened it will. And the last thing I want to do is create a family feud.'

'But would that stop you going ahead?'

'No. Nor Alex either, at least from what he tells me. Anyway, coming back to getting a place of my own, I'd like to talk to your parents and Uncle Fon about it. Aren't your sisters staying with friends tonight?'

'Yes.'

'Then maybe that's a good time to talk things over.'

Carmen kicked at the jammed drawer, which miraculously shot into place. They both laughed.

To Sarah, it was almost symbolic, as if her life was suddenly clicking into place too.

CHAPTER THIRTY-SIX

* * *

'SARAH! I HAVEN'T SEEN YOU FOR AGES!' SARAH IMMEDIATELY RECOGNIZED her parents' former maid in the square. 'Gabriella! How lovely to see you! How have you been? I've been in hiding for so long, I haven't seen anyone for ages, at least not in the village. I've been in safe houses for years, constantly moving from one to another, and half of them weren't even safe with the Boches and the Milice snooping about.'

'Well, I'm really glad you're safe now,' smiled Gabriella, wondering if she should ask about Sarah's parents, deciding that it would be heartless not to, but fearing the worst.

'I suppose you haven't heard anything about your parents yet?'

'No,' said Sarah. 'Nothing. I can only pray they're safe.'

'And I will, too,' said Gabriella. 'They were lovely people.' She was suddenly embarrassed that she had used the past tense, though relieved that Sarah didn't seem to notice.

'Incidentally, Sarah, I've still got the keys to the château if you ever want to go there, or perhaps go back. If you like, I can drop them through your letterbox. Number 36. Rue de Pasteur, isn't it?'

Sarah nodded.

'Okay, I'll bring them round in the next day or so.'

'No, knock on the door and come in for a coffee.'

'Thanks, I'd like that.'

Two days later, Sarah had the keys in her bag and was on her way to the château with Pedro, four years since she had been there last. And reaching the gates, which Pedro had considerable difficulty unlocking, brought back a flood of memories.

At last they were inside the hall, and the two of them then wandered round the all but empty house in silence, until Sarah could take no more of it, picturing her parents' last terrifying moments there.

But just before leaving, and now outside the gates, she decided on impulse to check the postbox, surprised to find a letter addressed to her among a pile of old circulars, and in faded handwriting she didn't recognise – with a Metz postmark.

She looked up at Pedro. 'Good Lord, this letter's for me.' She tore it open.

Pedro was shocked to see her go deathly pale as she read it, and tears suddenly streaming down her face.

'They're dead,' she whispered, looking up ashen-faced.

Pedro knew instantly that she meant her parents, and for a moment he was rooted to the spot.

'Here.' He opened his arms to give her a hug, but Sarah shook her head. 'It's okay,' she said in a faltering and tiny voice. 'I've pictured it in my mind a thousand times, and somehow I've always known. I kind of knew deep down that they wouldn't make it.'

She wiped away her tears before handing him the sheet of notepaper with a shaking hand.

Pedro read it with mounting shock, as Sarah went and sat on a rock, clutching herself and keening in misery.

Dear Sarah,

I really hope this letter will somehow reach you, but I'm afraid it brings terrible news.

I've agonised many times about whether I should tell you, but I made a promise to your parents that I cannot break.

I met them in an awful holding camp called Drancy just outside Paris and we became friendly, mostly talking about art and music. I was alone, my wife having died that year. After a few weeks we were suddenly ordered to board a train. It was made up not of SNCF coaches, but rough cattle cars. And we were all crammed in – men, women and children. The journey took three days, standing up without food and water. Many people died on the wagons, so Isaac and I feared the worst. We knew that if they were treating us like that and just on the journey, they obviously didn't care about our lives. So he and I memorized the addresses of each other's loved ones and promised to try and get in touch with them if either of us survived.

Eventually we arrived at a place that I later found was called Oswiecim, or Auschwitz in German. There were dogs and shouting men everywhere, forcing us off the train. And then a Nazi officer stood on a box and shouted something like this:

'This is Auschwitz Concentration Camp. Any resistance or disobedience will be ruthlessly punished. Anyone disobeying or trying to escape will be sentenced to death. Now, men on one side, women and children and old men on the other!'

Then, with someone who was probably a doctor, they started separating us all out with the men on one side, whom I later realized were going to work in the I.G. Farben factory, and the women and children and old men and anyone sick on the other. But your father refused to be separated from your mother. An SS man shrugged and said, 'So be it!' And they were both marched away. I never saw them again. I was devastated. Nobody ever came back from that end of the camp.

I did survive, by working as a slave for two years. And when the Soviets got close, most of us were sent off on what turned out to be a death march. But in the dark I fell into a ditch and was miraculously rescued by some Poles.

Eventually, I made it back to Metz, and now I'm near a postal system. That's why I can send you this letter, although I truly wish it wasn't to bring you such heart-breaking news. But as I said, I made a promise to Isaac and Véronique, one I could't break.

Please, if you want to be in touch, write to the above address.

Yours sincerely, and with my deepest condolences,

Israel Gluckstein.

Pedro handed back the letter wordlessly.

Sarah suddenly yearned for Alexandre, knowing that he was about to tell his parents that he was in love with her that very same day, and realizing that she could lose him too if he caved in to their fierce anti-Semitism. He had readily admitted their strong dislike of Jews in all the safe houses they had shared over the last few years. His words rang in her ears, 'They'll kill me if I marry you, but I'll kill myself if I don't.'

'I need to be alone,' she said, looking deathly pale.

Pedro was hugely relieved to walk her upstairs, clinging to his arm for comfort, although she was now unable to speak.

No-one said anything at supper that evening. There was only the sound of clinking cutlery until Maria broke the silence.

'Do you think Sarah will come down?' she asked Carmen, glancing upstairs.

'No, I think she needs to be alone. In fact, I *know* she does. I'll take up some soup for her later.'

* * *

It was May in Saint-Hippolyte, warm and beautiful, with the trees all gloriously green and the flowers coming out.

Judging by the radio reports, it was obviously a far less pleasant picture in the blackened, smoking wreckage of Berlin, and finally the longed-for news came through. Hitler, who had brought such untold misery to the world, was dead, killed by his own hand just before Russian troops closed in on his last bunker, but not before he had made his deluded people go on fighting to the last street and house.

And soon came the wonderful announcement that the war in Europe had ended at last, changing the atmosphere across France overnight. For most French people, this meant the return of their loved ones, their menfolk – both the soldiers who had been languishing for years in prisoner-of-war camps and also the civilians who had been forced to work in Germany. But many others did not return, bombed in Germany while trapped doing the dreaded 'Service Obligatoire'.

Pedro pointed out a real irony to Alfonso.

'I'll bet when Hitler said back in 1940 that he wouldn't release our fellows 'until all hostilities ceased', he was talking about brow-beating the British into surrender, and not about Germany's defeat and his own humiliating death. And I see Pétain ran off to Germany.'

'I don't blame him,' said Alfonso. 'He must fear for his life here. Think of all the people who'd like to get their hands on him. They're certainly going after the Vichy small fry with *l'épuration sauvage*, as the French are calling it. Nothing very pure about it, from what I hear. I think it has a lot to do with sheer shame. An awful lot of people were at it – collaborating.

Even Coco Chanel was openly living with a German officer, and in luxury for years. And I'll *bet* they don't go after *her*.'

* * *

After three hours non-stop drilling to get to the steel box in Pierre's old stone outhouse, and in the boiling heat of summer, both Alfonse and Pedro were exhausted and covered with sweat, but the worst was over as they felt their drills slide and rattle across its steel lid.

'Phew!' said Alfonso, wiping his brow and dropping his drill into the pile of rubble. 'I think it's time for a break.'

'Me too,' agreed Pedro, also tossing down his drill and wiping his face with his sleeve. 'This heatwave doesn't help. Must be nearly forty degrees out there.'

'And more in here,' laughed Alfonso. Six empty bottles of water were lying at their feet, and already they were thirsty again, suddenly glad to see Sarah at the door again bringing them even more – though irritated by the name on the bottles – VICHY.

She was delighted to notice they had at last reached the lid, and thanking them yet again for their patience and hard work, suggested they come inside to the cool of the farmhouse. 'Pierre's made some baguettes for you. Why not take a break for a bit? You'll boil to death out here if you go on any longer, or die of exhaustion.'

Both of them readily agreed.

Secretly, Sarah wished they would carry on, desperate to find out whether the paintings had survived and knowing what a difference it could make to everyone if they had. But she knew it wasn't fair to ask them to continue right now.

One hour later, which seemed like four to her, the steel lid was finally levered open revealing the scrolls. Sarah ran her hand gingerly over them, hugely relieved to find they were dry. 'They seem okay, not even damp, thank God.' She took out as many as she could carry back to the house and laid them on the kitchen table, soon relieved again to find that every painting she unrolled appeared to be in perfect condition, with not a trace of fading, let alone spotting or mildew.

Finally, all the scrolls had been carried in and inspected, then gently rolled up again. Not one of them seemed to have suffered in any visible way, although Sarah knew she was no art expert and that professional auctioneers might well disagree.

'I can't thank you enough,' she said to Alfonse and Pedro. 'And you,' she turned to Pierre, 'for giving them a safe house. And really luckily, a dry one. And on that note I think we should have a little celebration. I'll be back in a second.'

A couple of minutes later she returned with a bottle of champagne which she'd left in the van, hoping there would be a good reason to drink it, while fearing the worst.

'Here, I brought this just in case the paintings had survived. And my goodness, they have. And far, far better than I ever expected!' She handed the bottle to Pedro. 'You do the honours, and I'll fetch some glasses.'

As they sat around the kitchen table, nobody minded that the champagne was far too warm or that the smell of sweat in the kitchen was a bit overpowering.

'A votre santé!' said Sarah raising her glass.

'A votre santé!' chimed in Pedro, Alfonso and Pierre.

* * *

Early August brought tumultuous news from the Far East. For months the British had been steadily advancing through Burma, and by sea the Americans had been closing in on Japan, with island after island falling to them, with strange blood-stained names like Saipan, Iwo Jima and Okinawa filling the newspapers. Pedro, still acting as the town's unofficial military expert, said that judging by the way the Japanese fought almost to the last man on these small islands, the prospect of fighting millions of them in Japan itself must be really worrying the Americans.

"I wonder what the hell they'll do.'

But on August 6th, came the answer, with news came in that was almost impossible to believe. Just one single bomb had destroyed a whole city in Japan called Hiroshima. At first, the American announcements mentioned a 'Cosmic Bomb' but then suddenly they talked of an *atomic bomb*, apparently quite small but with the astonishing power of 20,000 tons of explosives.

Two days later the Japanese directed messages in French towards Europe, protesting the 'unfair and immoral' use of this new weapon on what they rather strangely called a 'ville démilitarisée'. They confirmed the shocking news that nearly every Hiroshima resident had been killed, with 'practically all living things, human or animal, literally seared to death'. The Japanese were advised from Potsdam to surrender, to avoid what the American President Truman called 'a rain of death'. On the radio, French listeners heard that, despite the unimaginable carnage, the Japanese had rejected the ultimatum.

'I wonder what's next?' said Pedro, switching off the radio, while picturing the utter devastation.

They did not have to wait long to find out – just two days. A second bomb had been dropped on the industrial port of Nagasaki, with equally devastating and horrifying results. What is more, the Russians had broken their treaty with Japan and had declared war, invading Manchuria. Surely now the Japanese would realize they were beaten and would surrender? To everyone's overwhelming relief, they did.

'LE JAPON OFFRE DE CAPITULATION!' screamed the headline in *Le Nation*.

Japan's God-like Emperor, Hirohito, had apparently recorded a broadcast to his people, the only time they had ever heard his voice. The French were almost incredulous when they heard that he had begun by saying, and in a masterly piece of understatement – 'The war situation has developed not necessarily to Japan's advantage'. He then urged his people to accept the ultimatum from Potsdam 'to endure the unendurable and suffer what is insufferable'.

Now it really *did* appear that a war that had killed tens of millions and had destroyed whole countries might be over at last.

THIRTY-SEVEN

* * *

'**Y**OU WILL ABSOLUTELY NOT MARRY THAT GIRL. OR IF YOU DO, OVER MY dead body! What's more, you won't inherit anything from us if you do. I can't stop you marrying her if you're fool enough to do so, but don't expect a penny coming to you. *Is that understood?*'

'Perfectly,' replied Alexandre. 'But even if you had all the money in the world, it wouldn't stop me. I'm in love with her, and I know I always will be.'

'You *can't* know that. No-one does. Time changes people.'

'Well, has time changed *you?*'

'That's not a question I'm prepared to answer. All I can tell you is that marriage isn't easy, and if there's a profound difference – like a different religion – that won't help. And I wouldn't have thought her parents would like the idea of her marrying *you*, either.'

'They're not around to care. They're dead. Murdered at Auschwitz.'

Alexandre was at least relieved to see that his father was shocked.

'I'm sorry about that. But if they *were* alive, I'm sure they wouldn't want *you* as a son-in-law.'

'Why not? From what Sarah tells me, they were both extremely open-minded people, and deeply intelligent ones.'

'Are you saying your mother and I are stupid?'

'No, only about Jews. And you don't even *know* any. All you've ever done is listen to that damn Pétain and go along with him. And you're probably not even sorry that so many Jews have been wiped out. Probably millions – including children.'

'Who says that I'm not?'

Alexandre was about to say 'Me', but decided not to. But he did continue. 'And it's particularly sad that you're so anti-Semitic, living in this region – one that's been so good at hiding the Jews. It's saved so many of them, thank God. Including my future wife. *You* may not mind what's happened to others, but many do – including me. I'd be utterly ashamed if I didn't.'

'Well,' said his father, 'go ahead with the wedding if you want to, but don't expect *us* to attend. And don't expect us coming round to the idea either in the course of time. It just won't happen. And another thing. Don't assume you can live here any more until you've changed your mind. And if you won't, you're out of this house *and* a job, and right now.'

'So be it,' said Alexandre. 'But don't ever say I didn't ask you and Maman to come.'

It was all exactly as Alexandre had expected, almost word for word.

Thirty minutes later, going down the path back to the road, he felt a huge weight off his mind, and longed to see Sarah more than ever, delighted to find her in the café where they had arranged to meet, even though he was twenty minutes early.

'How did it go?' she asked tentatively, knowing he had chosen that morning to talk to his parents about her.

'As expected.'

'You mean they're totally against it.'

'Well, Papa was. Maman had gone out – probably on purpose. So, my darling, I'm now homeless, jobless and an orphan. I've been kicked out, totally. Not exactly a great prospect for a husband.'

Sarah smiled. 'You still are to me. But, what do we do now?'

'Go ahead, get married, and do it without them.'

'But Alexandre, are you absolutely *one hundred per cent* sure you still want go ahead? I mean, without your parents' consent?'

'No,' replied Alexandre.

Sarah looked crestfallen, until Alexandre laughed and stroked her hand. 'I'm *two* hundred per cent sure. I've never been surer of anything in my life.'

'Even if it means converting to the Jewish faith?' asked Sarah, nervously. 'Then we could be married in a synagogue and I'd love to do that for my parents. But I can't expect you to do that for me.'

'Why not?' smiled Alexandre. 'I'd do anything for you.'

Sarah suddenly burst into a flood of tears, struggling to tell him she was only crying with gratitude and relief.

* * *

'This is a very fine château,' said Edgar Drouille, the estate agent in Saint-Hippolyte, looking at the graceful high ceiling in the hall and the beautiful wrought iron staircase in front of him. 'Do you know its history?'

'Not really,' said Sarah. 'We didn't really live here very long, and I never found out much about it with the war starting and everything. To be honest, it became a place of fear, not happiness.'

'Of course. I understand.' He knew about her parents – and had met them – indeed he had sold the place to them, and now felt deeply sorry for her, eager to get her as good a price as possible for her as well as himself, but knowing there may not be a market for such a sizeable property after years of depression, job losses and deprivation.

'It's a copy of a villa in Rome called the Villa Napoleon, built around 1880. The architecture is far more Italian than French and very rare around here.'

Sarah suddenly remembered her father telling her that.

'The symmetry is also unusual, again Italianate, similarly the height of this hall and that superb staircase, again very rare in this region.'

He walked around a little, checking the state of the walls, and disappearing into the salon for several minutes, where Sarah's mother always had huge vases filled with flowers. She decided not to join him, knowing it would bring back a rush of painful memories.

Returning from the salon, Drouille wrote a few notes on his pad.

'It may have a market with say, an art dealer in Nîmes or Montpellier who wants a country retreat. It's certainly perfect for someone with many paintings.'

'I know,' said Sarah. We used to have lots all over the walls here. My grandfather was an art dealer in Paris, and it was like an art gallery here.'

'What happened to them?'

Sarah thought quickly. 'I don't know. Stolen by the Boches, and their lackeys here.'

'I'm sorry.'

Drouille went off to inspect the kitchen and came back a few minutes later. 'May I see upstairs?'

'Of course. But if you don't mind, I'd rather stay here. I don't really want to see my parents' bedroom.'

'I understand. I won't be long.'

Ten minutes later he was back. 'It's all in reasonable condition, considering. There's no serious architectural work required, thank goodness. That always tends to put buyers off, particularly if they're buying second homes.' He looked at his notepad briefly, then put it in his pocket. 'Anyway, I think I'm done. And thanks for showing me around.'

'I didn't,' smiled Sarah.'

'Well, for bringing me here, and for involving me in the sale. My estimate is that we could probably sell it in the region of twenty million francs, depending as I said, on the state of the market. There are only a few people around now who can afford such a big place and its maintenance.'

Twenty million francs? Sarah couldn't believe her ears. That would be enough to get a place for herself and Alexandre, and to help everyone who had helped her, and still there would be money over. And she knew that her parents would have approved of her plans. Once again, she tried not to picture them in Auschwitz, a constant struggle.

Drouille interrupted her thoughts. 'Well, I'll let you know if there's any interest. And before that I'll need someone to take good photographs as soon as possible. Would it be possible to have the keys?'

'Certainly,' said Sarah taking them out of her pocket. 'I don't need them any more.'

THIRTY-EIGHT

* * *

I T WAS NOW THREE MONTHS SINCE SARAH HAD SHOWN THE ESTATE AGENT, Edgar Drouille, round the château, but she had heard no word from him. Now, passing his agency in the square, she looked at the photograph of it in the window, one of several there, partially faded by the sunshine, hugely surprised to see a sticker across it announcing 'UNDER OFFER'. So someone had made a bid for it? She immediately wondered why she had not been told and went inside, relieved to see Drouille sitting at his desk.

'Bonjour.'

'Bonjour, Mademoiselle Levy!'

'I've just seen that the château is under offer, and wondered why you haven't told me.'

Drouille smiled. 'I've hardly had time to. The offer only came in yesterday, just when I was closing up. I would have come round to tell you today, but now you've beaten me to it.' He got up from his desk to shake her hand and offer her a chair.

'And the good news is, it's very close to our asking price. As I told you, not many people can afford a place like yours these days, but this potential buyer clearly can. He's a successful art dealer from Nimes, Xavier Donnadieu, and clearly managed to keep going through the war. And now he's looking for a country retreat, and especially one where he can display his collection of antiques and paintings. In that respect, your château is a rarity, and I'm relatively confident he won't pull out. We'll have to cross our fingers for a while. I'll let you know immediately if there are any developments.'

Sarah was suddenly excited, and not only because they had received a firm offer. She realized that an experienced art dealer might be another blessing, someone who might be able to help assess her parents' paintings, now hidden in Auguste's shed – that's if they'd survived.

'What kind of paintings does he sell?' she asked, hoping the estate agent might know.

'He didn't really tell me. But I guess they'd have to be fine art to be able to afford a property like yours. And the Germans might have been good customers, even if the French weren't. A lot of them were like Goering, mad about paintings.'

'*And* stealing them whenever they could,' added Sarah.

'Yes, that too, from what I've heard.'

Sarah got up to leave and shake hands with Drouille. 'Well, thanks for your hard work. I'm really grateful.'

'A pleasure,' said Drouille, getting up from his chair and accompanying her to the door.

'As I said, I'll be in touch as soon as I know more.'

Sarah returned home, delighted. At long last things were suddenly falling into place. She pictured herself and the art dealer going through the paintings together at the farm. Surely, as a top professional, he would be interested? She told herself not to be too optimistic, but couldn't help smiling at everyone she passed on the way home. What a difference from when she hardly dared to look at people, or was terrified if they looked at her!

* * *

Two months after the sale of the château had gone through, Sarah chose to go round there, hoping that Xavier Donnadieu would be in and that she had given him and his wife enough time to move in. She had purposely picked a Saturday, assuming that he would be working at his gallery during the week.

Now, after knocking at the door, she was relieved to hear someone coming, and even more so to see Donnadieu open it. He, too, seemed pleased to see her – as was his wife when she had come downstairs, especially as Sarah had bought her a bunch of flowers as a moving-in present.

She had liked the two of them immediately when they had been at the solicitor's office in Ganges eight weeks ago, and was pleased to have sold to two such pleasant and polite people.

To her delight, they asked if she would like a glass of wine in the salon, and she accepted, despite the strong association of that room with her mother.

Now, as she was sipping an excellent white wine she turned to Xavier. 'To be honest, it wasn't just to give you the flowers that I'm here. I have something to tell you that you may find interesting. My father, as you may know from the estate agent, had many fine pictures here, and particularly in the hall. His father was an art dealer like you, back in Germany, and then Paris. He lost a good deal of his collection to the Germans, but what he managed to salvage he left to my father.

Well, before my parents went to Auschwitz, my father became very afraid, and rightly so, that the collection he had here would be stolen by the Boches. So he hid the lot before that happened. But he kept all the frames, and put cheap paintings in them from the market. And now I have the original collection, hidden in a place near here.' Donnadieu was clearly astonished and didn't answer for a while.

'Do you know what they are?'

'Some. I know there's a Monet and a Matisse, and a Berthe Morisot.'

Donnadieu was stunned. She *couldn't* be right. Three of the most famous painters in France, and not just France, but now all around the world? There had to be some mistake. Reproductions, surely, albeit probably very good ones.

'Are you absolutely sure?'

'Yes.'

'And you say that the collection was once in beautiful and original frames?'

'Yes. It used to be.'

Donnadieu's mind was reeling, as he suddenly remembered the two unlikely men who had brought all those paintings to his gallery years ago – cheap paintings, but in surprisingly valuable frames. He had never understood that conundrum. He also remembered buying the frames – and a lot of antique furniture, bluntly telling the two men that the paintings were worthless.

He took a deep breath. 'Did you also have a lot of antique furniture?'

'Yes. That was stolen too.'

Donnadieu nodded gravely. 'I think I may just know what happened to it. Several years ago, a couple of men came to my gallery in Nîmes with a van full of furniture, some of it quite lovely. But what was odd, they also brought a number of truly lovely frames, but with pictures inside that were worth nothing at all. Cheap stuff, probably from a local market. It didn't make sense. But it just might make sense now. And if it does, we're holding on to your rightful property. Not the frames, sadly. We've sold those. But I still have several of the antiques left. Tell me, did you by any chance have a table with a drawer on each side which you could turn upside down and use as chess boards?'

'Yes. My parents used to love chess. And we had a table just like that.'

'And did you have a very elegant chaise longue, upholstered in golden fabric?'

'Yes.'

'And a very tall armoire in dark wood, with leaf and flower carvings?'

'Yes, that too.'

Donnadieu turned to his wife. 'I think we should take Sarah to the gallery and see what's rightfully hers. At least, from the items we haven't sold. And Sarah, it appears we may owe you money.'

'I don't want your money,' said Sarah, 'And I don't need the furniture. But there's one thing I *do* want. Someone to look at the paintings I've got and help me sell them.'

Donnadieu nodded. 'I'd be delighted. It's the very least I can do. And again, I'm immensely sorry if I've been selling stolen property.'

'It's all in the past,' said Sarah, suggesting they meet the following Saturday. 'The paintings are hidden in a farm quite near here, but it's a bit of a hike. I'll ask one of my guardians to take us there in his van.'

'No need to,' said Donnadieu. 'We can go in my car. And Sarah, would you like to stay for lunch?'

'Well, if you're sure. You're probably still unpacking things.'

'Quite sure, it would be our pleasure. And frankly, it would be like unpacking guilt.'

* * *

Xavier Donnadieu had now spent half an hour silently scanning the first five paintings brought down from Auguste's bedroom, carefully spread out along the kitchen table and weighted down on all four corners by pebbles which Pierre had collected, cleaned and dried the day before.

Alexandre and Sarah waited nervously in silence for his verdict as he scrutinised each one, perturbed to see him shake his head at intervals, not gathering that it was in awe and astonishment and interpreting it as rejection. Finally he laid down his magnifying glass on the kitchen dresser behind him, and turned to give his verdict. 'Well, I can hardly believe what I'm looking at. I really can't. Frankly, I'm totally overcome. Do you mind if I sit down for a moment?'

Alexandre immediately fetched him a chair.

'Well,' continued Donnadieu, rubbing his back before sitting down, 'I've seen many fine paintings in my life, but never have I seen ones of this quality in a private and unknown collection. And if the others are anything like as good at these, you're looking at a fortune.'

Sarah and Alexandre were both stunned.

'Would you like me to tell you what they are?' he asked.

'We certainly would.'

Donnadieu scanned the table again. 'All these landscapes clearly come from a period called French Romanticism, which came to the fore in the first half of the nineteenth century.'

He pointed to each of the paintings in turn. 'This one is by the artist who started that movement, Théodore Rousseau. And this one is by Diaz, who liked to paint in strong fiery colours like these. And these two are clear examples of work by two rather more subdued painters – Dupré and Troyan. Both of them were intent on painting nature in a revolutionary new way, and settled in a village called Barbizon, near Fontainebleau. In fact, they started what was called 'The Barbizon School'. Have you heard of it?'

'I seem to remember my father mentioning it,' said Sarah, with the familiar pang of pain she always had when thinking of him.

'It's extremely famous,' continued Donnadieu, 'especially for landscapes like these.'

He now turned to another painting. 'And this one is by the greatest, and in my view, most fascinating artist of that period, Camille Corot, who was in frequent contact with the Barbizon School. It's a typical example of his style, with the pronounced tonal effects and the way he masters light.'

He pointed to another canvas, this time a drawing of a copse. 'And here's another Corot, clearly signed. But the real signature is in his style. You see the way he's done the trees? That's typical Corot.'

Donnadieu wiped his brow. 'Do you mind if we take a break? I'm sorry, but I'm rather in a state of shock. As I said, I really didn't expect to see paintings of anything like this quality. And we've only just gone through, what is it, one roll? Perhaps we could take a pause before the next one and have a glass of water.'

After another two hours, Donnadieu had identified and explained paintings by both Monet and Manet and one by Baudelaire, and the painting that Sarah had always loved in the family collection – an exquisitely tender painting by someone called Berthe Morisot that she knew Carmen had also loved. At that moment, she resolved to keep that one canvas, no matter what it might fetch at auction, unable to part with it.

And at that same moment, Donnadieu decided to call another halt for the time being. Again, it was all too much to take in – the experience of a lifetime, but as exhausting as it was exciting.

'Well, what a day!' he concluded, letting out a low whistle. 'And what a collection! But I can't rush it, not with paintings as fine as these. What if I come back next weekend when I'm down here again, and the one after that? I could probably make both Saturday and Sunday, And I'm sure my wife won't mind. In fact, if you wouldn't object, I'd like her to come along too to see it. I know she'd be fascinated, and thrilled for you.'

'She'd be most welcome,' smiled Sarah.

'Thank you,' said Donnadieu. 'And now I must urge you to wrap all these canvasses up with the greatest of care, preferably wearing clean gloves, and put a lock on the room they're stored in as soon as possible. And perhaps it's best not to tell anyone outside the family about them. As I said earlier, you're looking at a fortune. There's not a leading auction house in the world that wouldn't jump at the chance to sell them – that's if you really want to sell. London, Paris, New York, they'd all be clamouring to do it.'

Sarah shook her head in utter disbelief, shocked that she had lived with the paintings for years without ever truly appreciating them, and picturing a packed auction room in a capital city with frantic bidding. It was all too much to take in.

'And if you like,' continued Donnadieu, 'I could be your representative – free of charge. I'd know which auction houses to trust, and those I wouldn't. An amateur, if you don't mind me saying so, would be on dangerous territory, not knowing how to get the best price, and fixing the reserve prices, and not fully understanding how auctions work. And I'd be more than happy to help.'

'But I don't see why you should do that for free,' said Sarah.

'That's the least I can do after mistakenly selling your frames and family furniture. I still feel very badly about that.'

Sarah was about to protest again, but Donnadieu put up his hand to stop her.

'No. No arguing. It would be enough of an honour to be involved with such a sale. And it certainly won't do my reputation any harm in the art world. That in itself will attract more customers to my gallery.'

He got to his feet and stretched, stiff after leaning over the table for so long. 'Well, what a day! And now I think it's time for a glass of champagne in the château to celebrate – if you'd both care to join us. But let's get these paintings rolled up again first. And then, as I said, first thing tomorrow you should get a good, strong lock on that bedroom door.'

THIRTY-NINE

* * *

S ARAH HAD BEEN TO SEE MADAME PUGET FROM THE OLD DRESS STORE
in Saint-Hippolyte several times, who was now widowed and retired
but still living in the town. She was relieved that the dressmaker still
recognized her.

'Sarah, my dear, I'd never forget that mane of red hair – well, before
you changed it!'

For some weeks she had been busy making the wedding dress, and
at last it was ready, hanging in Maria's wardrobe. The wedding was now
only days away.

And for months now, Alexandre had been visiting a Rabbi in Nîmes
in order to convert to Judaism – never once doubting that he was doing
the right thing, but often worried about the complexities of what he was
hearing and whether he would ever be fully able to take it all in. It helped
that he had never been a practising Catholic and that religion had never
been a part of his life, but nevertheless, the challenge was still immense.

And without the gentle encouragement of the Rabbi and the huge
support of Sarah who often accompanied him to his lessons, he knew he
would never have made the grade. But at last he did – with the wedding
date only weeks away.

Those final weeks were then spent discussing what wording and
customs would be acceptable to both Jews and Christians. They were
told that the lighting of a 'unity candle' would probably be considered
acceptable to both faiths, in which the mothers of the couple each
light a candle and then light a larger one together – a role that Carmen

and Maria offered to perform in the absence of either mother. So too could be 'circling', in which one member of the couple circles around the other, and the use of a 'huppah' – a canopy under which the pair could exchange their rings, and the traditional Jewish custom of the groom breaking a glass under his foot and the use of the words 'Mazel Tov!' to say congratulations. Nevertheless, they were reminded that much of this was extremely unusual with a predominantly Christian congregation.

Back in St-Hippolyte everything was a flurry of activity. Alfonso had fished out his old camera and polished it up, delighted to see that it was still in good working order. Maria had made an amazing three-tier wedding cake, topping it with the two little statuettes of a bride and groom that she and Pedro had used at their own wedding – mementoes she couldn't bear to leave behind in Igualada. The wine and flowers had been ordered, and the wedding and everything had been paid for by Sarah out of the proceeds from the sale of the château – as was the rental on the flat in town where she was now living with Alexandre, ever since he had been kicked out by his father.

Now, coming into the synagogue on Pedro's arm, to the sound of a recorded and beautiful Hebrew psalm, Sarah thought of her parents again, wishing they were there and suddenly afraid she might start to cry. But as soon as she saw Alexandre, she managed to keep back the tears. After all, she reminded herself, *he* had also lost his parents, even though they were still alive.

One and a half hours later, by which time Juanita was suppressing another yawn, they were husband and wife.

Thank God, they both thought, they'd found a Rabbi, *and a surviving one*, willing to teach Alexandre so patiently.

* * *

'Absolutely delicious!' exclaimed Carmen, resting her chopsticks over the bowl in front of her. She had almost finished her choice of cha ca – 'a classic dish from Annam' as the menu described it, made with white fish, dill and spring onions, and served with noodles and peanuts. Although she was rather disappointed that Pierre had immediately opted for exactly the same dish. It seemed so unadventurous of him.

Pierre had come round to the house that morning to see if she wanted to try out the new Indo-Chinese restaurant in town. Now, at eight o'clock, they had almost finished their first course, or rather Carmen had. Pierre's bowl was still half full, and he wasn't touching it.

'It's a shame you don't like it.'

'To be honest,' said Pierre, 'it's not really my sort of food. Too fancy for me. I prefer the kind of things I grow on the farm. Potatoes, not noodles. Local Cévennes onions, not spring onions. And plain grilled fish, not all spicy like this.'

'Then why did you bring me here?'

'Because I thought *you'd* like it.'

'That's nice of you. Especially if *you* don't.'

An awkward silence fell over the table, only broken by the clink of chopsticks until Carmen placed them over her now empty bowl.

'Where's Annam, anyway?' asked Pierre.

Carmen looked up at him, startled. 'Oh Pierre, you *surely* know that. It's one of your French colonies – part of French Indo-China, and has been for over a hundred years!'

'Is it? Well, I never really did geography. Or history.'

'More like general knowledge!' laughed Carmen, suddenly ashamed of flaunting her superior education, at the same time worried about sounding unkind – even cruel. She knew that Pierre had left school early to help his father out on the farm, and that it wasn't fair of her.

'Anyway,' she said, 'it's really kind of you to bring me here, especially as you don't even like this sort of food.'

'Well, as I said, I didn't know I wouldn't until we got here, although I suspected I might not. I guess, deep down, I'm just a country lad at heart, not into fancy things.'

The main course soon arrived, and again he looked in awe in the way that Carmen was handling the chopsticks, extraordinarily deft for someone who was using them for the first time. She had picked up the technique almost instantly.

'Incidentally, you're very good at using those.'

'What, these chopsticks? It's not that difficult. You should have practised a bit instead of asking for a fork!'

She picked up the untouched chopsticks beside Pierre's still untouched bowl and demonstrated how to use them. 'Look, you put them in your hand like this between your thumb and forefinger, and then you balance the bottom stick against your third finger. Want to have a go?' She handed back the chopsticks, but Pierre didn't take them.

'No point trying if I'm not going to eat any more, or try this sort of food again.'

'I suppose not,' said Carmen, disappointed, again wishing he was more adventurous.

Pierre waited before speaking again.

'To be honest, I'm not really hungry. Look Carmen, I need to say something. It's been on my mind for some time, and I can't keep it in any longer.'

Carmen looked at him startled, suddenly feeling her heart rate rising and terrified that he was about to propose as he placed his hand over hers on the table and took a deep breath.

'The fact is, Carmen, I've changed since the war started. And so have you. I guess that was inevitable. Both of us went through too much to stay the same. And now, to be absolutely honest, I don't think we can get things back to where they were before. Anyway, *I* certainly can't, and I don't think *you* can either.'

He noticed that Carmen suddenly looked amazed.

'I'll always love you Carmen, and I hate saying this, but I think we've simply grown apart. And as you know only too well, I find it really difficult coming to terms with you as an armed soldier. I'm sorry, but I find it impossible thinking of you using a gun. I have done ever since I got back, and I just can't get used to the idea of a woman shooting people. It's – well, not natural, at least not for an old-fashioned fellow like me.'

He paused for a moment, frowning. 'Tell me, did you *really* do that?'

'You *know* I did. I had to.' She suddenly thought about the Gendarme she had inadvertently killed, hugely relieved that he didn't know about *that* too.

'You didn't *have* to. You *chose* to. But it's not just that, I just don't see you as a farmer's wife any more. And I don't think *you* do either, and that you're afraid to tell me.'

He was about to take a sip of wine, but sniffing it with distaste, put the glass down. 'And other things aren't right. You've told me often enough that you want to travel and see the world. And to be honest, I don't. Frankly, I just want a quiet life. And I can't travel anyway, not with a farm to run. That's what I want to do, really make a go of it. And you'd soon get bored. I know that now, and there's no point fooling myself. If the war hadn't happened it might all have been different, but we can't turn the clock back.'

Carmen sipped at her glass of wine, but like Pierre, quickly replaced it on the table, suddenly alternating between equal waves of sadness and relief, and overcome by the irony of Pierre being the one to break off their relationship, something she had never envisaged.

Both sat in silence for a moment, until Pierre broke it. 'I'm really sorry.'

'Don't be,' said Carmen, still in a state of shock. 'Look, do you mind if I have another glass of wine? I could certainly do with one after what you just told me.. But not this ghastly rice stuff, it's quite revolting.'

'I agree,' laughed Pierre. 'At least we still agree on some things.'

'Lots,' smiled Carmen, pleased to see him smiling.

Pierre ordered two more glasses, this time of local French wine – and they sat in another silence for a while, both lost in their own thoughts and thinking back over the years since they'd first met.

'So you think I'm right about what I said?' asked Pierre.

Carmen paused intentionally before she answered, knowing that a hasty agreement would be both hurtful and inappropriate, and that above all that she had to hide her relief. He more than deserved her respect.

'Sadly, yes. I'm really, really sorry I've changed. But I suppose I couldn't help it. And sorry you've changed about me. But I'll be even more sorry if we don't stay friends. That would *really* upset me after all these years.'

'We'll always be friends. Or I hope we will be. But I think we need a break from each other for a while. You're welcome to come to the farm if you need to, but perhaps it's better not to go out together, at least not like this, to let the dust settle.'

Carmen nodded.

Half an hour later, with two more glasses of the better wine finished, they walked back to the house arm in arm, and in silence, both thinking about the past – and the future – and sad, but relieved. And it was the first time that there was no kiss at the door, just a couple of chaste pecks on Carmen's cheeks.

'I'll see you when I feel ready to,' smiled Pierre, 'that's if you feel ready to see me.'

'I'm sure I will be.'

Carmen watched him walk down the street as she had so many times before, but this was the first time he didn't turn around at the corner. And when she closed the door, it was like closing it on a whole chapter of her past.

* * *

'There are so many things we could all do with the money,' said Sarah, chatting excitedly over supper after the day at the farm. 'For instance you, Maria, could get running water and electricity for here. You, Pedro, and Pierre could really get the farm going again, and with decent machinery. You, Uncle Fon, could expand the garage and get a new van. Carmen, you could get your own place and your own car. And Alexandre and I could get a place in Montpellier or near it, so he could study maths. And Oti, you could even come and live with us if you like, and go to art school, if your parents let you.'

'And what about me?' asked Juanita frowning, and feeling left out.

'What would *you* like?'

'I don't know.'

'Well, one day you *will*,' smiled Sarah, patting her hand, 'and then you can ask me for help.'

'It's all very kind of you,' said Alfonso, 'but what about you? What do *you* want to do?'

'The most amazing thing about today,' Sarah continued, 'is that I suddenly *knew*. There we were in the château celebrating over a glass of champagne, and it suddenly came to me out of the blue. Before the war I thought I wanted to be a pharmacist, but I certainly don't now. I want to do something far more fulfilling, and now I'm in a position to do it – or hopefully will be after the auction.'

'What?' asked Juanita.

'Start an orphanage for Jewish children. All these years we've been hiding them – or not hiding them enough. Loads of them have lost their parents and relations, and may have nowhere to go. And when all the men get back, they'll want their *own* children, not other people's.'

'But aren't you counting your chickens before they're hatched?' asked Maria. 'What if the auction *isn't* a success?'

'Oh, Mamá,' groaned Otilia. '*Of course* it'll be a success. I think it's a terrific idea!'

'So do I,' agreed Juanita. 'A wonderful one.'

'But won't it all be a bit of a handful if you and Alexandre have children as well?' countered Maria. 'And what does *he* think? Not all men want to have loads of children running all over the place. It's tough enough with just three!'

'Oh, Mamá!' groaned Otilia again. 'You're so *negative*. What an opportunity lost if Sarah *doesn't* do it!'

'Well, anyway, I think it's better not to get too excited until *after* the auction,' answered Maria. 'Remind me. When is it?'

'In two weeks time,' said Sarah. 'Monsieur Donnadieu and I are going up to Paris when we've settled what are called 'the reserve prices' – the ones we're not supposed to go below. And then I'll be back here, hopefully with the finest bottle of champagne I can buy.'

Noticing that Maria still looked a little glum, Sarah suddenly realized why, and to her profound shame. Perhaps she had gone much too far suggesting that two of her children could move out. Maria was a born mother, and an excellent one, and she would certainly miss them terribly. She instantly resolved not to bring the subject up again, or only after very careful consideration and consultation with Carmen. The very last thing she wanted was to create a rift in a family that had saved her life, and the thought of losing *another* family would be unbearable. How *could* she have been so tactless?

'I'm really sorry about that, 'Sarah said to Carmen later that night.

'What?'

'Going off at the mouth about all my plans. It was really stupid – and worse, showing off. And I really regret mentioning that you and Otilia could leave home.'

'Not your fault. And you meant it for the best,' answered Carmen. 'To be honest, I'd really love my own place – a bit of space to breathe. And I don't think Otilia wants to stay here, not with her reputation in tatters. I'm sure even Mamá would see that. But perhaps it's better not to bring it up again until *after* the auction, and then to take things really carefully.

The fact is, Mamá's very simple. I don't mean stupid, just wanting a simple life. A husband, children, an uncomplicated existence. It was the way she was brought up, and the way she always will be. There's no changing her, and change frightens her, and all the money in the world won't alter that. And nor should it. She's the way she is, the way she always will be, and we love her for that, however old-fashioned it is. Part of the old world maybe, but no less admirable for that.'

'I'm sorry'. Sarah was crestfallen.

'No need to be,' replied Carmen. 'Just remember who she is, what she is, and what she's been through. And still going through, struggling to speak French.'

'I will. Thanks.'

'And one more thing,' added Carmen. 'I really don't like saying this, but, as you've said yourself, money is what often worries people about Jews. They think you're too clever, too successful, and in many cases, too rich. They get resentful, and even jealous. So I'd watch out for that, too.'

Too successful? Not so successful that millions of us didn't die in gas chambers, thought Sarah, but chose to stay silent.

* * *

It had been a frantic two weeks of research and organisation as Xavier Donnadieu looked into several Parisian auction houses, all of which he already knew, though he was keen to check out their recent records and find out which had survived best during the wartime years. One stood out markedly: the famous Galeries Charpentier, making his decision easier. He had also had to source a good local photographer to photograph the paintings in colour for the catalogue, with close-ups of important details like the painters' signatures, and then send up the photos to Paris by recorded mail, as well as have all the paintings professionally framed. And on top of that were the hotel arrangements for two nights' accommodation for him and Sarah, covering the ones before and after the auction, as well as running his own gallery.

In the meantime, Sarah had been no less busy, organising their return train tickets, a van from the Galeries Charpentier to coincide with the arrival of their train at the Gard du Nord, and something respectable to wear at the auction – although that had now been sorted out by Brigitte who had brought down a flame silk dress to the salon on her last visit.

'You'll look marvellous in this, Sarah. It never did much for me, but you'll look great in it! Why not go upstairs and try it on?' Sarah had done just that – delighted.

All of it had been made more difficult by the fact there was a waiting list to get a telephone. And on top of that, she had needed to find time to write to everyone who had bought them wedding presents, telling herself that couldn't wait.

But at last their plans were in place, and they could relax in the salon before dinner in the château where Sarah would be staying that night.

Sarah had left Xavier to make the hotel arrangements and was now in for a pleasant surprise. 'Where are we actually staying? I quite forgot to ask you.'

'Somewhere I think you'll like,' smiled Xavier. 'I've decided, since it's such a big day for you, in fact for both of us, to splash out on somewhere really nice. And it's on us, Sarah. We'd like you to think of it as a late wedding present and a thank you for involving me in the sale.'

Sarah smiled. 'You don't have to give me a wedding present. You've already given me so much of your time.'

'We'd like to,' Xavier replied. 'If it all goes well the day after tomorrow – and there's no reason it shouldn't – you'll add a great deal to my reputation, and as a result, almost certainly to my financial situation. *Of course*, we'd like to give you something special in return!'

'Well, that's very kind of you. Thank you! What hotel is it?'

'The Crillon. It's a magnificent one on the Champs Elysées, where we spent our honeymoon, and I've always wanted to go back there again. If it's anything like I remember, I think you'll love it.'

'What's it like?' asked Sarah. 'I've never ever stayed in a hotel, let alone a famous one.'

'It's beautiful. It opened at the beginning of this century, but in a building very much older, dating back to the early 1750s if I recall correctly. It's really more of a palace than a hotel. Built by a very fine architect called Ange Jacques Gabriel, who was commissioned by the King himself, Louis XV, and…'

'Darling,' Brigitte cut in, patting him on the arm. 'Don't bore the poor girl with a history lesson! But he's right, Sarah. It's a gem. As Xavier said, we went there on our honeymoon, and it's our ruby wedding anniversary this year. We thought we might go there again, but not before he checks it out. So this is the perfect opportunity to do that. It's always awful to go back somewhere and find that it's completely different.'

'Gosh,' said Sarah, thinking about their ruby wedding. 'Forty years married? Alex and I have barely made forty days!'

Xavier and Brigitte smiled, remembering the recent wedding to which they had been invited.

The following day, after the initial panic of getting the pictures safely aboard the train, and a long, and uncomfortably hot journey to Paris followed by supervising the loading of the van, Sarah was astonished by the luxury of the Crillon. The architecture outside was stunning enough, but the grand foyer took her breath away. Dozens of fashionably-dressed Parisians were sitting over drinks in the cavernous, gilded surroundings as if there had never been a war at all. It was a different world and a somewhat disturbing contrast with life in Hippo.

And when she was ushered to her room by a smartly-dressed bellboy carrying her case, she was totally astounded. The carved wooden four-poster bed was enormous, with a beautiful overhead canopy with ornate hangings and tassels – and the adjoining marbled bathroom took her breath away. After years of fetching water out of wells at safe houses or washing in streams, she could hardly believe it.

She suddenly realized that if the auction went well, such luxuries would not be beyond the reach of her and Alexandre, but immediately felt guilty, knowing that so many people in France – indeed all over the globe – had lost everything – millions of them their lives, too. It was an uncomfortable comparison with her own position, a deeply sobering thought.

The very same feeling hit her again that evening in the hotel dining room, over a lavish three-course dinner served by immaculate waiters. Sarah had chosen oysters, a chateaubriand steak and an exquisite lemon soufflé, none of which she had ever tasted before. Nor had she ever seen what Xavier had ordered; paté de foie gras, veal cutlets, and an exotic compôte de pommes et pêches with crème brulée.

It was a all in such staggering contrast with life in Saint-Hippolyte, and she wondered how many fashionable Parisians had ever been there – probably none, preferring fashionable resorts like Nice, Cannes and Menton – that's if they bothered to leave Paris at all. Certainly, she decided, none of the people around her would have been content to have a coffee in the local café, mixing with people with strong local accents who considered Paris almost as a place on another planet.

'Are you alright?' asked Xavier, a little concerned that Sarah was so quiet.

'I'm fine,' she smiled. 'Just a bit overwhelmed. I've never been anywhere like this in my life. Or eaten like this, either.'

Xavier picked up his glass and clinked it against hers. 'Here's to tomorrow! My cautious guess is that everything will go well, especially as so many paintings have been looted by the Nazis. Do you know, it's said that about five hundred million francs' worth of fine art has been stolen by Goering's team alone? Probably more.'

Sarah almost choked on her champagne.

'And it's lucky, Sarah, that Goering didn't steal your property too – in fact, incredibly lucky for both of us.'

FORTY

* * *

'**H**OW DID IT GO?' ASKED ALEXANDRE EXCITEDLY WHEN SARAH, AFTER her long train journey, made it back to their flat that evening. In fact, he already knew the auction had gone well from Alfonso, whom she had called on his new telephone right after the event, although they were cut off after a few seconds. But he wasn't going to let on, wanting Sarah to tell him herself. It was a shame she hadn't been able to call *him*, without a telephone at home, but there had been so many other things to organize, without the hassle of getting on the waiting list for a telephone.

Sarah took off her coat and tossed it on to a chair. 'It was amazing. Quite astonishing. To be honest, I'm still in a state of shock.

Everything went. *Everything*. And it all went so fast! I thought we'd be there for ages in the auction room, but it was all over in about an hour. The room was absolutely packed with bidders, and the prices just kept going up, in fact through the ceiling. I just couldn't believe it. We were in the front row, so we couldn't really see what was happening behind us, but apparently if anyone in the audience makes the slightest movement, it's interpreted as a bid by the auctioneer and pushes the price up. I was told they couldn't even scratch their hair or adjust their ties or anything. And we couldn't even turn round to see what was happening. And the auctioneer was totally professional and in control, obviously with the eyes of a hawk.'

'So you actually *beat* the reserve prices?' asked Alexandre, astonished.

'*More* than beat them. It was unbelievable!'

'So how much did you get?'

'You're not going to believe this, but incredibly, about fifty-five million francs.'

Alexandre was stunned. 'Sorry, I must have misheard you.'

'No you didn't.'

He let out a low whistle. 'Good God! I think I need to sit down. Never in my wildest dreams did I think you'd get *anything* like that, although I suppose I don't know much about fine art. It's unbelievable. Goodness, neither of us will ever have to work again!'

'No, but we will,' chuckled Sarah. 'I don't want a lazybones under my feet all day. You'll be a maths teacher like you always said you wanted to be, and I'll have my orphanage. And the great thing is that we can have as many children as we like without worrying about how we can pay for them.'

Alexandre suddenly looked concerned.

'I hope nobody will ever say I married you for your money. I'm sure that's what my father will say when he knows about it. Presumably an auction as big as that will be all over the news.'

'Yes, I think it will be. Certainly all over the Paris papers – and probably on the radio. And maybe even in the local papers down here. With all the reports coming in about what Goering stole, it'll be terrific news that the bastard didn't grab it all.

But it isn't entirely terrific news for us. What scares me is making people jealous, and people like your father saying the same old thing about Jews: that we're too rich for our own good. And if you're *young* and rich, that might make things even worse. We'll have to keep it quiet, or at least as quiet as we can.'

'Not that easy if we buy a big house for the orphanage, and people know who we are.'

Both of them reflected for a while about their changed circumstances, until Alexandre broke the silence, thinking about practicalities.

'Incidentally, where's the money?'

'It'll be in Xavier's bank account at Crédit Agricole in Nîmes first thing in the morning, and then he'll pay me after that.'

Alexandre laughed. 'God, I hope he does!'

'Of course he will – don't forget he's already stolen from me once, albeit without knowing it, and he still feels guilty about that. And the auction was far too widely publicised for him not to play fair. And he's already rich, and bound to be even richer when people hear about the auction. People with good fine art to sell will be flocking to his door.'

'Tell you what Sarah, why don't we go round to Alfonso's and give everyone the good news, and then go and celebrate in that new Annamese restaurant – you know, the one Carmen told you about in the square?'

'Love to, but I don't have a bean left on me. I'm down to a few francs.'

Alexandre laughed at the irony of it. A millionairess without any money on her?

'Hang on a moment. I'll go and see what we've got in the kitchen jar.'

FORTY-ONE

❊ ❊ ❊

'**C**AN *I* DO THE THROWING?' ASKED JUANITA.

'Well,' said Pedro, 'I'm not sure you can throw far enough, and I certainly don't want you standing too close to the bonfire.'

Juanita moaned in frustration, stamping her foot.

Pedro looked down at his youngest daughter, sometimes defiant like his second one, Otilia, and occasionally with the same flashes of temper, though far easier to control.

Thankfully, she could usually be placated at a time like this, though he knew that none of his children would ever end up as compliant and traditional as Maria, not sure if that were a good or bad thing.

'I'll tell you what. We'll get as close as we can, and then I'll help you swing your arm.'

Juanita hopped up and down with glee.

In common with so many other towns and villages throughout France, St. Hippolyte was staging a ceremony for burning the hated ration books, and nearly everyone had turned out to join in, although Maria had chosen to stay at home with Otilia, Both were still traumatized by the horrors of the recent head-shaving ceremony, even though Otilia had escaped that ultimate degradation.

'I'm sorry,' Maria had told him. 'I just can't face going out in public yet – and certainly not if there'll be crowds of people. And Otilia *definitely* won't want to go out – not after that baying mob the other day. I'll stay at home with her.'

Now, brushing the steps outside the front door, she listened to the cheering coming from the square and turned to see another huge plume of smoke billowing into the sky. It was like the past being blown away, but sadly not for Otilia.

Suddenly Pedro and Juanita were joined in the throng by Sarah and Alexandre bringing their bag of ration books. After the usual embraces, they too started throwing them into the flames to a further burst of cheering, and it was impossible to hear Sarah talk about the auction, her words continually drowned out every time she tried to do so.

But at last it was over, and as the flames and the noise died down they decided to go to the café, lucky enough to find the last table free in the fountain area opposite. Juanita immediately ran off to splash about in the water as she always did.

'So, tell us more about yesterday,' said Pedro to Sarah. 'I'm really delighted to hear it all went so well.'

'Better than I could ever have dreamed of,' smiled Sarah. 'In fact, I'm finding it all rather difficult to take in.'

'Well, don't rush things,' said Pedro. 'Take your time deciding what you want to do.'

Sarah nodded. 'I will. But I certainly still know *one* thing I want to do.'

'Start an orphanage?'

'Yes.'

'I've been thinking about that,' said Pedro. 'You know you very kindly said you might be able to take in Otilia?'

'Yes.'

'Well, I'm beginning to think that could be a very good idea. But only if you really mean it.'

'I do,' said Sarah.

'The fact is, it's going to be very difficult for her to go on living here,' continued Pedro. 'Reputations don't die down that easily, especially in a small town like this, and I can't bear the thought of her being vilified every time she appears in public. It'll be a wretched life. But I don't think we can simply up sticks and move to somewhere else for her sake. Another move could *kill* Maria. She's had enough of it. If you *really* don't mind having her, and you too Alexandre, it would be a huge weight off my mind. And no doubt, Otilia's. And It'll be up to me to persuade Maria that it's the best possible answer. But don't forget, you two, Otilia's quite a handful, and sixteen isn't an easy age.'

'I'm sure I can cope,' said Sarah, but wondered if she really could with other troubled children to look after.

'Me, too,' added Alexandre.

'Well, on that note, I'd like to thank you both with a glass of wine.' He looked over to the fountain where Juanita was playing with another girl, then back to them. 'And not a word to Juanita when she joins us.'

Sarah and Alexandre nodded.

* * *

Otilia had been in the art class in Montpellier for around an hour without moving, her turn to pose for her classmates – a task she always hated – though it was interesting to see how they had interpreted her at the end of the session when she could walk around and see what they'd done. She was often pleased to see the influences of artists like Picasso and Serrano – Spanish artists rather than French ones, especially when she had been the muse.

Furthermore she was sometimes flattered to be chosen as the sitter. She knew that her slim frame and her thick black hair made her stand out as a good subject, and that her eyes, often described by her father as 'defiant' would make her a challenge to the class. She was relieved, too, that she had allowed her hair to grow again, now down to her shoulders, though often remembering with horror how easily it could have been shaved off in that appalling ceremony in the square – something that still gave her nightmares.

And she was relieved, furthermore, that none of the class were ever allowed to pose in the nude – a task that was always left to professional models, and one that must have been dreadful in winter when the classroom was so cold and the heating was rarely switched on to save money. She had often wondered how they could stay in the same position for so long without shivering, and supposed that they must be pretty handsomely rewarded for their ordeal.

Now, walking round the paintings at the end of the session she came to one by a boy she liked – Felipe, also Spanish. 'Goodness – I look a bit sad, don't I?'

'You do, sometimes. I don't think you know, but you do. You're laughing one minute, then suddenly a look comes over you as if you're suddenly remembering something.'

'I probably am.'

Felipe looked up at her. 'A boy?' He asked.

'Probably.'

Felipe smiled. 'Tell me when you get over it.'

'If I ever will.'

'Of course you will. We all do in the end. Get over things. That's life.'

'Not always. Depends on who it is, and how you break up.'

He studied Otilia's face.

'How *did* you break up?'

'None of your business.'

Felipe smiled. 'Anyway, do you want to go to the cafe?'

'Si.'

He was relieved to see this often-morose girl smile.

'Le Perroquet' had become a hugely popular venue for the art students – a local coffee bar nearby with a parrot on its perch just inside the door whose owner André had taught it a stream of obscenities. From there, it squawked out raucously to anyone who came in, much to the amusement of the regulars, and the art school flocked there as a result.

Better still, the premises were at last free of Germans, infuriatingly always drinking coffee with sugar unlike the locals, presumably fixed up by their Quartermaster with the proprietor. Everyone else used to make do with revolting low-quality saccharine.

Felipe knew that there had been over 11,000 Germans of the 18th Infantry division billeted in the city, part of a quarter of a million Germans stationed in the south of France. Now, to his vociferous relief – and everyone else's, except curiously, that of Otilia – all of them had gone. And so had the fear of the city being bombed like Nîmes, and with heavy casualties.

'We'd better go soon, or we won't get a table.'

'Okay,' said Otilia. 'Wait there, and I'll get my coat. I'll be back in a few minutes.'

She really liked this boy. Tall, handsome, with a shock of thick black hair like hers, and always with a merry twinkle in his eye and a fun story up his sleeve. But she wondered if she'd ever completely get over Hans, in many ways the very opposite. Blond, self-contained, and for obvious reasons, a lot more serious. And what made it harder was suspecting her older sister probably knew something about him that she didn't, even that he may have been killed at La Madeleine. Would Carmen ever tell her if she knew that? Probably not. And she would always be left wondering what happened to him. That depressing thought was never far away.

The parrot eyed them up as they walked into the café, and especially Otilia, cocking its head on one side to get a better look at her and strutting about on its perch.

'BLOODY BOCHES!'

'BLOODY BOCHES!'

'KRAUTS OUT!'

'KRAUTS OUT!'

Felipe roared with laughter, wondering why Otilia didn't, and not for the first time, why she had left home so young to live in an orphanage, even though her parents were clearly still alive. Indeed, she often mentioned them. Why hadn't he asked her? Something had just stopped him. And if *she* didn't want to talk about it, he wouldn't either.

A mysterious girl.

FORTY-TWO

* * *

I T WAS A CRISP AUTUMN DAY IN 1945, AND CARMEN WAS WALKING TO the local library in the main square in Saint-Hippolyte where she now had a job.

It was not work she much liked, being a librarian, especially as there was little custom. But it at least gave her time to get on with what she had decided to do – write a book about the role of the Spanish in the French Résistance, something everybody already seemed to have forgotten about or didn't want to mention, as if it belittled their *own* participation – or lack of it. In fact, she was beginning to worry that Spanish support would one day be conveniently and unfairly erased from history. Even British help was being forgotten. Carmen's former comrades had joked cynically, 'Remember *all* Frenchmen were in the Résistance, and *all* résistants were French!' Moreover, Charles de Gaulle had tried to pretend that Paris was entirely liberated by her *own* citizens, rather than the Allies led by General Leclerc's French armoured division – spearheaded, she happened to know, by its 9th Company, 'La Nueva'– made up of *Spanish*, formerly Republican, troops. The embarrassing fact that their capital had been liberated by Spaniards had been quickly hidden from the French, indeed the world.

She was determined to write it all down while her memory of events was still fresh, hoping that in the course of time it would be remembered and honoured. After all, it was hard to imagine a battle as successful as that at La Madeleine, largely thanks to her countrymen. But it wasn't helping that nearly all her comrades there had immediately left for Spain, taking their own personal stories with them, and not around to remind people of their contribution. And God knows what had happened to them. She often feared the worst.

Few people came into the library, but one did – often – an attractive middle-aged blonde woman who sat reading quietly in the corner. It was only when she signed her name in the list of those borrowing books to take home that she realized it was Marianne Koenig, Charles' wife, who had harboured Sarah up in the mountains near Cros three years ago.

'Madame Koenig, how nice to meet you! I'm Carmen, the one who asked Charles if he could give my friend Sarah Levy a safe house somewhere, which you kindly did.'

Marianne was delighted. 'How is she? It was such a shame she had to go. She was such a lovely companion. And so sad I couldn't go to her wedding either. My husband Charles and I were invited, but we both went down with that terrible flu so we couldn't make it.'

'She's fine. In fact, she's run off her feet. She's just started up a Jewish orphanage near Montpellier.'

'Good Lord! What a wonderful thing to do!'

Carmen paused. 'You know her parents died at Auschwitz?'

'Yes, Charles told me. Terrible. The whole thing makes me ashamed to be German.'

'Well, her parents had a pretty valuable art collection, which we managed to save from the Germans and the Vichy people. She sold it, and used the money for the orphanage. I think she's got about thirty children already.'

'Heavens, she must be run off her feet! If you give me her address, I'll write to her. And maybe I could even help out a bit, with time on my hands.'

'I'm sure she'd really appreciate that. Especially as I've just heard she's pregnant. Even more reason to go and help her.'

Marianne looked at Carmen, liking this somewhat serious-faced girl.

'And how are *you*? Are you married, too?'

'Not yet,' Carmen laughed. 'Not ever, probably.'

'Oh, don't say that. There's plenty of time, and you're young yet. You'll find the right man.'

'I have already, but I'm not sure what'll happen now. He was a British officer who helped us in the mountains, and in those battles in the summer, but then he went off to help the resistance in Italy. He's been in touch. But I don't know what he'll do now it's all over and he gets back home. *If he gets home.*'

'I'll pray he does.'

'Thanks.'

Minutes after she'd left, Carmen's thoughts turned to her own immediate situation.

On the very few dates she'd been on since Sean's departure, now over a year ago, her escorts had found it hard to believe that *any* Spaniard had played a part in victory, let alone a woman and an armed one at that – all of them immediately assuming she'd have had a passive and menial job like a cook. It might have been better *not* to have told them, but it annoyed her to keep silent and simply listen to *them* and *their* achievements. Women, she conjectured, still had such a long way to go. All sorts of other battles lay ahead.

Increasingly she yearned for Sean, remembering how easy it was to talk to him, and how difficult it was to do that with any man now, especially someone French – and about the war.

At times she wondered if she'd ever manage to complete the book, or if she did, whether anyone in France would read it or believe it. Maybe too many people were still embarrassed by their previous enthusiastic support for Pétain.

In fact, the book was going well, but it was all the harder to write it picturing Sean and wondering where he was. She felt lonely not being able to discuss it with anyone. Her mother was proud, of course, of the Croix de Guerre displayed on the mantelpiece, but was still horrified about what her daughter had been up to. Pedro was also proud, but seemed to want to put it all behind him, probably for Maria's sake.

Now, as she looked at the rows of dusty unread tomes, she wondered if her book would one day be one of them, but decided to persevere, at least for the time being. Certainly the rabid Pétainists wouldn't be interested, more likely embarrassed – but the Spanish might be one day, with their role in the Résistance and underground movements probably about to be under-estimated and unappreciated for decades to come. And it could, she felt, one day have a market with women, inspired by the fact that life didn't, at last, have to be dominated by men and the kitchen sink.

But there had been so many D-Days, not just one. Days of Danger. Doldrums. Denial. Deprivation. Desecration. Death. Disease. Disaster. Displacement. Despair. Desperation. Devastation. Denial. It was almost as if the whole world was littered with D-Days.

Would anyone *want* to read about it any more – since Deliverance?

FORTY-THREE

* * *

'Carmen, a letter for you,' said Pedro, passing her an envelope. He glanced at the stamp, surprised. 'From England.'

'England?'

'Si, it's got their King on the stamp.'

Carmen felt a rush of excitement, almost snatching the letter from her father's grasp. She recognized Sean's writing at once, and ripped it open immediately, picturing him when he had turned up at the house many months ago.

Except for a couple of hurried letters written from the battlefield, at least telling her that he was alive, she had not heard from him, and had begun to think that with the war over, their relationship might be too.

Now, reading the letter with mounting joy and relief, she knew it wasn't.

My darling Carmen,

Well, the fighting's in Italy's over at last and here I am in London, waiting to become a civilian – English or Irish, I'm not sure.

I'm sorry I only sent you a few scribbled notes since I've been away, but I wasn't with the regular army as I told you, but up in the hills with the Maquis – Italians this time. So it wasn't exactly easy to keep in touch.

London's quite a bombsite, I can tell you. Streets with vast gaps and holes everywhere. But there's a much bigger hole in my life, and that's why I'm writing.

I'm really missing you and want to see you, and desperately
want you to come to England. That's if you're not married to
someone else by now. I very much hope not.

Please write back as soon as you can.

I love you,

Sean xxx

Carmen suddenly burst into tears, flooded with relief.

'Are you okay?' asked Pedro, immediately worried.

Carmen nodded, struggling to speak. 'I don't think I've ever been happier.'

Being traditional Spaniards and from another generation, she had never told her parents about her relationship with Sean in the mountains, knowing that they would disapprove, and also not sure whether he would get in touch once the war was over and he was back home among his own people. Perhaps he would want to put that all in the past.

'It's from someone I worked with up in the mountains. An Irishman called Sean O'Neill who I really liked, the head of our group. He wants me to go and see him in London.'

'*London*? Por Dios! That's a bit rash, isn't it? You can't just rush off to see someone you haven't seen for ages. And who *is* this man? You've never mentioned him before.'

'I've just told you. A British Captain, our commanding officer for a while up in the mountains. And someone you'd really like. And , Papa, someone I absolutely *know* is for me.'

Pedro thought for a moment shaking his head, but suddenly smiling.

'Well, at least he was on the right side, unlike a certain friend of your sister's. So I *will* probably like him. But why didn't you ever mention him before?

'Because I was afraid he might be dead.'

* * *

Carmen was genuinely fond of the owner of the 'papetière' – the book and stationery shop in the square – the engaging Pascal Coularou. He had such a natural affinity with people. Not many shop proprietors would come round the counter to greet their customers as he did, or if you were buying someone a present – say a calendar or a diary – wrap it with such attention and care.

But she was surprised by his choice of the new assistant – a shy, small and rather timid girl about the same age as her who seemed to find eye contact difficult, and always twisted her hair nervously round her fingers when anyone spoke to her. On the few occasions when Carmen had, it made her wonder if she had become *too* tough in the Résistance, a bit battle-hardened perhaps, now perfectly at ease with strangers and so unlike this girl.

Perhaps, she thought, his new employee had applied for the job for that exact reason – to try and overcome her innate shyness – and considering that, and also admiring it – if that were her ambition – Carmen resolved to be especially gentle when talking to her.

Today she had come to the shop to find the girl on her own behind the counter, and sporting a name badge for the first time announcing that she was called Geneviève.

'Bonjour, Geneviève.'

The girl smiled nervously, immediately twisting a strand of her hair around in her fingers.

'Bonjour.'

'I'm Carmen, by the way. '

The girl smiled again. 'Then bonjour, Carmen. How can I help you?'

'I wonder if you have any books on England? I've had a look around, but I can't see any on display. I'm going there in a few weeks and I really need to know more about it. What I'm looking for mostly is a book on London and an English-French dictionary – oh, and a common phrase book in English and French if you've got one.'

Again, the girl twisted a strand of hair.

'Well,' she replied, 'we do have some, but they're in storage at the moment at the back of the shop. There's not been much call for travel books for a long time now as you can imagine, and we had to make space for other things. You know, things like books on how to cook with rationing. But I suppose, now the war's over, people will be on the move again. That's if they can afford to.'

She suddenly blushed, realizing that she had inadvertently suggested that Carmen was flush with money.

Carmen immediately came to the rescue. 'I'm lucky enough to have been given a ticket.'

'Mon Dieu, that's exciting! I tell you what. It might take a little time to see what we've got. But what if you come back after we close today, say at six, and we could go through the store room together? It would be a whole lot faster with the two of us.'

'Well, if you really don't mind.'

'Not at all. I'm not doing anything after work. And Monsieur Coularou would be pleased if I could add to our sales figures. Well, that's if we find something.'

At six o'clock in the dusty store-room, and just as Carmen was about to give up, she was thrilled to discover exactly what she wanted, and also pleased that the girl had become a little more chatty.

It turned out that Geneviève lived on the road to Ganges where her mother ran an olive oil business, and that her brother, like Pierre, had just returned home from a prison camp in France. She didn't mention her father, and fearing the worst, Carmen didn't ask about him.

'I really admire you going off alone, and to a city you don't know,' she had said before Carmen left.' I don't think I'd ever dare to do that. I'd be terrified, especially if I didn't speak the language. In fact, I'd be scared to death.'

Carmen wondered how she'd react if she told her she'd been in the Résistance. The thought would have appalled her, as it had Pierre.

* * *

Sarah had thought long and hard about a birthday present for Maria, wondering whether a puppy would be a good idea or not. With Otilia away and living with her and Alexandre, Juanita still at school, and Pedro and Alfonso at the farm and garage, life would clearly be getting more lonely for her – especially when Carmen left. And with Maria's still limited grasp of French, making new friends had never been easy for her.

But she knew only too well that Maria was house-proud. Would she really want a puppy in the house? She had driven to the house in her new Renault car to talk things over, and was delighted – and surprised by Maria's reaction.

'Well, maybe it's rather a good idea. I do get a bit lonely with you and Otilia gone, and with Pedro and Alfonso out all day. And of course, Carmen's off soon. And Juanita's mostly at school or with her friends. I'm already rattling round like a pea in a drum.'

A few days later Sarah was delighted to hear Maria on the phone, even more enthusiastic about the idea.

'Well, if you're really sure, Sarah, I think I'd love a dog to keep me company. But not a big one, something manageable like a miniature poodle.'

Now Sarah was even more pleased to see Maria on her next visit, getting on so well with the new arrival that she had delivered herself on the birthday – a wriggling poodle puppy, a few months old.

Now it bounded into Maria's lap in the sitting room, with her making no attempt to push it off – clearly un-fussed by dog hairs. And Sarah also noticed instantly how well Maria looked, suddenly appearing far younger.

The reason for that soon became clear, as she cuddled the puppy.

'With Rosa here – that's my name for her – I'm getting out a lot more and meeting more people. Everyone's coming up to admire and stroke her. And funnily enough, that's really made me change. Think about myself a bit more, and my appearance, and spoil myself a bit. I was really beginning to look as if I'd gone through the wars.'

'You did. Two of them!'

'And I sometimes walk Rosa to the school to pick up Juanita. The kids love her, and as a result, I've got to know some of the parents.'

Sarah was delighted, also to see that Maria's hair was now back to its former glossy black, albeit artificially, and that she was even wearing a bright floral dress rather than the usual funereal black ones. But it was her enthusiasm that was the real breakthrough.

'Do you remember your parent's maid?' asked Maria.

'Who, Gabriella? Yes, of course.'

'Well, she's teaching me French again. And we often go out walking with Rosa on my lessons and talking French. It's not as difficult as I always thought it was. And these days, to help me, we speak less and less Spanish in the house. In fact, I'm rather proud of myself!'

'And so you should be,' smiled Sarah, delighted. She suddenly remembered Carmen saying her mother would never change. How wrong she was!

'And I can't wait to take Rosa to the beach in the Camargue when we get a place down there, thanks to you. I think she'd love the sea. And next time we go house-hunting, I've even decided to try and learn to swim. If even Juanita can do that, I'm sure I can!'

'And drive maybe? Never too late.'

'Probably. But before that I'll have to learn to read. There's not much point in driving if I can't read the signs and don't know where I'm going!'

Maria suddenly became more pensive.

'My only real regret is not doing it all years ago, and before Carmen and Oti left.'

'You couldn't, not while looking after all of us, and this place. And when they come home to visit, they'll have a lovely surprise.'

The idea of Carmen and Oti receiving letters from their mother was a wonderful thought, and now not impossible.

'Incidentally, how's Oti?' asked Maria.

'Doing really well. And I think she's got a new boyfriend, although she's not admitting it – maybe just a friend. A Spaniard called Felipe, at the art school like her. He came over for lunch with her the other day. Really nice. In fact, I think he's a bit in love with her.'

Maria smiled. 'And how's the orphanage going, Sarah?'

'Fine, but we do have a few problems. Alexandre's teaching them maths – something he always wanted to do, and sometimes woodwork – he's really good at that. Oti does the occasional art class when she can, and now we've got someone to teach them French and English. But there's absolutely nobody we can find to teach them religion – now the Rabbis have nearly all gone. And the children always want to know why their parents were so hated and taken away. Some of their faces are absolutely heart-breaking.'

Picturing them in her mind, Maria didn't know how to reply.

* * *

Sarah was now checking the children in the orphanage bedrooms as she always did at eleven o'clock at night, long after the children should have fallen asleep. And as was so common, one or two of them were still awake and crying – increasingly for the same reason. 'I can't remember my Maman and Papa any more.'

Faces had blurred in their minds, and memories of family life had disappeared along with them. Constant horror about being separated had entered their dreams, making further sleep impossible. All she could do was soothe them by stroking their hair, holding their hands, drying their tears and tucking them up again, while never making the promise that their parents might one day return. Comfort from her was almost always soundless, not least so as not to wake the other children. It was bad enough that their crying and nightmares frequently did.

She was often exhausted and wondered if she were able to carry on, but knew she had to for the sake of these wretched orphans while knowing it would be impossible without Alexandre's constant support. And now, *effectively* an orphan himself, he understood what they were going through – or at least much better than he might have done otherwise – and never once questioned if they were doing the right thing.

But the smiles and hugs they both got made up for the depressing moments that the children would almost certainly go through for the rest of their lives.

The thing Sarah found most difficult was the deadness in some of their eyes, as if the light had gone out. This was partly helped by bringing in children's entertainers like conjurors, when that light, to some extent, seemed to return. But even so, some children were so badly damaged that she had brought in regular counsellors. There were simply too many of them to talk regularly to each one, especially when they sometimes found it so difficult to respond, and getting anything out of them was like trying to get blood out of a stone. Those were the ones with 'dead eyes', because they had simply seen too much.

But now, one thing had *really* made a difference: pets to look after. Cats to stroke, the comforting sound of gentle purring, the affection that they silently returned, the warmth of their fur. Even more mouths to feed, but every franc was more than worth it. Thank God, she thought every night, she had the money to make all this possible. And especially for the tragic youngsters who had not only lost parents, but sometimes siblings as well – now fostered by other families, but far from secure if returning husbands couldn't afford them if they now wanted children of their own.

So far she hadn't had any applications like that, but she was sure it was only a matter of time, with a baby-boom ahead in a Catholic country opposed to contraception. And moreover, she realized that if returning men started resenting looking after Jewish children – and the cost involved – they would hardly be likely to pay anything for them at the orphanage. But again she reminded herself that, even without fees, she had the money to cope.

Thinking about her priorities for the next day, her thoughts suddenly turned to Israel Gluckstein, the man who had met her parents on the train to Auschwitz – guilty that she had never got around to replying to his letter. He deserved to know that she had received it – and might like to know about the orphanage and what it was doing – or even pay a visit. And perhaps, lonely and bereaved himself, he could fill a gap – someone who could teach the children about art history and music. She remembered him saying in his letter he shared these passions with her father. It was worth a try, and if she didn't reply to his letter, he might well fear what had happened to her – that's if he hadn't heard about the auction in Paris and connected her name with it. And, leaving that aside, she knew she should have written back to him ages ago to acknowledge his letter, too painful at the time, even if only to confirm that she was still alive, and heartily relieved that *he* was. She would write in the morning.

Thankfully, in all the crowded muddle of the orphanage – where she was always mislaying things – she knew exactly where his letter was – safe in the drawer of her bedside table.

And there was another person she wanted to contact, Marianne Koenig, the kindly woman who had harboured her up the mountain above Cros. She remembered her saying that she had yearned for children. Maybe she'd like to visit, or perhaps show the girls how to weave? Being German in post-war France, she was probably horribly lonely and might relish some company.

FORTY-FOUR

✻ ✻ ✻

CARMEN WAS AT LAST ON THE WAY TO THE STATION, DRIVEN BY HER father, first to catch the train to Nîmes and then the express to Paris. After staying a night in the capital, she would then have to board the famed 'Flèche d'Or' to Calais where she would cross the Channel and take another new train, 'The Golden Arrow', to London.

Making the arrangements had all been something of a nightmare, but now she was only worried that her phrase-book English would never be up to it, and that somehow she would get lost on the journey.

Suddenly she noticed a couple walking hand in hand down the hill towards them, and to her surprise realized that it was Pierre with the timid girl from the stationery shop. But she didn't look timid now, far from it, happily chatting and looking up at him. To her surprise, Carmen felt a little pang of regret.

'Did you see who I just saw?' she asked her father.

'Yes, but it was *you* who split with him, wasn't it?'

'No, not really. He dumped *me*.'

'Only because he knew he wasn't right for you. That was bound to happen. Both of you have changed too much. Maria and I know that now. He's not the man for you. He *was* once, but not any more.'

Pedro paused for a minute, touching Carmen's hand. 'Try and be glad for him. As I'm sure he'd be glad for you. And try and remember that if we hadn't been able to hide the pictures on his farm, you'd never be on this trip.'

'Did you know about it?'

'What? That he had a new girlfriend? No. Or I'd probably have told you. But, as I said, I think we should both be happy for him, as I'm sure he'd be for you. Typical woman! If you don't want someone, you don't want anyone else to have them either!'

Carmen laughed, knowing that there was a grain of truth in that.

'I'll call you as soon as I arrive,' she said, 'or as soon as I can get to a phone.'

'Do that,' replied Pedro, or we'll worry about you. It's a heck of a journey. And if anything goes wrong when you get there in any way, come back at once.'

'I will. But I think I know Sean well enough to know that it'll be alright.'

'It'll have to be *more* than alright,' said Pedro glancing at her. 'It's a hell of a decision.'

'I know.'

At last she was boarding the train with her case.

'Good luck, cara, and look after yourself. And as you said, call us as soon as possible.'

With her final wave to her father out of the window and settling down in the train, Carmen was in a turmoil of different emotions, leaving one familiar world to go on to a new one she knew so little about. But at the same time she knew that if she didn't give this trip a go, she would have regretted it for the rest of her life.

* * *

The whole journey had been a revelation. First, the express train from Nîmes to the capital and the superb lunch she had enjoyed in the dining car, and after that, Paris. She had never stayed in a hotel before, and that was exciting enough. But what had been the real thrill was wandering the streets and boulevards of the city and looking at the opulent boutiques and galleries. Thank goodness, she reflected, Paris had been declared an 'open city' and had not been bombed or shelled to ruins. She had seen newsreels in the cinema in Hippo of so many other cities reduced to rubble.

The 'Flèche d'Or', too, had been a wonderful surprise, a complete throw-back to the 'Roaring Twenties'– or what she knew about them – absolute luxury with its polished fittings and stylish furniture.

She had been a little bit concerned about a Frenchman in the Trianon Bar car, who had pestered her to have lunch with him, but had luckily backed off when she took the French-English phrase book out of her handbag, explaining that she had to brush up on her English before meeting her boyfriend.

The luxury train had its own steamer, the *Canterbury*, equally smart, that took the passengers across the Channel in less than an hour. Then once more she was in another glamorous train, in one of the cream and brown Pullman cars of the 'Golden Arrow', looking out of the window at a strange new land called England. At last she was passing through the endless suburbs of London, and thinking about Sean waiting for her with mounting excitement.

But there was nobody there.

At least, nobody for her. Carmen scanned the platform again, but there was no Sean, no-one to sweep her up in his arms and say that he was thrilled that she'd made it. Only a crowd of strangers happily embracing each other.

Telling herself to stay calm, but only just succeeding, she carried her heavy case down the platform and sat on the bench closest to the platform exit.

'Would you like help with that? She looked up, but it wasn't Sean, just a station porter.

'No thank you. I can manage it.' Her first words of English.

Suddenly the big green engine that had pulled them from Dover gave off a rush of steam. Startled, she turned round to see the driver grinning and waving at her, at the same time noticing a shiny plaque saying 'Lord Nelson' on the side of the engine. A bit insensitive she thought, to have trains pulled from France behind that name, suddenly remembering from her London guidebook that the English had another station serving France called 'Waterloo'.

Ten minutes more passed and still there was no Sean, and she was now getting really worried, suddenly feeling horribly alone and vulnerable in a strange city and wondering how much longer she should wait, and what on earth to do if he didn't turn up at all.

Now she watched as the gleaming Golden Arrow carriages were slowly shunted out backwards, almost wishing she was aboard again. Then her friendly driver backed out his steaming locomotive, too. It was almost as if two friends had departed, along with her confidence. Where was all that courage she'd had in the mountains?.

Ten minutes later, completely alone on the platform and as the tears suddenly came, she tipped the case flat on to the platform and leaned down to open it to take out a handkerchief, suddenly aware of someone standing over her. And looking up, she saw Sean at last.

'I'm really sorry, Carmen. I got horribly held up.'

Carmen couldn't keep back her tears, but at least they were ones of profound relief.

Sean looked at her, startled. 'You surely didn't think I wouldn't come?'

'I didn't know what to think.'

Sean shook his head smiling. 'Honestly, you know me better than that! Or I *thought* you did. I couldn't *wait* to see you!'

He pulled her up from the seat and rocked her in his arms, stroking her long black hair away from her tear-stained face. 'In fact, it was *me* who was a bit afraid that *you* might not come. Anyway, I've got a taxi waiting, and we'd better go quickly or someone else will take it.'

He picked up the heavy case with ease, and they walked through the bustling station to where the taxi was parked outside. She noticed he was dressed in a tie and blazer and his hair was shorter than in those rough days in the hills. Suddenly all that seemed a world away.

'The Ritz, please,' said Sean to the driver, lifting in the case and following Carmen inside.

'Heavens. That sounds chic!'

'It is! I thought we'd treat ourselves to a really nice hotel on our first night, and then after that, have a look around London for a few days, at least what's left of it. It's taken a real hammering in the war.'

Looking out, Carmen quickly noticed that for herself, with all the missing buildings and the gaps in the elegant rows of houses, suddenly reminding her of missing teeth.

'Will there be a telephone in the Ritz?' she asked Sean.' I told my father I'd call him as soon as I got here.'

I'm sure there will be. And then,' continued Sean, 'I'd like to take you to Ireland, my home. I'm sure you'll love it. It's beautiful – 'the Emerald Isle', as they call it – always wonderfully green. And better still, there's no rationing there. Butter, not filthy margarine. And beef, not spam.'

Carmen laughed. 'What on earth's spam?'

'A rather revolting sort of meat substitute. At least, you'll be spared that. And as I said, probably loads of times, the country's stunning – especially in Connemara where I come from. Full of lakes and wild horses and glorious empty beaches. Did I ever tell you about my place there right on the sea?'

'Yes,' Carmen smiled. He *had* told her numerous times.

She pictured it – the two of them together again at last, walking along the beach, making a completely new start, and hopefully a life together.

'I think we need to get away,' said Sean. 'Right away. We've both been through too much. Two wars too many.'

He placed his hand on hers.

'And Carmen, when we get there, there's something I want to ask you.'

PERSONALITIES

* * *

Otilia Casalès, on whose family this book is loosely based, lives in Saint-Hippolyte. Her affair with a German soldier is entirely fictional.

Maurice Bertrand was imprisoned at Eysses, where he led a revolt of Résistance fighters. Transferred to Dachau concentration camp, his life was saved by the Germans guards needing a trumpeter for the camp orchestra. He returned to Saint-Hippolyte, where there is now a street named in honour of him.

SS Obergruppenführer Wilhelm Bittrich later commanded the SS Division, unfortunately where the British parachutists landed at Arnhem (his role was acted by Maximilian Schell in the film *A Bridge Too Far*). A French court exonerated him for the hanging of the 17 French at Nîmes, blaming other German officers.

Cristino Garcia, and many of his companions, just after their well-planned and heroic action at La Madeleine, went back into Spain to try to fight the Franco regime. He was captured, tortured and shot in February, 1946.

'Patrick O'Leary', real name Albert-Marie Guérisse – a Belgian medical officer – created several escape lines, 'Pat Lines', down which hundreds of British and Americans escaped. Captured and then imprisoned in Dachau, he survived. Awarded the Distinguished Service Order, the DSO, by King George V1, he served gallantly in Korea, and retired as a Belgian Major-General.

'Captain Whitney Willard', in reality Squadron Leader Whitney Straight – the American business man and racing driver – was repatriated 'on health grounds', returned to combat flying in the RAF, and after the war became Chairman of the British Overseas Airways Corporation (BOAC).

Gabriel Perez, who commanded the battle at La Madeleine, went to Spain and took part in the Aran Valley operation in October, 1944. In 1945, he was arrested and shot by the Franco regime in Santander.

Joachin Arasanz went back to Spain, was arrested, spared from execution under pressure from France, and spent many years in prison until liberated after the death of Franco.

Eoin O'Duffy, a leader in the Irish Republican Army in its struggle for Irish independence, was a fanatical anti-Communist, who brought 700 men to Spain to fight for Franco. However, they saw little fighting. Hitler turned down his similar offer to raise an Irish Legion to fight in Russia. Somewhat disgraced by his Spanish adventure, O'Duffy was nevertheless given an Irish State Funeral in Dublin in 1944.

Benito Mussolini, Dictator of Italy, was captured by partisans in 1945, and shot and ignominiously hung upside down with his mistress, Clara Petacci, in the main square of Milan.

Adolf Hitler, Dictator of Germany, committed suicide in his Berlin bunker on 30th April 1945 with his wife Eva Braun. The war he had started killed about 60 million people.

Francisco Franco ruled Spain for four decades, until his death in 1975. Spain then became a democracy with King Juan Carlos as Head of State.

Josef Stalin continued to run the Soviet Union and its satellite countries with a ruthless iron grip until his death in 1953.

Hermann Goering became less and less successful as the leader of the Luftwaffe. He committed suicide in 1946 in Nuremberg before he could be hanged for war crimes. Thousands of artworks that he had stolen were recovered– though many were not. In 2000, it was estimated that he had looted no less than $30 billion in modern prices.

'**Bonny-LaFont Gang**'. Many of the French leaders of this 'Gestapo Française' were executed at Montrouge prison in December 1944, including the corrupt ex-policeman **Pierre Bonny** and the gangster **Henri Lafont** (real name Henri Chamberlin). The French investigating officers were ordered to suppress the files 'because the nation's weakened morale would not support the shock of such devastating revelations'.

Philippe Pétain fled to Germany in September 1944, returned to France, and was arrested and tried for treason in August 1945. His sentence of death was commuted to life imprisonment. He was stripped of all ranks except Marshal of France and died in July 1951. Charles de Gaulle later wrote that Petain's life was 'successively banal, then glorious, then deplorable, but never mediocre'.

Charles de Gaulle was made head of the Provisional Government of France in 1946, resigning in 1949 and writing his *War Memoirs*. He returned to power in 1958, ended the war in Algeria, and helped to create the beginning of the European Union, while favouring a Europe of sovereign nations. One of the political giants of the post-war years, he resigned in 1969 and died a year later.

Manuel Valls, Prime Minister of France and **Anne Hidalgo**, Mayor of Paris, both Spanish-born, insisted on the belated celebration in August 2014 of the 70th anniversary of the liberation of Paris (on the same day as the battle of La Madeleine) by Spanish troops of 'La Nueve', the 9th Company of General Leclerc's 2nd French Armoured Division.

FACTS

* * *

August 1944

The Kübelwagen, the German equivalent of the Jeep, was made by Volkswagen. German citizens who had paid for their promised Volkswagen 'Beetles', or 'people's cars', never got them.

Chapter One

- Agricultural wages in Spain in 1935 were 90 pesetas a month, 45 for women – but often lower.
- The largest landowner in Spain in 1935 was the Duke of Medinaceli, with 74,146 hectares or 183,000 acres of land.
- Religious murders included 4,184 priests, 2,365 monks and 283 nuns.
- 200 to 300 civilians were killed in the Condor Legion's bombing raid on Guernica.
- There were at least 500,000 deaths in the Spanish Civil War, half in combat, the other half by murders or executions, of which it is thought 40,000 were killed by the Republicans, and 200,000 by the Nationalists.

Chapter Two

- 500,000 Spanish refugees crossed the Pyrenees into France in 1938/1939. About half were soldiers.

Chapter Three

- Saint-Hippolyte-du-Fort did not have running water until 1950, relying on its fountain system.
- The Military Preparatory School was one of four in France, designed to provide officers for France. It was closed in 1927, but all the buildings still exist.

Chapter Four
- The Fort at Saint-Hippolyte was a relic of France trying to contain the Protestants, including the 'Camisard Revolt' of 1702-1715. Such religious strife ensured that the area was very familiar with the concept of resisting outsiders.

Chapter Five
- In March 1939, Hitler, flagrantly breaking the promises he had given the year before at Munich, annexed the rest of Czechoslovakia.
- The train service to Saint-Hippolyte only closed in 1982.

Chapter Six
- The name of the Rue Pasteur commemorated Louis Pasteur's four-month stay there, trying to cure the 'Pebrine' disease that was threatening silkworm rearing.

Chapter Seven
- On 1st September 1939, Germany attacked Poland, starting World War 11.

Chapter Eight
- Former Republican Spanish soldiers were housed in several French 'concentration camps'. The biggest was at Argelès-sur-Mer, which had 70,000 at one stage, on a freezing windswept beach without shelter or latrines.
- Poland was defeated by Germany in only 37 days.

Chapter Nine
- The French consumed 200 litres of wine per head a year, meaning probably 400 or more for men.
- The Maginot Line was a 500 km line of complex forts on the French-German border, designed to deter or to divert any German attacks, south through Switzerland or north through Belgium.

Chapter Ten
- Germany's Jews came under increasing pressure in 1935, with laws banning them from working in many jobs. If they could leave the country, 90% of their wealth was confiscated.

Chapter Eleven
- There were huge and unpleasant French right-wing media attacks on the Spanish who had come to France and were now working there.

Chapter Twelve
- Although succeeding in their invasion of Norway, the Germans lost

so many ships that later they would be too weak to invade Britain unless they won absolute air superiority, which they failed to do in 'The Battle of Britain'.

- When the main German attack burst through the Ardennes, bypassing the Maginot Line, Winston Churchill discovered with horror from the French Generals that they had no armoured reserve ready to attack them, as he had expected. 'My greatest surprise of the war.'
- France, that had resisted Germany for four years in 1914-1918, collapsed in just six weeks.
- Marshal Philippe Pétain had been Ambassador to Franco's Government in Burgos, so his sympathies were hardly going to be with former Republican Spaniards.

Chapter Thirteen

- The sinking of the French Fleet was partly caused by the friendly third option, 'to sail your ships to the West Indies', being inexplicably and tragically left off a signal to the anti-British Admiral Darlan, by mistake, by Admiral Gensoul.

Chapter Fourteen

- In Poland, the Jews had been confined in ghettos, while plans for their fate were being prepared.
- The 'Blitz' on London would eventually kill 40,000 civilians.
- The claim of 183 German planes lost was indeed an exaggeration, the true figure being about 70. But it was a huge morale boost for the British, and the RAF being obviously intact and still fighting made Hitler call off his planned invasion of Britain.

Chapter Sixteen

- 'Détachement W' had already managed to organise 220 successful escapes when in Marseilles.
- British escapes were helped by the local resistance, who provided bicycles, and trips to Nîmes or the Pyrenees by an ambulance/taxi.

Chapter Eighteen

- Dr Erich Gritzbach, Press Secretary to Hermann Goering, as well as his biographer and artwork-finder, survived the war and lived on a pension granted to him after evidence that he had helped anti-Nazis.
- Goering was found to have personally looted 1,400 paintings, 250 sculptures and 168 tapestries.

- The campaign in Greece, triggered by Mussolini's vainglorious attempt to imitate Hitler's successes, ended as a disaster for Britain once German troops had come to the Italians' rescue.

Chapter Nineteen

- Thanks to their airpower, the Germans captured Crete, but lost so many parachute troops that they were never dropped again. Curiously, Crete played little part in the rest of the war.

- By staying on in France and setting up the 'Pat Line' for escapers, 'Patrick O'Leary', or Albert-Marie Guérisse, became one of Belgium's great heroes, later awarded the DSO by King George VI.

- For the German advance into Russia, Franco, to avoid going properly to war, had offered Hitler the 'Blue Division', a token force of Spanish volunteers. Between August 29 and October 8, it set a world record of military advances on foot, 620 miles (1,000 kms), or 15.6 miles (25kms) per day.

- The Japanese sneak attack at Pearl Harbor, without declaring war and without sinking the American aircraft-carriers, proved – as Admiral Yamamoto admitted – that that 'they had merely woken a sleeping giant and filled him with terrible resolve'.

Chapter Twenty

- Hong Kong was attacked without a declaration of war eight hours after Pearl Harbor. The garrison, outnumbered four to one, held out for 17 days. Among many atrocities, 10,000 Chinese civilians were killed in the next three years. Japanese General Sakai was tried and shot in 1946.

- Rationing in France was theoretically better than in Britain. For each person a week: 300 grams of meat, 500 of sugar, 200 of fats and 50 of rice. But rations were often not available and prices went through the roof.

Chapter Twenty-One

- The fall of Singapore was one of Britain's greatest and most shaming military disasters, in that the victorious Japanese were outnumbered three to one.

- On March 17th, 1942, 'Détachement W' was taken by train to the 'more secure' Fort de la Revère, near Nice. The escapes did not stop.

Chapter Twenty-Three

- The egotistical and over-confident General MacArthur had said of

Corregidor, 'They have the bottle, *I* have the cork'. Ordered to leave, typically he said 'I shall return', not 'We shall return'.

- Air Marshal Sir Arthur 'Bomber' Harris assembled 1,047 bombers to raid Cologne on 30th May, 1942. As he had said, '*The Nazis entered this war under the rather childish delusion that they were going to bomb everyone else, and nobody was going to bomb them. They sowed the wind, and now they are going to reap the whirlwind*'.

- The Battle of Midway, with four Japanese carriers sunk and hundreds of pilots lost, was the turning point in the Pacific, a disaster not revealed to the Japanese public until *after* the war.

- In August, 1941, 4,232 Jews were sent from Drancy to their deaths in Auschwitz, the first of 67,000. The last transport left on 31st July, 1944, just a fortnight before Drancy was liberated. In fact, thanks to the efforts of her citizens, *only* 25% of France's 330,000 Jews were killed, the best survival rate in Europe, although horrifying enough.

- The battle of El Alamein, a decisive British victory, is regarded with Midway and Stalingrad as one of the war's turning points.

- The Anglo-US invasion of North Africa (Operation Torch) threatened to trap the Germans and Italians there, and was also an obvious threat to southern France, triggering the German take-over of the Vichy 'Free Zone'.

- In Toulon, the French, as they had promised to do, scuttled 77 vessels including 4 battleships, 7 cruisers, 15 destroyers and 12 submarines, denying their use by the Germans.

Chapter Twenty-Four

- The Milice Française, formed by the Vichy regime in January 1943 to help fight the Résistance, numbered 30,000 at its peak. Some miliciens later joined the *Charlemagne* Division, the French Waffen-SS division and the only unit to enter Berlin *voluntarily* before its fall.

- The Carlingue was a para-military French force set up by the Sicherheitsdienst (SD) and the Gestapo. Incredibly, mostly staffed by criminals, it featured in the film *Lacombe Lucien*.

Chapter Twenty-Five

- Coco Chanel lived at the Ritz with Hans Gunther von Dinklage and was herself a German spy, Abwehr number F-7124. After 9 years in exile, she returned to re-invent herself as a fashion queen.

- Despite Hitler's last minute dispatch of men and equipment, over

100,000 Germans and 200,000 Italians surrendered to the British and American forces in Tunisia.

- Spain's 'neutrality' was very patchy. The people were starving while Spain exported food to Germany, and imported food from America.
- Spain's Blue Division, after suffering 4,954 dead and 8,700 wounded, withdrew from Russia in October 1943, although some volunteers stayed on. Hitler said, 'Spaniards are a crew of ragamuffins. But they have never yielded an inch of ground. One can't imagine more fearless fellows.'
- Cristino Garcia Grandas, aged 30, commanded all the Spanish maquis, about 750, in the Gard, Lozère and Ardèche.
- The Bren Gun, the British light machine-gun, weighed 10.5 kilos, and fired standard .303 inch rifle ammunition from 30-round magazines at an effective range of 600 metres.
- The Sten gun was a very cheap, simple sub-machine-gun, firing 9mm ammunition from a 30 round magazine. An ideal insurgency weapon, over 4 million were made.
- To fight the Résistance, 'The Carlingue' was a French paramilitary force set up by the Gestapo, and comprising many criminals. It was often simply known as the 'Bonny-Lafont Gang'.
- With Italy suffering so badly in the war, Mussolini was denounced by the Fascist Council and then deposed by his King. He was later to be rescued from a mountain fortress by Hitler.

Chapter Twenty-Eight

- Operation 'Snow White' flew in 9 SOE parachutists and 58 containers of arms and explosives. They fought with French and Spanish maquisards until the liberation of Montpellier on August 28th before going to link up with British and U.S. forces in Lyon.

Chapter Twenty-Nine

- The Chateau de Planque, first built in 1596, still exists and is the home of an international Christian movement, 'Youth with a Mission'.
- The Irish Guards, created by Queen Victoria after the Boer War in 1900 in recognition '*of the bravery of my Irish soldiers*', is one of the five Foot Guards regiments of the Household Brigade.

Chapter Thirty-One

- Allied bombing, by the Americans by day and the British at night, would eventually kill 600,000 German civilians and destroy nearly every major city.

- While technically superior, Germany's arms production was sometimes feeble, with 7,000 'Panther' tanks and only 1,347 'Tigers', as opposed to 38,000 American 'Shermans' and 43,000 Russian T-34s.

Chapter Thirty-Two

- The D-Day Normandy invasion was the greatest amphibious landing ever made. 156,000 men initially landed on 5 beaches from 7,000 ships, under the cover of 11,000 aircraft.
- Nîmes was bombed in July 1944, killing 300 French civilians. During the war, Allied bombing tragically killed about 60,000 French civilians, roughly the same number of British civilians killed by the German Luftwaffe.
- The same SS Panzer Division, *Das Reich*, carried out both the atrocities at Tulle and Oradour. Its commander, General Heinz Lammerding, escaped extradition to a Bordeaux court by a legal technicality and died in retirement in 1971.
- 'Operation Dragoon', the invasion of southern France, was controversial, opposed as a distraction by many, including Churchill, who thought he'd been 'dragooned' into it. But it cleared France of Germans, and Marseille and Toulon soon became vital supply ports for the overall Allied advance.

Chapter Thirty-Three

- There is a monument at La Madeleine that commemorates this extraordinary but little-known success by a tiny group of Spaniards and French against a huge German force.
- The De Havilland DH.98 'Mosquito' was one of the world's outstanding aircraft. Twin-engined and made of *wood*, it was even faster than a 'Spitfire'. It operated equally well as a fighter, light bomber, night-fighter, fighter-bomber, pathfinder and photo-reconnaissance aircraft.
- The decision by Cristino Garcia's group to go back into Spain looks, in hindsight, to have been brave, but foolish. Nearly all of them were caught, imprisoned or executed in Franco's Spain.
- The shaving of the heads of perhaps 20,000 women was the least of the unpleasant acts in *l'épuration sauvage* ('Savage purification'). Perhaps 10,000 suspected collaborators were killed before *l'épuration légal* sentenced 120,000 collaborators.

Chapter Thirty-Five

- The first concentration camp to be found, Majdanek, 1944, was in July, followed by Belzec, Sobibor and Treblinka, all in Poland. Although dismantled and empty, it was obvious what they had been. In Auschwitz in January 1945, the Soviets found 800,000 women's dresses neatly folded. The horrified Americans liberated Dachau and Buchenwald and the equally shocked British (including Colonel John Cowley, later General Sir John, the author Liz Cowley' father) Bergen-Belsen.
- The German losses in the last-ditch Ardennes offensive were 100,000 men, 700 tanks and 800 aircraft. This fatally weakened any defence against the Red Army, which then struck from the east with overwhelming force on 16th January.

Chapter Thirty-Six

- With British help, the Americans had developed the 'Atomic Bomb' in complete secrecy. The first was detonated in New Mexico on July 16th and the next two were dropped on Hiroshima (August 6th) and Nagasaki (August 9th). It was fortunate that Japan surrendered, because there were no more bombs available.

Chapter Thirty-Seven

- Despite being the first European country to emancipate its Jews, anti-Semitism has been a major factor in France for centuries. 'The Dreyfus Affair', in which a Jewish officer was falsely accused of treason, was a vivid example of prejudice. With the world's third largest Jewish population, France is now considered by Jews as an increasingly dangerous place.

Chapter Thirty-Nine

- French Indo-China consisted of the Vietnamese regions of Tonkin, Annam and Chochinchina, and later merged with Laos and Cambodia.
- The Galerie Charpentier in Paris was a centre of French artistic life for many decades. Its building is now the French home of Sotheby's, the famous auction house.
- The palace of what is now the Hotel Crillon was built in 1758 as government offices by order of Louis XV. The Count de Crillon later owned, it but it was confiscated during the Revolution and Louis XVI was guillotined right in front of it.

Chapter Forty-Two

- The 9th Company of General Leclerc's 2nd Armoured Division, 'La Nueve', consisted of Spanish Republican veterans.

Chapter Forty-Three

- The Italian Resistance movement was one of the greatest in Western Europe. Partisan forces hit enemy communications, tied down seven German divisions and provided tactical support for the Allied 5th and 8th armies.

- Unlike the cross-Channel sleeper trains, which actually travelled on the ferries, the Golden Arrow passengers left their trains at Dover or Calais and crossed the Channel on their own luxury ferry.